BOOK TWO

BOOKS OF
BEFORE & NOW

THE JAWBONE & THE JUNKMAN

Jason Fischer

THE JAWBONE & THE JUNKMAN:
THE BOOKS OF BEFORE AND NOW BOOK TWO
Copyright © 2023 Jason Fischer. All rights reserved.

Published by Outland Entertainment LLC
3119 Gillham Road
Kansas City, MO 64109

Founder/Creative Director: Jeremy D. Mohler
Editor-in-Chief: Alana Joli Abbott
Senior Editor: Scott Colby

ISBN: 978-1-954255579
Worldwide Rights
Created in the United States of America

Editor: Scott Colby
Cover Illustration: Steve Firchow
Cover Design: Jeremy D. Mohler
Interior Layout: Mikael Brodu

Printed and bound in the United States of America.

Visit **outlandentertainment.com** to see more, or follow us on our Facebook Page **facebook.com/outlandentertainment/**

To Kate, Logan and Lottie,
you are my everything.

— PROLOGUE —

He was a boy who'd gone by ten or more names before they put a noose around his neck. The boy had left these names discarded like snake skins in his wake, and when they told him he was going to die, the town clerk recorded his final name with the hammer strikes of a rebuilt typewriter, punching these words into the fibres of the parchment, trying to force permanence into this identity with ink and clacking strikers.

The boy had kicked away his last meal in a clatter of cursing. When they came for him, he burst out of his cell, cutting up one of the jailers with the sharpened edge of a spoon.

The boy was wild, and tough, and perhaps fourteen years old. Even he didn't know. He spat and swore, laughed and mocked the crowd and his jailers, giving various opinions on laws and those who would hide behind them.

Those who served the townlaw nudged the boy onto the trapdoor, next to a more experienced criminal, the one who'd led him into this noose. The man saw the hard edge in the boy's face and nodded once. Respect, and the boy drank it up, even here at his end.

The boy was observant, and even in all the clamour he noticed three things as his life came to an end.

The man who passed the sentence in the court room was the one who reached for the lever.

A girl even younger than the boy, half-hidden behind the gallows post. Well-dressed and well-fed. Forced to observe this execution.

Then the crack of a rifle, startling the whole crowd, the same second that the executioner pulled the lever.

The boy fell, and kept falling, down into the dank pit beneath the gallows, but where he expected a broken neck or a prolonged minute of choking, he struck the damp clay, his noose trailing around him.

A bullet had severed the rope as it stretched to its fullness, the noose gripping his throat for only one painful moment.

He watched as the older man fell next to him, his own noose working, but his neck did not break. He twitched and choked, eyes locking onto the boy's.

The boy set himself beneath the man, let him push down and finally stand on his shoulders to ease the choke of the rope. He deserved to hang, they both did, but the older man still wobbled and fought for every breath.

"The boy is down there!" someone cried, and faces peered down from above.

"Don't you leave me," the older criminal rasped, fighting for balance on the back of a child outlaw.

Survival. The boy ran with his noose flapping, leaving his old boss to dangle and choke in the darkness, his last word a gurgled curse against the boy that the slipknot thankfully interrupted.

A passageway led into a room with two coffins waiting for two bodies, and the undertakers were interrupted mid-cigarette by a boy running full-pelt.

He was wild and resourceful, the boy with ten names, but the cry had gone up, and the lawmen were out in force to hunt him down. Dashing headlong through an empty tannery, the boy drew up short as someone caught his noose, pulling him down by it.

The boy fought to get to his feet, even with his hands bound, and saw the man who clutched the other end of his noose. In his other hand he held a rifle, a good one, one that could have made the shot from the windows up in the tannery roof.

The man appraised him with a heavy eye and let go of the rope. Setting aside the rifle, he pulled a Bowie knife out of a battered old sheath on his belt, cutting the cord around the boy's wrists.

In later years, the boy would carry the heavily worn knife as his own and kill this man with a rock, but today he was grateful for the liberty, unaware that he was speaking with a Jesusman, that most despicable of characters.

"A nice lanyard they fitted you with," the man said, and introduced himself as Bauer. The boy took off the noose and put on that most heavy and final of names.

PART ONE
JAWBONE

— 1 —

Fifteen years from the day that he murdered a god, Lanyard found an intruder lurking by the tradeway. A puppet in the making, it was a hideous arrangement of bone and skin, as if someone with only the vaguest idea of a human was trying to make one. It lurched across the scrub, hailing them, reaching out with a knotty club that was meant to pass for an arm.

Lanyard's prentices circled it like children baiting a mad dog. They rode motorbikes and bicycles scavenged from the bleedthroughs, and the younger ones slapped around in sandals carved from old tyre treads.

They jeered and poked at the beast with sticks, none of them game to get any closer. Lanyard stood back, watching, arms folded. He had a shotgun slung over his shoulder, an ancient and most holy weapon, but this was a failsafe.

Today, he'd given the kids a devil to practice on.

"Please," the thing said. "I'm lost. Let me share your water, your food."

Someone threw a rock then, cracking the beast in the ribs. The creature drew down low, limbs scrabbling out like a spider, and it shrieked, a yipping and yiking that was half pain and half warning. The prentices scattered, daring each other to do more.

"Why do you hurt me?" it mewled, sharp fingers bent backwards, drumming at the clay, and then it found its own rock. It whipped an arm forward, a limb made of four joints, a trebuchet of meat and sinew.

The rock flew like a bullet and struck a girl in the temple. She fell from her motorbike, the machine bouncing across the ground. The girl rolled, screaming, a tangle of limbs, blood, and dust.

"Mal, enough," Lanyard called out. An older boy was waiting outside of the circling pack of kids, seated on the back of a riding bird. His mount still had tufts of chick down and was barely eight feet high at the crest, just big enough to ride. Lanyard had bought the bird the same day he'd freed the boy from a slaver, and he often found the pair daydreaming together, the boy muttering into the bird's ear, the bird clacking and parroting what words she could glean from her young master.

Mal turned at the sound of his name, stirred from a distant thought. When he saw the look on Lanyard's face, he reached down to the bird's flank, slowly drawing the lance out of its sheath.

"C'mon, Collybrock," he told the bird. She loped forward, screeching and nipping at the other prentices until they cleared out of the way. The younger prentices waited at a safe distance from the creature and pretended not to be relieved.

"Please, friend," the man-thing said to Mal. "I mean no harm. I'm in terrible danger."

"Friend," Collybrock squawked, breaking off into a warble of laughter. Mal licked his lips, setting the lance in the crook of his arm. The strange creature raised itself upwards on arm and leg bones, the whole mass clicking and shifting until it was almost the height of the bird. It swayed in time with the bird, skin stretched taut and slick with sweat.

Its mouth was obscenely wide, and the lips curved up into a smile, revealing row upon row of teeth.

"We can be friends," it told Mal. "I can tell. You have a good heart."

At that point, the creature struck forward like a whip, knobs of sharp bone reaching for the boy's face. Mal whistled through his teeth to Collybrock and the bird danced sideways, kicking out at the pin-wheeling monstrosity.

Mal drove the lance through the monster, the sharp blade instantly piercing that weird flesh. Lanyard had crafted the lance-head from a truck spring, hammering the thick steel flat, grinding the edges and the point into something he taught young Mal to shave with.

Lanyard had etched the ancient marks into the steel, crude copies of the sorceries carved into his old gun. Enough to do the job of binding and killing these things, and that was good enough for what needed doing.

Mal held the creature at bay with the cross-piece of the lance, even as the creature wiggled and tried to free itself from the foot-long spike. Digging his heels into Collybrock's flanks, Mal drove the intruder back, herding it left and right, until it tripped in a tangle of confused meat.

Mal drove the lance down as hard as he could, pinning the intruder to the earth. The chittering thing howled then, more from the loss of liberty than from pain.

"Make with the marks and the words, quickly now," Lanyard told the younger prentices, who had gathered around the monstrous thing. They used sticks and knives to carve into the clay-pan, making the marks of binding, the closing fingers of an invisible fist to hold the monster in place. At the very last the creature tried to withdraw back through the world veil, but it was trapped, flesh and foul spirit both.

"Enough!" it finally cried, limbs curled in around the lance, unable to free itself. "Cry pardon."

"No," Lanyard growled. He walked around the circle, checking on the work. One of the marks was weak, so he added another to reinforce the ward, digging into the dirt with a yellowed thumbnail.

"You are vermin. Squatters," the creature cried, staring at Lanyard. Its eyes resembled those of a dead fish, alien orbs that tracked the old man as he paced around it.

"You should not be here. None of you!" it continued. Lanyard shrugged the old shotgun from his shoulder, checking the breech action. He snapped it closed with a sharp click and brought the barrels to bear on that squirming face, a pancake of features that did not have a skull to lend them shape.

"End me, but there are so many more of me, and every day we tumble through the holes in the fence," it crooned. "I do not fear you!"

Lanyard considered the gun in his hands, the ancient pictures of the Crossing, the threats and promises carved into every inch of the weapon. The weapon of a Jesusman.

"You're not even worth a bullet," Lanyard said.

He brought the gun down like a club, cracking bones, grinding that alien flesh into the dust, knowing that the sigils carved into the stock were causing the creature a deep agony.

"Cry mercy," the thing finally bleated. "I fear you. I fear!"

"Good," Lanyard said, gore running from the butt of his gun. He stepped back, breathing heavily from the exertion.

"You kids, get in there and finish the job," he snarled, and the prentices waded in, hefting knives and clubs marked with the old killing signs. The trapped monster bleated with terror, and later pain, and then it was just a smear of dead meat.

"Pay attention," Lanyard said that night. He drew a stick from the cook-fire and scratched at the air with the hot coal on the end. He spoke a word and gave it just enough emphasis to leave a track of fire where he drew lines and shapes.

Soon he had drawn out a map in flame, a chart that hung in mid-air where his students could see it.

"Up here is the Overhaeven," Lanyard said, pointing to a circle at the top. "The gods live here. The Jesus, your bossman. John Leicester, too, he looks after the statue-lovers. We got no other friends in that place."

He drew a line downwards, marking out another circle. "This here is the Greygulf, the world between worlds. There're shadow-roads there, quick ways to get around. You'll walk here one day, but not till I say, and even then only for a moment."

He looked around at the eager faces, hungry for their legacy, and he felt a weight of sadness settle over him. He shook his head.

"Too much time in that place will ruin you," he said. "Remember, all of the Witches used to be Jesusmen."

"Beneath the Greygulf is the Aum. It's a place of endless night, a darkness that speaks to mirrors and madmen."

The kids watched him intently as he drew with fire. He wondered what it had been like in the Before, when people watched their televisions. Every bleedthrough spat out endless TV boxes, all of it useless now.

Going by everything the Boneman had ever told him about that marvellous old world, this was a low age, humanity reduced to bare-arsed survival in a shit-hole.

"Right at the bottom of this whole mess, you'll find the Underfog," Lanyard said, circling around the lowest part of his diagram. "This is the place where dead spirits go, preparing to die their Twice-Death. Don't any of you ever try to go there while you are alive. I mean it."

Left and right of the Greygulf, he drew shapes, a cross-arm to the vertical axis of his burning shape. He drew circle after circle, as far as he could reach.

"This is our world, the Now," Lanyard said, pointing one out. "We came here from the world called the Before. It's dead now, killed off by Papa Lucy, and he nearly killed this place, too."

He snuffed out one of the circles between thumb and forefinger, a blank spot in that fiery map, emphasised by all of the bright shapes around it.

"These other worlds, they all touch on ours. Especially now that Papa Lucy has weakened the world veil. Creatures and spirits sneak into the Now, and it's your job to kill them."

He saw the bright eyes of his prentices, lapping up the call to adventure. *I'm bloody telling it all wrong!* he berated himself.

"There's no glory for you lot! Just murder and madness," he snarled. "The towns will shut you out, or they will pretend to obey the Boneman's new laws, but they will shun you."

A few of the excited faces dropped away, but there were still too many. He pressed on with the hard truths.

"The moment you swore to serve the Jesus was the moment you crossed a line. You're not *human* anymore, and that scares the wall-huggers."

So much talking hurt Lanyard's throat. He sipped at his billy-tea and let the prentices walk right around his burning diagram, wide-eyed as they took in the structure of the universe.

It will grind the life out of you kids, he wanted to say. *Nothing marvellous about all that misery.*

"Mister Lanyard, when do we get guns?" one of the prentices said, which stirred him from his grim reverie. She was the girl who'd taken a tumble from the motorbike, a bloody wad of cotton still strapped to her head. For a moment he searched for her name, sifting through dozens of dead faces, kids who'd followed him from towns and shanties, who'd escaped from the crooked mobs to join his service. Every night their screams tore at his nightmares, new ghosts to add to his collection.

Kirstl. This girl was called Kirstl. She was Mal's sweetheart, and this romance was a new thing, all clandestine kisses and stolen tender moments. Tilly knew of course, and thought she was keeping this secret from Lanyard, who knew in his own way, both of them ready to chaperone the moment it was needed, just one more task when it came to shepherding the prentices through their education.

Would it be wrong to cut the kids loose? To let them have their happiness? A life away from violence and fear?

Kirstl looked to him hopefully, eyes alight with her imagined future adventures, and Lanyard was already digging a grave for her in his mind.

"You're not ready," he said. "Mal doesn't even have a gun yet. Stop worrying about that. Focus on your marks and words, on learning your trade."

He waved a stick at the diagram, accidentally smudging the lines. Grunting with annoyance, he snapped his fingers, and the burning chart dissolved into smoke. Rising painfully to his feet, Lanyard left the campfire and prentices both, limping out into the darkness of the plains.

Too much talking. Too many faces.

He watched from a short distance, unseen. The prentices grumbled and settled down for the night, whispering and joking as the fire crackled.

Some of the kids stared vacantly and did not join in this quiet camaraderie. Mem and Lyn, twins he'd rescued from Witches' Nest on another bloody day. Rella, a wild brawler at ten who often screamed in her sleep. Seidel, a lad who started at loud noises and often cut himself, or others.

Mal, who kept his own counsel, sharpening his lance-head on a whetstone. Lanyard worried about this swarthy young man the most.

Lanyard knew this look, and marked these children well. If you gave these prentices their guns too soon, more than one would simply blow their brains out. He'd learnt that lesson the hard way, over and over.

He felt the tear in the world veil, but they were too late to stop an attack on a farmhold. Lanyard and his students were greeted by smouldering ruins, dead sheep, and no people to be found anywhere.

"Look here," Lanyard said, pushing some tin sheeting with his boot. "Not with your eyes, the other way."

He pointed out scar after scar in the world veil, all the weak points left over when someone or something had gone through. Footprints, drag marks, and bloody clumps of dust led the way to each scar, and then nothing.

"Witches," he said, pointing out the way that the footprints changed from man feet to a dog's paws, to a bird's talons, to the coil of a serpent.

Mal and the other prentices perked up at the word and puffed themselves up, wicked little hand weapons at the ready. Lanyard shook his head.

"They'll kill you," he said. "At least twenty of them hit this place. You'll end up in their greypot if I send you lot through."

Trying to calm the rising tide of panic in his mind, Lanyard sought access to the Aum, to that black place of mirrors and prisons. He felt at the edges of it with his mind, unable to grip it easily, but he frowned and pushed forward with a brute effort rather than the relaxed method the Boneman had tried to teach him.

He was in. He focused his mental energies towards the walled city of Crosspoint, towards his first prentice. She was working at the Lodge of the Jesumen, perhaps one thousand miles away from the dusty Inland.

Tilly. I need you here. Witches.

He felt the thought bounce across that endless darkness. There were other things in here, lost creatures, insane from the isolation, and they hunted words sent across the Aum, fed from the energy, came hunting for the mind that dared to brave that place.

The alternative was days of dusty riding, swapping bikes for camels and birds, and ending up with a chapped arse for no good reason.

Tilly!

Lanyard, I hear you, the girl said over that impossible distance, her voice distorted and weak.

At least twenty Witches, he replied. *They are feeding now.*

We come, she said, and broke off the tenuous connection. Lanyard blinked and emerged from that internal darkness, his eyes once more drinking in the daylight.

"You kids, move away from there," he said, pointing to the spot that made his skin crawl. A moment later, a silver light slashed through the air, a doorway irising open from somewhere else. He saw that monochrome light, the connection of a shadow-road, then shapes emerging from the Greygulf.

Men and women, kitted out for killing. Everyone was marked with scars or burns, and some had lost limbs, others their souls. They moved with a quick nervous energy, scanning for threats, rune-carved guns at the ready.

The Jesusmen.

At their head was a woman with fuzzy brown hair, pulled back tight in a ponytail. She wore Lanyard's old slouch hat, pulled low, and a canvas dust-coat. A pistol hung from her hip, heavy black iron, etched with forgotten words, just marks that Lanyard and Bauer and countless others before them had copied, etched over and over until they no longer meant anything. She flashed a smile at Lanyard, her lips marred by a split scar that ran over the edge of her chin.

"Bossman," Tilly Carpidian said. She led the way into the wreckage, cradling a pike she'd marked in the same ways as Mal's lance. She watched carefully for survivors or for hidden killers, noting each shimmer that marked a tear through this reality into another.

"Let's go," she said, and the Jesusmen spread out, pushing through the scars in the world veil.

Some places led to the Greygulf. Others entered worlds of searing heat, of snow and darkness, or into planes that made Lanyard queasy just looking through their tears.

Even as the holes slowly puckered shut behind each of the Jesusmen, the cracks of gunshots drifted back into the Now, the shouted words of their rite. Bind, unmake, destroy. There used to be more tricks in the Jesusman's kit, but they'd lost so many things.

"You'll be like them soon enough," he told the prentices behind him, who thrilled at the action, the confidence of the gun-toting knights. "Then you'll wish for this day, when it was someone else going through."

"Through," Collybrock warbled. Mal leaned against the bird's neck, ruffling its feathers, watching the older Jesusmen do battle with the predators. When he met Lanyard's eyes, he did not look scared or excited.

The boy was simply sad, and already weary from a thousand burdens. Lanyard would add a thousand more before he was done, and he wondered if it might have been kinder to leave young Mal in chains.

The guns of the Jesusmen roared justice and defiance, but mostly they barked out in futility, crackled with vengeance for those too dead to care.

— 2 —

Two Jesusmen lost their lives fighting over that nameless farm-hold. Old Jacob surprised two Witches who were elbow deep in a man's intestines, but a third one surprised him and tore out his raspy throat. He'd been dying of lungrot. His was a good death.

Polline followed a Witch through a scar, but she'd been tricked. Her prey had opened a false door, and she'd stepped into a world of puce-tinted fog, unseen pressures crushing her from every angle. Her ending was an agony that took hours. None of the others could extract her, either with magic or with ropes.

Polline had been a child-killer, sentenced to either serve the Jesusmen or choke on a noose. Trapped in that fog, she begged for a bullet by the end, and was given one. When she'd first entered his service, Lanyard told Polline she should have gone to the gallows.

She did not have a good death.

The Jesusmen and the prentices kept camp by the smouldering ruins, waiting, watching. Here the world veil was battered and might take years to heal. Distant eyes might see the boundary shaking, sense the weakness in this spot, and creep through it, hungry and bold.

The Jesusmen drank, but they were not raucous. Those who shared stories were quiet around their cookfires, the cracking of coals louder than their wary words.

Lanyard had set sentries on the camp, pacing figures that lit their way with the twinkle of star-glass. Whenever the Taursi entered Crosspoint to find grog, these giant, spiked creatures left gifts of the glass on the Lodge doorstep. The Order of Jesusmen had more Taursi glass than it knew what to do with.

These wild Taursi were prisoners, as much as the human settlers were, and these gifts were the equivalent of cigarettes in the exercise yard. The other Taursi served the Lords of Overhaeven, and wore armour of glass plate. Despite fighting on Lanyard's side during the battle for the Waking City, they were not friends.

Some of the Jesusmen rested that night, but none slept. The prentices were sent to stack the rifles into neat piles, and others gathered around a star-glass where they were shown how to carve binding and killing symbols into newly cast bullets.

Lanyard kept a small fire on his own and boiled a billy of tea. He scowled when someone approached his spot, relaxing only slightly when he saw it was Tilly.

"Girl," he said. She sat down across from him, saying nothing for a long moment. They'd travelled together for years, in this world and others, and knew each other down to the bones.

He lifted the billy from the coals when it was ready and poured out a cup. He only had the one, and he offered it to Tilly first. She took a sip and grimaced.

"What are you boiling in there, dirt?"

"Liver-root," he answered. "Anything else, I'm up all night pissing."

Coals ticked and spat in the fire, and in the distance came the clinking of someone working on a motorcycle. Lanyard sipped, the barest movement of lip, tongue, and mouth. He was a creature of the hot places where economy of movement was survival.

"We are drawn thin," Tilly finally said. "We need you at the Lodge."

"No."

"You can't?"

"Won't."

They'd had the argument before, but still Tilly wore at her old master, knowing the patient ways she could bore through his stubbornness.

"We get reports of attacks over the telegraph now. The Boneman leans on us more and more. We can only do so much, but with you there..."

Lanyard snorted and sipped at his bitter brew.

"Why do you hide out here?" Tilly said. "A man your age deserves a bed and proper food."

"Girl, I took your bloody prentices on," Lanyard said. "What more do you want?"

"I need you," she said, voice small. For a moment, Lanyard didn't see her as the scarred veteran of a thousand deadly encounters, and she was once more the lost little girl, the foundling of a doomed tribe.

His charge, but more importantly, his salvation.

"No, you don't bloody need me," he said, and it broke his heart to say it. "Grow a backbone, girl."

She waved away his gruff words.

"You don't have to do this anymore," she said. "Come home with me."

"I'm not gonna moulder away, living under some roof," Lanyard said. "We don't get to retire, girl. We kill them, and then we get killed. That's the way it's always been."

"It's not the monsters that will finish you, Lanyard. Maybe you'll have another stroke, except this time you won't recover."

She looked him over, and Lanyard felt like a bird in the sale yards. He'd aged badly. His hair had turned grey and he'd grown a full beard to hide the droop in his face from the palsy. One eye had clouded with a cataract, the other gone cold and mean. Every movement now came with a hitch or a pain, and he knew the day would come when his strength would finally fail.

"Girl, my insides haven't been right since the Boneman fixed them. Figure I'm living on borrowed time."

Tilly rose to her feet in one smooth movement. She gave Lanyard a final look, equal parts love and frustration.

"You won't have a glorious death out here, just a pointless one. Time you called it a day."

He said nothing, sipping at his disgusting tea, and did not look up as Tilly walked away.

Morning, and nothing had crept through into the Now. Perhaps an intruder had smelt the guns on the far side, heard the whisper of the waiting wards and traps. Told its friends to look elsewhere for easier pickings.

The Jesusmen struck camp in moments, snuffing out fires, stowing swags and bedrolls. Guns and pikes were fetched, motorbikes and buggies cranked into smoky life.

"We go," Tilly said, opening a doorway back into the Greygulf. The black tongue of a shadow-road rested against that disturbing mouth, and with no further ceremony, the hunting party stepped from this world into another.

They took the prentices.

Lanyard remained behind, watching as the Jesusmen left for Crosspoint. A few offered him a salute or a nod, and he raised his mug in return, coughing, a stubborn old man remaining in the desert.

"Go with them," he told Mal, who was crouched across the fire from him. The sullen boy poked at the ashes with a stick. Collybrock was pacing around in her hobbles, hunting lizards in the spinifex.

"No," Mal said.

"There's nothing for you here, boy. Go back to your lessons. You'll get your gun, in time."

"No."

Bemused, Lanyard resumed his vigil, waiting until the last Jesusman walked into the Greygulf and the razor-sharp hole in existence winked shut.

The two of them were alone in the vastness of the Inland, with the whisper of the grass, the baking stillness of the gumtrees that clung to a creek bed, the sense that everything suffered under this sun. Lanyard stood then, and with a muttered word and a pass of his hand, he instantly extinguished his cookfire. The coals were as cold as if the fire had died a week ago.

"Alright, then," Lanyard told Mal. "Stay."

The boy looked up, surprised that the old Jesusman had given in so easily. He called for Collybrock, uncinched her hobbles, and scrambled up into the harness. The boy didn't bother with whips or the knout, and Lanyard felt a pang of pride.

Lanyard stowed his bedroll in the back of his buggy, a vehicle cobbled together by a Tinkerman from Mawson. He shifted a tarpaulin to reveal canisters of fuel, a tank of water, and a fat cluster of guns.

"You can watch my last days. Let's go."

Lanyard took them to an old tradeway that headed south, the buggy sliding from loose sand onto the packed earth of the track. After hours of jogging across the desolate landscape, Collybrock grew tired, and Mal slid into the seat beside Lanyard. Above them, the bird gripped the tubular frame of the buggy with her claws, sleeping like a chicken at roost.

"What do you feed that bird?" Lanyard muttered, eyeing how low the buggy was riding to the ground.

"Meat. Eggs. Damper. Potatoes and onions, mashed and boiled and fried up until they are burnt. She won't eat them any other way."

Lanyard looked away, fighting back the twinkle in his one good eye.

He continued to teach the boy as they crossed over from the Inland into the Overland. Desert gave way to bush, and the tradeway took them past well-defended farm-holds, past packed wayhouses that stank of grog and kennel-weed.

They spent a strange evening observing a group of Taursi undergoing a ceremony. One of their elders had fallen down and could not keep up with their group, so they set him upright and began crafting him a type of glass splint, but they did not stop there. Spines huffed out and glowing with the extreme heat, the creatures completely encased their elder in glass, sealing over his snout.

"They're making a Spire, boy," Lanyard whispered.

Within the glass, the old Taursi finally broke into panic and thrashed about, punching ragged holes in his prison. The other Taursi simply added more layers of hot glass over these wounds until their Elder was finally dead and entombed on his feet, observing the road.

"That's awful," Mal whispered.

"No more awful than the greypot," Lanyard replied, and then the Taursi spotted them and chased them away with sharp glass and curses.

Once, Lanyard felt the ache in his bones that meant a bleedthrough was about to slice into the Now, so they kept camp outside of an abandoned tin mine. That awful moment came, and both man and boy felt it, the pushing at the world veil. Then a trio of buildings emerged from the dirt, separated by a crossroads made of the black tar from Before and a blinking traffic light. There was half a car, the edge of the bleedthrough dissecting it lengthwise like a razor. Newspapers spilled out of an open storefront, and a fridgerator full of ice-cold beer tempted them through the melted toffee of the windows.

"Wait," Lanyard said, looking at the boy. Wistfully, Mal kept back from that treasure, and when he saw the look on Lanyard's face, he drew his lance, holding it ready.

A beast burst out through the shop windows, equal parts spider and horse. It came at Mal with dozens of furry limbs, each tipped with a hoof.

"Meat and mouth, meat and mouth!" it cried, breaking into a whinny. The long snout split apart to reveal row on row of fangs and a trio of tongues. It had eight eyes fringed with soft brown lashes, nictitating and blinking constantly.

It caught Collybrock a glancing blow with a hoof. She squawked, flapping and hopping to keep out of the reach of those flashing legs. Mal scored its ribs with his lance. The horse-thing squealed, wary now of the marked blade.

This gave Lanyard enough time to circle around the thing. When the creature finally realised, it turned to see the double-throat of the Jesusgun, barely feet away.

It lunged, and Lanyard fired, and again, the thunderous crack of his god-cannon at work. The horse-creature fell to the ground, twitching, dragging at the dirt with what limbs still worked.

"No mind, no mind," it squealed. Lanyard followed it calmly, feeding two fresh shells into the breach of his weapon. The creature was marking out a door now, tracing a shape with trembling hoofs. Mal used the razor edge of his lance to slice away one hoof, and then another, but still the creature tried to summon its escape, lifeblood spurting out of its various wounds.

"Here then, here then," the creature said. "Cables cut, mouth for the meat. Just so."

"Be careful," Lanyard said, and Mal narrowly avoided a hoof to the face. Even on death's door, the creature was eager to kill them, and it neighed in defiance.

"Your world will end," it boasted. "I serve the Dawn King! Master of all places! I fall into his mouth. So shall you!"

Mal stared at the monster, the grim words marking him in some way.

"You're done, mate," Lanyard said, and fired the shotgun into the monster's face, turning that foul facsimile of a horse head into mincemeat and bone.

Later, they built a pyre around the body, the huge legs still twitching even as they roasted. Lanyard built their own little cook fire upwind of the stink.

"Liars. They'll say anything," Lanyard told Mal. "There is no Dawn King. There's nothing but this hungry filth."

Mal kept sharpening the edge of his lance, and his eyes looked past the hot coals, to some place where Lanyard could not reach him.

Before he slept, Lanyard covered the bleedthrough with marks and words, an instruction to return from whence it came. That little slice of another world was half-gone by morning, and man and boy stood silent witness, letting the cold beers and the magazines sink back down into the earth, back to the Before.

It was still a trap, and far from safe.

"The instructions were set a long time ago, to haul supplies from the Before into the Now," Lanyard explained. "Those old sorcerers planned to bring everything over from the world they killed."

"Papa Lucy," Mal said numbly, tapping his lance on the tip of a roof tile. *Ting ting*, the metal rang merrily as the building sank down beneath a bank of dirt, like a ship swallowed by a wave.

"The bleedthroughs will dry out one day," Lanyard said. "We'll have to make our own things then."

The horse-thing was a charred mess of bone and burnt flesh. Lanyard passed his hand over the fire, whispering a word that made his throat clench, and his stomach almost rebel. By the time he finished, everything on the funeral pyre was dry, the non-colour of dog-shit that had spent a hundred years baking in a hot sun.

He clapped his hands, and the monster's remains collapsed into dust, a foul little sand that danced away in the light breeze.

A wave of relief washed over him. One more job done, another intruder dead or evicted from this world. It was the closest he ever came to being happy, and he knew it wouldn't last.

Lanyard felt it then, the darkness on the edge of his vision, the chimes from a far-off place. He resisted the pull into the Aum, wondering if some adversary was trying to trap him in that vast darkness.

Lanyard! he heard Tilly call. He fell into the Aum then, his eyes closed to the dawn and the camp and the boy on his bird. He walked in an endless night, watching for danger.

She appeared as a speck of light, bright but unable to part the gloom, and then came upon him in a rush, a falling star that shivered and shook around the edges. He saw her in two ways here: the scarred warrior, his lieutenant, a leader in all but name; then he saw flashes of her as a young girl, facing a brutal world with pluck and dignity.

Lanyard! she shouted, the voice almost impossible to pick up. *Beware!*

"What is it?" he said, his voice eaten up almost instantly. This was very bad. If she was unable to skip a message across the Aum, a predator was listening in, siphoning away all sound, sucking at noise and light like a dog rooting marrow from a bone.

Do not - Crosspoint - danger

He pressed in close, trying to read her lips. Her image flashed and fluttered, then grew transparent.

"Get out of here, now!" he shouted. "Run!"

Dawn King! she managed, and then she was a star falling backwards, a light fleeing to a distant point. Lanyard felt them pressing around him, felt the brush of something against his shoulder, his hands—

Lanyard opened his eyes to the world of Now, and Mal was shaking him, slapping him across the face. When he saw Lanyard's blinked confusion, he stepped away, a guilty look on his face. He'd struck his master, his hero.

"No, boy, you done good," he mumbled. "I almost didn't make it back out."

He shared Tilly's cryptic message with the boy, wanting his perspective on the problem. She'd looked terrified, desperate to tell Lanyard something—risking her very life and soul to do so.

With a click of his finger and a bark of command, Lanyard opened a spiralling door into the Greygulf. He could be at Tilly's side in moments.

"I should return," he said, "to the Lodge."

"Miss Tilly was warning you," Mal said quietly.

Lanyard considered the silver nitrate landscape, that world between all worlds. He saw shapes moving on the shadow-roads, eye-twisting forms that were far from human. Then he realised strange structures had been raised in the Greygulf, entire cities of geodesic domes and steel towers, metal fingers scratching at the sky. Several roads were shifting, converging on the gate he'd just opened, and he slammed it shut, locked it, and burnt the door with his mind until it was utterly ruined.

Whatever these new visitors were, the Greygulf was completely overrun by them.

"Looks like we're travelling the old-fashioned way," Lanyard said. "We go now. Two minutes."

Grabbing his bedroll and canteen, Mal vaulted into Collybrock's saddle and watched nervously as Lanyard packed his gear back into the buggy, checked the tyres and the engine. Then they were on the road and moving, the bird loping along the tradeway, the buggy's engine whining and coughing blue smoke in their wake.

Lanyard stared towards Crosspoint with his one good eye, willing his machine to move faster, his old guts churning with worry. If Tilly was in great danger, that was exactly where he needed to be.

— 3 —

He drove them hard, day and night, carving across the dust of the Overland. Only once did he draw camp, and only then because the buggy's engine overheated.

"Sleep, boy, I will watch," he told Mal, and boy and bird crept into a tangle of feathers and brown skin, snoring and purring by the fire.

Lanyard sat on a rock, shotgun across his lap, and he fumed with impatience. His girl was in danger, and here he was, resting by a warm fire!

The old Jesusman never slept on a watch, but the weight of the world pulled on his eyes. Soon he was in a dream, but not the foggy kind where he crawled around in the maze of his own thoughts.

He saw things with a clarity greater than his own waking days could ever give, which told him he no longer dreamt in his own head. Lanyard Everett walked once more as a boy, a wretch with ribs showing and tousled hair, the severed noose still hanging from his neck.

He walked barefoot through the empty streets of Crosspoint, the First City. He saw the great buildings of old, the houses and temples that Papa Lucy and the sorcerers had raised for themselves, the Moot, the plazas and parks. There was another city hidden behind Crosspoint in this vision, a place of gleaming, golden towers, transparent visions that could only be seen from the corner of the eye.

The Waking City, he realised. The place where he'd killed Papa Lucy and saved the human race.

His feet brought him to the Lodge of the Jesusmen, as he knew they would. There was a logic to these meaningful dreams, and he was not surprised when he entered the inner sanctum to see the Boneman.

He was a skeleton that still held the soul of a man, his bones scored and charred, held together by a dark secret art. Only his eyes remained, brown orbs that seemed kind and always a little sad.

In ages gone he'd been the flesh-and-blood brother of Papa Lucy, both of them great magicians from the lost world of Before. He'd been Sol Pappagallo, an unwitting partner in the wholesale murder of billions and the destruction of the Before, and before he came to his senses, he'd almost burnt the Now to feed his brother's ambition.

The Boneman did not sit in the ancient seat of the Jesus, but he squatted on the steps below it, wrapped in a plain woollen cloak. He wore thick shackles on his wrists and his ankles, a dark metal fused directly to his bones. The chains sagged down around his feet, running down the steps until they pooled on the floor below. A distant, coiled snake.

"Lanyard," he said, rising shakily. "I have been permitted to speak with you this once. On a legal matter."

"What the hell is this?" Lanyard said. "Who has chained you?"

The Boneman made to talk, and then he wheezed, eyes darting about in fear. He shook his head.

"Certain topics cannot be discussed here," he finally managed. "There are rules to this place. Observers."

"Is this the Aum?"

"No," he said, gasping in pain. The skeletal man seemed to shimmer around the edges, and he fought this off with great effort.

"What is happening at Crosspoint?" Lanyard insisted. "Is Tilly in trouble?"

"This I can tell you: the lords of Overhaeven have judged me, and now they sit in judgement upon humanity itself. I am mounting a spirited defence on your behalf. I cannot help you in what you must do."

"You are in Overhaeven," Lanyard said. "Not Crosspoint."

The charred skull nodded once, eyes twinkling with pain.

"So you've left Tilly in danger?" he growled and made to leap upon the old lich. He crashed into something that he could not see, a body that was at once soft but unyielding. He felt a crushing blow land in his solar plexus, and he fell on his backside, winded and gasping for air.

"I beg you," the Boneman said, his voice trembling. "Be still. Listen. We are both in terrible danger."

Lanyard struggled to speak, to curse out the old sorcerer. His pain felt real, yet still he did not wake.

"We can die our Once-Death here, Jesusman. Yes, even me. So listen. I name you my heir, my agent, and my attorney. I cannot return to the Now."

Lanyard blinked at this news. The ancient sorcerer was their greatest champion and ally, and he was abandoning his post!

"I should have killed you when I killed your brother," Lanyard managed.

"Perhaps," the Boneman said. "My strength fails me, so listen carefully."

Dragging his chains behind him, the Boneman descended the steps and crossing the floor to where Lanyard lay. He knelt down, cradling the Jesusman's young face with the bones of his fingers.

"Seek out the Dawn King," the lich began, and then he shook in pain, his very bones vibrating with a frequency that hurt the nerves in Lanyard's teeth. Shaking his head from the pain, he struggled to speak.

"Overhaeven seeks to end us. It seeks to destroy the human race!" the Boneman blurted out, and the walls of the temple instantly began to shake, plaster falling from the ceiling. The Boneman cried out in pain, and his cloak burst into flame, surely a horror to the man who'd been burnt alive twice. The chains drew tight with a squeal of metal, his wrists and ankles already cracking from the force as the shackles pinched down. Lanyard felt his own flesh sear from the heat, and he fought to free himself from the Boneman's grip.

The sorcerer pressed his nails into Lanyard's temples, and the Jesusman felt a bright flash behind his eyes, as if he'd stared into the sunlight. An afterimage remained for a long moment: the shape of a key, a thing of bone and teeth, a jawbone stretched into a new purpose.

"Go to the scar of the Crossing! Run!" the Boneman shouted, pushing Lanyard towards the entrance. As his hands and feet snapped loose, dozens of small bones fell to the floor. The chain was now a long metal whip, striking at the Boneman, destroying the rest of his body with every pass.

Lanyard ran from the Lodge of the Jesusmen, the building shaking and collapsing around him. He turned back once to see the Boneman in complete agony, his limbs and ribs shattered into dust, his spine broken in a dozen places. When his skull fell to the ground, the metal chain fell upon it, crushing it flat with one blow.

Lanyard ran then, and he felt the blows of a dozen invisible fists, striking him about the head, neck, and shoulders. He willed himself towards the Papa Gate, the lurid mouth that guarded the oldest part of Crosspoint, the place at the very edge of this dream.

Then he felt the noose around his neck snap tight, and he was hauled off his feet, crashing to the cobblestones. Choking, he looked up to see the loose length of rope pulling upwards, drawing the slipknot tighter around his throat. What might have been feet or hooves cracked against his ribs, but he only had eyes for that severed rope, for the end of his life.

He wore the rags he'd worn to the gallows as a young boy, and nothing else. Throat burning, he began to see stars float in his vision—and then he saw it again, the afterimage of the thing that the Boneman had buried in his mind.

Lanyard reached for the image desperately, and then he was holding the jawbone in his hand. He drew the fangs and teeth across the leftover scrap of noose, carving through rope fibre like a razor, and then he lay about with the jawbone key, feeling the resistance as he cut through his unseen attackers. Their screams were an awful din, church bells and chainsaws, and they bled fat splashes of golden light wherever he struck at them, brilliant and blinding.

Finally, he was through the Papa Gate, and then he was sitting on the rock next to the campfire, gasping and clutching at his throat, staring wide-eyed at the real world. In the next heartbeat he was on his feet, kicking at Mal and his bird, yelling at them to get up.

"No more rest!" he shouted, already yanking on the ripcord that started the buggy's motor. "We go to Crosspoint, now!"

He saw the smoke long before he saw the city—and the swirling clouds of cockatoos hanging overhead, thousands strong. Soon Lanyard heard the birds, the screeching washing across the plains, and their joy could only mean one thing.

Lanyard and Mal crossed the last foothill and found Crosspoint in ruins. Fires raged in the shantytowns, and big sections of the outer wall had been pulled down, despite the ancient protections laid by Papa Lucy and the Family.

Lanyard opened up the throttle as much as he could, launching his buggy towards the breach in the walls. Refugees fled the city in all directions, by bike and car, by bird and by foot. Stumpy lizards hauled pagodas and wagons overloaded with terrified survivors, and as he weaved through the traffic, they looked at Lanyard with disbelief: who would drive *towards* that?

This close to the city, the dead were thick on the ground, and he drove over them without a care. Somewhere behind him young Mal was shouting, but he heard only the thick beat of his own heart and the protesting whine of the engine as he pushed it to the limit.

His tyres chewed up the bodies of the Boneguard, the sorcerer's personal garrison, as well as the militia, coin-riders, and even the crooked folk in their man-skins and hair vests. The corpses of monsters lay thick here, many of them Witches that had melted into pools of waxy goo.

Bouncing across rubble and dead meat, he sped over the breach in the wall and into the streets of the First City, the wheels fighting to grip in all of that gore.

Just before the Papa Gate, a scaly beast as high as the outer wall lay dead, its flanks seared with brands and Jesusman marks. It was equal parts lizard and siege engine, and dozens of tentacles reached forward, tipped with iron hooks the size of wagons. The creature had carved through the city walls, crushing buildings and people underfoot, heading unerringly towards the older districts.

Towards the Lodge of the Jesusmen.

Here the bodies of the Jesusmen lay thick, and he recognised some of the dead faces, good people who'd sold their lives to put down this colossus.

As he rounded the dead beast, the buggy's motor finally died with a bang, and then Lanyard was out and running through the streets, clutching a bag that clanged and rattled.

"Bossman!" Mal called to his right, Collybrock huffing as she pulled alongside. "Listen!"

The crackle of gun fire, the cries of the dead and the dying. A screech that drowned out all of this, inhuman and wavering, and it sent thousands of cockatoos away from their bloody meal and back into the sky, squawking in terror.

The noise came from the direction of the Lodge. Lanyard snatched up at Collybrock's harness, clutching to the bird's flank. He tossed the canvas bag up to Mal and pulled a pistol out of his belt.

Face set in a grim line, the prentice urged the riding bird onward. Collybrock struggled under the extra weight, and she slipped and slid over the corpses of monsters and men, through the rubble of destroyed buildings.

"Tired. Stop!" the bird moaned, but she kept picking a way forward, flinching when the deafening cry echoed again. They were close now, and they passed the ruins of Lady Bertha's manse, her mad disciples laughing with glee at the chaos all around them, one woman dancing around a courtyard with the body of a dead boy.

Here they saw the bodies of Taursi blocking an entire street, evidence of them fighting on both sides. The natives lay in spiny heaps, still grappling in death with their cousins from the Overhaeven, these ones clad in their glass armour. Sharp battle glass lay everywhere, and Collybrock suddenly cried out in pain, hopping on the spot.

"Mind that," Lanyard shouted, sliding out of the harness. "Your bird will go lame if you don't pluck that out."

Taking the bag from the boy, Lanyard ran forward, leaping over corpses. He slid around in the sprawling guts of a dead man and fell painfully to the ground, jarring his knees. Movement, and he raised his pistol, sending bullet after bullet into the face of an enemy Taursi, its glass apron already starred from gunshot. It fell, but not before it drove a freshly-cooked sliver of glass through Lanyard's hip.

White hot agony. Lanyard dropped gun and bag and fought to pull the long splinter of glass free. No sooner had he drawn it out of his own flesh when another creature came at him, another horse-spider like the one they'd killed. This one struck Lanyard with its hoofs, hoping to knock him senseless before finishing him off with its fangs. Lanyard stabbed out with the Taursi glass like a bayonet, drawing blood from those flashing legs and finally lodging it deep in the creature's brain.

Only then did he notice how badly he'd sliced up his hands on the glass. He fumbled the bag over his shoulder and gripped the pistol hard, welcoming the pain.

Other stragglers roamed here, alien beasts that were wounded or lost, and he murdered them with efficiency. Then came that most ancient of enemies: a Witch. The corrupted Jesusman came at him with white talons and a wide smile. One bullet, two, but the waxy creature had hidden its heart well, and then the hammer fell on an empty chamber. Lanyard struggled to reload his pistol, but his bloody fingers could not grip the bullets that fell around his feet with a tinkle.

"He's here! Lanyard is here!" the Witch cried out to its fellows, smile growing so wide that it reached almost right around its face. It made to pounce, and then a foot-long blade punched through its chest, the edges of the wound bubbling and retreating from the marks graven into that steel.

Mal stood in Collybrock's saddle, pressing down on the lance with all his might. Whistling, he ordered the bird forward, and it lashed out like a fighting rooster, clawing away at that corrupt flesh.

"Get that out of me," the creature groaned, trying to flow away from the lance. It shifted into the shape of a dog, a boy, and then a great serpent, but it could not free itself from the marks on Mal's blade.

"Stay clear," Lanyard barked to Mal, dodging the scaly coils that tried to fall around his head. He wrestled the old shotgun from its sling across his back, and he emptied two rounds into the enormous pale snake. The second shot found its twisted heart, and the Witch fell away from Mal's lance like warm marshmallow, a foul slurry with all the life driven out of it.

Again came that wavering screech, answered by a scatter of gunshot. Man, boy, and bird raced into the old town square, the trail of the dead and dying leading up to the front stair of the Lodge.

A rough barricade protected the entrance, built of toppled statues, doors, and even furniture lashed together. Behind this he saw dozens of terrified faces, and relief washed over him when he saw Tilly among them, handing out rifles and pikes.

There were others there, good people to have in a pinch. Yulio, a heavily moustachioed rifleman with a dead-eye aim, raining down bullets from the roof. Yulio's uncanny trigger skills had saved Lanyard more than once, which he raised every time Lanyard cuffed him for stealing or being drunk.

Bogle Hess, the last survivor of a leper colony, who was nothing but an eye slit in a pile of rags, and whispers of thanks during mealtimes. No one knew if Bogle was a man or a woman, but Lanyard sniffed them out as a Jesusman and employed them all the same, knowing what it was like to be despised, distrusted, turned away.

Dogleg, Rochelle, Piper, and Isembolde, Jesusmen who'd bled with him more than once. Stavros, who liked to share his smokes and gallows humour. Perhaps not good people, but good enough for this trade.

Then Tilly, his Tilly, his girl, the one who kept the lights on and gave him what purpose he had left. As bad as this day was, she drew breath, one small kindness.

There were many more, but to his shame, Lanyard did not know all their names. He had once, but many had died, and new recruits had come, and the bloody business went ever on.

The desperate shouts of the defenders gave way to a glad cry as Lanyard was spotted. He ran forward, scanning for enemies with his gun at the ready, and drew up short at a bizarre sight.

Near the feet of the Lodge steps stood two small boys, pale-faced and thin, dressed in matching black outfits. The fashion was strange, ruffled jackets, tights, shoes with buckles. The boys seemed to be brothers, and they held hands, pacing around in a small circle on the flagstones. Blond curls ran down to their shoulders, and fastened around each brow was a tiny crown, a circlet of purest black.

Surrounding this empty space, the plaza was filled with carnage. The corpses of the Jesusmen lay thick here, churned into a bloody mess, their weapons snapped into useless splinters.

Closest to the boys were the corpses of children, broken and stomped into paste. Small hands were outstretched to the circle, and

Lanyard saw enough to recognise his prentices, the kids he'd been teaching out in the bush.

I didn't teach them nearly enough, he thought.

Years back, the Boneman had compiled a book for Lanyard, explaining that when the gods dwelt in Overhaeven, they appeared as concepts, images like all the gods were. The Cruik was seen as a hooked staff, the Jesus a pair of fluttering hands, John Leicester the image of a slouch hat, and so on. There were many others, a litany of sigils and marks that stood for those terrifying immortals, in a realm without the laws of physics and time.

When the gods walked in one of the lesser worlds, they needed to take on a shape, a form. Lanyard searched his memory and remembered seeing the image of two black crowns, joined in a figure of eight.

The Smothered Princes.

"Mal," Lanyard warned, but his last prentice was already out of Collybrock's saddle, lance forgotten, walking towards the Princes like he was asleep.

At the top of the steps, Tilly and the others were screaming and shouting, but still Mal walked forward, slipping in the gore, rising, slipping again. The two boys in black turned as one, offering Mal the sweetest of smiles. They beckoned, and he came on, lips turned up into a vacant grin.

Lanyard crash tackled him, and man and boy fell into the gore. Mal bucked underneath him, wailing in denial.

"GIVE HIM TO US," one of the Princes said, speaking with the volume of ten men, and then they both stood there with mouths open, unleashing a hellish din that sounded like steel scraping on steel, a sound that reached right into Lanyard's bones and made his joints ache.

Then silence. They were anything but children, and the creatures eyed him hungrily, pacing around in a circle that they could not cross.

He dragged the struggling Mal away from the Princes, fighting to hold him still. He traced a sign on the boy's forehead, a Mark of Clarity, so forcefully that his thumbnail broke through the skin.

Mal's eyes opened wide, and he drew in quick gulps of air, looking with terror at the screaming Princes. He fetched up his lance and looked to Lanyard, who shook his head.

"WE CALLED THEM TO US," the older Prince mocked. "ALL YOUR LITTLE ONES."

Lanyard ignored the creatures and fetched up his shotgun from the ground. With shaking hands, he fed more shells into the weapon, and he paced around the Princes, sensing the sorcerous barrier that held them in place. Many Jesusmen had spent their lives to hold these monsters still, and already he could sense that the trap was failing.

"YOUR LITTLE WIZARDS SHOULD HAVE GIVEN YOU UP." Here the smaller boy scratched at an invisible boundary, wincing as the energy stung at his fingers.

"Who sent you?" Lanyard said.

Again the metallic screeching. Lanyard walked right up to the wards and emptied his shotgun into the Princes. The pellets did not break their skin, but the gunshot sent them reeling, and they closed their mouths, looking at the shotgun warily.

"Who sent you?" Lanyard repeated, feeding in fresh shells.

"THE DAWN KING."

He frowned at the name and held the shotgun level with the older Prince, aiming right between his eyes.

"WE SHALL BREAK THROUGH YOUR LITTLE NET," he said, face twisted into a snarl.

"Tell me about the Dawn King!" Lanyard shouted, punctuating this by pulling both triggers. The Prince clapped a hand to his face, howling metallic pain, and the younger one cowered, scratching away at the invisible wall.

Although the shells were marked with signs and the gun was holy and incredibly old, the shot did not even pierce the Princes' skin. Years ago, Lanyard had killed Papa Lucy with this same gun, and it seemed the gods had learnt a lesson.

"THE DAWN KING IS BELOW, AND ABOVE, AND LEFT AND RIGHT," the Prince said, glaring pure hatred at the man. "HIS HOUSE IS GLORIOUS, AND WE HAVE SWORN TO HIM."

"SWORN," the smaller Prince said.

"FETCH THE JESUSMAN, HE SAYS, AND SO WE FETCH YOU."

"I've heard enough of this," Lanyard said, turning his back on the pair. They screeched and mocked at him, hands now ending in talons, and they scratched away at their bonds, slowly tearing loose.

He fetched up the canvas bag from where he'd dropped it and hauled it towards the Princes. It clanked and rattled, and Lanyard walked right up to the invisible barrier before he tossed the bag through it.

It landed with a thick, metallic clang.

"Can't shoot you dead," Lanyard said. "So here's what I've got for you. That bag has got a dozen sticks of dynamite. Pipe bombs. Molotovs. Some old hand grenades."

He fed two fresh shells into his shotgun, his blood dripping along that ancient stock, and he snapped the action shut with an ominous click.

"Everything has been marked with the old signs. The dying signs, the binding signs, the ones that will keep you in pain long after that bag turns you into a mist of blood and shit."

He held the gun level with their faces and then pointed it downwards, lining up both barrels with the bag. The Princes panicked, scratching away for freedom, keeping as far from the canvas satchel as they could manage.

"Enough boom-boom there to take out you, me, the front of the Lodge there, everyone. Still worth it, I reckon."

"YOU CANNOT. YOU DO NOT DARE!"

"You've got two choices. Fuck off out of my world...or die in it."

The muscles in his forearm tensed as he slowly put pressure on the triggers. The Princes let off one final, terrified shriek, and then they instantly vanished from sight. Two black crowns clattered against the flagstones, stretching into the linked loops of their sigil, flaring out in golden light, and then this too was gone.

Lanyard stepped forward into the empty circle, scuffing at the ground with his boot, looking for anything they'd left behind. Slinging the gun over his shoulder, he picked up the canvas bag. Throwing open the flap, he slowly lifted out an ancient tin of baked beans.

"Shit. Grabbed the wrong bloody bag."

— 4 —

T he Boneman gave you a key," Tilly repeated.
   "Yep," Lanyard grunted.
   "Where is he?"
"Told you. He's gone."

Their small party was in the hills above Crosspoint, investigating the ancient scar in the earth that gave the place its name. Perhaps three hundred years had passed since the survivors of the Before staggered out of the gate here, driven mindless and low by their journey across the world veil.

Only a handful of people outside of the Family kept any knowledge of that dead world, of the billions murdered by Papa Lucy in his ambition. Those who were then called the Hesusmen also remembered—and wished they had not.

Below, the city was a smouldering ruin, and from here the refugees looked like ants, streaming away in all directions. Bands of crooked folk had made camp in the old slave yards, watching the surviving Jesusmen through binoculars, waiting to prey on the survivors.

Lanyard eased himself up from the scar in the bedrock and stood, wincing at his various aches and pains. Tilly had gathered together every pair of hands, every bird and bike, every gun, and still the number was woefully low.

The Jesusmen were forced to seize a big, stumpy lizard at gunpoint from the surviving Boneguard, and for one tense moment there was almost a second bloodletting in the streets. They did not believe

Lanyard's story of the Boneman's death, and they scoffed when he insisted he was the sorcerer's heir.

The Jesusmen left with the giant reptile, with a pagoda on its back that housed a working machine gun. A trade instead of death, and both Lanyard and the Boneman's soldier kissed the tradestone, an ancient tablet once belonging to the Boneman himself. For the stumpy and the gun, the Jesusmen were to turn over their Lodge and never return to Crosspoint.

"Enjoy it," Lanyard told the man, "before the crooked folk take it from you."

So now they waited before the scar, a caravan of the lost and beaten. Tilly had saved some of the prentices from the Smothered Princes, and they were pushing barrows and handcarts loaded with food, bullets, firewood.

The girl, Kirstl, was one of the surviving kids. Her face was a mess of bruises and lumps, wrists marked where someone had pinned her when the Princes called. She was craning her neck up to speak with Mal on his bird, and she smiled at the boy through a fat lip.

When Mal answered her, he didn't quite smile, still guarded as ever, but his shoulders relaxed a fraction. Then he leant down and pulled the girl onto his bird with one smooth motion.

Best tell Tilly, Lanyard thought, and then remembered that of course she knew. Tilly was aware of everything under the Lodge's roof.

"You sure it's here?" Tilly said to Lanyard.

"It's pulling at me like a fish-hook, right between my eyes."

"What does it open?"

"Dunno."

Lanyard rubbed at his forehead, worrying at a spot. He pinched hard at the skin and pulled, breathing hard between his teeth, refusing to cry out. Between thumb and forefinger he drew out a thick jag of bone, a sharp sliver that grew inch by bloody inch. Out came a tooth, and another, and then the whole thing fell out of his head like a newborn on the last push, the savage wound puckering closed almost instantly.

In his hand lay the jawbone, the key of bone and teeth that had cost the Boneman his life. He showed it to Tilly, who set her mouth in a disapproving line.

"There's nowhere safe that can take us," she said.

Lanyard arched an eyebrow.

"The Greygulf, the Aum, everywhere is overrun by this enemy. Quarterbrook and Rosenthrall sent for help over the telegraph before the lines came down. Lanyard, we've already lost."

"What would you do, girl? Think."

"Regroup. Hide our people in the Inland, and we keep moving. Dog our attackers for as long as we can."

"Is that an answer?"

Tilly frowned. Lanyard turned the key over in his hands. It was heavy, as if the bone was a patina over lead, and the teeth were a mixture of fangs, human teeth, even the peg molar of a horse.

"Those monsters came to Crosspoint looking for you," Tilly said, an edge to her voice. "They killed everyone because of you, and you weren't even here!"

"Are you done?" Lanyard said. The look in her eyes said she was far from done.

He raised his voice. "Listen. You all swore to this cause. Would you go bandit, watch city after city fall while you skulk around the desert?"

"That's not what I meant," Tilly said. Behind her, a wall of waiting eyes watched the old man put his lieutenant to rights.

He saw the sullen looks, the fear on the men and women drawn up before him. They'd been beaten and knew it, and now he was asking for the last of what they had.

"You bunch of bloody cowards. I'll go on my own if I have to."

He saw the grudging twitch around Tilly's mouth, the sign that a smile would win through. It wasn't the first time they'd butted heads, and Lanyard could still picture her as the little girl with oversized boots, dogging his steps, never afraid to stand up to the old man if she thought he was wrong.

Lanyard held out the key towards the scar in the rock, and it twitched in his hands like a divining rod. He followed the movement, scanning left and right, and then finally he slid the key forward, into an empty space in the air.

He felt the teeth pushing against unseen tumblers, the grip of keyhole against key. He turned the jawbone clockwise, and then a latch turned, one piece of the universe shifting just so, a movement of less than an inch. A force pushed back from this movement, a vibration so strong that Lanyard felt it in the back of his eyeballs, down to his bones, dancing along his marrow.

Long fused shut, the scar of the Great Crossing teased open, as if a scab peeled free from the rock. A curtain of purest white oozed upwards, both milk and cloud, and it settled into the form of a great arch, wide enough to admit thousands.

There were thirty-three Jesusmen left. Including the prentices.

"Gonna find this Dawn King," Lanyard said. "Then I'll rip his fucking head off."

He stepped through the milky gate. All thirty-three followed.

They moved through a world of dense fog, so thick that visibility was less than ten feet. There was a light source somewhere above, and everything was diffused with the purest white. The cold wormed its way into every joint, chapping at any exposed skin, but it was completely dry, and felt like it was wicking away moisture rather than providing it.

Lanyard remembered trips across the Drift, the sandstorms limiting visibility even more than this. The Boneman had given him a gift long ago for times like this, a way of seeing his people no matter what, and it was one of the few secrets he kept from Tilly. But staring around the fog, he was just as blind as everyone else.

Wherever they'd landed, the rules had changed.

He hollered out names and told everyone to draw in close.

"Ropes if you've got 'em. Everyone stays in contact. Tilly, I want ten stout fellows on the hand-wagons there. You kids, I want everyone holding hands, a human chain. No bloody complaining, you lot."

The fog seemed to swallow up sound, and the Jesusmen had to repeat these instructions. One of the kids set to sobbing, and his neighbours mocked him relentlessly.

"Shut your faces," Tilly barked. "Another hour of this, and you'll be crying, too."

Then they moved. Lanyard followed the growl of the motorbike in front of him, figuring it was heading in as good a direction as any. Birds paced alongside, left and right, ropes trailing from their harnesses for people to keep a hold of.

Finally walked their camel, a honking, rude beast with fangs and attitude to spare. Heavy with baggage and supplies, it had nipped at the children and spat at Lanyard, but even this beast fell to quiet terror, honking to itself and eagerly following the tug of the ropes.

The big lizard with the pagoda was a hulking shape in the mist, its feet and tail scraping over the ground. They walked upon smooth rock, almost a white milk stone, and if Lanyard was correct about where the Boneman had sent them, no tool would ever mark that substance.

When Lanyard thought to call a stop, hours might have passed in that endless trudge, or even a day, but nothing in the endless swirl changed, and the diffuse light grew neither stronger nor weaker. Lanyard lit a small fire for cooking and for billies of tea, and the light and heat seemed to barely penetrate the endless gloom. Ten steps away, and Lanyard could barely see the fire at all, just the wink of a bright spot that could have been a star.

"We've lost two," Tilly said, appearing at his elbow. "Eli and young Tara."

They formed a search party, and they called out into the mist, their voices muffled and weak. Lanyard tied ropes together until they had one line that was fifty yards long. They sent one fellow out on the rope, a man with good hearing who'd been a poacher in a previous life. When they reeled him back into their little camp, he shook his head.

The missing people could've been within a mile, but they were as good as lost. Lanyard fell into an uneasy sleep, his mind chewing over the fact that his people were going to wander, lost and scared, calling out for help until their throats were raw. They were going to die of thirst in here.

He hoped that Tara and Eli found each other. He hoped that they cursed his name, that they made their peace before Eli turned the gun on the child and then upon himself.

Lanyard strained his ears for the sound of gunshot, but he heard nothing. The oppressive white murk swallowed even the crackling of the cook fires, and he heard nothing.

Sleep, and endless trudging. Lanyard had an old wind-up watch, looted from a bleedthrough, but the mechanism had seized up the moment they'd crossed the gate. With no idea of the hour, they set up camp whenever the birds grew tired and snappy, or whenever the stumpy sat on its haunches, refusing to move.

Despite their best efforts, each campfire revealed another person missing. Birds that had turned aside for a moment, bikes that stalled and sputtered to a stop, and in the blink of an eye they were lost to the endless fog. Lanyard snapped out orders, and the Jesusmen strapped all of the supplies to the already overloaded lizard. They took axes to the handcarts, breaking them apart for firewood.

"Lanyard, I'm worried about the prentices," Tilly told Lanyard as he boiled his liver-root. "Fevers, diarrhea. Tomil is having his seizures again."

He grunted, looking over the misery of their camp. Even the strong and the grizzled looked exhausted, washed out. Beyond that, shapes hunched around the winking firelight, the silhouettes of men and women dying by inches.

"The Boneman sent us here," he said. "Helping us killed him. Keep faith, girl."

"But we're blind in here!" Tilly said. "I'd give anything for another Turtwurdigan. Doubt we're even walking a straight line in this place."

"We will survive this," Lanyard said. Tilly merely shook her head, the weight of the lost visible in her haunted stare.

Shifting his billy as it finally boiled, Lanyard felt the heft of the Boneman's key on his hip, the jawbone wedged into a spare gun holster. He'd not spared it a thought since entering the fog, all of his energy devoted to keeping his people together and alive.

He drew out the key, the sharp teeth scoring the leather. Now that it was a real thing, removed from his soul and his mind, it simply sat in his hands, inert and dead. It did not draw him in any direction, did not speak to him in the Boneman's voice, did nothing but weigh heavy in his hand.

There was no way back into the Now. All they had was this foggy nightmare, sapping all the life and will from his mob.

"Bloody Boneman," Lanyard snarled, and hurled the key out into the gloom, where it clattered and bounced across the stone, like a dice-throw into oblivion.

"No!" Tilly said, jumping to her feet. "Give me that rope."

"Waste of time," Lanyard muttered, handing over a hodgepodge of rope and cord, twine-baling, even plaits of string. Tilly shook her head, making sure to tie the ragged fibres around one of her belt-loops.

"Hold this end. By the Jesus and John Leicester and everything else that you hold dear, do not bloody drop this."

Alarmed at the determination in her face, Lanyard did as instructed. He held the rope tight, wrapped it around the healing wound on his palms. Two, three strides, and Tilly was lost in the drifting cloud, a gloomy shape, and then there was nothing left of her.

"Don't you wander off, girl," Lanyard called out, his words instantly swallowed. He fed the line through his hands, felt it jerking left, right. Drops of his own blood clung to the fibres, dripping down onto the milky stone. One of the knots started to slip, and he snatched at the rope, retying the hitch as quickly as he could. Tilly jerked impatiently at the line, and he let it slip through his fingers, praying the knot would hold.

When the line fell slack, Lanyard's heart lurched, and he thought he might be ill. He inched the line backwards, teeth clenched, mindful of the knots. He hoped to meet resistance, as if fishing for the meal that might save his life.

It felt like long minutes, and he called out to the Jesus, to the dead Boneman, even Papa Lucy, begging that they bring back his girl, bring back his heart before it broke.

If he lost her now, doomed her to this slow, pointless end, Lanyard told himself that he would feed a fresh shell into the shotgun, hold the god-cannon up to his chin, and evaporate his pain in one fiery instant.

The rope grew taut, and then slack again. One tear fell down the leather of Lanyard's cheek, lost in his beard. Hauling in the line, he felt a final resistance, and fed the line hand over hand, drawing his Tilly back into light and life.

She emerged from the gloom, holding up the abandoned jawbone, her face as dark as a thunderstorm.

"Do you know how far you threw this damn thing?" she yelled. "You damn fool. Our ticket out of here, and you threw it away!"

Untying herself, she wrapped a loop of twine around the middle of the jawbone and let the bone dangle underneath her hand, the fibres turning, spinning, the bone slowly unwinding from that tension.

At the end of that movement, the bone key turned slightly, the lightest of movements. Tilly moved the rope and bone left, then right, and each time the point of the key settled into the same direction.

"It's not just a key," Tilly said. "The Boneman gave you a compass."

Tilly led that chain of people and beasts out of the mist, the jawbone pointing their way. After a few hours of travel, the fog around them lessened, and soon Lanyard could make out all of his people, if only with his normal vision. Those who lagged behind could be heard as they cried out for help, and Mal swept back and forth on Collybrock, tossing out ropes for the weary to clutch onto.

The pure white stone underfoot began to show irregularities, ripples and marks, and then it became first rock, then clay, and finally a pale soil. Soon Lanyard paid little attention to the swinging jawbone and advanced forward with shotgun handy, ready to speak the words of binding and breaking.

The change in the Jesusmen was immediate. They'd gone from victims to wiry hunters, survivors in a strange land. Bird riders rode in close, lances and guns held ready. Those children who were fit ran alongside the gunmen, hatchets and slings to hand.

The stumpy lurched out of the mist, tongue flicking, and the machine gunner watched in all directions, the chatter gun ready to unleash murder on any enemy.

The fog faded away, and the Jesusmen set foot into a field of bone-white wheat, with rolling hills stretching off into the distance. Small wisps of the fog clung to the landscape, a reminder of the thick bank of cloud that they'd finally emerged from.

Even as they watched, a hill slowly rose from the landscape, turning into a craggy mountain and then sinking just as quietly back into the earth. Around them the wheat shrivelled and died, and pale flowers began to grow underfoot, petals uncurling and scattering as the Jesusmen pushed through.

"Look there," the machine-gunner shouted, and Lanyard saw a cluster of figures on the horizon, watching their progress. They weren't friendly or unfriendly, they just were.

He called for a far-glass and climbed up into the pagoda, focusing on the distant figures. Men and women, but they were pale, weak around the edges, no matter how he focused the lenses on the far-glass. Animals, but none like he'd ever seen in the Now, or heard of from the Before. Strange creatures like thorn bushes that seemed to shiver and glide, others that floated like box-kites, and more were appearing now, each weirder than the last.

These beings did nothing but wait there, watching their progress, bearing a silent witness to the intruders in their land.

"Set up camp," Lanyard called out to his mob. "The locals will come to us soon enough."

The light in the sky was diffused from some unseen source. No sun, no moon, no stars marked the passage of time. It took perhaps an hour to raise their tents and cook up a meal, and the sky changed from a sepia hue to a bruised purple, enough to suggest dusk or night-time in this strange place.

The perimeter sentries raised a shout, and the camp exploded into action. Prentices ran about, handing out rifles and pikes, and the bird-riders formed up into a tight line, ready to set up for a charge. Two of the bikers revved their engines, gunners and crossbowmen aiming from the sidecars.

A trio of creatures approached their camp.

"Stop right there," Tilly shouted. The three figures halted as instructed. One took the vague shape of a man, as if a statue had weathered centuries of rain, the folds of face and limbs and clothing more suggested than defined. It had something that might have been a beard and shallow pits to pass for eyes and mouth.

A rodent squatted down by the man's feet, a creature of large, quivering ears, face filled with eyes of midnight black. It scanned the camp nervously, as if ready to bolt for its life.

The third creature was the size of a large wagon, a mass of branches and thorns that grew dense at the centre. Something moved in there, a pulsing shadow that might have passed for its organs. Even at rest, the thorn-beast moved and flowed like a jellyfish, its thousands of sharp points moving like cilia, forming shapes that made Lanyard's eyes swim.

They waited, staring at the Jesusmen as if ogling a curiosity. Lanyard ambled forward, ancient shotgun resting across his shoulders. He held his murder in check, riding on that long moment when a stranger was neither friend nor enemy, even as every fibre urged him to unleash lead and death, to send round after round thundering at anything that defied instant understanding.

"No need for your guns," the man who was barely a man said. "I am here as a custom and a courtesy. To welcome you."

"Welcome us?"

"To the Underfog. Stranger, you walk in the lands of the dead."

I have seen four other living souls enter the Underfog," the man said. "Gretel of the House of Torana. The Gravedigger. And of course, Papa Lucy and the Boneman."

Their host was bleached by centuries of existence, his flesh little more than driftwood or stone. He'd introduced himself as Paeter but had long forgotten any other name or detail about himself.

"Necromancers and fools. The Underfog is a dangerous place to the Once-Dead, and even more dangerous to the living. Never has anyone entered in such numbers. You invite trouble, Lanyard Jesusman."

Lanyard and Tilly sat with the trio, well clear of their own camp. They'd left the other Jesusmen in a state of high alert, and the men and women were digging into the pale soil, carving out trenches and piling up an earth rampart for defence.

Plucking at the soil in the centre of their parley circle, Paeter set out the suggestion of logs and a circle of stones. With thumb and fore-finger, he teased out a pale blue flame, weak and dancing, offering almost no warmth.

"Do you have the means to turn around? Perhaps you should return to the world of the living."

"No," Lanyard said. "No going back."

"Well, then," Paeter said, the gouge that passed for a mouth curving up slightly. "I offer you the counsel I give to all the newly dead. All these lands are free to you, between the Edgemist and Shale."

"Shale?"

"The final shore."

Lanyard had heard the Boneman's tale, how he'd pursued his brother to the stony beach at the edge of life itself, how he had cast Papa Lucy into those dark waters. To fall into that ocean meant the final end for these lingering spirits, the Twice-Death.

"Those who have suffered the Once-Death can survive for a long time here. There are philosophical pursuits and teachers with centuries of knowledge. There are lords in the Underfog, cities and associations, salons and festivals. Visit the House of Avadon, and see the Palace of the King of the Birds! It can be a most *glorious* world."

Lanyard looked down at the weak campfire, lips drawn thin.

"I don't see any glory here. Just husks of men, reflections of better places."

"Ho! This one sees the right of things, Paeter!" the rodent creature said in the man-tongue. It sat on its haunches, weighing Lanyard and Tilly with eyes of pitch black. Every few moments it quivered, after-images of it moving left, right, running, waiting, even as the main creature at the centre of these possibilities sat perfectly still.

"This is Bilben of the Iron Nest," Paeter said by way of introduction. "The first Queen of her people, whom she serves even in death. Watch how she considers every outcome and frets herself into never acting."

"Untrue," Bilben said, and the thorn creature bristled in what must have been laughter.

"How would you educate these fools, then?" Paeter said.

"You, girl. Attend me!" Bilben said to Tilly and scurried around the fire, flashes of the hopping rat leaping in a dozen different directions. At the last they all combined into the one figure, which sat before Tilly's crossed legs, looking up at the girl with questing eyes, long snout sniffing, whiskers twitching.

"I look upon you, and I see warmth, the flush of blood, the electricity dancing around in your brain. You have life in you, and it stands out like a beacon. Any of us Once-Dead will know that a living creature walks in our lands."

She lifted a delicate paw and pointed out the busy camp, the lumbering of the giant lizard, the fluffy preening of the birds.

"So here you come, a whole tribe of living folks. You will draw the curious and well-meaning spirits, who wish only to hear your tales, learn about the living world you visit us from. Then, there are the others."

Paeter raised an arm, seeking to silence her, but Bilben drew back her lips, hissing and snarling in the old man's direction.

"There are creatures here, monsters who think nothing of tearing apart the Once-Dead, especially the new ones that Paeter sends their way. Oh don't deny it, you greedy thing!"

Lanyard noticed how the man-thing played at laughter, clapping together his crusty old hands, but everything about his body spoke of sudden tension. Danger.

"Vampires of a sort, and they live here, siphoning off the souls of these new spirits, making them weak," Bilben continued. "Those whom the vampires catch have no choice but to enter servitude, or else they will march to Shale, with nothing left to resist its pull."

"A fanciful tale from the mind of a mouse!" Paeter scoffed. The enormous thorn-beast flared up a little at these words, perhaps a threat display, and it rolled slightly from left to right as if shifting on its feet. Paeter held up a hand in submission, wary of the creature.

"So, now you know how the villains of this land treat the Once-Dead," Bilben continued. "How do you think they will treat you, those of living body and soul? Will they shelter you and offer aid and advice?"

She paused, ears twitching as she gauged her listeners. Across the faux campfire, Paeter shook his head and began to offer denial and complaint. The rodent stood up on her haunches, as high as she could, and when she spoke it was with the volume of ten men, drowning out the statue man's voice.

"They will tear your souls out and wear your skins as their own. Many here seek to leave the Underfog, and they will take centuries of dread knowledge into the worlds of the living. I say to you, human folk, if any of your company falls and is worn as a skin-puppet, murder it instantly."

Lanyard watched Paeter reach for the fire, plucking it free from the ground. With a twist of his hands, it was suddenly a long knife, the blade flickering with a blue light. He moved swiftly, reaching for Bilben, his sliver of mouth twisted down in hatred.

Even as Paeter took the first step, Lanyard already had his shotgun up and tracking, that murderous god-cannon barking. One shot, two, and then Paeter was falling backwards from the campfire, wailing, his body like a papier-mâché shell punched full of holes.

The thorn-mountain bristled a little at the murder, but did not move, as if considering the living invaders. Bilben could only watch wide-eyed at the sudden violence, quivering and running about in a tight, nervous circle.

Paeter bobbed across the landscape like a balloon, little dribbles of his life-stuff splashing to the pale ground, giving off flashes of blue light that were soaked up instantly. His feet scrabbled against the pliable soil as he floated off, fighting to get a grip on the land, but he could not fight the force that dragged him away.

Soon Paeter did not move at all and merely drifted towards the horizon, arms and legs limp, head hung low, but he let out a pitiful cry so strong that it made Lanyard shudder. Lanyard got the old Witch-aches then, little hooks in his teeth and his joints, and from the cries behind him he knew that the other Jesusmen felt it too.

"That one was old, very strong from the lives he has stolen, but even he could not withstand that," Bilben said, eyeing the smoking shotgun, face wide with fear. "Paeter is on his way to Shale now."

"Speak true or you will join him."

Bilben shook with a dozen ghosts. One laughed, one lunged at Lanyard with fangs bared, but the rest ran, darting in all directions. These images coalesced into one terrified rodent, who bowed her head in agreement.

"I swear to speak the truth, Jesusman, painful as it always is."

Now that they were clear of the Edgemist, their makeshift compass stopped working. The jawbone spun as before, but it did not settle on any direction, simply unwinding until the twist of cord gave out.

"Tell me what you seek here, Lanyard Jesusman," Bilben said hopefully, whiskers twitching. "Perhaps I can help?"

"Don't know you," Lanyard said. "Don't trust you."

Bilben eyed the shotgun on his shoulder, the one that had punched holes in old Paeter.

"You are right to not trust me," she said. "Trust no one in this land, for all will seek to use you."

"So what will you use us for?" Tilly said.

The rodent moved in a twitching blur, all of her instances climbing up until she rested on Tilly's shoulder.

"I offer my service as a guide, translator, and voice of wisdom and caution," Bilben said. "In return, I hope to call upon you for a future favour."

"We owe you no favours," Tilly said. Even still, she scratched the spirit under the chin, and it preened to this attention.

"This is true," Bilben said. "I can only hope to win you to a good cause."

"Even the darkest villain thinks his cause is just," Lanyard said.

The enormous bundle of thorns rolled around their camp, keeping a wary distance ever since the shooting of Paeter. Bilben introduced this creature as The Serene.

"There are exactly ten of these thorn-spirits in all of the Underfog," Bilben said. "Few have bothered to learn their language, but I have devoted two centuries to understanding this one."

Drifting past the picket-line of birds like a huge tumbleweed, The Serene pulsed twice, forming brief flashes of limbs and shapes.

"It says you carry a special glass with you, one that drinks the light of stars. It begs me to abandon you and flee for my own safety."

"It's star-glass," Tilly said. She fetched one from her shirt pocket, and it blazed on her palm like a miniature sun. The Serene puffed up in a threat display, doubling in size and retreating to a safe distance.

"The Serene says that is an Overhaeven crafting. Are you gods?"

"We're not gods," Lanyard said, "just idiots with some leftovers."

"Show your godly things to no one here," Bilben warned. "Those who live in the shining lands are not beloved in the Underfog."

Tilly tucked away the glass, her pocket instantly dousing the clear light. All around them, the sky was a dark purple, almost black, and beneath that the landscape slumbered, hills and ranges slowly shifting as if the land itself breathed in and out.

It creeped the hell out of Lanyard. He wanted to fetch out every star-glass they still had, to set a bright light against this bizarre land, even as common sense told him their fires brought attention enough.

His mob was exhausted from the trip through the Edgemist, and he was unwilling to push them any further until the sepia light returned. He saw men and woman sprawled out on swags, dozing like dogs around their fires. Tilly went to check on the prentices with Bilben still chattering in her ear, and Lanyard was glad of the peace.

Mal appeared on the other side of Lanyard's little cook-fire and took it upon himself to prepare his master's liver-root tea. Even though the lad looked drained, he shared the silence with the old Jesusman.

"You should rest with the other kids," Lanyard said. *Spend what time you have left with your little girlfriend.*

"Nah," the boy replied.

The precious firewood cracked and spat. Lanyard remembered another campfire like this, when he was barely older than Mal and just as broken inside. In a moment of madness, he'd leapt across the fire, murdering his old master with a rock.

He'd damned old Bauer for dragging him into the life of a Jesusman, for gifting him with that maddening knowledge. Killing the old man did nothing but interrupt his education.

Lanyard looked at young Mal, at the way his dark eyes soaked up the firelight, and wondered if one day the boy might finally break and end his life in the same way.

"Hey, bossman," Mal said.

"Yeah?"

"Will we get home after this?"

"I don't know, boy."

Silence, interrupted by the metal tinkling of the spoon against the billy, as Mal stirred in the medicine.

"Long as we get those bastards what killed the other kids, guess it's okay," the boy mumbled, serving the tea to Lanyard.

"True," Lanyard said. "We're not good at fixing stuff, but we're pretty good at revenge."

There was a sudden clamour on the other side of the camp, near the sleeping lizard and the tents of the prentices. Lanyard was instantly on his feet, a pistol drawn, Mal at his heels.

"Lanyard!" Tilly yelled, and then his careful approach became a run. He fought his way through a group of onlookers standing around the flaps of a tent, and sent one laggard reeling with a boot to the backside.

"Girl, I'm here!" Lanyard grunted. Tilly was kneeling next to one of the prentices, a girl tangled up in her bedroll. A corpse, damp with sweat, staring blankly up at the ceiling of the tent.

Standing over the body was the exact image of the girl, but pale and washed out, less *there* than the living body it had just stepped out of. A Once-Dead spirit, fresh from a corpse, and she looked at Lanyard with a mixture of confusion and hatred.

"Stand clear!" Lanyard ordered, aiming his pistol at the heart of the spirit.

"Stop!" Tilly cried, putting herself between Lanyard and the ghost. Snarling with frustration, he stepped back, but he would not put the pistol away.

"I got here just as Rella was in a seizure," Tilly said. "She caught sick in that fog. Went downhill fast."

Lanyard watched the girl-ghost pacing around in the tent, looking down in horror at her own dead body. She looked mistrustfully at the adults who hadn't saved her life, and clenched her hands into small pale fists. Rella had been a wild little thing, and Lanyard remembered breaking up more than one fight between her and the other prentices.

"Rella," he said, holding the gun down by his side. "Don't do anything stupid."

The fight went out of the girl-ghost. She broke into tears, little blue splashes that fell down her face. One droplet fell from her nose and splattered onto her cooling body. The corpse twitched at the touch, a little shiver that made her back arch, her dead feet drum against the bedroll.

"Keep back!" Bilben said, the rodent appearing between Tilly's feet. It stood on the girl's body, snarling up at the ghost. "This isn't yours now."

Rella hunched before her own body and tried to push the rat creature aside, a dark hunger written all over her face. Bilben snapped teeth at the girl's fingers, driving her back.

"You can't go back in," the tiny creature said, not unkindly. "You have to let this body go."

Rella howled, a lost sound that sent a shiver up Lanyard's spine. She curled up in a corner of the tent, bawling hysterically.

"Take the body outside," Bilben said, looking up at Lanyard. "Burn it quickly."

He nodded, wide-eyed, scooping up the small corpse. Rella leapt up then, lashing out with her ghost fists, and it was all that Tilly and Bilben could do to hold her back.

The awful cries of the newly dead thing chased Lanyard out of the tent, and he trembled as he pushed through the horrified onlookers.

He carried the body through the camp, past fires and empty swags, and found a bare spot behind the latrine pit. Here he placed her, a little child asleep, and then he was stacking armloads of wood over her, precious fuel that he was now drowning in rotgut spirits, soaking the pyre with an entire flagon.

"No! Please!" he heard Rella cry. She was fighting hard now, three or four grown men holding her back. Her spirit stuff was slick, like holding in an armload of intestines, and she almost wriggled loose. Lanyard looked to Tilly, who nodded.

"I'm sorry you died like this," Lanyard called out, striking a match. Instantly the blaze of a funeral pyre burst to life, and the ghost of the girl sank to the pale ground, sobbing in defeat.

The spirit of Rella stood by her own pyre for hours, watching the fire burn away her flesh, char her bones. The stink of her burnt meat washed over the camp, and the living Jesusmen kept well clear of the scene.

As the purple night gave way to a fresh sepia dawn, Rella finally turned away. Without another word or a look to the living, she climbed the rampart, navigating her way through the rough trench-work.

Lanyard kept vigil through his far-glass, watching the spirit as she ran across the landscape, untiring, the slow-shifting hills finally swallowing her whole.

"She heads to Shale," Bilben said from his shoulder, cleaning her whiskers.

"Don't we all," Lanyard said.

— 6 —

No one else died that night, but the fog-sickness was hard to shake. Half of the prentices were listless and could not keep down their food. Yulio coughed constantly, his long moustache slick with phlegm and vomit.

"He is our best rifleman," Lanyard muttered to Tilly. "Damn this place."

They broke camp swiftly, wanting to get away from the stink of the pyre. The bikes kicked into smoky life and mosquito whining, the birds quarrelled and snapped at the camel, and the lizard rose with a groan, unwilling to leave the bed it had scratched out for itself.

"That way," Lanyard said, pointing where Rella had crossed deeper into Death. They left that sad camp behind, and Lanyard realised they would never pass back this way.

I kill all of us to do this, Lanyard thought, the smoke of the pyre still painting the sepia sky behind them.

There is only revenge now, and then we end.

The fire had drawn more of the Once-Dead here, curious observers that dotted the landscape in twos and threes. Diluted creatures from a hundred different worlds, watching them pass by.

The survivors moved in a nervous pack across that breathing landscape. Fingers lingered near triggers, and when some of those spirits began to keep pace with their caravan, the machine-gunner let loose a burst of warning shots over the heads of those who lurked nearest.

Lanyard whistled through his teeth, glaring up at the pagoda. The gunfire stopped. Tilly climbed the lizard's rigging and sent the trigerman packing with a swear word and a boot to the arse.

The commotion drew even more of the curious dead, but they kept a cautious distance. The rolling ball of The Serene returned, and Bilben darted away to confer with her friend.

"The Serene says these ones were drawn by the body," Bilben told Lanyard when she returned. "All of these Once-Dead, travelling through the night to get here. Mark this, Lanyard Jesusman: had you not burned the corpse, one of them would be wearing your lost girl like a coat, causing mischief and woe."

Lanyard caught a sudden movement out of the corner of his eye, and he whistled in alarm. A spirit about the size of a big dog had been stalking their caravan, keeping its barrel body low to the ground, but now it was loping towards the rear-guard, blue spittle flying from a face full of fangs.

One shot rang out. Even in his shaking sickness, Yulio the moustachioed rifleman put a round between the beast's eyes. It staggered sideways and then turned tail and ran, yipping and shrieking as it bypassed the entire caravan, heading for Shale at a fast clip.

Lanyard ignored the beast, scanning the landscape for further threats. Under the weight of all those staring eyes, he realised this first attack was a test. There would be more.

"The House of the Accurate Count is closest," Bilben said. "They have stability there, and laws. The House provides a service to all, and none molest them."

By the hungry twinge in his gut, Lanyard supposed they had been travelling for hours. There was no sun to track, just a diffuse glow in the sky, and anyone with a watch reported it to be frozen, the mechanisms seized.

All around them, hundreds of spirits dogged their passage. Above the lizard, Lanyard leaned over the edge of the pagoda, scanning the groups with his far-glass. Some of the creatures were too bizarre to read, but there were groups of human spirits here, and he could pick their moods well enough. There were those who were simply curious, here for some distraction from their endless ennui.

Others watched them hungrily, the shades of people burnt pale from centuries of survival. They bore pikes and long knives forged with the blue spirit stuff. They kept other creatures in chains made from the same material and prodded them along with whips. Larger spirits were bound in blue-laced harnesses, and they rode upon these like horses.

"Bilben," Lanyard called, and the creature leapt from Tilly's shoulder, shifting across the ground and up the lizard's flank in a ribbon of rodent shapes.

"That group there," he said, holding the far-glass for her to use. She pushed it aside with a paw.

"My eyes see well enough," she said. "They are Chain-Folk. Slavers or criminals when they were alive, and death did not improve them."

Lanyard knew their type well enough. As a young man, he had run with the slavers of the Riverland, trading in that misery. The pay had been good enough to buy his silence, and there was grog to drown out the rest.

He saw Mal out by the perimeter, keeping watch with the other bird-riders. His little friend Kirstl rode with him, clinging to his waist, and the boy chatted easily with her.

They were sharing an apple, and their simple back and forth with the fruit caused Lanyard's heart to ache. Lanyard had never known anything like this in his own life. He'd had women of course, but it was always a jaded exchange, tawdry. Little affection and no connection.

He'd doomed Mal and Kirstl's lives, but he'd also doomed this young love, and it was just one more sin to add to his growing list.

Freeing the boy had been a token gesture compared to the sins of his past. When he rode out under the Boneman's law and put the gun to the last of the slavers, he'd recognised one or two of the men he shot, blood brothers from his criminal past. Without the curse of the Jesusman's life, his own spirit would have been here by now, riding with those monsters below.

"Do not let them seize any of your people," Bilben said. "No telling what they will do with a living body."

Lanyard grunted. Next to him, Yulio swung the machine-gun on its pivot, tracking the largest group of Chain-Folk. One rode on the shoulders of a creature that looked like a skinless bear, save that it walked upright. The rider lay about with a whip of bright blue light, lashing at prisoner and ally alike.

"You want I put some of them down, bossman?" Yulio said, focusing the gun on the warlord. He broke into a sudden coughing fit and hacked a gob of something over the side of the pagoda.

"No," Lanyard said. The gun was etched with fresh killing marks, and the prentices had scratched more onto the bullets in the canisters, but when these were fired, the big gun would be useless. No supply train followed and no caches waited ahead; there was nothing for the living in this place but pale lands and hungry eyes.

"Girl," he called out, and Tilly climbed up the side of the lizard, resting the crook of an arm over the pagoda railing. Wary of Bilben, Lanyard leaned in closely.

"I want a full count of our supplies," he said. "Food. Water. Medicine. Ammo. Do it quietly, and get it to me quick."

Tilly nodded gravely. She paused as if to say something else, but then there was a shout from below. The whip-lashing slaver was leading a large group of spirits into a trot, and soon they would cross the Jesusmen's path, forcing them to stop or divert.

"They are in range," Yulio said. Lanyard watched as the Chain-Folk began to head them off, all lashing whips and hooting laughter. His neck prickled with suspicion, and he turned to see the real threat, an even larger group of human souls, bearing pikes and long knives, blades wreathed in blue.

Behind them were more, and these spirits bore chains, open shackles and iron collars.

There was no time for words. Lanyard reached past Yulio, wrenching the machine-gun around, and when the moustachioed shooter saw the charging horde, he opened fire. Lanyard jerked his hands away from the heat of the barrels and fumbled for his pistol.

As they'd done in countless exercises, the Jesusmen stopped, instantly forming into a defensive posture. The bikes peeled away from the core group, a whining cavalry that was joined by the bird-riders. *Demons and monsters always strike fast. Indecision is death.*

Lanyard's master had taught him this, and he'd passed it on to Tilly, and then to the others they found.

Rifles fired, panicked at first, but the seasoned hands took over, taking measured, precise shots. The Once-Dead fell like rabbits, howling and bleeding out in blue, but still they came on. The bikes swept across the enemy line, chatterguns punching the unnatural life out of them. The birds were a heartbeat behind, feet kicking up the pale dust, their riders holding lances and hatchets.

"Aim higher, boy!" Lanyard called out to Mal, using a mark to increase the volume of his voice. The boy corrected the angle of his lance and put the sharp point through the throat of a spirit holding open shackles. Another spirit was upon them, trying to chain up boy and bird. Collybrock tore out its entrails with her talons and pecked out the eyes of another that tried to clap her in irons.

"Everyone, back!" Lanyard roared, the dull mark that throbbed over his larynx already failing. Those on bikes and birds turned from their mad dash, retreating to the square of rifles and pikes. Yulio swept the machine gun just above their heads, slowing the pursuit.

Then another ghost dashed forward and snatched at a motorbike with uncoiling tentacles, and it snagged a man around the throat, yanking him out of the sidecar. The horde of spirits ceased their pursuit to turn on the living man in their midst.

"That's Rufus!" Tilly cried up from the ground. Lanyard remembered him, a dwarf he'd rescued from a gibbet. He'd been a pet to a crooked mob until they caught him moving a stone with his mind. He'd become one of Lanyard's most valued warriors, hunting down Witches and bad men with savage glee.

"Shoot him," Lanyard said, handing a rifle to Yulio. Tight-lipped, the sharpshooter nodded. There'd be no rescuing him now.

That was when Mal noticed the dwarf's capture. Forsaking the retreat of the bird-riders, he dug his heels into Collybrock's side and turned to face the mass of hostile spirits alone. Yulio tried to aim around the boy and his bird, and with a wet growl he gave it up as a rotten shot.

"Mal, what the hell are you doing?" Lanyard shouted, but the mark had faded, and the boy could not hear him. Collybrock raced towards the creatures, screeching a threat. The ghosts of men and beasts looked up at the mad charge, their irons and shackles forgotten for that moment.

Mal leaned forward, lance extended, bracing it with both arms. A savage thrust, and then he was turning Collybrock with his heels, holding something heavy and dripping.

He had the dwarf spitted on his lance. Rufus was already dead, throat torn open by something with fangs. Lanyard could see how the boy struggled to hold the corpse above the ground, his strength wavering.

Robbed of their prize, the would-be body thieves came howling, heedless of the gunfire that thinned their ranks. At Tilly's signal, those with pikes parted and let Collybrock through.

Only then did Mal lower his lance, and Rufus's corpse slid from the blade, the pale soil drinking up the last of his life fluids. Lanyard scrambled down from the lizard's back, heedless of the attack on all sides.

"We need a fire, now!" he shouted. The attack came in hard now, from all directions, and it was only a matter of time before more of his people fell.

Gritting his teeth, he passed his hands above the dead body and spoke the words that meant dryness, giving the cooling flesh the passage of a thousand days. He felt the heat pour down through his arms, felt his palms peeling, burning from the desiccation. In moments the body fell in on itself, mummified, the flesh ruined and crisp.

"A hammer, quickly!"

Tilly stepped forward, bringing down the butt of her pike, and with a sharp blow she caved in the body. It fell into dust, now merely the outline of a man.

They'd driven off the sneak attack, and the last of the Once-Dead fled, wailing and leaking blue flashes as they ran towards Shale, unable to deny its pull. Now the Chain-Folk came for them, slavers and slaves alike. Beasts in harnesses thundered forward, the spirits of men and women clutching to their backs, blue-limned spears and knives held at the ready. Above them, Yulio swept their ranks with the machine gun, chewing up the Once-Dead, but they were more afraid of their master's whip, and so they came over the twitching bodies of their comrades, eager to snatch, to slay, to steal.

Still woozy from the destruction of Rufus's body, Lanyard crafted a set of marks, drawing shapes in the air that became real, vicious little figures that were painful to hold. He tossed these out, and they dug into the dirt, joining, growing into a sharp palisade. The first of the Chain-Folk hit this barrier and caught on the sharp jags, but still they pressed on, tearing themselves apart to reach the living.

Everything was a desperate blur. Lanyard saw his people pressing against the onslaught with pikes and long knives. The enemy howled with hungry rage against these intruders. The Jesusmen spoke what words they knew, sending out flames, invisible fists, confusion, and madness. They did not know enough, and this baby magic did little to halt the advance. Guns roared, sending Chain-Folk reeling and fleeing towards their final death, but still they came on.

"A moment, Lanyard Jesusman," Bilben said, the rodent quivering on his shoulder. Lanyard ignored the little creature, firing his shotgun into that press of villains. Even faced with their Twice-Death, they threw themselves into the guns and blades.

Behind all of this, the warlord on his hairless bear, blue whip sparking and driving on the laggards, sent slaves and slavers alike to their ruin.

"Please, it is urgent," Bilben continued. "It is The Serene."

"What? Spit it out."

"The Serene wants to know if you will accept its grace."

"I don't have time for this bullshit," Lanyard said.

"It says it can only offer grace to you."

"Grace?" Lanyard said, fumbling fresh shells into the big god-cannon. "What the hell does that mean?"

"I only pass on The Serene's words."

"Fine. We die here, we are overrun. Grace then, whatever that means."

No sooner had he said the words than The Serene was in their midst, the thorny mass puffing up to twice, three times its size, and then still growing. Suddenly it lashed out with hundreds of thorny limbs, piercing the entire front line of the Chain-Folk.

The spiky creature held the enemy transfixed, then it gave a sudden twist. The Serene whipped its razor-sharp limbs through throats and hearts, butchering dozens of spirits in one economical movement.

Just as quickly it withdrew its spikes, releasing these ruined bodies to float and howl all the way to Shale.

Thick puddles of the blue spirit-stuff soaked into the ground. The Serene rolled slowly towards the Chain-Folk, spines reaching out, hundreds of legs testing the air. The survivors broke apart in terror, fleeing for their lives, even as their warlord raged and lashed his whip.

Within moments the slowly breathing plain was empty of all Once-Dead, with even casual observers finding somewhere better to be. Slowly, The Serene deflated to its usual size and rolled back towards Lanyard and the terrified Jesusmen, twitching and signing in its language.

"Such is my grace," Bilben translated. "Beware my disgrace."

Licking suddenly dry lips, Lanyard nodded.

"We have a problem," Tilly reported.

"Only one?" Lanyard said.

Once more the sepia skies had given way into the bruised night, but Lanyard drove his mob onwards, wary of camping anywhere that the Chain-Folk roamed. Many of the prentices were exhausted, and the outriders were run ragged, tense and flinching at shadows. Tilly had the bike-riders kill their engines and push the bikes to save fuel and to keep silence.

At the head of their terrified group, Mal and two other bird-riders swept the way, looking for traps or creatures lying in wait. From time to time these scouts would crack open the shutter of a lantern, letting out the glimmer of star-glass, and then just as quickly they doused this brilliant light.

Just behind their caravan, The Serene kept pace, an inscrutable ball of rolling murder. Bilben kept counsel with the spiky creature, the rodent appearing as a series of stuttering shapes as she flowed alongside it.

"Don't trust either of 'em," Lanyard muttered, still picturing the swiftness of The Serene, the moment it murdered dozens of foes with one movement.

"So I've done that count that you wanted, boss," Tilly said. "Three times now."

"What do you have?"

"Nothing."

Lanyard scowled at his lieutenant. She fetched out a star-glass lamp, eking out a sliver of light. In her other hand she held a slightly singed notebook, a near perfect scavenge from a bleedthrough. Lanyard had seen it before and knew it to be Tilly's constant companion. She kept records of all those sworn to the Order, records of monster sightings and kills, logistics, internal discipline, even tallies of flour sacks and bags of nails.

"Stop mucking around, girl. I need to know this stuff, now."

"Writing doesn't work."

"What?"

"I've written down a tally three times, but look." She rifled through the notebook, and every page was bare. Her fingers were stained with ink, but the ledger was free of even a single letter.

"Soon as I lift my eyes from the page, the letters are gone. Not even a scratch from my pen nib. Gets worse though. All our books and writings, every page has gone blank."

Lanyard blinked. In the Now, a book in good condition was worth a man's life. They'd brought most of the Lodge's library with them when they left Crosspoint, and still this only came to a small chest of books, everything from dictionaries to tatters of fiction books from Before.

"From cover to cover, everything was just...wiped away," Tilly said.

Lanyard had come into reading late in life and still struggled with his letters, but this saddened him as much as anything they'd learnt about the Underfog. The Boneman had gifted them with hand-written tomes, instructions for magic, hierarchies of Overhaeven, everything he'd had time to commit to paper.

All of it was erased, as if the ink had been blotted from the paper, right down into the fibres and lifted away. Gone.

"We can use the books for toilet paper and kindling," Tilly said. "It might have to come to that soon."

"How so?"

"We've got water for two weeks. Next to no grog. Food is little better; we'll be eating the birds soon. We stop feeding the lizard, it will start eating us. Barely enough fuel to keep the bikes going."

"Ammo?"

"Rough count has us down to half of what we carried in. Another scrap like that, and we'll be down to bayonets and pikes."

Lanyard felt a new panic jangle in his insides. He'd gone without before, but there was always a soakhole beyond each desert, always sheep he could steal and eat. His mob had nothing besides what they'd brought in with them. No grain grew here, and no water he'd care to drink.

He was responsible for everybody who'd followed him here.

Gotta find this Dawn King fast, Lanyard thought, *before death finds us all.*

7

C louds are rare," Bilben said, her snout up as a thick bank of
sepia rolled across the sky, making the dim light dimmer still.
"Beware that, Jesusman."

"Let's hope for rain," Lanyard said.

"You'd be a fool to put out pots and pans for that," Bilben said.
"Maybe those raindrops would be from Shale, or worse."

"Have you ever seen it rain here?"

"No, but I heard a story once. A rain that came long ago, sweeping
from Edgemist to Shale. Melted away the Once-Dead as if they were
spun sugar."

"Then who survived to tell the tale?" Lanyard pressed, to which the
rodent lifted her paws and shrugged.

Bilben led them out of that land of breathing hills and down into
a vast plain. There were roads here, well-tracked scars across the
landscape. In some ancient day the Once-Dead had attempted to
scratch an artwork into this ground, vast in scale, but all that they'd
managed were curlicues and random tracks, all of it incoherent.

Stranger still were the tattoos. Almost every image and piece of
writing Lanyard's people had etched into their skin was gone, as if
needle and ink had never been applied, but with one exception: every
image of the Jesus, every mark and sign of their creed, all of these
remained.

The tattoo on Lanyard's chest remained, a little worn away by time,
but still as bold as ever. Where once it had brought him nothing but
trouble, now it brought a flicker of hope.

As an experiment, Lanyard was able to make a simple mark in the clay, a sign for light, and it shone as brightly as it would have back in the Now.

"Well, that's a thing," he said, eyebrow raised.

He remembered the fate of Tilly's writing, of all of their books. The Underfog seemed to curse any attempt at keeping a record, which reminded Lanyard of his years in prison, chained up with the other villains in the swamps outside of Mawson.

Talk was discouraged. Writing a note or a letter brought a flogging, or worse. Records meant planning, and their jailers feared the prisoners getting organised, marking the passage of the guards and planning riot, escape, or murder.

Whoever was the true master of the Underfog was a warden. It feared the spirits who dwelt here and wanted to keep them stupid and biddable.

A weight rested on his shoulder, and then Lanyard felt Bilben's paws nudging the far-glass slightly. Lanyard now saw where millions of feet had beaten the tangle of tracks into a highway and supposed that this was the way that led to Shale. It ran as straight as an arrow until the track narrowed and pinched its way into a thick forest.

Trees loomed ahead, as grey and still as stone sculptures, with leaves that were the blue-grey of a dead man's lips. Ferns crowded underneath mushrooms taller than men, and ropey vines stretched across the empty gaps, slowly pulsing and shifting from branch to branch. Within a mile, the whole vile mess vanished into a thick bank of fog.

"That is the Oerwoud. The House of the Accurate Count waits for us on the other side of that," Bilben said.

"I hope this house is safer than its garden."

"Ho, the wit of the living! No, Lanyard, you won't find safety there, exactly, but you will find a place of measure, of reason." Bilben cleaned her whiskers in a blur.

"I thought you said that once we got there, none would molest us."

"Not true. I said no one dares molest *them*," the rodent quibbled, then disappeared through the trudging Jesusmen in a blur of possibilities. Lanyard slid the tubes of the far-glass together and let it hang from his belt.

"We're not getting all of the truth out of her," Lanyard said quietly. "Perhaps we should kill Bilben, or cage her."

"We need a guide," Tilly said, tapping the useless jawbone at his hip. "She has kept faith so far."

"Only because she wants to use us in some way."

"If we harm the rat, her large friend may kill us all," Tilly said. "Patience."

"Fine," Lanyard said in a tone that indicated the opposite. He'd forged Tilly's anvil of a will and had no one to blame but himself when he beat his own head against it.

Lanyard kept his mob in a tight knot, outriders in close, only a single scout ranging ahead for traps. Out here on the plains he felt vulnerable, his people exposed between the breathing hills and the forest. If the Chain-Folk wanted revenge, this was the place to strike in great numbers, regardless of what The Serene might do.

"Bossman," Yulio called out from behind the machine gun. Lanyard climbed up into the pagoda and pointed his far-glass towards the forest, where the man pointed.

Movement in the tree line. Contorting his hand into a painful twist, Lanyard pursed his lips once, a whistle that gave no sound. He almost swooned, a tiny piece of his soul given over to the magic, but he knew that all who answered to him heard his whistle, and felt their eyes drawn to the danger he'd seen.

Two dozen rifles swivelled to the exact spot he was looking at. He looked left, and the guns of the Jesusmen tracked wherever he focused his eyes. He scanned slowly, the effort of supporting dozens of hands, eyes, and minds rapidly draining his strength.

A heartbeat that ached to his core, and then another. Lanyard was on the edge of releasing control, his eyes swimming, when there was a snarl, the crack of trees snapping, and then it crashed out of the tree canopy, whooping and snarling. An octopus the size of a ship, but bred for the land, its tentacles draped in thick fur and moss.

Lanyard crooked his index finger once.

The Jesusmen met this monstrosity with a single burst of gunfire, every bullet striking the exact centre of its forehead in the same instant. The concentration of fire cracked its head open like a cannon-ball had struck it. The creature thrashed its limbs wildly, destroying the forest around it. It reached for Lanyard with the curl of a tentacle, and then it sagged on the trees underneath it, sluices of blue gore running down its face and dripping into the undergrowth.

The enormous beast sank into its Twice-Death. It broke apart before them, limbs and gibbets of flesh floating above the tree growth, drifting back and into the bank of fog. One angry eye glared at them, and then the beast was gone.

"Another one goes to Shale," Bilben said. "You did well to spot that one. When they find a path like this, they wait for travellers and gorge themselves."

"You knew of this?" Lanyard said, eyes narrowed.

"Not this one," the rodent said quickly. "The big hunters normally lurk close by Shale, waiting for suicides and cultists. Strange times, to find this one here."

"What do you think brought it?"

"You draw many fell things just by being here and breathing."

With a grunt of disgust, Lanyard waved away the creature, and she leapt onto Collybrock's harness, chattering to Mal. Lanyard sagged against the rails of the pagoda, head pounding from the strain of all that sorcery. As dangerous as waiting in the open was, he needed to recover. One look at his mob revealed that they were exhausted.

"Tilly, call a ten-minute break," he croaked to his lieutenant. Within seconds of her call, people sprawled on the ground around their dumped packs, chewing on hard biscuits and smoking. Lanyard felt the grind of his empty gut but was still queasy from the magic and did not trust his failing body to hold down any food. Beneath him, the lizard sank down onto its belly with a rumbling groan. Lanyard leaned against the machine gun and closed his eyes to Yulio's wet coughing.

"Hey, bossman," he heard. He opened his eyes to see Mal standing up in his saddle, looking over the rail of the pagoda. Collybrock was busy scratching at the rail, sharpening her beak.

"Bossman," the boy repeated.

"You need to climb down and give that bird a rest," Lanyard said.

"I'm on watch," the boy said. "Seen something."

Unloading a grumble that started from his bones, Lanyard got up—and then he saw it. Over the last crest of the breathing hills were thousands of the Chain-Folk, coming at them as fast as beast and foot could carry them.

"UP!" shouted Lanyard. Yulio found a hand-klaxon up on the gun deck, a leftover from the old owners, and he wound this fast, sending a keening wail across the camp.

Rest instantly forgotten, the Jesusmen leapt up and formed into a firing line. Tilly yelled at the bike-riders to start up their machines, and she waved them towards the narrow pathway that fed into the Oerwoud.

The Serene stood in the centre of the path, puffing up in a threat display of twitching spines. Lanyard leapt out of the pagoda, sliding and cursing down the lizard's flank until he was on the ground and running for the beast.

"Out of the bloody way!" he shouted at the creature. Bilben appeared in a darting stream of rodent images, putting herself between her large friend and the Jesusman's shotgun.

"Please stop!" she begged. "The Serene says that salvation is coming!"

"I'll give it salvation with my bloody shotgun if it won't move," Lanyard said, and then he felt every joint in his body throb, his teeth shiver in their sockets.

Something was coming through the world veil and into the Underfog. Something that didn't need to enter through the Edgemist like the dead and the necromancers.

Bright spots lit the sepia clouds far above them, miniature suns that danced and spun and grew brighter by the second. They spread like the pox until there were hundreds of golden lights, drilling, burning through the barrier.

The Chain-Folk had reined in beast and slave and pointed upwards, confused by the movement in the heavens. Caught in their final stand, Lanyard saw his Jesusmen huddle close, the prentices feeding bullets into the spare rifles, the bikers poised and ready to charge.

Then the clouds burst open. Golden beams shot down from the heavens, brilliant and blinding, and the landscape echoed with a deafening cry, a sound that carried screams and laughter, the smashing of glass, a glorious chord that went on and on.

When Lanyard could see again, he saw the Chain-Folk running for their lives, leaving pale dust in their wake as they retreated to the breathing hills.

In the centre of the plain lay a host, thousands strong. Taursi warriors, garbed in their glass battle-aprons. Some of these spine-coated humanoids were formed into a line of cavalry and rode on the horse-spider beasts he'd seen back in the Now.

At their forefront stood the Smothered Princes. The brothers stretched out into two, three times their own height, slender arms reaching out with wicked claws. Their faces spread out into fanged smiles that reached from ear to ear so that their heads seemed to split in half as they laughed.

"HO, JESUSMAN!" one of the Princes boomed. "ARE YOU LOST?"

"SEE HOW HE PLANTS HIS PEOPLE HERE," his brother scoffed. "TOO SCARED TO GO ON."

"SHALL WE PLUCK HIM?"

"BY THE ROOT."

The great host moved forward, a steady advance. Lanyard turned again to The Serene, teeth gritted.

"Out of my way," he growled. He tried to remember all the dirty tricks the Boneman had taught him, little sorceries for every occasion, but he wasn't sure what would work on the thorny alien.

"The Serene says that salvation is almost here," Bilben translated, voice trembling. "It asks if you will accept the grace of its cousin, and the cousin of its cousin."

"Yes, I accept your cousin's grace. I'd accept the grace of a bastard's cousin at this point. Now move!"

The edge of the Oerwoud shook violently, and then several of the thorny aliens chewed their way through the foliage, rolling onto the plain. The Serene's kin, reaching for the shining army with murderous thorns.

The creatures were enormous, puffed up into thorny balls that grew to thirty, forty feet high, lined with thorns of every colour, some even shining in a metallic chrome. The Serene was tiny compared to its cousins, and Lanyard supposed that The Serene had died and entered the Underfog as a juvenile spirit.

"The Serene says to follow now!" Bilben shouted. Lanyard saw the ball of the alien retreating into the Oerwoud, thorns flashing out rapidly as it picked at the vines and foliage around them. It was untangling a wider path through the dense forest and barely had to slow down to do so. Lanyard resketched the volume sigil on his throat and shouted across the noise of the battle, cutting through the furious cries of the Taursi horde as the murderous balls tore into their vanguard.

"Back! Follow me!" Lanyard shouted before his voice gave out altogether. Behind him, he saw his people retreating into the Oerwoud, leaving behind a scatter of packs and boots, and a motorcycle in pieces that a rider had attempted to fix.

In the centre of the plain, the forces of Overhaeven crashed up against the fury of The Serene's kin. The Taursi cast volleys of battle-glass, flashing brilliant golden light, but these hardly seemed to affect the thorny giants.

Some of them rolled across the enemy, crushing Taursi and horse-beast into a bloody paste. Others reached out like The Serene had against the first rush of the Chain-Folk, stabbing and twisting in a torus of barbed spines.

The last thing Lanyard could see of the battle was the Smothered Princes, now stretched out until every proportion was reed-thin. They looked like enormous stick-insects, towering above even the fray. The Princes caught one of the spiny creatures and pulled it apart between them like a chicken.

Behind them one of The Serene's cousins followed the escape, limbs flashing as it restitched the path closed behind them, a bank of thick growth blocking off all pursuit. Still the living ran, caught between two blurring balls of death, and no less terrified. All Lanyard knew now was the shifting chaos of the Oerwoud, the slow creep of vine and bough, a sick reflection of the life a typical forest held. He got the impression that this was simply an idea of a forest, compressed into a mimeograph or a woodcut, every aspect of the plant-life they walked through an exaggeration.

Nests that no bird had ever laboured to build. Grafted trees in orchard ranks and hints of vineyard trellis, crushed between trees thick in girth or lost to brambles and vines. Plump bushes of kennelweed. Lanyard backhanded the first fool he saw reach for the facsimile of that addictive plant.

"You don't have time for a stupid death!" he barked.

Ahead, The Serene bisected a path through a bank of strangler trees, parting that slow murder, and the living squeezed through the gap, watchful of the seeping thorns. Behind, the second spiky alien reunited these plants, trunks and branches caught in a seamless and fierce embrace.

There was no sign or track left to show that any had ever passed, but still The Serene forced the humans onward. To left and right, Lanyard could see the rolling churn of its larger cousins, having abandoned the battle and blasting their own path across the Oerwoud.

In the sky behind Lanyard's shoulder, more bright spots began to drill through the clouds, golden beams punching down into the Oerwoud at random points. The booming voices of the Smothered Princes rattled behind them, too far now to make out, but strident, angry at being denied their prize.

"The Oerwoud turns away prying eyes. Especially eyes of gold," Bilben chattered in his ear. Lanyard flinched at the sudden appearance of the rodent.

"Where is your thornbush taking us?" Lanyard demanded.

"The Serene is not mine in any way," Bilben said. "You have received grace upon grace from their kin, so they will take you where they please."

"I should shake an honest answer out of you!"

Bilben flickered through a hundred possibilities that included raking out Lanyard's eyes, leaping into the Oerwoud, and even submitting to injury. Eventually the rodent queen settled for sitting still on Lanyard's shoulder, preening herself.

"Lanyard!" Tilly called out, several places down their rushing line. "The prentices are tiring! We need to stop."

"No stopping, girl! Run or die!"

Then, a cry. One of the children stumbled over a tree root and fell underneath the enormous feet of the stumpy lizard. Yulio could only look down from the pagoda in horror as his beast crushed the life from the boy.

"Bring that body!" Lanyard yelled back down the line. "Do not leave it here!"

A shriek of horror from behind. The needle-beast to the rear had snatched up the corpse, instantly unravelling the body until it resembled a cat's cradle, guts and muscle fibres stretched out for yards in every direction. In its own inscrutable way, the alien absolutely had picked up the body.

Lanyard then seized Bilben by the neck. The rodent permitted this, looking up with wide eyes.

"Tell your bloody friend we are stopping. Right now."

"But they stop of their own accord."

A clearing appeared, equal parts village green and lonely moor. The Serene rolled to one side, its clacking needles finally at rest.

The Jesusmen filed into the open space, fearfully gathering together in a huddle of bikes, birds, and people. The stumpy lizard slunk in, tail dragging and head hung low, Yulio hacking phlegm over the side of the pagoda.

Mal was there, the smallest of small mercies, squatting next to Collybrock, checking his bird's feet as the tired creature panted and complained. By his side was Kirstl, his young sweetheart, slumped against a dead man's rifle, haunted eyes staring at nothing.

She finally got her gun.

Lanyard still held the rodent spirit, fingers squeezing. He wasn't sure that you could choke a ghost to its Twice-Death, but he was prepared to try.

"The truth. Now. Where is the House of the Accurate Count?"

"Great news, Jesusman," Bilben rasped. "Your foe has lost your scent!"

Lanyard looked up to see that the creature spoke the truth, even as it deflected his question. The golden beams were still crashing down from the heavens, but they were striking farther away from this clearing, like a lightning storm that had moved on to shake some other town. The Smothered Princes raged and wailed, but the noise was a distant thing, muffled by the thickness of the false forest between them, bouncing around in the fog.

"Do not quibble," Lanyard said, increasing his squeeze on Bilben's plump little neck. "Where is this damned House?"

"See past that bank of trees, where the skybeasts fly thick? They circle the House, waiting for scraps."

Through his one good eye, Lanyard made out what Bilben was describing, just above the fog. There was a cloud of flying creatures, perhaps birds or bats, circling in a pulsing, swirling formation. Many miles away, but close enough.

Lanyard threw the creature to the ground, and she scurried across to Tilly, who let her climb up her arm and rest in her shirt.

"Don't you hurt her!" Tilly scolded. "She saved us."

"Do you feel safe?" Lanyard said. More of The Serene's kin emerged from the forest then, some tangled with gore and golden slime, others with spines bent and broken. They rolled and rustled together in the clearing, a congregation of flicking needles.

Back in the dust of the Now, the magistrate who'd sentenced a young Lanyard to hang had a clerk record the whole sorry moment with a typewriter from the Before. Back then, the clattering and striking of the tiny irons as they struck the paper had burrowed into his soul. Now, The Serene and its kin sounded like a hundred of those machines, their needles constantly in motion, even striking angrily at each other like fencers with a thousand swords.

"What are they saying?" Tilly asked Bilben.

"There are so many of them. They are speaking too quickly for me to translate."

As Lanyard drew out a pistol, Tilly held up her hand and frowned. *Patience!*

"Risk. Great risk. Grace is permission," Bilben ventured. "That one there says the whole thing won't work."

"What won't work?" Lanyard said, but the rodent ignored him, now perched on the tip of Tilly's pike, the better to see the giants at their speech.

"Oh. Oh no, that will not do," Bilben said. "Unacceptable."

The Serene separated from its elders and rolled over to speak with Bilben, the many limbs flashing, clicking, knitting at the air.

"I regret to inform you that The Serene's people want your lizard," Bilben said.

"Like hell," Lanyard said. "That's ours. Transport, and then meat when it finally gives out."

"You gave grace," Bilben said, nose twitching as it watched The Serene speak. "You then gave grace upon grace. It is either this trade, or you and yours shall fall into disgrace."

Lanyard picked it then, the movement behind the word. *Disgrace* was a sudden expansion, with all the limbs stabbing outwards. Remembering the way The Serene had dealt with the Chain-Folk and the hunters from Overhaeven, Lanyard felt furious.

"Yulio, get down from there. Bring the gun."

The moustachioed gunman nodded. He'd packed the pagoda full with the smallest of the prentices, and they clambered down from the lizard as if they were ticks. Bags and boxes came down, and finally the big chattergun, which Yulio mounted on a motorbike with a sidecar.

Lanyard seized the reins of the lizard, and only now did the stupid beast realise what was happening. It started to panic, tongue flicking nervously as it was led towards the spiny aliens.

"Here's your bloody lizard."

Lanyard dropped the reins in the dirt and walked away, ruing the bargain he'd made for this creature. *All the Jesusmen, banned from Crosspoint forever.*

The lizard hissed, equal parts threat and fear, and then it was off and running, making for the edge of the clearing.

Even as big as the lizard was, the rolling aliens dwarfed it. At the last moment the lizard slumped in defeat and was pierced in a thousand different places.

Then, a new strangeness. The spirit of the lizard emerged from its dead body, and then The Serene stabbed this too. With a flurry of needles it stuffed this soul back into its dead body.

Then, the eager little knitters started to unravel the corpse, their limbs stabbing in and out like the sewing machines sometimes found in bleedthroughs. Skin, muscle fibres, bones, nerves, guts—all of it came out in a dozen different chains of matter, and then the ball-creatures were knitting the dead lizard into a structure.

It looked like a giant sock, a tube big enough to accommodate the largest of their kind, and it was reaching up, snaking towards the sepia cloud cover.

"It's a tunnel," Tilly said. "They're trying to get out."

This grotesque construction was tissue thin, with everything that made up the giant lizard unravelled and then sewn into a fluttering nightmare.

Lanyard gave a signal, and the Jesusmen were up and ready in an instant, guns snatched from the stacks, everything stowed away and tied down. They'd been granted barely a minute of rest, but none of the men and women grumbled.

The tearing sounds. The clicking. The wavering of a tunnel of tissue, growing higher and higher.

Then, the lizard was completely gone, and it still wasn't enough. The needle-beast who'd picked up the body of the crushed prentice added this flesh to the construction. It inched ever closer to the heavens as the living swore at this desecration, this misuse of a person who'd died for no good reason.

"You bastards!" Tilly shouted, wheeling in every direction, pike hefted.

The Serene returned from the construction, gesturing to Bilben, but Lanyard did not need the interpreter.

"They get nothing more from us," he growled. "We've made our trade, and that's that."

"Grace upon grace," Bilben translated. "Your debt has been compounded."

"We're leaving."

More limbs flashed, and then The Serene rolled back and forth in front of Lanyard, preventing him from moving. Lanyard had his old shotgun out and held low, ready for that killing moment.

More limbs flashing, and that final signal. *Disgrace.*

"This–this was not what I agreed to," Bilben whined. "Serene, you must find another way. Don't make me ask this of them."

"What more do they want?" Lanyard said. "Do they want the camel? Some of the birds?"

"They ask for ten of your people, Jesusman. You have one minute to decide who will die."

8

I 've made my decision," Lanyard said, levelling his gun at Bilben. The rat leapt from Tilly's pike, disappearing in a flurry of possibilities and decisions, most of these avoiding the thunder of that great big shooter. Tilly tried to spit the rodent on her pike but did little more than turn over sods of sepia clay.

There was no time for instructions, but the Jesusmen knew this moment well enough to act. It was one heartbeat where the guns raised, in the next their barking thunder, and in a third heartbeat dozens of mouths spoke, hands contorted and tracing at air. Mark and word, the leftover workaround magic of their order.

All the defiance these lost humans could muster, and it barely gave the rolling leviathans any pause. One large beast sank in on itself as Yulio chewed it apart with the chatter gun, spines mere feet away from spearing the moustachioed gunman.

They took young Morris, a lad barely old than Mal. Then Dogleg, a Crooked Folk who'd gone apostate to follow Lanyard's doomed tribe. Next, a spined beast pounced upon Piper, a swift and sure bird-rider.

Three more heartbeats, and then these three were stitched into the tunnel, the far ends just brushing short of the heavens.

"You've got enough! Leave off!" Lanyard roared, binding one beast in a squeezing silver band that it shook off with one toroid twist.

The Serene's kin paused then, twitching needles at each other, making a swift measurement of their tunnel.

"Only two more needed to craft their escape!" Bilben cried out from the edge of the clearing. "Take the deal."

Lanyard looked to Tilly, who nodded. Laying down their weapons, they stepped forward. Tilly sought Lanyard's hand, and he took it, squeezed back hard, trying for one final moment of love and peace before doom.

"I'm sorry, girl."

"I'm not," Tilly said with a weary smile.

The Serene rolled straight towards them, spikes raised, clicking, measuring, speaking with its kin. Lanyard closed his eyes, only to feel the air shift.

The killer alien had rolled straight past them.

"No. Come back here! Take us!"

The Serene fell upon two others. Milosh, a stout man with a paunch, who fell into that blur of sharp edges without complaint.

Then it tore Kirstl from Mal's arms. She went with an awful, lingering scream that went on and on, as anguished as Mal's own. He held her, sobbed, even tried to leap into that death himself, but The Serene did not even nick the boy's skin, even as it unravelled Kirstl's fingers and hands from within his own.

The measure had been exact. The aliens only took what they needed to complete their structure, and soon the end of the writhing tunnel connected with the bank of sepia cloud above, bored into it, tore open a hole into their own world of thistles and honour.

Lanyard saw the look of pure hatred and loss in Mal's eyes, only to realise it was directed at him, not the aliens who'd snuffed out his sweetheart's life, who'd taken Kirstl's very soul.

One more black mark against Lanyard and the life he'd dragged Mal into. If they survived this massacre, would the boy ever speak with him again, or would he come for his master with a sharp stone in hand, much as Lanyard had done for his own master?

In truth, Lanyard would welcome that death, and call it a balanced book.

Tilly was upon Mal, who fought against the expected human contact, but she reached past the screaming boy, snatching up Kirstl's rifle. One shot into The Serene's centre mass, and the creature wobbled, but it did not pause in its mad quest to knit its escape from the Underfog.

Coughing until he was nearly bent double, Yulio fussed with the chattergun, shaking his head as he frantically worked to clear a jam.

As the other survivors paced around that knitting circle, emptying rifle and pistol, pestering the aliens with spells that they shook off, Lanyard realised the truth of things.

They could not hope to avenge their dead here. What little they had at their disposal would do naught but scratch at these mysterious beasts and burn through ammo they could not afford to waste.

Putting finger and thumb against his teeth, the old Jesusman let off a piercing whistle, a signal that meant everything from "stop for a cuppa tea" to "time to mount up and ride."

Here, it meant "cease fire."

A moment later, Mal came crashing in at Lanyard with his pike, seeking his master's blackened heart. The older man knocked the point aside with one hand, cuffing the boy with the other. They fell together, pike dropped and forgotten. Mal's fist thumped hard against Lanyard's leathery chest, and then he was scratching at his master's face, and then the man simply held the boy tightly as he howled and shook, feral with loss.

"None of us dies well, boy," Lanyard said, and Mal simply replied with a buh-buh-buh, over and over, until master and prentice were joined with a slick of tears and snot.

Collybrock danced about the pair with terror, parroting Mal's cries. He was trained to kill the boy's enemies with beak and claw, but the bird was unsure if Lanyard was threat or friend.

Both, bird, Lanyard thought.

With their escape route finished, the aliens completely disregarded the humans. The survivors could do little but watch The Serene lead its family into that writhing tube, a perverse birth canal leading from the Underfog back into their world, into whatever passed for life there. The aliens delicately stretched out each fold of skin and tissue on a thousand points and moved upwards in a gentle pulse, clicking and sliding on their path to freedom.

Tilly paced around The Serene's escape tube, her rifle still wet with Kirstl's blood. She fired Jesus-marked bullets into the tube at point blank, but her shots simply ricocheted, even though the tissue was thinner than an eyelid, completely translucent.

"Girl, I told you to bloody stop!" Lanyard yelled over Mal's bowed head.

She threw the gun down in disgust and tried with the pike. Enchanted as it was, sharpened to a point that could punch through steel, the pike could barely stretch that tough material. Above her, tickling along the tube's insides in peristaltic lurches, The Serene climbed higher and higher, reaching for golden light and escape.

Lanyard heard the resolute grumbling of a pair of his men nearby, who'd tossed down their weapons and were preparing a billy of tea. Even in the face of this strange disaster, a good soldier always knew when to put his feet up, and Lanyard was glad to see people being people, even here in the bowels of death. All around, others shrugged and made their own moment of rest, cigarettes and matches passing from hand to lip to hand in many stoic little circles.

Then, Lanyard saw one man scratching the sigil for flame and heat into the clay, summoning a rude flame to bubble his teapot. A Jesus Mark, the only writing worth a damn in this place.

He understood then, and he pushed Mal aside, even as the boy clutched at him, wordless in his need for comfort. The old man hitched into a run and turned Tilly back towards the writhing tube she'd given up any hope of harming.

"They made that," he babbled. "They *made* that bloody thing."

"No shit," Tilly said, but the next smart comment died on her tongue as she saw Lanyard reach out for the writhing tube, speaking frantically, drawing a jagged line with his fingers.

Eyes wide, Tilly joined in, even as she called for help. The grumbling of the soldiers at rest turned into frantic motion when they realised what the boss was drawing, over and over.

The Mark of Unmaking.

A simple magic that most prentices started out on, along with those for binding and holding. For the Jesusmen, it was the magical equivalent of a mop and bucket, used for cleaning up the remains of unwanted visitors after the guns and death spells did the real work.

With enough effort, you could break down a wall, a fence, a house, anything created or crafted by a set of hands. Once, Lanyard had set a punishment detail for Mal to unmake an outhouse, forcing him to stand in the sun for a full day until he'd reduced the shitter into a neat stack of planks and a filled in hole.

Unmaking took a darker meaning after the Jesusmen butchered some vile visitor to the Now. If the life had bled out of something, it was just meat, and meat was made, either in the womb or on the lips of a magician.

As a crafting of meat and spirit stuff, this escape tunnel was doubly intended. Craft upon craft, much as Lanyard had accrued grace upon grace.

The Jesusmen stood all about that squirming horror, hands jammed around their neighbours' elbows, between people's legs, prentices even standing upon grown men's shoulders. All the while tracing, whispering, unmaking.

"Let's unravel this fucking sock," Lanyard said, and then he found it—a loose thread that might have been part of the lizard's guts came loose, and with that, the whole tunnel quivered. A moment later it suddenly collapsed, snapping shut, squeezing, a sore gut closing in on a half-digested meal.

"Back!" he barked. The tunnel detached from the cloud above, mere moments before The Serene would have made its escape, and then it was all falling, miles of gut crashing all around the clearing, draped across the Oerwoud.

By some miracle no one was crushed by the collapsing tunnel, which fell and coiled all around their latest final stand.

Once, Lanyard had seen a big snake digesting a group of settlers. The lazy beast slept in the hot sun, a string of lumps in its guts where a family had once been. The Serene and all of its murderous tribe was trapped in a similar way, spines unable to pierce through that skin.

Then their tunnel of meat and murder squeezed and clenched until it was finally atomic thin, and these ones who'd thought to cheat death were utterly destroyed.

The construction broke apart, all of the stolen meat little more than dust and stink. A cavalry charge of blue spirit stuff emerged from the mess, gibbering and floating towards Shale.

The blue soul of the lizard, legs and tail dragging, eyes wide as it drifted to total destruction. The Serene and its kin floated by, ghostly spikes flailing, and these were falling apart from the centre, shedding needles like pine trees.

Finally, Lanyard suffered through a silent parade of every person that he'd just failed. Prentices and gunbearers alike drifted past, faces twisted in agony and horror, limbs limp. Humans painted in an eery blue, their souls dripping like blood.

Then it was Kirstl, doomed the moment she'd entered the Lodge, and she was reaching for Mal, mouthing his name.

"Kirstl! You can't leave me!"

Please, her blue lips formed. *Help.*

The boy reached for her Twice-Dead hands but found nothing to grip onto, and he was unable to stop her from drifting up and over the Oerwoud, toward Shale and her final unmaking.

Quick as thought, Mal snatched up his pike, leaping into Collybrock's saddle. Lanyard swore bloody murder at the boy, but Mal ignored him. The boy set his bird to a trot, riding low as he crashed back into the Oerwoud, chasing his sweetheart's ghost.

"Stop that," Tilly said. "The boy's gone."

Lanyard paced around the camp, scowling into his liver-root tea. He'd shared a half-baked plan involving a motorbike and a generous whipping with his belt, and Tilly had immediately ordered the bikers to pull out their sparkplugs and give them to her.

In times like these, Lanyard regretted dropping his bundle and forcing Tilly to take over the Order. He was still the old man, and they'd literally followed him into hell, but whenever there was a pissing contest between the grizzled relic and the strong-willed girl he'd raised, the men and women would go with Tilly.

They'd had many stupid arguments over the years, and she knew every chink in Lanyard's armour and had the patience to wear him down.

"You're not on your own anymore," she continued. "You do not get to simply fuck off whenever something goes wrong."

"He is out there! On a bird!"

"Mal made his own stupid choice. He's a man now, like it or not."

"It's not about that, girl. He's one of ours. We bring him back safe."

"You sound like a Leicesterite," Tilly scoffed, packing tobacco into her pipe. "Do you want to find this Dawn King? Or do you want to die alone out there?"

She pointed out at the oppressive Oerwoud, the cloud of flying beasts over the distant House of the Accurate Count, and even the odd beam of golden light in the distance, the Smothered Princes still on the hunt.

"We will find the Dawn King and end him," Lanyard said. "As soon as I haul that little shit back to camp by the ears, kicking his bird up the arse the whole way."

"Bullshit. You love that boy."

"I–" and here he lowered his voice, conscious of all the wagging ears nearby. "Of course I love him. He needs to be here with me, not risking his neck for a ghost."

"You would do the exact same thing," Tilly said, "if that was me, Twice-Dead and floating out to my ending."

"I'll find him," he said, looking in the direction Mal had left. A few years back when the cataract had turned his left eye into a blurry cloud, the Boneman had offered to repair it, which Lanyard knocked back with a scoff.

A man is supposed to wear out and die. I don't want to end up like you, Sol.

The Boneman and the Jesusman had come to a different arrangement regarding his ruined eye.

"Do your job here, boss," Tilly said. "That's all I've got left to say."

Lanyard tried to fight the point but knew he'd already lost the argument. Tilly was right, the way a punch to the face was frequently right. He scowled, even as his heart filled with pride and love for his stubborn girl.

Young woman, he corrected himself.

"I saved you once," he said. "Please, let me save him."

"He doesn't need you right now, Lanyard," Tilly said. "But I do."

Silence. He sipped his awful brew, and she set a match to her pipe, drawing in deep. Lanyard would have given anything for this to be another campfire in the Now, man and girl bickering over minor things. Back when it was just the two of them, wandering the world in search of monsters.

Their arguments never ended in a rock to the skull, and Lanyard guessed this counted as a successful apprenticeship.

A scuff of a boot against the strange clay, and Yulio approached them, coughing into his sleeve.

"Boss?" Yulio said when he could manage to speak. "It's back again."

"Well, do your job and shoot the bloody thing!"

"Waste of ammo if you ask me."

"I didn't."

Bilben was back yet again, lurking around the edge of the clearing, trying to catch Lanyard's eye. The first time it happened, he'd blustered and raged and sent bullets singing into the bush, with no hope of hitting the shifty time-swerving rodent.

Now, Lanyard ignored the Queen of the Iron Nest, and this had driven the creature into a frenzy of self-pity and begging.

"I am no traitor," the creature said. "Please, there must be something I can do."

"There is," Lanyard said, and hope lit the creature's furry face. "Stand very still and let Yulio shoot you."

Yulio started up the chattergun, chewing apart the tree line, and Bilben shrieked, darting off in a scatter of possibilities. Several of these ended in her catching a stray bullet, and this time her escape seemed final.

As the spent casings rang and tinkled, Tilly shook her head.

"Worth every bullet," Lanyard said.

9

They had no way of marking time down here, but Tilly forced a complete halt and let every man, woman, and child sleep their fill. Bilben had spoken the truth about the Oerwoud hiding them well, and the Smothered Princes and their golden army had moved on, their search for the humans fruitless.

The sepia clouds moved on, returning the sky to the bruised purple of night. Lanyard permitted the use of star-glass to light the camp, but without a true sun to draw in a charge by day, this light was dimming out, growing weaker. Weary fingers scratched marks in the damp clay of the clearing, augmenting the gloom with little blisters of magical light.

Apart from cookfires, Lanyard ordered the wood be spared. Shivering and grumbling, others summoned fire with Mark and Word, but these flames never lasted long, and took more strength to maintain than they deserved.

Theirs was a miserable camp, less than two dozen survivors shivering in that violet night. At one stage the camp rang with shouts, as Yulio and a man called Lugg fell into a furious brawl, fighting over ownership of a blanket.

Lanyard knocked both men to the ground with his own hammer fists and confiscated the blanket. He thought for a moment then of Mal, out there in the cold, and gifted the covering to a young prentice named Seidel.

Lanyard fought sleep, agonizing over every wasted second, but one long blink gave way to another, and then exhaustion drew him in the rest of the way. For the first time since he'd set foot in the lands of the dead, Lanyard slept.

Almost immediately the dream came on, once more a thing of clarity and meaning, but instead of visions of the Boneman's destruction, Lanyard stood outside the front gates of Carmel.

More than fifteen years ago, he'd taken a job from these people, and was betrayed and left to die. All for water, rare and worth the violence in the dry Inland. Now, instead of tradestones and handwringing from the wall-huggers, Lanyard looked on empty walls, the streets silent beyond the open gate.

Then they came, fluid in bronze and marble, watching him from the high walls. Leicesterites, tall and grim, stone rifles in hand. Dozens of carved soldiers, judging him from above.

Then a red hand seized the edges of the gate, pulling it completely open, and ducking through the opening came the gigantic statue he'd last seen at the Waking City, cracking the parched clay beneath each footstep. Daubed with blood from boot-tip to cowlick, the statue had contained the very spirit of John Leicester, that long vanished magician.

"Ho, Jesusman," the statue rumbled.

Once more, Lanyard was the starved boy, severed noose around his throat. He said nothing, but met that blank red stare calmly.

"You hold peril at your bosom, and worse peril on your hip."

Lanyard looked down to see he wore a fine gun belt, and sure enough the holster contained the jawbone, the last gift of the Boneman. The key to this dead land, to vengeance and the destruction of everyone who walked by his side.

"I have wisdom for you, if you would hear it," John Leicester said through ruddy stone lips.

"Speak," Lanyard said, with the rasp of a near-hanged teen.

"Turn from vengeance. Leave that thing on the ground and return to the lands of life. Let the Smothered Princes have their toy."

"They want *this*?"

He drew the jawbone as if it were a pistol, looking down that row of jagged teeth and fangs. The red giant nodded.

"No," Lanyard said. "We ride for the Dawn King."

"Fine. If you won't hear me, then listen to your master."

Above the empty town rose a fluttering bird, enormous in scale, and then Lanyard saw it for what it was: a pair of hands, each pierced through the centre with a ragged hole, one marked BEFORE, the other NOW.

The Jesus, a terrifying symbol, the author of every scrap of Lanyard's misery. It came down until it eclipsed the city, statues and walls forgotten, and then Lanyard was in a place of pure night, the hands a pair of mountains fluttering above him, fingers curling inwards, the palm wounds a pair of empty eyes staring upon infinity.

"LEAVE THE JAWBONE."

A gunshot.

Lanyard sat upright, the fog of dream washed away with an instant sense of threat. He was up and moving through the panic of those stirred from slumber, his Jesus-marked shotgun at the ready.

He swore. Lugg was still slumped against the tree he'd emptied his brains against, pistol clutched in one hand. His Once-Dead spirit was already gone, running through the trees on a path to Shale and oblivion.

Kicking the pistol away as if it were a snake, Lanyard gave Lugg's corpse over to the blistering heat of his desiccation magic, bleaching and cooking it into dust, until even the tree behind the man's body started to char and smoulder. Even so, the wood did not catch, and the sickening smoke made Lanyard rethink his sudden plan to harvest local firewood.

"No one else do this!" Lanyard finally barked, turning to address people who were suddenly looking to ground and sky, anywhere but at the boss.

"If you tire of living, I will kill you myself. With my hands. We need the bloody ammo."

Lanyard picked up Lugg's pistol and put it into a pocket. If he found Mal, he would give this to the boy as his first gun, along with the tale of the previous owner.

If Mal was man enough now to chase ghosts, he deserved one more horrible gift from his master.

The false daylight of the sepia-tinged dawn drove back enough of the fog that Lanyard's group could navigate the Oerwoud, weaving through the plants that weren't plants. Without The Serene to untangle a path for them, they were reduced to hacking away at the vegetation with hatchets and bayonets. Every miserable foot was hard-won, and Yulio spent an awful moment snagged on the thorns of a strangler, swearing at the sting of the venom.

"Feels worse than a real strangle-thorn," he said, pausing to hack up more phlegm. White muck pooled out of the wounds, which Tilly pressed and massaged until the blood expelled all of it.

"Keep that clean," Lanyard ordered, for all the good it did telling a man who rattled wet sounds with every breath.

Everything was the rise and fall of small blades, sharp edges wet one moment and dusty the next. Tilly sent the prentices to scooping up the cuttings and stacking them in a barrow.

"Wood's bad, girl," Lanyard barked. "Won't burn."

"We may need to build things," she said testily. "Stretchers, barricades, bloody lavatories."

He shrugged and set to pulling back more vines, wincing as the sharp-edged leaves parted his skin as they slid through his grip.

Then the first mercy of the day came as their ragged crew forced their way out of the thick brush and back onto the main path through the Oerwoud.

Above the trees, Lanyard could see a straight run through to the distant pillar of flying beasts. Tilly handed back the sparkplugs to the bikers and sent a pair of scouts rattling and whining down the path, leaving a cloud of blue smoke for Yulio to cough upon.

"Watch for more lurkers," Lanyard said, remembering the octopus-thing that had lain in wait. He hustled his troops forward as fast as he dared, and even sent a pair of bird-riders back to see that nothing threatened them from behind.

Only one bike returned, bearing both the riders.

"Boss, trouble ahead."

"Where's your bike?"

"A girl took it. Girl with hooks for hands."

"Right. You lot, wait here."

"Lanyard, I-" Tilly began.

"Stow your tongue, girl. I know what lies ahead."

"Have you learnt bloody nothing down here? Don't go alone."

"I won't."

Lanyard waved another bike forward, the one with the chattergun mounted on the sidecar. Evicting the rider with a grunt, Lanyard looked down at Yulio in the sidecar, who sat sweating behind the triggers.

"You good?"

"Yep," Yulio said thickly.

"Bullshit," and Lanyard twisted the throttle, the machine coughing as much as the dying man, and he launched them down the path, false trees whipping by to the left and right.

He remembered that day in the Waking City, hours before he put both barrels through Papa Lucy's head. Lucy had sent his agent in, bearing the corrosive staff known as the Cruik, *becoming* the Cruik, and he remembered her flowing forward, more wood than girl, hands curling out into hooks as she nearly killed him.

He'd bled her out, his rune-marked knife driven deep into fibre and sap, turning her back into the Cruik. As for her spirit, he'd sent that into death. Sent her *here*.

"You aim true, Yulio," Lanyard shouted against the wind. "Blow her fucking head off."

Yulio nodded, tense and ready. The path swept in a long rightward curve, both sides now a neatly trimmed pair of hedges, and then he saw her up ahead, Papa Lucy's killer standing in the centre of the path.

Holding the stolen motorcycle up over her head.

Yulio filled the air with fury, barrels spinning and barking, while Lanyard poured on the speed, no hesitation in the face of this dangerous foe.

Then her arms grew, forming an incredible lever, a living trebuchet, and she threw the stolen motorbike at them with great velocity.

One heartbeat of panic, and Lanyard swerved too far to the right, grinding the bike against the thick hedges, struggling to keep the whole thing upright. Then the missile slammed into them, and Lanyard's valiant charge fell apart into spinning, bouncing, and then that final, painful slide.

Oil dripping. The ticking of the stalled engine. The weight of the bike and sidecar, pinning him to the damp clay of the path. Lanyard looked up past the spinning front wheel to see the girl stalking toward him, hands curled into hooks.

"Killed you once," he gasped, freeing a pistol from his hip, and sent round after round into that advancing monster. He sent out a word that made her stagger, long enough for his next shot to hit true.

Papa Lucy's killer sank down into the pathway, cradling an arm that was all but severed, now leaking blue soul-stuff instead of the sap he remembered. Worried, she was attempting to restore the limb, ignoring Lanyard for the moment.

"Yulio. Yulio! Get out of there!"

The man lay curled underneath the sidecar, the chattergun and its cracked mounting the only thing that had saved him from a broken neck. He stirred, moaning, awareness still moments away. Too long.

The wooden girl had reattached her arm, but it hung by her side, the hook uncurling until it was once more a hand. Lanyard madly fought free from the wreckage of the bike, something catching on the clay. His old shotgun, still slung to his back. The girl took one unsteady step, her good arm rising, stretching, the hook now a spear tip. Wrestling out his Bowie knife, Lanyard sawed away at the leather strap, finally winning his freedom. Barking out a word that filled her eyes with searing pain, he stepped aside from the spear thrust, slamming his gun butt against the searching limb.

It had been Bauer's gun once, and his father's and grandfather's before that. Each generation had filled the stock and the barrel with every etching they knew, marks, signs to bind and hurt.

The girl withdrew with a bloodcurdling scream, smoke and flame rising from the wound.

"Come on, then," Lanyard yelled. "You don't have Papa Lucy here to protect you. I killed him too. And now, I'll kill you again, as many times as I need to."

"You—you killed Papa Lucy?" she said, voice thick with the memory of sap, her rooty tongue no longer suited for speech. Lanyard nodded.

She withdrew the reaching limb until it was an arm, point forming into a shepherd's crook and then once more into a carved hand, fingers clenching and releasing. An angry fist.

"The Cruik is gone too. Cast into the last ocean by the Boneman, back when he gave his brother a dunking. You're a fool to wear that shape."

"It's all I know now," the girl said quietly. "If I'm going to destroy Papa Lucy, I need every weapon I've got."

"Destroy–girl, do you have sap in your ears? He's gone. His brother threw him and his bloody walking stick into the dead waters."

"No. No, he is not gone," she said. "I can taste him in the air. Feel him with these," she said, reaching out with curled fingers.

"I can't see how anyone could survive that," Lanyard said. "Lucy is gone. You're hunting a ghost."

"You know nothing, Jesusman. He walks, and I will end him!"

"Why fight us then? We had common cause."

"I want your machines. Your guns."

"We'll be lucky to fix this mess here into one working bike!"

"Well then, I want a body to wear, if one goes begging."

"We burn our dead down here. Find yourself a different puppet."

She eyed his shotgun, and then the knife that had long ago ended her first life. The wooden girl nodded.

"You should not have come down here. It's very hard to leave."

"No shit," Lanyard said.

A long pause.

"Do you have a cigarette?" the girl said. "I miss those the most."

Eyebrows raised, Lanyard fetched out a crumb of tobacco from the near-empty pouch, then brought out the rolling papers. One economical movement, fingers squeezing and rolling, a quick lick of the paper edge. She took the cigarette, eyes wide as Lanyard summoned a flame on a fingertip to light it.

"I'll remember this," Lanyard said, "when I face my final moments, and all I want is a damned smoke."

"Thank you, Jesusman."

"Lanyard."

It wasn't the first cigarette he'd shared with someone who'd just tried to kill him, and he preferred to spend these moments with people who kept silent. When they got chatty, it pissed him off.

A groan from the bike. Yulio would be fine, or he was dying, and it was all the same at this point.

"I don't know how long I've been down here."

Lanyard set his jaw. The wood-girl was chatty.

"Fifteen years."

"I remember you," she said, looking at him through the hollows of her wood-knot irises. "Not a man. A boy. A rope around your throat."

Lanyard raised an eyebrow. Lucy's killer looked through the cigarette smoke and right through him, as if staring into the past, and he thought he understood what was going on. Old memories came easier to people near their endings, and the Underfog was nothing if not an ongoing ending.

Or perhaps death and the branchings of death were easier to see down here, and as the cigarette passed back and forth and their fingertips brushed, more memories came to her.

"When my father pulled the lever, someone shot your rope. You ran."

"Your *father*? You were Rider's child."

He was caught in that old memory, where a girl watched him from behind a gallow's post. Her father was the Selector of Mawson, a dying man from a Before-time tower, the man who both passed the sentence and yanked the death lever.

"Rider," the girl-thing said, trying the word on her grainy tongue.

"Your name was Jennifer Rider. You were the Selector's Daughter. You were meant to take over that bloody big tower one day."

Memory. Her eyes went wide then. Now that the killing moment was all tobacco and the distant groans of Yulio, Lanyard felt pity. The wood-girl was just the latest in a long line of fools who had fallen for the Cruik, fallen *into* it, and now in death she still aped that exiled god-in-a-stick, still hunted a master who had died in the most absolute way, wasting her afterlife on a folly.

Should have been me down here, he thought, *neck stretched out as a kid, and you living on to see the world above end. Now, we are both monsters and it's all Lucy's fault, Jesus's fault, Sol too. Lay blame for this ongoing mess at their feet, that whole wretched gang of bastard magicians!*

"We got grog, too, if you want it," was what he actually said.

A shout, and then the air filled with the hammering chatter of gunfire. Jenny Rider staggered away from Lanyard, bullets punching into her torso, sending away bark, wood chips, more of the blue fluid. Yulio was limping away from the wrecked bike, chattergun torn from its mount and barking.

"Stop!" Lanyard said, waving his arms furiously, but Jenny was already gone, parting the hedge and wriggling into the Oerwoud.

"I got her boss! Got her good!"
"We were having a bloody cigarette!"

As the sky once more shifted towards violet, the path took a sharp right and then abruptly spilled Lanyard's people out of the Oerwoud. Ahead, a cracked plain that ran toward a fuzz of hills, their peaks shifting with a peristaltic flexing from left to right, and then back again.

The plain itself breathed around their feet, the broken edges of the cracked clay clicking, rustling, shifting. Tipping. Each footstep became a drunken lurching for this line of doomed soldiers, the birds seeming to have the worst of it. They chattered and flailed their wings, shared the swear words they'd stolen from human lips.

Ahead, the only exception to grace this barren place. A building, grand as a palace, a tight cluster of turrets, minarets, towers, and cupola, a thin structure reaching impossibly high.

The House of the Accurate Count.

"Move fast," Lanyard said, remembering the Smothered Princes, their army of gold and glass. "That odd forest will no longer hide us from prying eyes."

Tilly sent the bikers forward to scout, and they did better than the others, floating across that breathing clay like whining boats.

Three motor bikes were left to their expedition, one cobbled together from the pair ruined by Jenny Rider. Yulio huffed along under the weight of the big gun, walking with the others as punishment.

Death within a day, Lanyard thought, marking the thick rattle of Yulio's phlegm, the coughing that sent him kneeward more than once. *Perhaps a kindness, to walk the last bit of life out of him.*

"What are those damn things?" Lanyard grumbled. Putting a telescope to his good eye, he scanned the flock of beasts flying above the House.

Moths. Thousands upon thousands, bumping and darting into each other as they spiraled out of the spires and towers of the House, their dirty paper wings carving at the sky. Once clear of the building, they moved easier, like the flexing murmuration of a bird flock, and then they flew away in all directions. There were others dancing among them, small specks of dust, and they moved like smaller clouds within the greater spiral. These too were moths. Lanyard realised with a creeping horror that the creatures he could make out from this distance were the same thing on an enormous scale.

Those flapping wings, those quivering antennae, it all drove a giant insect the size of a camel, and they swirled above in their *thousands*.

"Those big ones. Some of them are carrying people," Tilly said, and they trained their spyglasses at the heavens, marvelling at the sight. Once-Dead souls, cocooned in those furry legs, the moths emerging from House windows in a mad flutter upwards.

"Prisoners?"

"Passengers. I think."

"Hmm."

The turning gyre of moths worked in both directions, some of those on the descent suddenly darting into the House as if given a signal.

They circle the House, waiting for scraps, Bilben had said, neglecting to mention what those scraps were. She'd also mentioned that the House was a place of law and custom, but he'd seen enough of that to know that a magistrate could murder you just as well as the foulest of the crooked folk could.

"We're mad to go towards that," Tilly said. "I say we veer wide and keep quiet."

"Look there," Yulio coughed, spotting a Twice-Dead soul passing on their left, translucent skin in the shape of a person. Floating, drifting towards the final shore, and the House was in its path.

Lanyard thought of Mal, pursuing the shape of his own beloved sweetheart, chasing the outline of Kirstl towards that final shore. To Shale.

"Perhaps whoever lives in there knows where we can find this Dawn King," he said, and Tilly saw the lie, set her own lips in the thin line of disapproval she'd learnt from him. She knew him down to the bones, could see the longing for Mal in how he followed the travel of that lost soul.

"What does your jawbone say?" she finally managed, using the butt of her pike as a walking stick against the shifting clay. "Get advice from the Boneman if you've lost your own common sense."

Drawing out the jaw, he set the line to untangling, and saw it act in a bizarre way. First, it pointed at the House, but then after a long moment, it jerked around on the tether, pulling away from him as if a fish fighting the hook in its own jaw.

Suddenly, it swung up, a pendulum that struck Lanyard in the face, over and over, drawing blood, seeking to peck out his eyes. Not even the frantic manhandling by Tilly and a pair of other Jesusmen could get the sinister jawbone under control. Lanyard swore at the thing, blood streaming down his face.

"Tie that up," he swore. "Lash it to the camel for all the good it bloody does."

It fought the whole time, moving under its own power, and it even took a man's hand off at the wrist, sharp teeth sawing away in mid-air. Finally they rammed it snout-first into a rifle bag, lashing it down with much rope and cursing, even as they shifted and slid around on the tilting clay.

"What the hell," Tilly huffed as she bandaged her lacerated forearm. "It brought us here. Led us out of the mist."

"Bloody Boneman," Lanyard mumbled. It made no sense to him. A dream of that sorcerer, the gift that was a key and then a compass, only to find all of Overhaeven hunting for it, even John Leicester and the Jesus ordering him to leave it.

They were Jesusmen! An order of warriors, sworn to vengeance against a hidden warlord. The Jesusmen had never turned from their own endless war, never running from fights they'd already lost at the outset. Illegal for hundreds of years, still fighting for those who spat at them. Now, ordered by their holiest figures to simply give up.

All the Jesusmen knew, all they ever breathed was the opposite. Dig in. Fight on. Die, and die gladly.

And now, the jawbone itself meant them ill, turned to malice and injury. A gift from the Boneman that had turned dangerous. In the last fifteen years, Lanyard had only seen that ancient necromancer practice his art a few times, and not once did that sad-eyed relic so much as touch a bone without grace and respect.

Lanyard still thought like a half-starved criminal, even after all these years, and one of the first things you learnt was to watch others for that moment where they might turn on you, that smiles and good words meant nothing when you held something that others wanted.

We're being played, Lanyard realised. *Someone is lying to us. Hell, to all of us.*

"Boss," Yulio wheezed. "Over there. Chain-Folk."

The dying rifleman had seen true, as a whole horde of the slavers burst from the shifting clay, riding forth on the spirits of horses and even stranger things. Lanyard ordered a ragged defence, but the Chain-Folk were not riding for them.

They rode on the House itself, holding up spears and whips of blue.

"Let's see how this House defends itself," Tilly began, even as the charging horde drew short, marking some indistinct line in the ground. Then, they looked upwards, to the moths and their cargo, the enormous fliers scattering in all directions.

The Chain-Folk worked efficiently. Spears, to bring down a flyer. The whip to beat the wounded moth senseless. The chains, shackled to both moth and passenger.

They repeated this assault three times before one of the slavers set a boot-heel across that unmarked line, finally drawing the ire of the House.

The man was hauled in by unseen hands, dragged toward the walls of the House, and for a moment his comrades grabbed at him, fought to save him, before giving up and releasing the man to his fate.

He hit the nearest wall, pinned spread-eagled to the bricks as though he were a moth collected by a house of moths. Then his arms and legs stretched out, impossibly long, and then some unseen thumb worked on the unlucky raider, smoothing out his skin, stretching and kneading it, spreading out that spirit-flesh across the bricks, grinding and smoothing it out until the tower bore a tissue-thin face of the man, a look of horror realised across an acre of stone.

And then, the flesh fell into the stone, absorbed, increasing the whole structure by some miniscule fraction of an inch.

The Chain-Folk had already left with their wriggling prizes, not looking back as they returned to their secret ways, parting the clay and riding back below the surface.

"Boss, we cannot go there," Tilly said. "We will be gobbled up into that building!"

"Too right. Pasted into the bloody bricks and mortar," someone grumbled.

Lanyard had a passing moment of regret that he'd sent Bilben packing, reinforcing this exile with a barrage of gunfire. He'd been angry then, and felt betrayed, but he admitted he could have used the rodent-spirit's counsel, even if it was inevitably self-serving.

As per usual, it was his decision to make, and he made it.

"Shut up. We're going," Lanyard said. "No one touch those bloody moths, and we'll probably be fine."

Then the clay shifted beneath Yulio, and he went down hard, falling across his machine-gun. He hit the trigger bars by accident, sending out a rapid burst of bullets before he could stop it. Lanyard watched in horror as the rounds whizzed across the plain, stitching a neat pattern across the enormous front doors of the House.

"You idiot!" Lanyard roared, hauling the man up to his feet. Yulio looked at him through a haze of blood and mucus, dropping the big gun with hands that could no longer hold it.

"Sorry, boss," he hacked, falling into a sharp fit of coughing. Lanyard assessed the man and came to a decision.

"Tilly, check my bag on the camel. Good bottle of grog. Some tobacco. Yulio, it's time, mate."

"No," the man protested. "I can still shoot a rifle, better than you, better than anyone."

He hacked up a lump that was dark green and bright red and spat it onto the tilting clay.

"Besides, I already knocked on their front door."

There was no more time for words, only whistled commands and forming up into ranks. Over at the House, that double-door split into a gap-toothed smile a hundred feet high, as if humouring the insult the living had delivered.

Figures emerged, people followed by a flurry of moths. Some of the insects swept the ground for Yulio's bullets, claiming each one with reverence.

Many more people emerged, a great host that slid eerily across that shifting plain, and Lanyard passed his telescope across a parade of the caped and the mitred, each with a different sash or chain of office. There was nothing uniform about their finery. He saw Phrygian caps, berets, staves, and symbols of office bobbing and wavering. Beneath that paste-gem pomp were dozens of smiles, dead and wide. They came for the living, relentless and sure.

When Tilly handed Yulio a rifle, Lanyard did not object.

— INTERLUDE —

To exist in the Overhaeven was to be a symbol floating in a sea of golden light, a complicated ballet of hierarchy, predator and prey, and always feeding, glutting on that shining ocean. It was called Aurum, that heady stuff, and the Lords of Overhaeven had schemed long and hard to squeeze and steal every drop that was here.

Other times the Lords of that high place went deeper and were a commune of thought and information without form, a mind compartmentalised against itself in a million shifting ways.

Rarer still, the Lords allowed themselves a physical shape, carved out an area that was both *place* and *idea* and *culture*, and these were often reserved for great parties, for wars and sport, and sometimes for secret meetings, either to take on flesh and caper and rut as the lower creations did, or to plot.

John Leicester stepped out of golden thought and into a grubby flat from the Before, a facsimile perfect down to the takeaway containers and the feeling of fear. Luciano Pappagallo's place, where the Family hatched their desperate plan to escape a world ending.

This décor was not lost on Jesus, who entered the same physical space, sitting down on the same chair he'd selected on that day. A disgraced professor then, in a roomful of dear friends, long before the madness that destroyed their fellowship.

"Are we safe?" he asked. John shrugged. This physical bubble was as safe from eavesdropping as either of them could make it, but these old friends were low in this immortal hierarchy, still learning the rules. Novices and outsiders, frustrated at every turn.

"I'm still on probation," Jesus ventured, testing their paper-thin shield and finding it wanting. "You've got probation and disgrace. Still, we may as well speak openly."

"The Boneman is gone," John said simply, and Jesus nodded.

"I can't see Sol anywhere. I've tried everything."

"Who would hurt him? If we're the wardens of the Now, he's just the turnkey."

"The Now is ravaged. Sol might have been able to stop this Dawn King, but he wasn't there."

The Dawn King. At the words, the pair fell silent. The very concept of this being had driven a schism through Overhaeven, with parties swearing for and against him. Even so, no one was quite clear what the Dawn King was or what he stood for.

They had an ally or two of course. A being that went only by a rat sigil had raised their suspicions, suggested that John and Jesus meet and plan in a physical bubble. She would be arriving soon, and spoke of others who could act in the Dawn King matter.

"Do any of your followers remain? In the Now?" Jesus asked.

"Some. My faithful are scattered, hunted. They'll all be dead soon enough," the soldier-mage said glumly.

They'd seen Overhaeven hosts sacking the cities and towns in the Dawn King's name, and refugees who fled from their golden terror, facing even more danger out in the wilds. Predators from other worlds slipped through the world veil, glutting themselves in all the chaos.

Their requests for intercession were rebuffed, either with kind homilies or outright hostility. The civil war in Overhaeven meant that none cared about the last survivors of the human race.

"I am further troubled, old friend," Jesus said. He cracked open the idea of a beer, ending up dissatisfied with the taste of it. Old memories could only do so much.

"I had some still riding under my name. A Lodge again! Lanyard Everett and his students, still doing the work."

"Your half-formed magicians? You wouldn't have trusted any of them with a mop in the Collegia."

The Jesus ignored the old insult about his followers. He'd focused on making specialists with only three jobs–get survivors through the Greygulf, guide the bleedthroughs into the Now, and deal with any intruders.

"They have entered the Underfog. Every last one of them."

"Of course. It happens to every living soul."

"No. They have entered, bodily. Crossed into the land of the dead with their hearts pumping and their souls untaken."

"How did you do this?"

"I didn't do it, John."

"Well, get an answer out of this Lanyard. Use the Aum, send him a dream!"

Jesus arched an eyebrow. Of course he'd tried that.

"Something is blocking me," Jesus said. John tried, too, reaching out to Tilly Carpidian, who'd once served his grim-faced flock.

"How? Who could keep us out?"

"I think it's the Dawn King."

"Down there? I thought he was up here somewhere, playing chess with idiot gods in the golden sea."

"None here has ever seen him," Jesus said. "I have hunted extensively for clues, crept from camp to camp. He is an idea here, the whisper of a friend of a friend at best."

John said nothing.

"I do not think the Dawn King has ever set foot in Overhaeven," Jesus continued.

John Leicester made to frame an awful thought, even as the walls of their shelter collapsed. The symbol of linked circles forced entry, forming into a pair of smiling cherubs with golden hair. The Smothered Princes came for Jesus and John Leicester with arms spread, and those two old magicians of the Before found all escape suddenly cut off.

PART TWO
JUNKMAN

− 10 −

BEFORE

Ray Leicester stood on the train platform, toes touching the painted line. He inched forward, just a little, and felt rebellious.

In Ur-Sydney the civic magicians had placed barriers across all the main stations to prevent jumpers, pushers, and unfortunate accidents, but little towns like Shadrach couldn't afford much in the way of safety. Just a line of paint, and old Alf Simpson with his whistle, rarely leaving the conductor's office unless he saw some kids mucking around.

Ray slid backwards, once more behind the safety of paint. Unlike his celebrated brother, John, Ray never put himself in danger, and he approached any sort of risk with analysis and then paralysis.

He'd never even been to Ur-Sydney and had only ever caught the train the other way, out to Duntrune. There was a monthly swap-meet out there, good for stocking up his workshop, and of course the Military Academy. He'd seen John's passing out parade there, back when Mum and Dad were still alive, and felt envy, pure and thick, even as he clapped with all the others.

Ray still kept a faithful scrapbook of his brother's adventures, newspaper clippings documenting every military success, the Order of the Collegia Medal, and then his appointment to the Collegia proper, that bright city placed high in orbit by the powers of a thousand magicians.

He'd started the scrapbook with his Mum back when John's photo first got into the local newspaper (John's twelve-year-old hands, yet to be soaked in blood, clutched around a small trophy on a tennis court). Ray only kept adding to it for the sake of her memory, and because he was a bull-headed completist. Ray Leicester could no more leave a task unfinished than his brother could avoid falling arse backwards into success.

Ray couldn't afford a visit up to the Collegia, and when John offered to pay for his ticket, he'd refused. That was the last time he'd ever spoken to his celebrated brother. Ray was great on the tools and could fix just about anything, but he wasn't quite sure if he could ever fix their strained relationship, or if he even wanted to.

"Hallo there, Junkman!" he heard someone say, and he came out of his reverie to see Max Colley with his equally stout wife, both dressed in their Sunday best for the train journey.

He hated the nickname, but took the handshake anyway and did his best to make eye contact and smile like his Dad taught him to, back when they were worried about the lad not playing with other kids, a little slow on learning his speech.

"Hi, Max."

"Finished fixing my record player yet?"

"Sorry. I'm missing the right stylus."

"You're bound to find one in Ur-Sydney," Max said. "That place has got everything."

The train arrived with a blat of its horn. The engine was the newer kind, humming and spilling out golden light, and it approached with next to no sound. More than one person had wandered out in front of these new trains, their ears still trained to the sound of diesel or even steam engines.

Ray liked everything about engines and tools, but he did not like this new technology. This power didn't come from a steam turbine or the reassuring rumble of an internal combustion motor.

Aurum, the golden light the Collegia was siphoning from Overhaeven. The same as the power stations on most street corners, usually paired with the nearest phone booth, humming cheerfully as they powered homes and businesses.

He handed over his ticket to be punched and climbed aboard, finding his assigned seat. Normally he declined the treasures of the tea-cart, but he purchased a sandwich, a newspaper, and even a cup of tea.

It felt like a maiden voyage, going away from everything he'd ever known, but views of endless farmland soon bored Ray. He turned to the newspaper and found more of the usual worry-worting and celebrity nonsense. Measured temperature climbs in the power stations. The rollout of the new refrigeration modules, which seemed to be keeping these climbs to manageable levels.

"Shouldn't be tampering with that stuff," Ray told the empty cabin. "No telling what might bloody blow up."

He spent most of his first day in Ur-Sydney in a continuous panic attack. So many people. Buildings and skyscrapers that loomed higher than any work of man had any right to do.

He clutched his Dad's old hat to his head against the windy passage of a tram, struggling against the weight of the canvas duffel bag across one shoulder. In his nervous state he'd overpacked the bag, and that was without intent to even stay one night here.

These city folk moved at a mad clip, and every block of Ur-Sydney felt like wading through mud. He missed Shadrach then, missed the quiet streets where he could walk as he wished, everything laid out in a sensible way, the people terse and polite and always, always predictable.

Then, an excited rush around him, and he was pushed by the crowd, heard the sounds of someone yelling into a megaphone, an official ordering a crowd to disperse. Then, the single whoop of a police car's siren.

Red and blue lights reflected in the shop windows. Ray did not want to get involved in anything illegal. He grabbed onto the nearest lamppost, scrambling up it like he did when he spent one summer working for the telephone company as a linesman.

Over the excited crowd now, he could see the whole scene laid out before him. An illegal roadblock, with a stage set up. Angry people with placards, clashing with police officers in riot gear.

SHUT IT DOWN, the signs read. POWER OFF!

Above this chaos, figures were on the stage, screaming over the police megaphones. He recognised many of the figures there, infamous in the news. The Pappagallo brothers, Sol and Luciano, a pair of magicians now ejected from the Collegia and denounced for their extreme views. Luciano was the figurehead of the movement, and he set a sorcerous mark upon his throat, overcoming all of the noise.

"WHAT HAVE THEY GOT TO HIDE?" he roared at ear-splitting volume. "THE SCIENCE DOES NOT LIE."

He was a striking figure, the man who was nicknamed Papa Lucy in certain corners of the press. Tall, with a handsome roman face, and long, spilling Robert Plant hair. As he swept his gaze across the crowd, his piercing eyes seemed to fix each person in place, and for a heartbeat Ray felt the heady charisma of this man.

"SHUT DOWN THE POWER STATIONS," he declared. "NOW. OR EVERYBODY WILL DIE."

At that point, the protestors' blockade fell. The police had their own magicians, who parted the crowd with mark and word. The Pappagallo brothers did not resist, and Papa Lucy laughed the whole way, head held high, and this moment was captured by photographers and reprinted often in the coming months.

Ray barely noticed this historical moment, as he saw the last of the ring leaders led off in handcuffs. John Leicester, celebrated soldier-mage, recipient of the Order of the Collegia Medal, estranged brother. John had publicly thrown his lot in with Papa Lucy, and Ray watched as his brother lost everything.

It was an awkward reunion in the bailiff's office, Ray clutching his duffel close, John still wearing his blood-stained uniform. At some point he'd been beaten badly, and his left eye was almost closed over, his lip split and weeping.

"I am sorry," Ray finally said.

"Sorry?" John answered.

"I could only afford to post your bail. Your friends will have to make their own way out."

A long moment, and John clapped Ray on the shoulder. A pained smile.

"They will be okay," John said. "What are you doing here?"

"I came to pay your bail."

"No. In Ur-Sydney. Your whole life, you've never travelled more than twenty miles from Shadrach."

"I'd rather not say. I have to go."

Ray turned around and left the building, not giving his brother a second glance. He heard the footsteps behind him as John Leicester caught up to him.

"Ray! Wait. We haven't spoken in nearly twenty years!"

John only paused to refer to a piece of paper, looking around in bewilderment for a street sign.

"Ray. This place is going to eat you alive, mate," John said. "At least let me help you find your way."

"My business is private," Ray said tersely. "I wish you well."

"Bullshit. You never did."

The two brothers eyed each other in the street, held together by the weight of family history, expectations, and failures.

"Lucy is right," John said. "About the power plants. It's all about to go tits up."

"Language," Ray said, in the voice of both dead parents.

"I know you hate those plants. The new engines. Endless power, but it has to come from somewhere, right?"

"I don't believe the fear-mongers," Ray said finally. "Look, I have an appointment. If you can leave your criminal associates, you are welcome back to stay at Shadrach."

"You don't mean that."

"I do. You are family and that always means something."

"Family," John said, chewing over the word. Ray finally found his bearings and headed down Goulborn Street.

"I know why you're here," John yelled out, and Ray stopped in his tracks.

He's at you again, Ray, he thought. *Ignore him. Walk away.*

"You won your ticket. You're here for the treatment."

Ray turned towards his brother, and as he looked at the soldier's beaten face, the last of his resolve failed. He nodded, genial mask slipping aside to show genuine fear.

"You're really going through with it?" John said.

"I've won my spot," Ray said. "Waited ten years on the list. I'm getting it."

"Don't see the point. Two, maybe three years, and the whole shithouse is going up in flames."

"Language."

They'd reached the facility, a heavily guarded wing on the outside of the Royal Meschach Hospital.

"What did it feel like?" Ray asked.

"The treatment?"

"Yep."

"It's–it's cold. Very cold. After a few months, you start to feel warmer, but you'll never get it back. Everything's always just a little colder."

"I don't mind."

"The army put my unit through an experiment. Seven hours in a shipping container set at 110 degrees. I did not even break a sweat."

"What else?"

"Your thoughts slow down. Just a whisker, but noticeable."

"Little difference here," Ray said, a note of bitterness falling out. He'd heard it all as a lad: *Slow. Dense. Simpleton.* A kind-hearted circuit doctor once mentioned *Asperger's* and Mum sent him packing, in tears and denial. Nothing then but lessons on handshakes, and the solace of tearing apart machines, a world of junk and tools instead of proper friends, a proper life.

"You know I don't mean like that," John said. "Just a little lag. I could still pilot a Nhulunbuy fighter craft afterwards."

A few years ago, the treatment facilities had been surrounded by semi-permanent protestor camps, but today they only passed one old woman who glared at them through cataracts, waving a sign that read "LIFE IS MEANT TO BE SHORT."

The brothers passed the first of several cordons of security, the security guard looking with surprise to see the celebrated soldier-mage on his doorstep.

"Saw you on the news, Leicester," the man said, checking their papers and marking John's injuries. "Why'd you let them do that to you?"

"They were just doing their jobs," John said. "No one deserves to die for doing that."

"Should have seen the other guys," Ray said bluntly, and as always his humour fell flat. The guard waved them on, and Ray fell deeper into panic, his whole passage through the hospital a myopic hyper-focus of corridors, white coats, and upside-down timepieces. At one point they paused as John spoke to a veteran in a wheelchair, the man's legs transformed into those of a new-born baby's. *Mage-mine.*

As the minutes passed while John checked in on his fellow soldier, Ray began to seriously fret then, breathing heavily, close to vomiting, and he paced back and forth, scratching at his forearms with his workshop-roughened fingernails. When John realised this, he begged leave from the wounded soldier and hustled his brother forward.

"It's okay if you don't do this," John said. "I know these places scare you."

"I have to," Ray said.

"I hope you realise something," John said after a moment. "Right now, you are being as brave as any soldier I've fought beside."

"It's just a procedure," Ray said brusquely. "I'm not a hero like you."

"I'm glad you never had to be," John said. "I'm glad you got Shadrach, your workshop, living on your own after Mum and Dad. I–I worry about you a lot, Ray."

"I can look after myself."

"Not saying you can't."

They'd arrived. Here was a legitimate guard post, with a pair of soldier-mages who saluted John as they arrived. If any protestor or thief made it to this corridor, Ray knew that they were authorised to destroy said person in one of the many awful ways that they knew.

METHUSELAH TREATMENT FACILITY, the sign above the double-doors read.

"Last chance," John said.

"Yes. Yes it is," Ray replied, and took a step forward.

In all of his panic, Ray had forgotten to book somewhere to stay, and then thought he might simply get on the next train home, but the Methuselah procedure took many hours, and he missed the last departure. Shivering in his brother's arms, Ray let John guide him back to his city apartment. It was a run-down place in Paddington, and there were signs that others had been staying here. Plans pasted to the walls, the table strewn with maps and stacks of paper.

John made a move to cover these plans, stopping when he realised Ray simply didn't care. The Junkman from Shadrach only had eyes for the big colour television, pulling it away from the wall so he could inspect the panels and wires on the reverse.

"You won't be able to stay here much longer," Ray said, muffled behind the big wooden set. "They'll cut off your pensions, dispensations, bursaries, sponsorships, etcetera."

"They already have," John said. "Army cut me off when I returned my Order of the Collegia Medal."

"Oh. At least you have a good television."

"You'd think so, for what it cost. Bloody thing goes on the fritz half the time."

When the post-treatment shivers got to be too much, John ran his brother a scalding hot bath, and Ray slid into it awkwardly. He only ever showered at home.

"I'm still cold, John," he called out.

"Perfectly normal."

The cold was marrow-deep, the tips of his fingers and toes pulsing with pain. Already, the treatment was working upon him, wriggling into every atom, every corner of his body. Changing him. He'd tried to read the material about the hardening of telomeres using the application of a new Overhaeven theory, but gave himself a minor headache just trying to understand it all.

John stayed by his side throughout the first night, pouring kettle after boiling kettle into the water, and it still wasn't enough to ward off the chill of eternity.

By dawn he wanted to die, but knew he couldn't.

His bones still throbbed with a deep x-ray ache, even as the chills faded into a refrigerator cold seeping out from his core. Ray was a bundle of blankets in front of the radiator, its heat cranked so high that the cheerful golden glow of the Aurum winked out from its innards.

"I still don't understand," John said, sketching out fire symbols with dancing fingertips, setting them to dance around Ray's head.

"I won a spot. I was entitled to this."

"People are selling those spots. There's no point now, not to any of it."

"You want to know why I took the treatment?"

"Well, I mean no disrespect, but you–Ray, you live a simple life. Even if the power stations weren't failing, what would be the point?"

Ray could not truly explain the urge to spend eons in the dust of his shed, working with his hands. Taking everything apart. Understanding everything. Having nothing but time.

"You were away in the war," he finally managed, "when cancer took Mum. When Dad's heart failed him the next week. You didn't see what I did."

"I couldn't be there. You know why."

"Listen. I'm not blaming, just trying to explain. I know machines. The human body is a marvellous machine, and I saw it fail twice. I cannot accept my own machine failing."

"The Methuselah treatment won't stop you from burning with the rest of us."

"Those power stations are machines, too. With enough time, a machine can always be fixed."

Ray did not go back to Shadrach. Lucy and Sol had been bailed out by supporters, and John arranged for Ray to meet the infamous brothers at the Beatles concert the following night. This plan fell apart at the last hour, Ray falling into an extreme panic attack at the thought of the crowd, of all the noise at the Ur-Sydney Stadium.

John shifted this meeting to his place, where they watched the concert on his television, even as the actual concert shook his windows and most of the neighbours were pinpoints of cigarette out on their balconies, straining to hear the music from across the bay.

Then an imperious knock on the door, before it simply opened by itself, locks disengaging by an unseen hand, handle turning. Luciano Pappagallo swanned in, all curls and attitude, followed by the ever-faithful Sol.

"John said you were a Beatles fan," Lucy said by way of introduction.

"I am."

"I hope you understand that I pulled a big, big favour. We were going to meet the fucking band."

"Lucy, please," his brother Sol pleaded, and Luciano Pappagallo sighed. The infamous magician patted Ray on the shoulder, swapping scorn for a toothy smile that didn't quite meet his eyes.

"Never mind. John owns a very good television."

The two sets of brothers crammed onto the couch, watching in colour as the group took the stage. Paul and George on the left, a perfect V of guitar necks. To the right John Lennon loomed large, while Billy Preston's organ was pushed behind the guitarists, fighting for space with Pete Best's ever-sprawling drum kit.

"Dear gods, I hope they don't just play all their new shit," Lucy groaned.

"Is Hesus coming?" Sol asked John, who shrugged.

"Baertha sends her love to all," Lucy said. "Out hitting up her old folks for cash."

"I thought they disowned her?" John said delicately. Sol's mouth worked into a very thin line. The marriage had destroyed him professionally, and the Hann family was continuing to sabotage their anti-power movement.

"We're just that desperate, mate."

Ray was transfixed as the band worked through their early hits, still note perfect after all these years. It seemed fitting to swim in nostalgia as his body changed, every moment feeling more important now, more resonant.

In John's apartment, they were draining energy like a box full of vampires, with the big TV, the heater, the lights, the fridgerator, and the fondue-set, everything drawing out of that miraculous power station on the street corner, which pulsed suddenly, causing shadows to dance across the walls. The television sparked and spat and went black, halfway through *"Band on the Run."* The room erupted into chaos and jeers. Lucy went out onto the balcony, placing a magical sigil on his ears so he could hear the distant concert. It was still not enough, and he swore some more.

"Maybe we should have gone to the concert," Sol said quietly, looking out to his brother raving and shouting on the balcony.

Ray stood up calmly, opening up his duffel and extracting a small selection of tools. He unscrewed the back of the television and tinkered with its innards.

"Shouldn't he unplug that first?" Sol said, a little worried. Since switching his studies to necromancy, the younger Pappagallo was always a little gloomy and risk averse.

"He knows what he's doing," John said. Within a minute, the TV was repaired and once more showing the Beatles concert. Ray reattached everything, adjusted the rabbit-ear antennae to get the best signal, and returned to his seat, visibly uncomfortable as the others cheered him and clapped him on the shoulders.

Lucy arched an eyebrow at the speed of Ray's practical skills, but he sank back into his seat in a kind of sullen annoyance. Three exiled superstars of the Collegia, masters of the magical arts, not one of whom could mend a broken television.

"Oh, here we go," Lucy said. "Bloody *'Imagine.'* The nerve of these arseholes."

"*'Imagine'* was *the* standout song of their 1972 reunion album *Dovetail Joint,*" Ray recited. "Molly Meldrum said so. The single spent 12 weeks at number one."

"Says the loser who could have met them in person."

"Enough, Lucy!" John said sternly.

On the TV, Billy Preston worked through the recurring organ line, even as Paul and George harmonised, and Pete Best played with brushes and a light hand. It was syrupy Beatles sweetness and as near perfect as a song could be. John Lennon was true to form and worked in a protest lyric.

"Imagine the fucking Collegia/
Switching the power off!"

That brought howls of laughter from Lucy and kept the press busy for days. Even as the band closed off with three songs from their newest album *Chess in a Golden Sea*, Lucy was in a much better mood.

"You know, I've heard a different version of '*Imagine*,'" he told Ray later, over plans and conspiracies. "John Lennon, singing on his own, backed by piano only. He did it better without the Beatles."

"I don't know if you're lying. I can't read faces."

"Just trust me. It sounded much better. And don't even get me started about Ringo!"

"What's a Ringo?"

Hesus had a van, and they took Ray's experiment on the road, testing any power station they could get to. Every time that he popped open a panel and tinkered with the insides, Ray and the magicians were bathed in golden light. Anyone without protective gear or who hadn't taken the Methuselah treatment would be in severe pain working so close to all of that radiating Aurum, but they were fine, passing around tools and instruments.

"There," Ray said. "Here's the problem. It's just a loose thread."

"What do you mean?"

"Like in the cartoons, where a loose thread can unravel an entire sweater. Someone is pulling out a thread, a big one. From the other side, wherever this feeds into the Overhaeven. They don't want us nicking their Aurum."

It took a simple repairman to point out the obvious to that cadre of celebrated magicians, but now it was all they could see. All their instruments spoke to this as the problem.

Sabotage. Someone or something in Overhaeven had detected humanity stealing their Aurum. This was simply an economical way to wipe out the power thieves.

Humanity was a whole planet of power thieves, but the principle was sound enough in Ray's eyes.

Lucy made special friends with Ray, made good their initial rough meeting. They worked alone many nights, Lucy always making excuses to the others. Ray did Lucy a favour, and with a mixture of precision tinkering and magic they pulled out a golden thread of their own, a thread with the potential to unravel the entire world.

Lucy paused for a moment then, looking deep into the golden light. Looking through it. If Ray had been able to read faces correctly, he might have recognised a sudden ambition, an idea that had seized Lucy so completely that he did not think to disguise his greed. Ray interpreted this pause as a frustrating interruption to his own work process, and this was the only thing that saved his life that night.

"We're going to tie these threads together, right? To fix the hole?"

"Again with the Beatles? We're not fixing a fucking hole."

Lucy eased Ray's worries and refusals, first with words, then with lies, and finally with magic, enough to get the job done. He massaged the event from Ray's mind and sent the man wandering away with pleasant thoughts of the Beatles, his toolkit, the love of his brother.

"Fuck this place," Lucy said, and yanked the golden thread.

It almost worked.

NOW

In a nameless stretch of grassland, a lone Taursi stalked an animal and was the only witness when the world tore open and all of the humans poured out.

They wailed. They babbled. Some no longer knew how to walk. Thousands upon thousands, a great host of refugees driven to blank-faced madness, literally reborn in this new world.

Some survived this journey with minds intact, and they cared for the inflicted, rounded up the livestock, and tried to make a beachhead.

Crosspoint was first a great medical centre, with rough tents and shelters stretched out to cover grown adults who were no longer toilet-trained, did not respond to language, and had to relearn every-thing. Many of the refugees went catatonic and never came out.

It was a rough few years.

While Lucy, Baertha, and Sol set to building the First City with their magic, John was less useful. He spent most of his time at his brother's side, acutely aware that everything that made Ray special was gone.

Ray Leicester stared at the tent ceiling for hours on end. He knew no words. He had to be spoonfed and have his arse wiped. He never once responded to his brother's ministrations and had no recollection of his face.

The Family and the Hesusmen brought a wave of people back, the first to relearn speaking and walking, and then they were tasked with helping others. Slowly, the human race began to wake up.

So, so much was lost.

Ray was in that last group, the ones slated for euthanasia should they not recover. The catatonic were still consuming precious calories, and everyone else was surviving on the bare bones of their arses and getting desperate.

Then John put a shifting spanner in Ray's hands, and everything changed. Ray began adjusting the shifter, back and forth, and other recovered tools had a similar effect. He relearnt walking just to reach his tools, much as a baby would be drawn by a favourite toy.

Speech came slower. Ray became frustrated with the lessons and eventually refused to speak when John was in the room, seeing him as a source of frustration, never really understanding the word "brother," which he seemed to assume meant teacher or therapist. For the second time, the brothers were strangers, and it broke John's heart.

Papa Lucy, of course, saw this as an opportunity to get his favourite soldier-mage back to work. He gave John a following, the devout Leicesterites, and sent them out to find and tag the bleedthroughs, recovering precious goods for their new civilisation.

Ray was put to work in Crosspoint, once more repairing machines, his operation equal parts muscle memory, instinct, and relearning everything that once more fascinated him.

Whenever John visited, he was greeted with rage and thrown tools. "Brother!" Ray would scream, over and over, until John left in tears.

Years passed.

The newer settlements and in-between places needed repairmen, their scavenged goods failing more often than not. Many came to learn from Ray, who now only answered to the name of Junkman, and these students were sent out as the Tinkermen, fixers of the found, rebuilders of the recovered.

More time passed. One day, shortly before the madness of Sad Plain, Sol sent Ray out on a Tinkerman wagon, and the Junkman simply vanished into the Now.

Many Beatles records were recovered in the bleedthroughs. Before he fell into a soldier's statue and never came out, John Leicester paid a small fortune for a pristine copy of *Chess in a Golden Sea,* and he listened to this most evenings, drinking alone in a dark room.

Over many hundreds of years, the Junkman broke every Beatles record he ever found.

— 11 —

UNDERFOG

Jenny crashed through the brambles as bullets sizzled around her, leaking from a dozen deep wounds. Behind the bark of the machine gun, she heard Lanyard Everett yelling out in anger, but whether at her or his own man she could not tell.

She splashed out brilliant blue across leaf and vine, her own soul feeding the greedy landscape. *Aether. Essence. Psyche.* She'd heard it called a dozen things in her time here, and it was the only economy in the Underfog.

As she ran into the Oerwoud, she bled out a fortune in the wake of her crashing passage. She'd fought for every drop, crushing the weak and the lost, a necessary cruelty in the face of what drove her.

She knew that Papa Lucy was alive. Felt him in the air, smelt him wherever she went. His stink was even in this forest, faint but true.

She'd tried carving a type of calendar into her own wooden limbs, hoping to mark the days she'd spent prowling the Oerwoud. Hunting Papa Lucy, knowing it as a place where some came to hide. Each sepia dawn removed the marks from her limbs, her attempts at a record erased, and so she hunted anyway, unknowing if she'd been here weeks, or even months.

It didn't matter. As long as she kept her will strong and her spirit body intact, she could avoid destruction and being drawn to Shale.

Jenny Rider had failed in life, talked into madness by a madman, but here in the Underfog, she had her second chance.

Ever since she'd slipped out of the Cruik's trap and followed Papa Lucy into the Underfog, she was driven by one purpose: revenge against that liar, the smiling face of a small girl's dreams, that lurker in mirrors.

It didn't matter that Lanyard and many others had told her that Papa Lucy was gone, destroyed by his brother at Shale. Even Gretel of the House of Torana had stood with her by that rocky shore, as close as either spirit dared to go.

"See there?" Gretel had said, back when she had House and name. "The scarring is thick in the world veil. Papa Lucy came to this shore, dragging and scrambling, and he could not escape. This is the point where the Boneman threw him in."

"I do not believe it," Jenny had said, testing the air with her hooks. "He is still here."

"There were seven witnesses. One of them was the Gravedigger himself. The act is recorded at the House of the Accurate Count. The Boneman pushed his brother into the water with the butt-end of the Cruik. He paused for exactly forty-seven seconds before throwing in that foul staff, and once broken by the dark waters, the Cruik gave out every soul it ever captured. Then the Boneman returned to the lands of life."

"I don't care. They are all wrong."

"I had five moths arrive that day! Five!"

"Each one sent by a fool."

"Waste your time here, then," Gretel had seethed. She was all mass and menace, and was not above dragging victims here to dash upon the rocks at the water's edge. Worse still was if she took them to the House of Torana—or if the House of Torana came to them.

After the killing moment passed, the two went their separate ways, Jenny on her fool's quest, and Gretel onto her own much swifter destruction—and of course the Jesusman connected them both. The Jesusman was connected to *everything*.

Jenny had never doubted her course, not once, and a chance meeting with the killer of Papa Lucy's fleshly body confirmed a few things. Of course, the blast of the Jesusman's shotgun had sent an echo throughout the Realms. Even fifteen years after the killing shot, she'd caught a sniff of that moment of thunder and fear, when Papa Lucy was betrayed by his own brother, powerless to stop the pulling of the trigger.

The shotgun was holy and most ancient, and she'd only had a moment to see it tangled up in the wrecked bike, but it was there. A connection between the murder weapon and its most celebrated victim.

Just a thread, but it led out and into the Oerwoud, the tangle lost to her hunter's senses. Even in her panicked flight she'd been following the thread, snagged on branch and thorn, taut and leading back to wherever the Jesusmen had come from.

Then she lost that thin thread, the magic of the Oerwoud hiding yet another secret. There was nothing left for her then but to slump to the ground, pressing against her wounds, willing the life back into her barky flesh.

She'd lost the trail, but a trail meant a target.

She'd absorbed so much of the Cruik in her final weeks, and even in death she was as much the memory of wood as she was the spirit of a wilful young woman. The Oerwoud did little to hinder her, perhaps seeing her as kin, and traps of vine and thorn slid aside, granting a grudging admittance.

Jenny Rider hunted with her every moment and her every movement. She stretched herself into a crooked staff that reached high above the canopy, piercing the fog with one unblinking eye. She drove a sharp foot into the ground, tickling at the roots of the trees with another type of eye, leaping across that network of roots like pain through a nervous system.

She found the place where The Serene had met its end, traced out the murder of Lanyard's people, saw just how close that rolling ball of mystery had come to escaping from death.

No Papa Lucy here, but there was another thread, many threads bound into one. Jenny chased it like a greyhound after some small animal, plunging through that all-forest with purpose, and she enjoyed the simile so much that she took on the form of a dog crafted from shepherd's hooks to speed her passage.

She came upon a panicked rodent, already aware it was being pursued, and Jenny recognised Bilben of the Iron Nest immediately. They played a game for many long hours, the hunter having the help of the Oerwoud, while Bilben fell into her usual tricks, sending possibilities in all directions, some turning back to fight defiantly, others hiding, but a consensus sending most of what was Bilben onwards in a typical rodent fashion.

Triumph, and the hound pounced upon the rat.

Jenny Rider seized up Bilben with the grip of a dozen hooks, but always the creature wriggled loose, and their chase fell into a farce, a great wooden hunter patting her own body for a rat that wriggled around it in dozens of different ways. Her wooden fangs clacked against air, even as the rat nipped at her, more nuisance than threat.

"You'll not eat me today, you awful lost girl!" Bilben cried. "I will not permit it!"

"I did not mean to snap at you," Jenny said. "I fell into a role."

"Don't we all," Bilben said, still dodging the snatching curls of hooked fingers. She ran on tirelessly, even joyfully, and Jenny knew she would never capture the Queen of the Iron Nest.

"Fine! Your freedom then, but do not flee from me."

"I so enjoy a good chase," the rodent said, now perched upon her outstretched fingers.

"Information, and we can part ways," Jenny said. "The Jesusmen were here. A whole crowd of living folk."

"Ho! If you seek a body, look elsewhere! They are angry and capable. You will only lose that fight."

"I–I do not quarrel with them." And even then, she was unsure if this was true. "But there was a link from his gun to one I must find. Point me to where they came from."

"Ah. You are the one still hunting Papa Lucy. Have you tried going to Shale and sticking your head into the water?"

"I will trap you in this place, tangle you in a bower even you cannot escape from. Do not mock me!"

"'Tis but gentle guidance. You are misled. None can survive that dunking, and that magician was no more special than any soul."

"Papa Lucy lives!" Jenny yelled, a thousand shepherd's hooks erupting out from a central point, quivering with anger. When she regained control, she fell back into a girl shape, the rodent still on her finger.

"I am sorry," Bilben said. "It is the way of a small beast in a large world. To wound someone already in pain is not a noble thing."

Jenny stood still, trying to find peace. Seeing that smiling face in every whorl of tree bark, still tasting his ambition through the lace of her crooked fingers, as if the very atoms of his scheme washed across her grainy fingertips.

"Let us approach this differently," Bilben continued. "An agreement, to work together. I will help you as best I can, if you reciprocate."

"What do you want?"

"What everyone else wants, but for a different reason. The leader of the living folk drove me out, but he needs me. The House of the Accurate Count will connive him into destruction."

"Lanyard," Jenny said, still remembering her former mission. Being driven out of her comfortable old life and sent to kill the Jesusman. Failing. The grip of those fingers, the feel of the knife across her throat.

Further back, and their first shared moment, when two children in Mawson were linked by a moment at the gallows.

"Ah," Bilben said, flitting around her head for a dizzying instant. "That is an awful tale. No wonder you need closure."

"How did you-"

"I can only divine what is on the surface. It's rude to pry any deeper."

"Do not intrude into my thoughts. Never again."

"Indeed. As long as we are companions, I swear I will not dip into your thoughts in any needless way."

"That is no answer."

"This, then: bring me to Lanyard. Help me win back his trust, and I will find you the truth of Papa Lucy."

"Why bother? The moths went out on that day. I am a fool."

"I received my own moth," Bilben said, and whispered a long parable into Jenny Rider's wooden ear.

Mal rode low in Collybrock's saddle, chasing his sweetheart's ghost. Behind, the cursing of the old man beckoned him back, and he pressed down his need to please Lanyard, burying it under a tombstone of hatred and fear.

Please, Kirstl had mouthed at him. *Help.*

The bird weaved left and right, finding a path through the thick tangle of the Oerwoud. Above, a pale blue parade of Twice-Dead spirits, drifting in one exactly straight line. In places they were just clearing the tree line, and Mal braved glances upward, spying the spines of The Serene's kin, the curl of the lizard's tail, the frantically flapping arms of a slain Jesusman, as if trying to swim away from the drag of that distant dead sea.

"Kirstl!" he cried, over and over, till his voice gave and his throat was some hoarse thing barking skywards. Collybrock took up the cry, but the bird had no proper words yet, and could only give a rough *kurgle!* that was as close as she could manage.

He looked skyward a moment too long and cracked his forehead into a low branch, almost falling out of the saddle. He remembered Lanyard's first lesson in bird-riding: *"grip with your knees if you get shot! Don't bloody fall off!"*

Wincing and gasping, he indeed gripped with his knees, hugging low to Collybrock's neck. The bird knew enough to keep up the chase and followed the shadows of the spirits, casting a weak blue flicker like a lit-match held behind thick blue glass.

"Kurgle!" Collybrock cried, crashing through a trellis of phantom vegetables, the fruit becoming dust beneath the bird's feet. Mal recovered in time to yank the bird's reins to hard right, narrowly avoiding impalement on a box-thorn, but the jags caught Collybrock's flanks, yanking out several feathers and scoring the flesh beneath.

Hide your trail, Lanyard admonished in the back of Mal's mind, but there was no time to retrieve feathers, to kick dirt over blood splatters. At last, he looked up through the canopy to see Kirstl looking down at him sadly, the girl blue-lipped and floating in an unseen current.

She spoke to him, a constant chatter, but he could not read a single word, only that her mouth moved in between the flashes of forest. He realised they'd never spoken much in their stolen moments, had shared perhaps a few dozen words in total between them.

Just sweet, young love, wrapped and invincible from time and everything that pressed from outside their pairing. Lanyard's expectations, Kirstl's own urge to find favour with Tilly and get her own bike and gun, fantasies of shooting it out with every kind of monster. Snuffed out, the whole lot, all of that potential stolen with Kirstl's life. They were meant to be old, with kids to mourn and celebrate their last stand, guns blazing their final tale.

Fucking Lanyard, Mal thought, hating the man who'd brought them to this rotten place, binding them to vengeance and doom. *He doesn't love me, doesn't love any of us. We're guns. Resources to throw at threats. An army for a man who does not deserve one!*

He didn't truly believe the thought, but it held him, hate as good as love when it came to throwing himself and his bird into danger.

"Kurgle!" the bird honked, knowing the instructions of knees and rein. Keep pace, always underneath the shadow of Mal's girl.

Hours of this rough ride underneath the shades of the Twice-Dead, the Oerwoud buffeting and scratching boy and bird in dozens of places, and then finally they were out of that bizarre forest and rocketing across a shifting plain of cracked clay. The Twice-Dead were like a school of pale blue fish descending until they barely floated above the ground, and Mal darted amongst their miserable parade, cursing as Collybrock fought to keep his balance on that breathing clay plain.

This new place was dominated by a lofty tower. Thousands of flying beasts circling it, but Mal only had eyes for Kirstl, who reached for him, her arms extended fully, Mal's hands jolting on the reins as Collybrock surfed the wiggling clay tiles.

Frustrated by the closeness of his sweetheart's ghost, Mal fought the objections of the bird and brought them straight into the parade of the dead, gasping from the shock whenever he brushed against their transparent forms. Each touch brought a sudden flash of cold like he'd never known, not even as a starving slave left out in the desert night.

He fought through it, kicked the bird forward, and then he was finally with Kirstl, who spoke and smiled and cried and reached for him with hunger, greater than he'd ever seen in life. They shared a brief kiss, electricity, heat and cold, and then they were apart again, the terrain sending the bird stumbling.

"Get back in there!" Mal grunted at the bird. He tried to seize Kirstl by the hand, to pull her from this parade, but while he felt the shock of touching her Twice-Dead shell, his hands passed through with nothing to grab upon.

"Please!" he begged her ghost. "Please take my hand. I can save you!"

Kirstl shook her head, resigned to whatever this ending was, waving Mal away. The intent was clear. *Go, live for as long as you can. I'm done and you're free from me.*

Mal came in for a last kiss, even welcoming the jellyfish sting as they managed to connect, but then Collybrock stumbled on the shifting clay, feet juggling to keep bird and boy upright and moving. Mal bit his tongue and his lip hard, drawing blood.

Something changed in Kirstl. Her kiss became insistent, and she was latched to him, drawing in greedily, the lips of ghost and boy joined in nerve-firing agony. She drew in the blood, sucking greedily from his wound, and only when Mal looked up from this strangeness did he realise he'd pulled Kirstl out of the parade of the Twice-Dead, drawn her aside from that floating destruction.

She'd stopped.

Licking a droplet of blood from her lower lip, Kirstl drew herself down to sit on the saddle in front of Mal. He pulled his arm around her, drawing his palm up to her mouth to kiss.

Elated, Mal was caught by surprise when she bored into his palm, his hand, his forearm, ghost teeth gnashing, drawing out his blood in a dozen messy ways. He struggled against her, unable to escape her attentions, even when she severed his left pinkie finger, gobbling it down.

"Please," he begged, not sure if this plea was to Kirstl, or to Lanyard, wherever he was. "Help me."

On the far side of the Oerwoud, golden lances once more pierced the sepia heavens and punched into the ground of the Underfog, revealing a new host led by the Smothered Princes, but other symbols appeared by their side. The Joyous Hound. The Blackstar. More and more, all sworn for the Dawn King and ready to march in his name.

Rather than getting lost in the ever-forest that shielded the Underfog from prying eyes, they simply razed it, one painstaking step at a time, burning a swathe through the eternal Oerwoud that would never be repaired.

The Joyous Hound swept a lash of golden light back and forth like a scythe, and each tree it struck remained as a bright memory for a heartbeat, then falling into ash. The whip was a filament of pure Overhaeven energy, unreeling over an incredible distance, and the trees were tough, requiring much lashing. This road was costing the Dawn King's followers a fortune, and one they would spend ten times over.

"ON! WE SEIZE THE JAWBONE!" one Prince commanded, the host slowly advancing through that smouldering pass.

The other Prince held a case of the strongest Taursi glass, and within it floated two Overhaeven symbols, as sullen as a pair of neglected goldfish.

The first was a slouch hat stamped in tin, worn and beaten thin. It shared the crystal prison with a fluttering pair of hands, thumbs linked as if a perverse bird, ragged holes in the palms. In the smallest of writing, the palms bore the words BEFORE and NOW.

— 12 —

UNDERFOG

Stop right where you are," Lanyard called out, a sigil of volume glowing on his larynx. "Send your bossman forward, but no one else."

Between the surviving Jesusmen and the House of the Accurate Count, a whole parade of councillors stood, grinning and weighed down by sashes and metal bobs. Staves of office bristled in all directions, and more moths, some as big as bats, others the merest tickle of dirty paper wings, whispering into certain ears and took messages back to the House.

"We have no bossman," one of the spirits finally ventured. This one wore simpler dress: a shirt and tie with a waistcoat, and rumpled trousers. A visor, made of a green transparent material, and under this a very tired face, yellow and lined deeply, with a permanent haze of five o'clock shadow.

"Well, how does this place work without a boss? Do you just bloody agree on everything and get along?"

A low wave of laughter from the spirits, little better than the rustling of the moths.

"Yes. Exactly that. We have a perfect agreement, which enables the House of the Accurate Count to exist."

"So who the hell are you when you're not dealing blackjack?" Tilly demanded.

"Girl," Lanyard muttered, but let the barb land.

"I am the Teller," the spirit said.

"Ooh! Do tell."

The spirit raised one eyebrow to Tilly's humour, waited for one beat, and then pressed on as if she had not spoken. She barked with laughter at this attempted dignity.

"It is rare that we encounter the living. Twice we have hosted the Boneman, and twice we have repelled the attacks of his brother, Papa Lucy. We of course have agreements with the Gravedigger and Gretel of House Toran. There have been other necromancers, of course, but they came here before The Count, and we cannot and will not verify these."

Lanyard spat into the dirt.

"I don't give a shit."

A scandalous murmur rippled throughout the welcome committee. The Teller held up a hand, and eventually silence resumed.

"We've had moths describe your arrival and your battles. The army from Overhaeven. You may not care, but we certainly do. Whatever you seek down here, you most certainly need our services."

"Moths and idiots in fancy dress?" Tilly said. "Fuck off."

"Girl's right," Lanyard said. "Step aside or you'll be counting bullet holes."

The Teller rubbed at bleary eyes, bemused at the threat of violence. He seemed to have heard every insult and wasn't impressed by their bullet-chewing ways.

"We have information. Accurate recordings. Within our walls, we have the answers to everything worth knowing."

Nods. Dead smiles.

A moment, when Lanyard paused on the edge of the wrong question, the one that would chip one more shard out of Tilly's stone Leicesterite heart: *Where is my boy? Where is Mal?*

He stepped away from love and put his boots behind duty.

"What do you know about the Dawn King?"

Conversation buzzed in that council of spirits behind him, of disagreement even. The Teller raised his voice.

"We are by agreement—by agreement, I say!— neutral in all matters relating to the Dawn King!"

More arguments. Worse still, Lanyard noticed the hunger in some of those eyes, and his rat-cunning kicked into high gear.

"That sound like a perfect agreement to you?" Lanyard asked Tilly, in a tone of voice that told her everything she needed to know.

"Nope, boss. Just sounds like more bullshit."

Tilly darted forward, touching the sharp tip of her pike to the Teller's throat, and Lanyard waved the double-mouth of the shotgun in his direction.

The milquetoast handwringing intensified, especially as the Jesusmen advanced en masse, all bayonets and grim stares. The Teller shrugged philosophically, even as Lanyard waved his gun right in the Teller's face, letting him get a good look at the old carvings and marks, the hundreds of years of misery and murder soaked into the very stock.

"This gun killed Papa Lucy. Let me know if you want to meet him."

A moth the size of a thumbnail flew by the Teller's face, and then another.

"Do you really want information?"

Lanyard snarled, making to grab the Teller by his braces and jam the gun into his teeth, but the spirit slid to one side in his grip. Lanyard found himself holding onto a bunch of moth wings, shedding filmy paper scales from between his fingers.

"Are you quite done, god-killer?" the Teller said, fixing his collar. "Because you'll want to come inside."

He pointed, and Lanyard looked to see a whole ring of Chain-Folk now, stealing out of the Oerwoud, emerging from hidey holes in the clay, some even riding on captured moths. They came in the dozens, hungry souls bearing chains and whips.

Lanyard saw that same Once-Dead spirit of a man, a figure that seemed familiar, and this ghost rode upon the shoulders of a bear that was no fur and all skin, its mouth a lipless chasm of teeth and fury. The rider pointed at Lanyard, and then the whole force advanced at a run.

"What will it cost us?"

"Such a cynic."

"Everything costs down here."

"Come, god-killer. Better to spend some than to lose all of it."

None of the Chain-Folk would pass the unseen barrier surrounding the House of the Accurate Count. Their furious charge fell into a silent watch, even as the last Jesusman slipped inside and the big double-doors clicked shut.

Lanyard had caught one last glimpse of the spirit riding on the bear. A leader of some sort, staring at him and specifically him with hatred, seething, unending.

Pissed off a lot of folks. Killed a lot of them, too, he reasoned. *Guess I'll get to meet most of them a second time.*

"Here," the Teller said. "Pay your way."

A bank of great spigots stood just inside the double-doors, intended for spirits to spit their palms against, with channels to catch a tribute of the blue spirit fluid. Pipes ran into the walls to send this bounty onward to a reservoir or some other purpose.

"Aether is needed. When the living visit, we expect a donation of blood instead."

"Boss," Tilly warned, and Lanyard set his teeth. They'd bought their safety, and it was time to pay.

Lanyard was the first to lance his own hand on the spike, and the House drank deeply from him for a full heartbeat before the point withdrew from his flesh. The Teller watched as every single man, woman, and child bled themselves to enter. He did not seem to want or care about their beasts, and so the camel and the remaining birds were not bled.

The parade of eager sycophants was nowhere to be seen now, vanishing the moment they re-entered the House, all slippered feet and the rustle of moth wings. In every direction stretched miles of corridor, but there was little order or sense to the interior of the house.

Grand stairs ended in mid-air or met blank walls. Ramps led upwards and downwards in a curlicue of creaking wooden floorboards and musty rugs, with rows of doors that flexed and fluttered like the plain outside, creaking and rubbing against their frames.

Whenever Lanyard shifted his good eye to watch for threats, small details changed when he looked back. The building was far from fixed, following the same rules as the outside.

Willpower. Thought becomes reality.

How many minds were concentrating on the shape of this House right now? One to focus on that wall, or the curve of a lintel, or the flagstones in the floor?

If a mind wavered too far, would the roof cave in?

"We've many a mile to wander before you get your answers, god-killer," the Teller said. "I would insist upon your civility."

"I've got more miles in these legs than you have miles in your House," Lanyard said. "Delay me at your peril."

"Peril," the Teller mused. "Yes. There is certainly peril in here. Come, our records are this way."

Whatever commotion they'd caused by their arrival had ended, and any who crossed the Teller's path swiftly found business elsewhere. The Teller took them along a main throughfare, a place that couldn't decide if it was a grand hallway or a cavern. The doorways they passed led into staterooms and halls as often as they were gaping holes that led into cubbies or monastic cells.

Every door they passed was a babble of chanting, facts recited, or a number slowly advancing. Sometimes, a runner would bustle out of one doorway, muttering "fifty-seven, fifty-seven," under their breath, running pell-mell for the next chamber.

"My greatest work," the Teller gestured at the system of rooms and runners. "The Accurate Count. We may not be able to mark a word or a date in any lasting way, but what of it?"

"What are you counting?" Tilly asked.

"All things," the Teller said, not bothering to look her way. "I can tell you to the second when I started the Count. When Gretel came to her arrangement with us and with the Gravedigger. How many spirits Papa Lucy destroyed on both of his journeys to Shale, including the journey he did not return from."

"You're an abacus," Tilly said dryly. "Hardly impressive."

"Yet here we are, receiving tribute from across the Underfog," the Teller said. "We have all of the data. We are information, in a place where records fail."

A long moment of their footfalls, answered by the whispering and the chanting coming from each cell. Lanyard had seen the operators of the telegraph back in the Now, hunched over their little switch, noting everything down and passing it on, and he guessed at the nature of this system. No wire here, and no notepad, just mouths and ears, runners to funnel the information to this corridor, some perhaps clutching to the big moths to speak a message to someone distant.

"Played a game called Telephone when I was a kid," Lanyard said, watching another runner drastically rush past, reciting a memory under their breath. "Whispered a message from ear to ear, and it was never the same when it got to the end."

"There is a risk," the Teller conceded. "Still, best system we've got. If we're not true, we're true enough."

Lanyard thought of Tilly's neatly erased notebooks and fell back into silence. The Jesusmen were mice creeping through this house of dead things, intruding with their footsteps, the mutterings of the prentices, the wracking coughs that Yulio no longer tried to hide.

Then, a faint tremor in the walls accompanied by a distant booming sound, and dust fell from somewhere above. The Teller stopped, head held high. A dog on the scent.

"The House holds," he said after a moment. "Come."

"The Chain-Folk outside, how long will they besiege this place?" Tilly asked.

"Forget them. You are safe here."

"That's not what I asked."

"Pay the blood price and none may harm you."

"We already paid that!"

Tilly punctuated this with an ugly stare and a hand on the spirit's arm. The Teller twisted away casually, leaving her with nothing but a handful of crushed moths.

"That was for entry. If you would lodge here, your brigade will give over yet another dribble in the morning."

"Girl," Lanyard warned Tilly, who was somewhere between fury and horse-trading mode. Closing her mouth, she frowned.

All around them, the House flexed and pulsed slowly, and they left the counting cells to see another attempt at recording. Spirits sat cross-legged here, each focusing on a bare stretch of wall. These observers brought forward sculptures, little tableaus of people at normal life, grand dioramas of heroes and gods, and always they fought to fix the images in place, lost within moments as the Underfog erased the record.

Muttering figures lurked behind each shoulder, describing everything they saw back to the artist, who would nod or correct them.

Runners would take the consensus of each image and run to some other place.

"Stand here a moment," the Teller said, as another spirit approached the living visitors, a wild-eyed figure with a beard reaching below the belt of his filthy robe, and he stared at them intently. Several hands snatched for gun grips, but Lanyard held up a hand.

"He's trying to take a photograph."

Nervous laughter, and sure enough the spirit found his own stretch of wall and brought forth a passable image of Lanyard and his doomed troop, wary intruders in death.

"We look tired," Tilly said to Lanyard, as the image shook and resolved to a bare clay wall.

The moths lived in a type of rookery, a fluted honeycomb that spiralled up the towers to let in both moths and sepia light. The walls were papered thick with the spread of wings and twitching antennae, the leafy patterns blending into one mass of false life.

Spirits rushed past with memories on their lips and brushed a likely looking moth until it detached from the wall. For a brief moment a nozzle was visible in that gap on the wall, still dripping the bright blue of Aether. Then the moth took up a passenger and drove off in a flapping blur, even as a new moth entered the House and took up the nozzle in its mouth, proboscis uncoiling to lap at it greedily.

This stairway leading up to the Teller's loft was narrow, and the birds and camel wouldn't fit. The bike-riders were performing a quick mechanical fix under Tilly's eye, and the last of the fuel cans were emptied to top them up.

Tilly knew the score. They might need to shoot their way out of the House yet, or go out in a blaze of sour grapes and defiance.

Both options were always fine.

"Boss, I can't," Yulio wheezed at Lanyard's side, and they paused often during the ascent.

"Stop it," Lanyard snarled. "It's just a bloody staircase."

Yulio nodded, thick ropes of foam and blood on his moustache now. When he staggered, Lanyard helped him upright, and took a moment to whisper in his ear, in this the house of whispering.

"Shoot straight, you bastard."

Another coughing fit, and Lanyard was unsure if the words sank in. He felt the tickle of a moth at the nape of his neck, and a small cloud of the lesser moths flew past the Teller, curving upwards into the top of the House.

"We are close," the Teller said. "I have many duties, so please do not tarry."

Lanyard grimaced and hoisted Yulio upwards by the elbow, himself starting to struggle with the climb. He could feel the Boneman's fifteen-year-old repair-work strain and pinch in his guts, and his old body was really taking some punishment.

Almost out of liver-root, he thought. *I'll barely be walking tomorrow.*

This thought came with anguish. Revenge burnt hot, but it was only as strong as the wood that it consumed. To know that his own body might betray him before he could take down the Dawn King did not sit well with Lanyard Everett.

Another distant crash. The space around them seemed to dilate slightly. A small moth came and whispered in the Teller's ear, who waved it away with annoyance.

"Come," he said, and led them through the door at the top of the stairs. It was a room, equal parts casino cash-cage, classroom, and office.

All around, wide windows let in light and yet more moths, many of whom perched on an outer railing, antennae twitching at the unseen light source above.

"Well," the Teller said, locking himself into the old cash cage. He spread his hands in a gesture that was equal parts *let's trade* and *I can't really help you.*

"Give us everything you know about the Dawn King," Lanyard said. "Then, safe passage to wherever he is. In return, I will give you a living man."

"He's hardly living," the Teller said, looking over Yulio, who was using his gun as a crutch, lips a worrying shade of purple.

"He's agreed to this. Use his flesh for your own. Walk the world again. Just do as I say."

"I think I will take everything. In return, I offer you...nothing."

Instantly Lanyard and Yulio had guns up and raining thunder, but the cage turned aside their fury.

Down the stairs, a crash as the main doors were thrown open. More gunfire, the shouts of Tilly and the others fighting to be heard over the cackling rabble now bounding through the halls.

"You bastard," Lanyard said. "You've let the bloody Chain-Folk in."

"We have common cause," the Teller shouted. "It will be hard to expel them from the House, but they should leave once they have most of your people."

Lanyard stalked the cage, looking for a weakness. He jammed a small pistol through the cash slot, blasting away. The Teller twisted aside, but not fast enough, and he was struck by at least one bullet. The man became a cloud of moths, a gyre twisting about in the booth, and then once more he was a man shape, this time slamming the cash slot shut. "BOOTH CLOSED," the sign read, with a cheerful picture of a card croupier alongside the text.

"You have something that doesn't belong to you," the Teller said.

"Open up the door and die like a bloody man," Lanyard muttered, stalking about the cage.

"Never mind, I found it."

A storm cloud of moths filled the stairwell, some of the insects as large as dogs, battering the two men. The cash-cage opened, and the Teller stepped outside, grinning as a moth placed something in his hand.

The jawbone, and it lay peacefully in his grip.

Lanyard let off one wild round of shot before the moths simply pinned him to the floor, a rustling blanket that stank of dust, pressing down on him like a thousand years.

"I will take him."

"You can have him," the Teller said. "Have all of them if you wish."

"Let me see it," the first gruff voice said.

"Do you think it's real?"

"Of course it is. We even have some golden visitors who come looking for this toothy piece of gristle."

Lanyard struggled to rise, but the furry grips of a thousand legs tightened around him, and the wings pressed in tightly.

"Give me that. I will take it to him," the gruff voice said.

"Unacceptable," the Teller said. "I shall bring the jawbone to the Dawn King. Keep all the prisoners, take the House itself if you want. But this, this is mine now."

The brief sound of a struggle.

"Do you really think you can put a chain on me? You can't even touch me. Accept that this is the best deal you can get."

"Fine," said gruff voice, in a tone that said anything but this.

"The Dawn King is below and above," the Teller said.

"Left and right," Gruff Voice intoned.

"His house is glorious, and we have sworn to him."

"Sworn to him."

"Take your trespasser. I have many miles to cross, and many enemies."

Then the moths were gone, and Lanyard was up and swinging the butt of his empty shotgun, but not quick enough. An enormous fist crashed into his head, sending him back to the floor. A bright blue whip followed, and he gasped as pain fired along every nerve in his battered old body.

Above him, the bear-rider, the Chain-Lord who spoke law for the slavers, looked down on him with lipless fury. Then Lanyard recognised the set of the eyes, the jut of the jaw.

This spirit was still as big as he'd been in life, back when they'd shared the gallows together in Mawson, the old criminal and the nameless boy who would become Lanyard, the last of the Jesusmen.

He'd run, scared, left this man to twist and choke to death on a rope.

"Hi, boss," Lanyard said, and the whip fell down again.

— 13 —

UNDERFOG

A miserable huddle of humanity was driven out of that place of whispers and moths, disarmed, wrists bound behind them in blue ropes of Aether.

The Chain-Folk capered in delight and made no secret to their new slaves that they were great prizes to be auctioned off across the Underfog. Blood, actual flesh, the means for the strong to re-enter the lands of life.

Lanyard stumbled along with his neck in a bright-blue noose, the slipknot held with just the right amount of pressure over his Adam's apple. He stumbled on the shifting clay shards, the noose cinching tighter for a moment.

"Careful, boy," the Chain-Lord said. "It's awful to choke out slow."

"You would know, boss," Lanyard said, and the big spirit yanked tightly on the noose, dragging him across the clay. He rode atop what was left of the Jesusmen's camel, which the hairless bear-thing wore as a suit now, stuffing itself in through the wounds, pulling on the limbs like the sleeves of an ill-fitted suit.

The butchering was quick and greedy, given the moment that the Chain-Lord claimed the beast as his own. Even as the knives of the Chain-Folk drew out the lifeblood of the camel, this blood was caught and stowed in pans and mouths. The spirit of the animal stepped aside, looking in horror at its own death a moment before the Chain-Folk butchered it for the second time. This time they took it apart for the Aether, giving it to spirits wounded in battle, using it to craft new whips, new spears. More chains.

The pressure around Lanyard's neck eased. The Chain-Lord had stopped dragging Lanyard across the clay, unwilling to offer such a quick mercy as death. The slaver let out the slipknot with a practiced wrist-flick, and Lanyard bucked around like a landed fish, gratefully gulping in air.

"I'll hear better words from you, boy," he told Lanyard. "Begging. Deal-making. Fear, oh yes, I'll draw words of fear out of you."

"Hey, boss. Got a question."

The noose tightened slightly.

"Can you teach me that dance you did? Jigging and kicking, down there in the dark?"

With a roar the Chain-Lord drew Lanyard off the ground, hauling him up by the hang-rope until he was bug-eyed and screaming in the Jesusman's face.

"You ran! Left me to die in your place!"

The rest of the Chain-Folk drew up in a loose huddle around their boss, muttering quietly, wagering sips of Aether over a type of rocks-paper-scissors game. Tilly looked on in muted horror, but even as Lanyard choked out, he threw her a wink.

The Chain-Lord jumped down from his camel and dashed Lanyard against the clay, drawing tightly on the noose, dreaming forth a thick blue whip for his free hand. The Chain-Lord slammed it into Lanyard again and again, beating him into blackness.

Sometimes you can win a fight by losing it. Lanyard remembered a distant conversation with Bauer around a campfire, an instruction that finally made sense as the oxygen stopped and all the lights went out.

He woke to a trickle of water in his mouth. Tilly, hard-eyed and wary, with a limp waterskin in hand.

"Be still," she said. "They think you asleep or dead."

"Did they take the bikes?"

Tilly nodded.

"What about the birds?"

Tilly pointed to the edge of the Chain-Folk camp. While some of the birds were chained to a ragged line of Aether, there were two who'd been claimed, and moved about awkwardly with the gait of someone learning how to walk.

"We tried magic," Tilly said. "Young Will spoke a word or two but could not fix anything into place with his hands bound. Now they butcher any who reach for a spell."

Sure enough, the balding old man they'd dubbed Young Will walked around with the Chain-Folk, now wielding a whip, his slashed throat still showing the bright blue of Aether stitchwork.

"He's gone?"

"Yep. Some other puppet walks around in his skin."

"What about you?" Lanyard said, looking to her freed hands.

"I'm the trusty," Tilly said with disgust. "I feed the birds. Keep the peace. Pass messages."

"I have a message."

"To whom?"

"To you, girl. Turn around. Open your bloody eyes."

The House of the Accurate Count was perhaps less than a mile away across the breathing plain, even accounting for Lanyard's terrible eyesight.

"The Chain-Folk are moving in a circle, like a maze," Tilly explained. "One step wrong, and a beast emerges, devours them whole. Your friend there is furious, says that the Teller tricked them."

Sure enough, the big spirit was raving to his followers, who were probing the clay, looking for safe passage.

"And so the Chain-Folk play their own game with the Teller. They've stopped all the moths."

A line of blue poles stretched out behind them, circling the House, knitted together until it resembled a rough facsimile of a spider's web. Spikes crafted from pure Aether, driven into the clay and stretching upwards into a mad tangle.

This gang of slavers had stolen an obscene amount of the spirit-stuff and were burning through it to prove a point. Every now and then the web gave off a brilliant flash, and Lanyard supposed this meant some moth had been drawn into a fascinated Twice-Death.

"What else have you learnt?"

"There are bright lights in the Oerwoud. Same spot, slowly drawing closer. Overhaeven comes."

"Okay, girl. Now, think. What do we have here? What can we do with it?"

He sat up, the hang-rope pulling tight. The Chain-Lord had pegged him to the ground with an Aether spike.

"Do? We're bloody stuffed, boss. We're slaves or dead or worse now."

"Girl, I raised you better than that. Look again."

Tilly looked around, tried to put the pieces together, and gave up after a moment. Lanyard smiled, even as the Chain-Lord came at a swift walk, drawing out a whip now that his favourite victim was awake. Lanyard leaned tighter into the rope, the slipknot slowly closing.

"What are you doing?" Tilly whispered.

"You forgot about Yulio," he said, and then the rope went slack, parted by a bullet, the gunshot echoing across the plain a moment later.

Yulio was close to dead and felt confused. Every play he'd ever been to and every story he'd read spoke of dying as some beautiful, dramatic, and drawn-out moment.

He was mostly tired. A little bit cold. Sometime soon he would simply wake up next to his broken body and continue being *here*, in the bloody Underfog.

Yulio was drowning on dry land, lung-muck rattling with every attempt to draw in oxygen. Half-starved, a rib or two broken somewhere between here and the lands of life. Now, at the end, he'd seen the boss finally fail. The jawbone stolen from him, and revenge revealed for what it was: a folly that drew more failures than a wedding cake made of horseshit drew flies.

Now, he was being smothered by enormous moths, and it made next to no difference because he couldn't breathe anyway. In a lifetime of habit, he'd slept with a rifle in his hands, and he found himself reaching for the curve of the gunstock as the sleep of death came in, pushing through the forest of moth legs, wings, and the slobbering proboscis that tasted his skin, intrigued by all the sweat and muck.

His fingers finally closed around the rifle, and he knew that this was the moment he could let himself go. Dead with a gun in his hands was not a bad way to go out.

When he could no longer feel that blanket of creatures pressing down on him, he supposed he'd passed out of his broken body, but then he coughed again, a big ball of dark blood, and he sat up with everything hurting.

The moths were all gone.

Still using the rifle as a crutch, Yulio got to his feet. Considering the empty stairwell, he realised that even walking downstairs was too far for him. He'd been a hunter before Lanyard found him, and ears that could hear a crack of a twig a mile off couldn't hear a damn thing. None of the whispering bean-counters, their footfalls, or even the grumbling of his own folks, the fussing of the birds.

He was the only one left in here.

Slowly, he hobbled towards the windows, open to let in as much light as could be drawn from the pale sky. A door led him out onto a balcony, and then a smile tickled across his face, finally leading to a painful laugh.

He saw the Chain-Folk trapped in a ridiculous maze. The moths trapped in a cage of flashing blue. And all of them stalked by the golden blaze burning through the forest.

Even as Yulio's heart squeezed painfully, he fetched out a handful of bullets from his pocket and fed one into the rifle. Leaning over the railing, he looked through the scope and picked his first target.

Lanyard Everett, stretching out a hang-rope for him to part, looking directly up at him with a hopeful grin.

BANG. He parted the rope as though he stood next to it with a blade. Yulio ejected the shell, but when he tried to load another, his fingers fumbled bullets all over the balcony, and they rained over the side.

Last shot, he thought, finally sliding in a bullet. He looked up, and saw it, a moth of perfect emerald, the same green as the Teller's visor, and it fluttered about in a maze of blue lines, struggling to escape with the jawbone.

BANG.

Yulio fell, the moth and the jawbone fell, and the House of the Accurate Count fell with them.

Peering through dust-grey ferns, Jenny Rider watched the building collapse from the edge of the Oerwoud, while Bilben perched on her shoulder, cleaning her whiskers. Jenny had had her own frustrating dealings with the Teller and his moths, but she felt a little sad at the destruction.

"Such a loss," Bilben said. "We have no memories now. Only stories, retold until worn through."

"Lies. Misdirection."

"Oh, the Teller shared enough of those. But all in the public interest, mind!"

"He lied to me. About what happened at Shale."

"At least ten observable lies were sent out that day. Yours was by far the kindest one."

"Ten lies about Papa Lucy? *Ten?*"

Jenny clenched her jaw, fingers joining, flexing, curling into the Cruik-shape. Bilben paused in her fussing to lay a paw on Jenny's cheek.

"Politics. You have the anger of any petitioner and constituent that ever was, as is your right."

"That–that liar. That bastard, and all his moths, and–"

"Be angry at that ruin there; it was civilisation, order! Tell me of any king, any government, oh even the rudest of village councils that does not push a lie when it serves them!"

Jenny tried to think of her own father, the Selector of Mawson, the man who dispensed law and justice from his Tower. Even as good and noble as he was, she'd seen him play at politics. He had lied for the greater good, had lied to protect himself and those he cared about, had even begun teaching her the art of lying well and fairly.

I have not seen him down here yet, she thought again. She'd prayed fervently for his survival back when she lived, and prayed doubly hard, knowing what awaited her father. Every criminal he'd ever sent to dangle and choke was down here, waiting for him, in this paradise of vengeance and endless patience.

The wooden girl and the rat watched the living prisoners rebel against the Chain-Folk, and heard the distant crackle of whips and gunshots.

"Ho, that one steps incorrectly!" Bilben crowed, as an enormous beast broke up through the clay, a beast that was all mouths and reaching tentacles, dragging a handful of spirits down into the earth to devour.

"We sniffed out the Teller's secret friend a long time ago," Bilben said. "Those clay shards are but the shed scales of that sleeping beast, a layer many miles deep. Ouroboros, it calls itself. The beast allowed the Teller to plant the House above it."

"In exchange for some of the Aether?"

"But of course."

Jenny stiffened in place then, and sent up a questing hook above the tops of the trees, a staff that Bilben quickly scrambled up. Even here, Jenny could see the flickering golden light, hear the blaze of destruction visited upon the Oerwoud. The rodent ran down, chattering with excitement.

"They come! They have almost blazed their pathway through it!"

Woman and rodent stepped out onto the clay maze, and Bilben spoke out the true path, knowledge squirrelled away by her people since a time before the House, before the first spirits of humanity walked the Underfog.

Then they saw the moth that was the Teller fall, and the jawbone fall with it.

"An unexpected advantage! Snatch up the jawbone, Jenny. Move fast!"

"Remember our deal, little one," Jenny said.

"But of course," Bilben said. "Do not show our hand just yet, Selector's Daughter. He does not trust either of us. But look at what his people are capable of."

The House of the Accurate Count was already gone, sinking through the shed clay scales of the hidden beast, a grand enterprise drawn down into complete and utter oblivion.

Jenny went one way, and Bilben another.

Mal took his own journey away from that plain that was neither clay nor a true plain. While the Twice-Dead spirits of The Serene and its victims continued on towards Shale, he reined Collybrock to a hard right.

They were cutting across another field of the white ghost-wheat that grew and died in an endless cycle. In the distance was a settlement, something like the memory of a village, a pulsing of barns and windmills, and dwellings that were more fungus than design.

With a squawk, Collybrock dodged around an oddly twisted ploughshare that had been dumped in the wheat field. It looked as if built from a second-hand description and given up as a bad idea. Mal wanted to ride toward that place and ask for help.

Kirstl disagreed.

The hand that held the bird's reins was Mal's, missing the smallest finger, but the flimsy spirit stuff of Kirstl reached through his skin, her hand joined to his, down to the muscles, the nerves, even the bones. Already they were married in a way the sweethearts couldn't have hoped to achieve in life.

Her feet tapered out to a tail, which was still drawn towards Shale and the destruction she was meant to face. Kirstl held tightly to Mal, and with each mile this pull grew less. From time to time she twisted around in his lap, nipping at his neck and his bare arms, drawing razor thin kisses that wept blood. Her lips were bright red now, and a faint flush was washing away from her mouth, as far as the high cheekbones he'd once brushed sweet kisses against.

"Please," Mal said. "This isn't right. Let me go."

"I need you," Kirstl said huskily. "You saved me."

Mal was a mess of bites, with entire chunks of flesh missing from his bicep, an ear severed close to his face, and three fingers missing. Even Collybrock had suffered injuries from Kirstl's greedy mouth, her feathery neck running with deep cuts, but birds would tolerate a whip to a point and she paid these nicks little mind.

They were cutting across another field of the white ghost-wheat that slowly grew and died in an endless cycle. In the distance was a settlement, something like the memory of a village.

"You are my hero," Kirstl said, looking on Mal with a confusing mixture of hunger and admiration. "We found a way past it."

"But you're hurting me."

"Hurt? You think you know hurt?" Kirstl said, eyes wide, her sclera flush with Mal's blood. "Everything is fire. The only thing that will douse it is the waters of that damn beach."

"Kirstl, I promise I will take you somewhere safe. Then, you must go—and let me go."

Kirstl dug in deep then, her spectral hands jangling all of his nerves. She pulled on that hidden tree, and he screamed at the sudden flood of pain throughout his universe.

"I should do you a favour and snip you out of that useless body," she cried. "You are never going back. None of you are!"

"I know," Mal said. "But Lanyard needs me."

She scoffed at the name. If Lanyard had been there, he'd probably have agreed with this assessment.

"Kirstl, I just need more time."

"We have all of time," she said, and then she struck like a snake, tearing into his neck and suckling.

He fought her. If Lanyard had given him his gun by now, he might have been able to destroy her. All he had was his pike, and deadly as it was, it was next to useless at such close quarters.

He whistled and clicked his tongue, and Collybrock responded to the command, striking backwards with her razor-sharp beak. Not once did the bird connect with his ghostly opponent, beak clacking and snapping at ghostly air.

It was a hopeless fight, and Mal fought to the end, just like Lanyard had taught him. He gripped his pike just behind the spear-point, and pushed it closer to his sweetheart's face, prepared to drive that holy steel through her temple.

When she realised the danger, Kirstl lashed out, reaching into his arm with ghostly fingers, plucking and pinching at nerves until his fingers fell open. The pike fell to the ground, and by some small miracle it landed point first, a steel signpost.

Small spatters of blood followed the terrified passage of Collybrock. The earth was greedy in the Underfog, and it also forgot fast, and soon the blood and bird prints were wiped away.

NOW

I n a land where a stranger caught in a lonely place was a potential meal, the Tinkermen were a protected species. They fixed broken cars, kept the ramshackle telegraph network together with spit and wire, and in those rare places that had electricity, they literally kept the lights on.

Most importantly, if a mad-eyed cannibal gave a Tinkerman a broken gun, they would fix it, no questions asked. And the cannibal would say "thank you," put away his weapon politely while paying the exact amount asked, and then leave in peace.

Few Tinkermen settled for the safety of townlaw, and they plied their trade all across the Now, usually one step behind the treasure hunters chasing Bleedthroughs. Often as not the mysterious leavings of that dead world were broken, or hadn't bled through true, and the first Tinkerman to come along could fix these things, or even trade for them outright.

The Tinkermen were a loose society at best, and frequently in competition with each other. Still, they would meet, trade knowledge and parts, take on prentices, and had a guild of sorts.

The records of that guild were meticulous, lodged in the libraries of Crosspoint and Mawson, but neither mentioned the Junkman. Hands who'd written of him were broken with hammers long ago, and certain early Tinkermen were buried in both the vastness of the Now and underneath the towns.

This was Sol's reluctant work, many years before he was the Boneman, and he was simply Lord Goodface, adjusting the settings on a newly minted civilisation. John Leicester had lost focus and needed a distraction removed.

For reasons of his own, Papa Lucy burnt some of the other Tinkermen into grease and dust, and no one ever raised an objection.

Ray Leicester was lost somewhere out in that vastness, and for a time was a legend, and then some time after that he was simply forgotten.

There were plenty of ways for someone to hide in the Now. The Junkman's earliest memories were of fear and confusion. Of the Brother, a constant bringer of bedside misery. Then, other kind faces, but always they wanted him to work, gave him instructions and tasks. No matter how much he worked and did as he was told, Brother would return, watching him from the doorway, and the very sight of the solemn-faced figure drove him into panic and then finally anger.

He'd been hidden, he understood that much. The man with a good face told him to go away, and to be very wary of his brother.

"Hide from Brother?"

"Yours and mine. Hide from all brothers."

The Junkman became secretive, and he was anonymous enough out in the Inland, out on the fringes of civilisation. Other Tinkermen worked the remote places, and some spoke even less than the Junkman did.

There were others who'd had the Methuselah treatment, and who had survived the Crossing with minds intact. They were great talespinners, repositories of knowledge and the workings of the old world, the Before. Typically folks such as these hid behind thick town walls and drank themselves stupid as often as possible.

When the Junkman took the Crossing with the rest of the survivors, the journey stripped his mind of anything but the faintest of troubling dreams, and so he did not have useful stories or advice, nothing but a quiet wariness at campfires, even as his clever hands worked whatever needed fixing.

Still, he had a great instinct for trouble, having survived bullies and worse, false friends who'd exploited his condition in the old world. If someone ever watched him too intently, or pressed him too closely, he simply vanished into the dust.

And so, the years and the decades passed, and finally a century or two crept past, marked only by the constant chill in the Junkman's marrow. He could no longer remember why he was always so cold, even in the punishing heat of the Inland.

Always, he thought of the instructions of the man with the good face, and he took measures to hide from Brother. With endless patience he carved out a series of secret caches across the dusty Inland. The digging machine was his own invention, and it used an old car engine to drive ploughshare blades directly into the soft sandstone.

Soon, he'd made over a dozen large underground complexes, with living quarters, huge cisterns, and sprawling workshops filled with half-completed projects. A dozen fortunes scraped together over a dozen lives, but the Junkman lived simply, even surrounded by an eye-watering amount of loot.

Sometimes, the Junkman could spend a decade or more on a single project, pausing only for meals and sleep, and never seeing a human face in all that time. Other times he went into a frenzy of travel and human contact, pushing through his discomfort to barter and gather equipment and goods throughout the towns and rougher markets, mingling with both townsfolk and cannibals to restock his hideouts.

Early on in his fugitive days, the Junkman made a stupid mistake, one that brought him close to discovery. He was picking through a box of assorted fanbelts when he heard the familiar strains of music floating across the market square.

The joyful harmonies, the backbeat, all of it instantly recognisable, and it was memory in a mind that held little but murk from the dead world. He remembered dancing to this music with a woman in a humble kitchen. Learning to use tools at an older man's elbow, the same sweet tunes playing through a tinny speaker.

Later, a less innocent memory. Listening to this music on a couch with a bad man, just as destruction came crashing in. Goodface was there, but Brother was there, too, and another Brother. There was great anger over this music, and it was all his fault, and then he—

"I did this. I did all of this," he said to the mystified seller, and then gently replaced the fanbelts, crossing the market to a record-seller, a wind-up gramophone playing the music at full volume to entice buyers.

The album cover was propped up against the side of the player, and he recognised the cover art immediately. Five men were sinking into a golden sea of light. Each was ramrod straight, bobbing around like buoys, but the light was dragging them in regardless.

"Chess in a Golden Sea," the Junkman read.

They were silhouettes, but he knew the outlines intimately.

"John. Paul. George. Pete. Billy," he mumbled, on his knees now, watching the record spin. The record-seller was rubbing her hands together happily. Many were waiting nearby and listening, but unable to afford this rarity.

"Near perfect condition," she said. "Only a couple of scratches on this one."

"I listened to this music," the Junkman said. "I listened to this music, and then I ended the world."

Seized with rage, he snatched the record from the player and snapped it in his hands, and then snapped those pieces, and when the bailiffs arrived, he'd slashed his hands up from the jags of vinyl, raving about destroying the world.

It took almost everything he'd gained from this trip to pay off the furious record-seller. He left with his head hung low, reeling from shameful memories, and he made himself scarce.

He'd made a scene. He'd been visible.

Bare minutes after he left town, a sliver opened in the universe, the tear rotating out to form a doorway. Two men stepped out, and were the Junkman still in the market to see them, he'd have been more terrified than the people in the market, who knelt in fear and worship, faces pressed into the dirt.

Both of the Brothers, and they were looking for him.

The Junkman was spared from the madness of Sad Plain and did not see his Brother fall into a statue and never come out. If Lord Goodface hadn't been clever enough to hide the Junkman, Papa Lucy would have quite easily used him to open his gateway to Overhaeven, burning the Now to the ground to fuel his godly ambitions.

Years after that old disaster and not so long before the Boneman emerged from his cairn, the Junkman went for a drive. It was a beautiful car, a warlord's machine that came with spikes and other menacing decorations, and the engine was a snarling thing of chrome and thumping pistons. It was simply too expensive for the warlord to run, and so the Junkman traded a small fortune for it.

He'd taken away the worst of the additions, grinding and smoothing everything back to as close to original as he could get. He'd added a few modifications of his own, and the car ran lean and fast now, on tyres better suited for sand. The Junkman had hidden all sorts of clever little tricks in his car; after all, a car itself was a prize, and the driver mere protein for the taking.

Up and downhill he went, leaning out of the window and looking through a set of binoculars. Dusk was the easiest time to spot them, and so he drove around through lengthening shadows, big aimless circles in the dust and sand.

Ray Leicester had failed his driving test, terrified of the policeman with his clipboard. He'd never so much as driven a car outside of a workshop. The Junkman had overcome this old fear over the past couple of centuries and found peace out in the empty places, engine roaring, wheels churning up dust and stones.

As with everything mechanical he put his mind to, he got good at it, and now that driving was removed from the world of people, licences, and road rules, he found beauty and joy in the act.

Right on dusk, the Junkman saw a gleaming light on the horizon, right near the top of a set of dunes, and he wove through the deceptive sands, trying not to get stuck.

As night fell, the glass spire glowed warmly, a peach colour that radiated light for a fair distance. The Junkman tried not to think about how much the spires resembled the Taursi, the spiky-coated creatures displaced and all but destroyed since the settlers had arrived.

The Junkman wrapped a heavy chain around the spire, attached the chain to the towbar of his new car, and applied foot to pedal until the whole spire came out of the ground like a rotten tooth.

He dragged it behind him through the dunes, the one working headlight on the car only illuminating the area just ahead of him. The

Junkman had fixed more than one axle broken by some idiot driving in the dark, and suspected that if he wrecked the car now, he'd have more trouble than a long walk home.

There. A wink of light to the left, as a sliver of the world veil tore open. Another, and another, and soon spears were raining down on his car as he slalomed along the crest of the firmest looking dune.

Taursi, drawn by the desecration of the spire.

Bang. Bang. Sharp points punching into steel, and somewhere behind him the breaking of glass, maybe one of the quarter-panels. For a moment he had a random memory of being a schoolboy, running in terror from other children who were pelting him with stones.

"Where are you going, Ray!"

"Get him!"

His one headlight fell across one of the creatures, its spines huffed up and glowing red. It was cooking glass inside itself, ready to turn it into a deadly weapon. Frowning, the Junkman jammed down on the accelerator, trying to find some way to dodge the figure. The dune fell away sharply to either side, and he'd either roll the car or bury it face first into the sands.

It was forward or nothing.

The alien creature riddled the front of the car with sharp battle-glass. The windscreen starred below Ray's eyeline, fully three inches of freshly brewed hurt had punched through the glass before it stopped, lined up with his throat.

"I'm sorry," the Junkman told the Taursi, who was now frozen in place, terrified as the headlight loomed large. The horn on the car still worked, and the Junkman beeped, a long warning note, but still the Taursi did not budge.

Closing his eyes and wincing, the Junkman ran the native down, and it crunched underneath, the whole car shuddering and bouncing as if it was eating the poor creature.

"Sorry!" he sobbed.

More Taursi came through the world veil, but the Junkman's new friend was right. They would come to the site of the spire, but their workaround sorcery wouldn't allow them to keep up with a fast Before-time machine. They could only use the Greygulf and the shadow-roads in terms of fixed locations, and all the Junkman needed to do now was run.

He could have made a weapon of some sort, but the gentle tool-loving man came up with his own answer to pursuit. Flicking a switch on the dashboard set up the racks of homemade smoke-bombs mounted on his roof, and a large spring-loaded device launched a stack of burning tyres from his trunk, bouncing across the dunes and billowing smoke.

He left the dangerous warriors in his wake, his prize bouncing and dragging behind him.

He hid the car and the stolen spire in the nearest of his refuges and did his best to hide from the legendary Taursi trackers. A sled-mounted fan wiped out the last three or so miles of car tracks. A wall of canvas covered the entry to the complex, stiffened with starch and painted to resemble the rockface of his hideout. Behind that, a twin set of portcullises, with cannisters of homemade tear gas.

The Junkman did not want to hurt anyone, but there were blank spaces in his mind, the memories of people who'd hurt him. The pain was there, and the fear, but he could not remember their origin.

Perhaps it was Brother.

The jagged edges of this pain drove him towards caution, to safety and even paranoia. Often, his new friend encouraged this mind-set.

"Gotta stay hidden," the Junkman said. "Keep everything safe."

It was heavy, but he dragged the spire into his workshop, and it glowed like a miniature sun, still shedding the light it drank in during the day.

He hooked it up to the other five Taursi spires he'd taken. He'd made them into a crude serial battery linked by copper wire, with pegs drilled deep into the glass. For a full five minutes all six of the spires lit up, and the light was blinding, overwhelming.

"Yes!"

But soon the light became dull, and all six of the spires glowed with a peach ember, and then nothing. One spire on its own would light up the plains until dawn, but tampering with it bled away the captured sunlight in mere minutes.

"It should work," the Junkman muttered. He had a similar serial battery on the bench, a chain of old car batteries. It would keep a charge for hours, even more with a running motor and an alternator. But whenever he attached a motor or any other machine to the spires, it fused into sullen silence, even as the light drained away.

He opened a random can from a teetering pile and ate it cold with a spoon. Dog meat, thick with jelly. Waited nervously for the sounds of Taursi breaking into his nest. Drank a can of Tab. Spent an hour working on a model aeroplane kit, but his anxiety kept pulling him away from the serenity these usually gave him.

He needed to talk to his friend.

For close to two hundred years now, the Junkman had covered the mirrors on every car and motorbike he worked on. An old warning, and he remembered it coming from the man with the good face and the kind smile.

Don't look in mirrors. Ever.

It happened by accident. A market stall with a complete mechanic's tool-chest, and when he looked up with a dozy smile, he saw himself reflected in a dresser mirror. His beard and hair were long, matted and tied back, and he was filthy with engine grease and old food, and it was the first time that Ray Leicester saw himself in a very long time.

A heartbeat later, and he was drawn into a place of pure darkness, where somebody spoke to him for a long time, gave a friendly smile that was too many teeth, and then sent him back into the crowded market, dazed and unsure of anything.

The Junkman took the dresser mirror with him and installed it on his wall. He'd been alone for so very long, and it was nice to have someone hear his ideas, and then introduce him to new ones, prod him along the paths towards exciting new inventions.

Best of all, he was given a very important job. He was going to help someone escape from a very dark place, and he would finally be a hero. An even bigger hero than Brother ever was.

It was nice to have a friend like Papa Lucy.

The Junkman was frustrated by the memory of the golden light engines. These never came over in the Bleedthroughs, and all he had left were the dimmest memories of trains and cars that ran on shining light.

"Aurum," he said, testing the unfamiliar word.

Others who'd had the Methuselah treatment and kept their memories spoke of what they knew, and when he found another old relic, he would drill them for information. Typically these ancients were lesser magicians, sometimes others like him who'd won the lottery and came through the tear intact. He could find no one still alive who'd actually built or worked on one of these machines.

He remembered hating the light-powered engines and misunderstanding them, preferring the noisy clatter of internal combustion. The light was humming, shuddering power, beyond control. His mind wouldn't offer up any more than that, as if protecting him from a bad memory.

There was a link between the golden light called Aurum, the Beatles, and Brother. In frustration he often slapped himself in the head for hours, hoping to dislodge the stuck thoughts. He remembered people trying to stop him from doing this. Sometimes the hands around his wrists were kind, but sometimes they were rough, and people shouted at him.

The pile of tins grew smaller. He completed dozens of model aeroplanes and ships. Read slowly through a library that would make the collectors at Crosspoint weep with envy. Every day he opened hatches to allow sunlight into his underground spaces and onto the spires, and he got the same result. Roughly five minutes of blinding light, and then nothing.

His friend in the mirror became darker, more insulting. Sarcasm at his lack of progress was the typical flow of the chat, until the Junkman removed the mirror from the wall, hiding it in a backroom under a thick shroud.

Decades passed.

Many years later, the Junkman was looking for a tube of superglue when he found the mirror and thought to check it. His friend in the mirror was simply gone, abandoning him like every friend he'd ever known. He wasn't to know that Lucy had awoken through other means and had found both the Waking City and utter destruction at the Boneman's hands.

All he knew was that he was so very lonely—and scared.

In all that time he'd kept the experiment with the spires going, unable to let go of a problem he hadn't solved, and the workroom was now a fat mess of cables and homemade components, resistors and capacitors, switches, and more.

The problem drove him half-mad. Every shifting stone was a Taursi come to reclaim its treasure. He barely slept, starting at noises, expecting a spiny echidna-man looming over him—or worse, Papa Lucy having emerged from the mirror, looking down at him with that cold smile.

One frantic morning he broke apart the battery leads, tipping over spires and breaking them up with a jackhammer. His plan was to bury the shards or scatter them far from his home.

The jackhammer got through the outer casing with ease, but the inside grew tougher, and the work became slower. Finally he hit a big chunk that the jackhammer could not break apart, and set the tool aside.

The Junkman looked down in horror at what he'd exposed. A full Taursi body, bones transformed into glass, the rib cage shattered by his tool. In the centre of this all, the heart of the creature, a diamond the size of two clenched fists. It shone weakly, but the light was not peach. It was gold, just like the energy he'd seen powering that dead world in his mind. Pure Aurum.

He broke dozens of drill bits installing pegs into the hearts, but soon he had six glass hearts connected in a serial battery, and this he connected to the frame, a simple welded rectangle.

The light in the glass hearts flickered, and grew, and then the doorway opened.

— 15 —

UNDERFOG

As the House of the Accurate Count sank beneath the discarded scales of the beast, the Jesusmen struck hard. When it came to that killing moment, that shift when wary patience fell over into violence, these friendless monster hunters were experts, and moved as one. They trained for this, over and over, knowing that hesitation was oblivion.

They'd been betrayed, ambushed, and captured in the House, but every Jesusman had been taught to make this the most dangerous possible time for a captor. Lanyard had a favourite story about being captured by Witches, and he'd been tortured in the Greygulf, nailed to planks of wood, with every humiliation visited upon him.

And the first moment the Witches had turned their attention away from him, Lanyard had torn his hands free, pushing away from the wood until the nails slid through his palms. He then seized his holy shotgun through the world veil, blew one Witch away, and hammered the life out of the other.

Sometime after Bauer had taken on young Lanyard, he taught him about bitter resistance, of fighting even to your dying breath. He'd given Lanyard this wisdom, which he'd paraphrased to his own doomed legion of monster hunters.

"Even as they put the noose on you, hold the gun to your face, set the knife to your throat, you're still in the fight. A condemned man accepts his fate, and the executioner carries out the sentence, lazy, cutting corners, like any man

who does a job. Do not accept your fate. The moment their attention wanders is when you strike as hard as you can. Dirty blows. Kill like a low animal, and you might just walk away."

The Jesusmen had spent almost two hundred years operating in secret, hunted by all. Even the members of this resurrected organisation still kept the flames of paranoia going, helped along by the old guard of Lanyard and Tilly.

Jesusmen were once fair game and could expect death at any moment. Even though the Boneman had changed the law and made them legal once more, they never expected this to last. The prentices were hazed relentlessly, punched and slapped at random moments, tied up and challenged to escape, everything that prepared them for a moment like this.

It might be a robber on a lonely road. A bounty hunter hoping to cash in on the old laws. Or something darker, a creature from another realm, toying with prey. Whatever it was, if you were captured, you were trained to resist, and pounce at the best moment.

Expected to take out as many as you could.

Lanyard was up and roaring, blue cord still flapping around his throat, and he shoulder-charged the nearest slaver-spirit, the old shade fumbling for a whip. It staggered backwards from the blow, feet falling onto a separate clay shard.

Instantly a beast punched up from below, dozens of tendrils rushing up through the scale like a trapdoor spider, seizing the unfortunate spirit and dragging it down an unspeakably long tunnel. The last tendril replaced the scale carefully, resetting the trap.

Something was lurking beneath them, some incredibly huge beast, and suddenly the shifting nature of the plain made sense. Each step promised the threat of the hidden predator, a waiting for the faint tremor of a footstep on its front door.

Lanyard felt the nick of a blade parting his bound wrists. Tilly had a wicked little knife in her hands, the slaver who'd seized it now a filmy scrap floating towards Shale. Some of the other Jesusmen had wrestled their guns away from their guards and were causing grievous damage this close to the enemy.

Lanyard tore out the stake the Chain-Lord had tied his noose to and used it to brain and stab everything that came near, careful of his footing. He barked out the words for smiting and breaking apart enemies, ignoring the sting of the whips that fell upon him.

It was a moment of surprise, but it told true. Soon the Chain-Folk were more than halved in number, most of whom were fleeing towards a safe scale, a known tunnel that did not lead to scrabbling tentacles and doom.

The living had taken losses, of course. Some had been murdered by their captors, who instantly climbed into the bodies and took them for their own. Others had stepped awry and been snatched up by the hungry beast far below, including all of the remaining birds, who'd scattered foolishly and fast.

Still facing the living were a small group of the Chain-Folk, unwilling to defy their Chain-Lord, who'd climbed up into the camel-thing's saddle, frothing with rage. Those spirits who had slain the living and climbed into the bodies clung close to their master, unwilling to risk their new skins.

"You will end here!" the Chain-Lord raged, whip raised on high. The twisted camel-bear beneath him shifted and lurched upwards onto its rear feet, braying awkwardly, face twisted out into a flat ursine snarl.

"Here's a funny thing," Lanyard said, taking his shotgun back from one of the prentices. "We're down to nothing. Boots and bare-arses."

He fed two precious shells into the shooter, clicking the action closed.

"So bloody what? If it comes down to it, I'll carve the marks on my knuckles and punch my way out."

The Chain-Lord was apoplectic, trying to spot a safe path across the clay to take on Lanyard's escapees. During the breakout, the slaver's camp spread out in all directions, and there were perhaps six clay shards separating Lanyard from the vengeful spirit.

"So we might be in strife, but that's normal for our lot."

The Chain-Lord lay about with his whip, ordering underlings forward, sacrificing them to find a safe path.

"But you? You're stuck down here."

"Go! Earn your skins!" the Chain-Lord yelled at the puppets. Finally breaking into movement, they lurched forward, ill-fitting into their stolen bodies, limbs moving wrong.

Twice the tentacles punched upwards and took an attacker who stepped wrong. Others the Jesusmen took apart with their recaptured guns until only a handful of puppets stood trembling around their master. Others took to safe tunnels and fled, routed and terrified.

"I don't even remember your name," Lanyard said to the Chain-Lord, who was fuming and sulking perhaps twenty feet away, too wary to close in. "Do you?"

"Names are nothing down here," the Chain-Lord finally snarled.

"Well, here's a new name for you: Unobservant."

At that moment a sea of moths buffeted everyone, as the enormous web crafted by the Chain-Folk came apart. Tilly and some of the prentices had crept close enough to work the Mark of Unmaking, and they took apart the web, letting a fortune in Aether drain into the ground.

The moths fell upon the Aether, the beast underneath them feasting freely upon the ones that touched its traps. The moths that knocked Lanyard and the others around were more confused than anything. Masterless now, message-bearers with nothing left to say.

One moth knocked a young prentice into a trap, the lad crying out in horror as tentacles drew him into some distant gut. The last sliver of the Chain-Folk turned and slowly retreated, whips parting the enormous flock of moths. Some that were handy with the whips used them to snag the enormous fliers out of the sky, hurling them against the ground. This revealed the beast's traps, and using this trick, the Chain-Folk started moving away quite quickly.

Lanyard watched with satisfaction as the enemy retreated through the moths, but this was soured by the fact that his force was down to a handful of survivors. No birds. No bikes. Few weapons, and even less to eat and drink.

"Lanyard!" Tilly cried out from the distance, the mark for volume etched on her throat. "They're taking the jawbone!"

Sure enough, the Chain-Folk had spotted it and were painstakingly veering course to claim the wretched jag of bone for their Dawn King.

"Let 'em have it."

"You bloody old fool!" Tilly yelled, and Lanyard winced at the sudden volume. "The Boneman gave it to you. It's all we've got."

Lanyard could only watch in dismay as the Chain-Folk closed in on the jawbone, but then a blur of motion came through the dust of the fallen House, a spider carved from hook-ended sticks, easily dodging the reaching tentacles whenever it triggered a trap.

One binocular was left to Lanyard's sorry expedition, and he demanded it quick smart. He tracked this new creature, and watched as it scooped up the jawbone, running right under the Chain-Lord's nose.

It reached the end of the dangerous clay plain, and the spider shifted into a girl shape, loping across the wheat fields with purpose.

"Jenny bloody Rider," Lanyard said.

Their own exit from the plain was long and dangerous, a careful advance that tested each new clay plate for safety. The Chain-Lord departed, swearing to return with many reinforcements.

"Well, piss off then," Lanyard yelled across the gap separating them. "Only cowards talk about fighting as much as you do."

The Chain-Folk had lost much that day. Lanyard supposed they'd robbed and murdered their way into that great supply of Aether over many years. They'd spent the lot to contain the Teller's moths, only to lose it to the cracks in the ground.

"Quick! They are getting away with our dead!" Tilly yelled. She fretted as a prentice tested the clay scales with a stick. Ahead, the Once-Dead spirits of many murdered Jesusmen trotted alongside their own corpses, possessed by their new masters.

They had one rifle left, and Tilly shot one of the dead prentices through the skull, a lucky shot that even poor old Yulio might have envied. The child's body flopped and ejected the parasitic Chain-Folk spirit out onto the clay, where the beast struck again.

Then the Chain-Lord threw up a crackling wall of Aether around their huddled group, and even with their magic the Jesusmen couldn't break through this.

"Look how deep the Chain-Lord reaches into his bread basket," Lanyard said. "Good. Let's bleed him dry."

Lanyard and Tilly watched as the Chain-Lord and his handful of skin-puppets fled toward the breathing hills, a pathetic huddle of raiders who'd just had their arses handed to them.

Inch by painful inch, they themselves stepped toward the edge of the clay pan, and then they were free and on solid ground, on the very edges of the wheat fields that led to the odd village in the distance.

Lanyard had three hard choices ahead of him, and he knew it. Hunt down the Chain-Lord and liberate the dead Jesusmen. Chase after Jenny Rider and retrieve the jawbone. Follow the trail of Mal, which of course he could see quite clearly.

Behind them, the clay shards were settling, and there was no sign that the House of the Accurate Count had ever stood on the plain. Lanyard shuddered.

He'd led thirty-three living souls into the Underfog, and only six remained.

Tilly, the girl he'd forged into a bullet-chewing woman.

Bogle Hess, all leper rags and whispers, scarred fingertips caressing the trigger-guard of a rifle.

Stubs, who'd eaten his own nose and ears to avoid starvation once. He'd been close to hacking off his own hand when Lanyard found him, curled up and dying in a broken-down car.

Mem and Lyn, twins with the gift, tortured in a Witch's nest for years until Lanyard and Tilly freed them. They rarely spoke, but dogged Tilly's heels in hero-worship. Lanyard intended never to give them guns, not even now.

Mal. His boy, the ache in his heart, a stubborn mirror that showed himself.

Doomed, but they never said a word of complaint, merely shuffled together and waited for his instruction.

"Our people had their bodies stolen," Lanyard said. "Their spirits are in chains."

Tilly set her jaw and nodded.

"We will avenge them. Drive out the thieves, burn our people's flesh so that no one else can do that to them."

Lanyard turned away from the hills, flashing with the occasional crackle of a blue whip, and he turned toward the wheat fields to the village nearby. He looked more keenly through his cataracted eye and nodded with satisfaction.

"But we've got a job to finish, and I need to rescue my boy," Lanyard said, and started through the wheat. Five people followed.

They found the abandoned ploughshare and then Mal's lance, which Lanyard plucked. Regarding it for a long moment, he passed it back to Tilly, who handed on her rifle to Bogle Hess.

"He would never have left that," Tilly said to Lanyard.

"I know."

"He might be gone. You need to be ready for that."

"Mal's not dead. He's ahead of us some ways, but I know he lives." Tilly scoffed.

"You're just being hopeful. He's alone, chasing ghosts, and now he doesn't even have a weapon."

Lanyard only had answers that led to painful discussions, so he kept his mouth shut. He looked to his people and saw the fruits of years of work. A leper. A woman with a smart mouth, who he'd once hoped would bury him someday, and not the other way around. A freak with half a face. Two silent girls, trailing their hands through the wheat in unison.

All that blood and terror, all those years living in Bauer's shadow, and this is the best I could do?

"Don't bloody eat those seeds," was all that Lanyard said, and the girls nodded in mute terror at the instruction.

The tiny group of survivors approached the village, and soon they were noticed. They held their weapons at the ready, only to find themselves greeted by an odd collection of figures.

A small community of the Once-Dead, from the recently dead through to those with the same eroded features as Paeter, the ancient robber who lurked by the Edgemist. Most were the spirits of men and woman, but there were other creatures here: a coiled worm the size of a large dog, a thin cockerel twice a man's height, a cube of flowing mercury which hummed, a minotaur, and even one of Bilben's kind, though it was scabby and half-blind and only shifted in weak spurts of possibility.

They clustered together, but did not radiate menace, and had taken on the appearance of humble farmers, with threadbare dresses and overalls. If anything, they were as terrified as any village Lanyard had ever stumbled into.

Here, existence was misery. The constant fear of predators. These people were too weak to leave, and too weak to better their lot. Apart from a scatter of scythe and pitchforks fixed in place with Aether, the village seemed unarmed.

"You should not be here!" a near featureless man warned.

"We offer no trouble," Lanyard said. "Just passing through."

"You don't understand, necromancers. She is coming, and she will blame us! You doom us just by being here!"

Another spirit, a woman whose features had been worn away to the merest suggestion of eyes, cheeks and nose, steered the figure away with kindness.

"If you can hide, do it," she said. "Please. Gretel is coming."

"Dunno who that is," Lanyard said.

"This is her land."

Lanyard remembered the tales of the Boneman, and how he'd had to pay his way to the various lords of the Underfog. Some would grant passage when asked respectfully, while others demanded great gifts.

Lanyard guessed that a warlord who kept her subjects poor and fearful would not settle for a cup of tea and a chat. Looking around at his poor crew, he had no real option.

"Hide us," he asked the group, who muttered amongst themselves. Their ranks parted, and an incredibly old spirit came forward, face washed nearly smooth, with the merest slit for a mouth and nothing more.

"You trespass," it said.

"Look. I said we're passing through. We're not here to nick any of your stuff."

"We cannot spare a drop. Nothing. This crop was useless."

Lanyard blustered.

"I said we don't want anything. Are you deaf as well as dead?"

"We are sorry," Tilly said, elbowing Lanyard in the ribs. "We will leave as soon as we can."

"If we are caught sheltering you, we–it will be a great penalty."

Lanyard squared up and tried to look this spirit in the eyes.

"I'm Lanyard. What's your name, mate?"

The slightest upward curve of that cleft that passed for a mouth.

"I lost my name a long, long time ago. I am Farmer now."

"Well, Farmer, our place was attacked by some arseholes, who hurt our loved ones and took our stuff. We've come down here to get justice."

"There is no justice down here," Farmer said in a low voice.

"No, mate, you misunderstand. We're the justice. We're going to find this Dawn King and wring his fucking neck."

At these words the villagers were in an instant uproar, but they fell silent as Farmer held up a hand.

"Lanyard. You speak of justice, of hunting the Dawn King. You do not understand anything of what you say."

Lanyard opened his mouth and then closed it. The sky echoed with a great snarling roar, and then again, and he could feel the vibration in his sternum, in the distance but getting closer. The villagers looked to each other in terror.

"Gretel comes!" one of them whimpered.

"Well, looks like you've got a choice to make," Lanyard said to Farmer. The old spirit looked over their group and came to a decision.

"Mina, hide them in the old school," Farmer said.

"But–"

"Quickly. They cannot be seen."

Mina led them forward, parting the muttering villagers with grace and poise. Where Farmer was a statue obliterated by time, Mina was merely a weathered spirit, her features less than distinct. As they pushed through the cluster of rude huts and around a granary, Mina took them through a low door frame, and Lanyard suddenly saw the truth of the place.

This wasn't a simple village. It was an entire town, wearing the appearance of a subsistence commune, and now that they'd passed through the veil of sorcery, they could see a town hall, a proper market square, even other civic buildings, all set in place with the tell-tale glimmer of Aether in mortar and brick.

Even stranger, there were places above the lintels where words would normally be carved, but these were perfectly blank. Others had foundation stones and commemorative plates, and these were as smooth as though a chisel had never been brought down to say who had cut what ribbon and when.

Sometimes, a building would pulse and shift, but this secret town was more set in place than anywhere else he'd seen in the Underfog.

The shifting never took, and these buildings always settled back into their fixed form.

"The school is over here. Hurry."

Another roar, this one echoing through the buildings, and Mem and Lyn cried out in unison. Mina opened the double-doors of the school, closing it once everyone was inside. The Jesusmen had captured and held buildings before, and they hustled into position through muscle memory. Tilly ready to defend the closed door with her lance. Bogle and Stubs pressed up to the sides of windows, guns at the ready. Lanyard spoke words of protection, of hiding, all of the makeshift magic he knew.

Mem and Lyn clutched together tightly, eyes wide as they took in the classroom, the small desks, the chalkboard, the bookcases filled with volumes erased by the Underfog.

"Look at all the toys," Mem said, and for a moment the twins seemed to forget the danger they were in, drawn to a big chest filled with colourful toy animals, cars, trains, and blocks.

Lanyard drew in breath to yell at the girls to return to their posts but caught the look in Tilly's eye. He let the kids have this moment.

"The noise has stopped," Bogle whispered, holding some dead man's pistol, deeply etched with the killing marks and notched with Witch kills. Stubs breathed wetly through his exposed nasal cavity, clutching the old rifle close.

A long, watchful moment, but so far they were safe. Hidden. Lanyard was about to open the door to check outside when he heard a faint whimper behind him.

He turned to see the twins backing away in terror, toys forgotten on the floor. At the front of the classroom was a heavy teacher's desk, and emerging from behind it with a stretch and a fang-filled yawn was an enormous she-wolf, pelt as grey as gunmetal, full teats dangling. It looked them over calmly.

"Girls, move back. Slowly," Lanyard said.

The wolf came towards the girls, padding across the floor, radiating menace. Lanyard and the others advanced, but a heartbeat before the killing could start, the wolf sat down, and then got down on her front legs.

She nudged one of the building blocks with her nose.

"You can play if you want," the wolf said to the children. "Just make sure to pack up the toys when you're done."

UNDERFOG

S top pointing your guns at me," the wolf told them. "You're making me nervous."

"Of course we're nervous," Tilly said. "You're a talking fucking wolf."

The wolf tilted her head upwards and *whoofed* lightly, lips upcurved in a smile.

"I will give you that, girl," she said. "Quite the visitors. Hardly anyone visits my classroom anymore."

"Your classroom?"

"Yes."

The twins shared a look, and decided that play was play, no matter how weird the playmate. Mem picked up the block the wolf had offered, stacking it, and Lyn added another.

"I am very sorry, those used to have letters on them," the wolf said. "We had jigsaw puzzles, too, but no one enjoys those anymore, now that the pictures are gone."

"Right, you lot. Back to your posts," Lanyard said, nodding toward the door. He sat down on his haunches, shotgun across his knees, and watched the surreal playdate for a moment.

"You got a name?" Lanyard said.

She huffed in a way that might have been a laugh or acknowledgement of the request.

"Give me ten thousand years and I'll forget it like Farmer did. I am Lupa."

"Lanyard Everett," he said, and offered his hand across the circle of toys. Instead of shaking it with her paw like a dog might, the wolf leaned in close, drawing in his scent.

"I know you now," Lupa said, and Lanyard was not comforted by this. She nudged one wet nose against the girl's tower, gently toppling it to the sound of their giggles.

"You are sweet girls," Lupa continued. "Twins! Rare and precious. Your parents must have sacrificed many animals in their joy!"

Lanyard didn't have the heart to tell Lupa the truth, of how the parents had sold them to slavers, and how these rough guardians had run when the Witches came to take the girls into their nest.

"I had two boys of my own, a long time ago," the wolf crooned, and she shifted to her side, one long flank of fat teats hanging to the ground. "Humans. Lost little things, and I gladly gave them a suckle to keep them alive."

"These two could have done with a wolf," Lanyard said. "They got me instead. But I took too long to find them."

"You found them as you were meant to. You girls will be well and hale now, won't you?" Lupa said, and Mem and Lyn nodded for yes, even as they completed another construction.

Doomed in the Underfog and coddled by a speaking beast, Lanyard thought. *I should have given them the mercy of a knife back when I found them.*

He considered the blank books, the chalkboard free of all marks. Once the criminal who'd become the Chain-Lord had sent him to learn his letters, and he'd been in a room like this as a young teen, squinting at books full of lessons, fingers filthy with ink by each day's end.

But this room looked much older. The books were precious and held to the shelf with Aether-bright chains. The desks and the chairs did not look like they'd come from the end of the Before, but from before the age of the machines. Some of the toys were new additions, but this building spoke of a distant age.

"Tilly, keep watch but listen good," Lanyard said. "Jump in if you have any thoughts of your own."

"Right, boss."

"So, I heard a legend of a wolf who suckled twins, back from the Before," Lanyard said. His mind was a trap, in ways both good and bad. "The Boneman told me once."

"The Boneman?" Lupa asked.

"Sol Pappagallo. Lord Goodface. Walking fucking skeleton."

"Language. There are children here."

"These kids have killed before. A hard word won't do much."

"True."

"So the Boneman told me the wolf suckling the twins was an old, old story. Long before their power stations and their other bullshit. Dawn of that old civilisation."

"Righto then," Tilly said.

"My old bossman had a dog once. Lived to be about twenty. Incredibly old. Can't imagine a wolf has much more life in it than that. So Lupa here, you must have died something in the region of two, three thousand years ago."

"That is accurate," Lupa said. "The twins held me down, in a cave underneath that city of the seven hills. They drew a blade across my throat. It was the way."

"And so, you came here."

"Yes. Farmer took me in. Gave me a name, and the gift of speech. I served him in this, the first town, though its name is gone now, even from my mind."

"You've always been the teacher here?"

"Others came to help me, but yes. I have always taught those who sought knowledge."

"You think about this building and everything in here, fix it in place with your mind?"

"Well, Aether sets everything just so, but I do have to maintain my thoughts, on the roof, the doors, the children's playthings."

"What about the books? Do you need to think on those to keep them from fading away?"

Lupa snarled and turned away.

"Answer my question, wolf. Why keep them here when the words went away?"

The wolf gave what might have been a wolfy frown and whimpered a little.

"I cannot part with them!" the wolf growled. "They gave such joy to the spirits of dead children."

The twins had moved on from the toys and the serious discussion nearby, and were madly defacing the blackboard. As fast as they could draw their people and animals, the chalk was gone, as if an invisible finger was wiping it clean.

"When did the writing stop working?"

"When the golden ones first came down," Lupa said. "Before your Papa Lucy ever thought to pierce the Greygulf. Long before the Teller planted his tower and his moths over the old lake."

"How long have your kids gone without?" Tilly asked gently. "When did they lose their picture books and puzzles?"

"Some four hundred years ago," the wolf admitted bitterly.

BOOM!

An explosive force, and close, and the sound of bricks collapsing, bouncing across the street. The dusty windows of the school shook, and Lupa was instantly up, standing protectively above the children. Her lips drew back into a snarl.

Once more that echoing roar, an animal rage, and the creature that hunted them emptied its great lungs, over and over. Getting closer.

"She's followed you here!" Lupa said. "Farmer should have turned you away!"

"So you can sleep in a room with empty books?" Lanyard scoffed. He clicked his fingers at the twin prentices, ordering them to Tilly's side with their little blades, and then he dared a glance out of the nearest window.

It was a car, purring up the street, engine snarling. Then Lanyard took a second look, and his blood froze in his veins.

The car was a woman's body, completely stretched out in all directions, a muscle car sculpted out of flesh and bone. The radiator was a great mouth filled with yellowing teeth, and even as it roared and wailed, Lanyard could spy teeth and tongue, and a throat that was deep and black.

The headlights were eyes, and they scanned left and right, looking for prey. The wing mirrors were ears that flapped and searched for the slightest sound.

This obscenity rolled on wheels that were the nubs of feet and hands, thick leathery skin that easily pressed against the rubble on the street. The hubcaps shone with the sheen of toenails. The flanks of the car were skin drawn taut above a ribcage, with an old tattoo faded and stretched to a blue smudge.

Above all of this was the roof, the cap of a skull that ran with long ropes of grey hair in all directions. Up front and centre was a hollow space, framed with bone. The windshield. Lanyard spotted a driver seated in that gloomy interior, hands gripped tight to a steering wheel that was all polished bone.

Everyone held still. Another roar, and this close it was an angry cry. A note of hunger that hung long in the air, a human voice that rattled with the rhythms of an engine.

Mem whimpered slightly.

"WHERE?" the car yelled. Lanyard slid away slowly from the window, heart thumping. He could hear the shifting of brick under tyres, and then the cry became a hum, the tyres spun wildly, and BOOM.

Across the street, the car made of flesh had rammed into another building, climbing the steps and punching into a column. The whole place came down on the car.

Lanyard rose, ready to order his people out of there, but stopped when he felt the wet huffing of the wolf's nose, right next to his ear.

"Stop," Lupa whispered, "The House of Torana is still dangerous. Don't go outside."

Sure enough, the car came whining and snarling out of the wreck, its skin and flesh barely marked. A small trickle of blood dappled the hood, which Lanyard now saw was a completely flattened nose. In moments the trickle had stopped, and the House of Torana was back in the street, searching and snarling.

Lanyard thought through his options. They could try the Mark of Unmaking, but the will needed to keep such a bizarre vehicle together would be hard to overcome. The Mark of Many Triggers he'd used against the enormous land-octopus was useless with so few guns to aim as one.

So, marks for fire and light, but he'd need to step out, show himself. The great magicians of the Before could send a mote of fire to lick against a distant foe, but the Jesusmen could barely set alight their cooking fires with the spell.

They'd lost or used all the bombs and grenades they'd brought into the Underfog. All they had left to take on this thing were bullets, blades, and gritted teeth.

The ears on the car were enormous, and this close he could see the nostrils near the front of the hood drawing in the air, sniffing for prey. Soon they would be discovered.

"Wolf," Lanyard whispered into Lupa's ear. "Get everyone out the back door and away. I'll keep the car busy."

Lupa nodded and pushed at people with her snout, herding them towards double doors that led to a schoolyard. Stubs and Bogle looked for permission from Lanyard and took the escape gratefully enough.

Tilly sent the twins on before standing next to Lanyard, lance at the ready.

"Just this once, I'm not going to try to talk you out of it," Lanyard whispered quietly. "I'm going to need you, girl."

"I know," said Tilly, and then they moved as one, kicking open the front doors to the school and running out into the street.

"HEY!" the car shouted, and it whipped around, fleshy tyres kicking up stones and dirt as it fishtailed, turning to face the two Jesusmen. The eyes at the front were human, green irises with blood-shot sclera. The car blinked with surprise at the sight of these living folks, and then it frowned.

"ON MY LAND," it snarled and revved. "THIEVES!"

Then, it came speeding forward, as fast as a real machine would. Lanyard whistled and pointed, and Tilly knew the command well. It wasn't the first time someone had tried to run them down.

They stayed together, watching, weapons held ready, and then at the last moment they split apart, running like rabbits. The House of Torana yelled in shock, and shifted left and right, trying to pick a target.

It went for Lanyard, who was a moment too slow, and it clipped him in the hip. He went sprawling and rolling, and his head bounced against a brick in the street.

"AH! YOU DARE!" the car screeched. Lanyard looked up to see the car wheel around for another pass, but blood ran from its flank, and from Tilly's lance. Lanyard watched for it to seal up and clot like the damage from the falling rubble, but the wound bled freely.

Whatever this was, Jesusman marks damaged it, and that was everything he needed to know.

This time, Tilly and Lanyard stayed apart, waiting for the car to make its move. It chose Tilly this time, and she held her ground, wheeling the lance around and dancing on the tips of her toes.

Then Lanyard ran forward, straight towards the car, which corrected to aim at him. He held the shotgun low, not even bothering to aim. BLAM!

The car screamed, its right eye in ruins, blood running out in a gush. This close he could see a driver inside, a figure behind the wheel that fought to keep it in a straight line, but the car disobeyed its driver and ploughed straight into the nearest building.

While the car lay trapped, Tilly walked around it, calmly piercing its wheels, and the car screamed and screamed, the marks telling true. The House of Torana spun its wheels in reverse, but the fleshy tyres were deflated and did little to grip the ground.

"Get it, boss! Shoot it again!" Tilly cried. Even as Lanyard levelled his god-cannon at the side of the trapped vehicle, the door opened, and the driver emerged.

The Once-Dead spirit of a woman, but where the other dead things changed their appearance with their moods and whim, this one was wearing clothes, real fabric, complete with broad-brimmed cowboy hat and boots. She had her own shooter, which was as real as Lanyard's, and she was out with a snarl, batting Lanyard's gun aside before he could fire. She was quick, and in the tussle both Lanyard and the woman had each other by the collars, guns levelled into each other's temples.

"You wrecked my ride. You wrecked my fucking ride, punk!" she shouted.

Lanyard didn't bother saying anything. In these moments, a steely glare and pressure on a trigger meant much more than bravado or negotiation.

"You okay, sweet girl?" the spirit said to the car.

"GRETEL, IT HURTS," the House of Torana said, still feebly trying to escape. Tilly laid her lance against the car's flank, pressing just enough to draw blood, and then the car stayed still, flexing and panting like a terrified beast.

"Okay, let's talk about this," Gretel said, and Lanyard smiled, a smile that Lupa might have recognised. Threat display and nothing more.

"Please. I'll let you stay on my land. I'll even give you protection."

"Do we look like we need protecting?" Lanyard snarled.

"Living folks down here draw trouble. You might have won here, but you look tired. Hungry."

"Hunger makes me sharp."

"For a few days, sure. Trust me, when I was alive down here, living was nothing but trouble."

"Wait," Tilly said. "You were alive down here?"

"Yep," she said. "And it drew all the wrong kinds of attention. The moment I found a way out of my skin and bones, all my troubles were over."

Gretel nodded towards her car.

"Turned out there were more useful things to do with my body anyway."

In the Oerwoud, the Joyous Hound swept the golden lash, over and over again, destroying tree and brush, carving a path through that ancient defence. In the golden sea of Overhaeven this being was represented by an ankh, but whenever the Joyous Hound wore flesh, it became a kilt-wearing man with a jackal's head, ears erect.

The Hound was sweating profusely and took a moment to rest against a tree. It cried out as a thorn pricked its skin.

"DO NOT TARRY!" one of the Smothered Princes ordered. "RESUME YOUR TASK!"

"The work goes hard," the Joyous Hound complained. "Let the Blackstar have a turn."

"DON'T YOU MIND THE BLACKSTAR. THEY HAVE THEIR OWN ERRAND."

"I was served by priests once. Now here I slave in a garden."

Still, the Hound picked up that unravelling filament and got back to work, severing tree trunks, destroying brush and vine, clearing a path wide enough for an army to traverse. Behind their force the golden filament unspooled, eventually reaching a point where it suddenly struck upwards, piercing through the sepia heavens and all of the realms between here and Overhaeven.

A great tank of energy, a stolen fortune, and they were spending it to ease their way.

"WE REMEMBER WHEN HE PLANTED THESE TREES," said the first Prince to his twin.

"YES. THE FARMER THOUGHT HE COULD KEEP US OUT."

"HIS SEEDS SPROUTED TOO SLOWLY."

"NOW THEY MERELY VEX."

"QUITE."

A commotion further back in their ranks, and a glass-plated Taursi came to the Smothered Princes with a visitor in tow. The Once-Dead spirit was obscenely fat, and so flush with Aether that it sweated blue muck from every pore. In one hand, the spirit held a long-bladed shovel like a symbol of office. In the other hand he held a blue chain, which led to a shackled and terrified man. This man was old and infirm, but alive.

"The Dawn King is below, and above," the spirit with the shovel said.

"LEFT AND RIGHT," the Smothered Princes said as one.

"His house is glorious and we have sworn to him," the spirit finished.

"HO, GRAVEDIGGER! YOU HAVE DONE VERY WELL!"

"This was not easy," the Gravedigger said. "He was guarded well, and we were pursued back through my tunnel. I lost most of my group."

"DO NOT COMPLAIN," one of the Princes said. "NECESSARY LOSSES."

"Well, here is your prize," the Gravedigger said, handing over the chain. "The Selector of Mawson, as requested."

"HORACE RIDER," the Princes said in gleeful unison. The living man was terrified, surrounded by this host of godlings and Taursi warriors plated in shining glass. The Gravedigger had stolen him out of his very bed, and he still wore his nightshirt, lower legs coated in an ointment meant to treat the bloated feet that came with riverlung.

"Please," Horace Rider said. "There's been some mistake. Let me go. I'll give you anything you want."

"YOU WILL GIVE THE DAWN KING WHAT HE WANTS," said a Prince. "HE WANTS YOUR DAUGHTER."

"Jenny?" Horace whispered. "Jenny is alive?"

"HO! HARDLY! NO, SHE IS DOWN HERE AND CAUSING MISCHIEF. YOU, WE SHALL DANGLE AS A MEANS TO TAME HER HOOKING HANDS."

The father slumped to the ground then, sobbing with grief, his worst fears realised. He hardly noticed as he was lifted to a spider-horse and lashed into a saddle. Behind him was the glass case containing the Overhaeven forms of the Jesus and John Leicester, swirling and bumping against the walls of their prison, but the old man did not notice or care.

"We break through!" the Joyous Hound cried up ahead, finally destroying the last of the trees with his golden whip. He released the filament, and it whizzed past the host, reeling back into the heavens and into that distant reservoir.

The Overhaeven forces stepped out of the forest and onto a cracked clay plain. Ahead, a field of blue-grey wheat beckoned.

The host moved forward.

— 17 —

UNDERFOG

Lanyard escorted Gretel and the captured House of Torana out of the secret settlement and into the village. Farmer and the others were emerging from their hiding places and looked at the scene with amazement. The small group of living travellers had both car and woman at gunpoint, and the vehicle was gravely wounded, all the fight driven out of it.

"Gretel, you are undone!" Farmer cried, his barely visible smile a curve of pure joy.

"Shut up! Know your bloody place!" Gretel said.

Tilly slammed the butt of her lance into Gretel's gut, winding her. Stubs and Bogle dragged her into the centre of the gathering villagers and dumped her to the ground.

"Here's your local fuckhead," Lanyard said. "I must say, we've had tougher fights."

Behind them, the façade of the sleepy village was hanging like a torn stage-dressing, showing where the House of Torana had simply crashed through the illusion while sniffing for prey. Some of the villagers were on ladders, using a paste of Aether and clay to fix the vista in place.

"I gave you protection," Gretel said vehemently. "I didn't ask for anything you couldn't spare."

Farmer gestured to Mina, who brought forward a bucket filled to the brim with Aether. He took it and stood in front of Gretel, who sat up with interest.

"I have farmed that field so long that I have forgotten my name. I was the first to learn that a trace of Aether can be found in the grains, and it can be extracted with great effort."

"So? You have enough to share," Gretel scoffed.

"Hardly. We can only trust our memories since the writing failed, but we know the yield is dropping. This bucket is all that we could extract from the last crop."

At the sight of the bucket, the House of Torana whined pitifully. The villagers lined up, and Farmer dipped a ladle into the blue swirl, letting each of them drink their fill.

They drank their entire store of Aether in front of Gretel, who stared darkly at the proceedings. The sated villagers stepped aside, flush with vitality.

At the end, Farmer cast the empty bucket at Gretel's feet, and the final drops fell into the ground before she could move. The earth soaked it up with a blue flash.

"These living visitors will move on soon," Gretel snarled. "But I will remember this. I will be back, and they will not protect you."

Mina came to Farmer with a big, jagged stone, which she cradled in both hands. It did not run with Aether, but it was fixed in place, as real as Lanyard's people and their artefacts. Farmer took the stone and stood above Gretel.

"I have existed ages upon ages. My memories are weak things, but I have kept this much. I was a farmer, driven from his first garden."

Farmer cradled the stone, running a thumb across a jagged point. Lanyard thought of his own stone, fetched at an old campfire and driven through his master's face, and understood the sudden wash of fear that came across Gretel's face.

"This rock was used by my first son to kill my second son. And now, it will end you."

"Wait, I—"

The rock fell, and again, and when the screaming stopped Farmer let the Aether splattered jag fall to the clay, the old spirit slumping until he was the very picture of weariness. Mina took his hands gently and licked the spills of Aether from his fingers and his forearms. Another spirit took the ancient lump of stone and wrapped it in a cloth, taking it away to store safely.

The entire village watched as Gretel's Twice-Dead scraps floated across the wheatfields, the warlord headed toward her final destruction.

The House of Torana pined over its dead master. Flinching every time Tilly pointed Mal's lance at it, it limped around dejectedly on its flat tyres, revving and babbling.

"You would do well to destroy that thing," Farmer said, his hand resting on Lupa's head. The wolf growled at the car-thing, daring it to move. "It is an abomination in my eyes."

"Got other plans," Lanyard said, looking over the House of Torana.

"Understood," Farmer said. "Our people are grateful for your help, but we cannot support you. If you mean to harm the Dawn King, we cannot aid you in any way."

"We don't kill monsters to make friends," Lanyard said.

The wheat rustled.

"I beg you, Lanyard Jesusman, please turn from your course," Mina said, gliding forward from the wheat field. "The Dawn King is a force for good! Please, turn away!"

"Can't do that."

As Mina got closer, Lanyard saw that she had a trickle of Aether running from her mouth, which she absently wiped away with her sleeve. Three other Once-Dead spirits followed her from the field, two people and a man with a bull head, dazed, clutching at their necks.

Lanyard instantly had his gun up and tracking, but Farmer and Lupa stood in the way.

"Step aside!" Lanyard snarled.

"Again, you understand nothing!" Farmer scolded. "Our ways are not yours to judge."

"You'd kill the car, but you live with your own monster," Tilly said, stalking forward with lance in hand.

"Yes. Mina is free to act to her truth, as long as no one is harmed by it," Farmer said. "All can live in that way."

He saw the dozy grins on Mina's "victims" and knew they'd been willing to follow that woman of poise and dignity out into the field, to offer their veins to her mouth. A vampire, as much as Paeter had been, lurking by the Edgemist, save she only took Aether from the willing.

"Damnit," Lanyard grumbled, and whistled between his teeth. *Guns down, but watch for treachery.* His handful of followers adopted that pose, a watchful pack of hounds ready to bare fangs at their master's cry.

"Your Dawn King brought war to us," Lanyard said. "We've sworn to end him. Don't you dare fucking oppose me."

"We're in no position to fight you," Farmer said. "Please, the Dawn King must have had his reasons."

"His House is above and below, and left and right," Mina said. "Who are we to comprehend such a mind?"

"He killed my kids," Lanyard said. "Laid waste to cities, drove out the living like cockroaches."

Mina had the grace to look away, but Farmer's age-smoothed face was resolute.

"There will be worse to come," Farmer conceded. "But ours is a righteous war. If the Dawn King took your cities, he had need of them."

"For the cause," Mina said.

"The cause," some of the villagers muttered earnestly.

"Why the damned and the dead want to fight the living is beyond me," Lanyard said, fishing out the fixings of a cigarette. "Well, try to explain it to me before I finish my smoke."

"I will explain nothing more," Farmer said. "We are sworn to the Dawn King, and you mean him harm."

"OH, GRETEL," the House of Torana cried, limping forward. Slowly but surely, the wounds on the car were closing, and the tyres were reinflating. Tilly slashed them once again, hobbling the beast.

"HURTS! STINGS!" the car bellowed.

"You need to start getting more helpful, Farmer," Lanyard said. "Otherwise, we leave the House of Torana behind when we go. Tilly, does it look hungry?"

"Yep, hungry," Tilly said. "Pissed off, too."

The villagers looked worried then. Lanyard doubted that their holy rock would do much against this unnatural vehicle.

"You need the history, then," Farmer said desperately. "To know why we have sworn to the Dawn King. He's the only one who stands up for us, who tries to better our lot."

"So what does he look like? Your glorious leader?"

The Farmer looked down at his hands.

"He was the light of dawn, blinding! A voice. He spoke of changing the way of things. That we could break out of our prison."

"Perhaps you all deserve to be here," Lanyard said.

"Some, of course. But not all. This is meant to be a land of bounty, of reward for lives well lived!"

Lanyard took in the shimmering blue wheat, the cracked ruin of the plain, the bare, breathing hills. Saw the point in the Oerwoud where a sparking flare was burning through it.

Those Smothered Princes are burning their way through the trees! he thought. *We don't have time for this.*

"Do you know where to find the Dawn King?" Lanyard demanded. "Quickly, and no riddles."

"I am sorry, but we do not know."

Shotgun up, stub of cigarette stuck to his lip, Lanyard repeated the question.

"This town, this field, this is all these Once-Dead have ever known. Perhaps I travelled once, but it was a long time ago, and I've lost my sense of this place."

Farmer pointed across the fields, to the former site of the House of the Accurate Count.

"There was a lake just there, before the Beast drank it dry from below, before the Teller made his own accommodation. Those waters fed the fields, and the wheat we grew there provided for all of the Houses."

There were barely enough spirits left to fill one of the buildings in the hidden town.

"We had bread and beer, and we raised our own House, though it's a nameless thing now. We had a shining civilisation that was meant to last forever!"

"The way you lot are going, I give you ten years," Tilly scoffed.

"And then another Gretel will come along and finish you off," Lanyard observed.

"This is why the Dawn King is everything to us."

"So tell me, Farmer from a House without a name, what does the Dawn King bloody want?" Lanyard said.

"To put things back to how they were. Once, the spirits of man, and things from other worlds, were all welcome here and wanted for nothing. Before this was the Underfog, it was the pinnacle of the universe, Gan-Eden, where all spirits came for their final, eternal rest."

Across the clay plain, the golden light burnt through the Oerwoud with a bright flash. The Smothered Princes were through.

"If you've got any sense, run," Lanyard told the villagers, and gave the twirling hand signal, instructing his people to *pack up quick.* "Those shiny golden bastards are coming this way."

"Why would we run?" Farmer said. "We invited them."

NOW/UNDERFOG

The Junkman stood before his doorway, mouth dry as he looked at what he'd done. In the middle of his cave was a welded metal door frame, hooked up by cables to a serial battery of six glass hearts, pulsing with golden Aurum.

The frame was filled with white fog, thick and clammy. The Junkman approached the situation like anything he didn't understand yet, and he experimented on it.

First, a stick, that entered the frame and came back unharmed. Though he thrust it in as deep as he dared to, it was not visible on the other side when he looked around the edge of the door frame.

A pot with a spring-loaded lid to sample the air, and it was a neutral smelling fog, harmless enough.

He tied a wrench to a rope and threw it through the frame as far as he could. He pulled out twenty feet of damp rope, the wrench clattering behind it.

Next, he wore a welder's glove and thrust his arm through, and then peeled it off to touch the fog with his naked skin.

The Junkman had seen the workings of magic in his strange second life, and even with his memory stripped close to bare he still despised and misunderstood it. Machines, tools, and science he could appreciate, and it was a simple circuit, powering an unknown effect.

He preferred facts. He'd opened a doorway into somewhere else, right in the centre of his workroom. Aurum powered it. The connection was stable, the glass Taursi hearts blazing away on his bench.

A less comfortable fact was this: by making a door and flooding it with that strange golden energy, he'd intended the door to open, and in certain circles intent was as good as casting a magic spell by chattering and waving your hands around.

He thought of getting the mirror and showing his new friend the results, but decided against it. His friend had been mean to him, and for just this little while, the Junkman wanted to enjoy his achievements, without the sarcasm and the constant instructions.

Much like when Ray Leicester took the train to Ur-Sydney, the Junkman packed a heavy bag. Food, extra clothes, and the heavy rattle of spanners and screwdrivers in case they were needed. A flashlight with good batteries, though the beam did little to pierce the white murk.

He tied the rope around his waist, tied the other end to a table leg, and walked into the mist.

Fog pressed in thickly, and within ten steps he could no longer see into his workshop. Eyes wide, the Junkman pushed through his terror and kept walking.

The rope suddenly went taut around his waist. He fell to his knees in a panic, the useless flashlight clattering away into the mist and never to be seen again.

Below him, the ground felt smooth and hard, like polished stone, and he'd banged his knee hard when falling, felt the blood pool in the knees of his pants. Was there something in here that could sniff out blood, like a shark–

What's a shark?

Or maybe like a hound bred to hunt slaves or criminals, he corrected himself, wondering where the odd word had come from.

There's a shark. There's a shark in here with me.

After hyperventilating on the ground, he realised he'd simply walked to the full extent of his rope, and that he'd either have to untie himself or go back.

He went back, running the rope through his hands, and then he'd returned to the safety of his workshop, the door still humming behind him. Frantically untying the knot, he ran over and disconnected the circuit, the white fog instantly winking out, the steel frame just a steel frame.

He woke up in a panic a week later, cursing his own stupidity. He'd gone through the door without timing the period in which the door *could* remain open. If it had closed on him, would he still be wandering around in that place, lifeline severed?

He connected the glass hearts and threw the switch, instantly powering the doorframe. There was indeed an intent in the Junkman's mind, planted there by his mirror-bound friend, and he opened a door that could have gone to many places, but instead opened the way to this one.

Fog. Thick and seemingly unending.

He sat there in his workshop, eating cans of beans and reading old detective novels, looking at the clock for hours on end.

The hearts glowed, and the door remained open until he was too tired to watch it. He moved his bed in front of the door and slept with an old comic book rustling across his chest.

He woke with a start to see the door still open and cursed his own stupidity again. There could be anything in that fog, and here he was, napping in front of its open front door.

He set his bed in the middle of the portcullises and locked the mechanism from the inside. He had a bucket for a toilet, a stack of tinned food, and enough books to keep himself busy. Mirrors were set at angles so he could see into the workshop, to the white rectangle of the mist-filled doorway.

It was fully six days before the power cut out, and the hearts lay still. He changed the wiring from serial to parallel, and there was still enough power to keep the door open. Only one heart was needed, and he increased the charge six-fold.

Opening his ceiling hatches to shine sunlight on the glass hearts kept them charged by day. In his extreme caution, the Junkman reached one full month with the gate still functional.

So the Junkman returned to that land of fog, this time armed with several ropes tied together, a full three hundred feet of neatly spliced rope connecting him to his workshop. He did not bother with the flashlight, and he took a handcart filled with essentials, enough to survive for some time should he get lost in the fog.

This time when the rope played out, he was expecting it, and he stepped back a few paces. He unpacked his equipment and set about his experiments, firstly capturing some of the mist with a bellows-powered air-pump and a small pressure vessel. Next, he used a hand-drill on the ground, breaking three diamond-tipped drill bits before conceding that it was close to unbreakable.

A week later he returned into the fog with a motorcycle. Back in his workshop was an enormous spool of telegraph line, miles of the stuff, and he slowly motored forward, surprised as all of the instruments on the dash failed. No speed, no odometer readings, nothing to help him make his calculations.

It was guess-work at best. He drove and drove and slept twice before he made it through the fog to see a bizarre land of breathing, flexing hills.

He got off the motorbike and drove a six-foot steel peg deep into the ground with a hammer. He fastened the telegraph line taut to this, knowing that with a carabiner clip he could safely travel between his workshop and whatever this place was.

"You'll want to be careful," a small voice said at his feet. "Old Paeter might be gone now, but there are others who hunt here."

The Junkman looked down to see a desert rat with big ears and a fuzzy tail, staring up at him with intelligent eyes. This rat flickered in place, dozens of possible movements and choices centred around one serene creature, cleaning its paws.

"You couldn't possibly be talking," the Junkman said. "This–you are impossible."

"Keep telling yourself that," the rat said, smiling up at him in a jitter of a hundred possibilities.

— 18 —

NOW

Even as the cries went up in Mawson that the Selector was gone, stolen from the Tower, the Junkman came puttering back in through his own impossible doorway on his motorcycle.

Unusual for him he'd taken a risk, running miles of unreliable telegraph cable across the stone without supporting posts, and he shook all over as he returned from that strange land and back into his sanctuary. He undid the carabiner clip connecting him to the wire, switched off the motorbike, and sat still.

On his hip, his bag twitched, and the talking rat climbed out, eyes wide with wonder. Instantly the creature buzzed and spiralled around his workshop, knocking over tins and upsetting his models. The Junkman snapped out of his fugue state, instantly irritated.

"That is a P-51 Mustang!" he shouted at the creature, who ignored the outburst. She climbed high up a bookshelf, and then she was sitting in the sunlight of an open hatch, drinking it in joyously. The rat was slightly transparent, and this made the Junkman queasy.

"Ah, it's starting to burn," the rat complained, withdrawing into the shadowy interior. "Too much of that and I'll burn away into nothing."

He'd been given a lot of information very quickly, which was bad enough. Mostly he was uncomfortable with how much this Bilben had shown him, the tiny creature ripping apart the curtain of his reality with her words. He'd thought he understood the physical universe, only to find that motors and mechanisms were a small part of it.

"So few of us come back," the rat-spirit crooned. "The Gravedigger more than most, and old Bauer did it once. And now I am walking in Life!"

The Junkman was reminded of double-exposures on movie film, the way she twitched in every direction, constantly calculating the best course of action. He could appreciate this, having been very cautious and indecisive for hundreds of years, in this world and another he'd all but forgotten.

She cleaned her whiskers in the sunlight, but then she paused in her glee, holding her hands over her belly.

"I can't stay here," she said mournfully. "It's not for me. In fact, you'd do well to find a way to close this door behind you, in case something truly awful follows us here."

Eyes wide, the Junkman fell upon his battery network, disconnected the golden hearts, and returned the white fog to an empty frame.

The severed end of the telegraph wire fell to the floor.

"No!" he cried. "It took me months to find a full reel of cable. A fortune!"

"It's still in there," Bilben said.

His vision swimming with panic, the Junkman opened the door again, and he reached in, feeling around on the ground in the fog. He patted around frantically, and then stopped.

"I smell meat in this one," Bilben said, worrying at a tin with her claws. "How do I open-"

"Please, be silent!" the Junkman said, and pushed his head through the frame, into the chill fog of that other world. There. He heard the distant *twang*, and a distinct sliding sound.

Miles of metal cable, pulled as taut as he could manage, and suddenly severed. It had probably been enough to pull the other end out of the ground, too, peg and all, the entire line bouncing around in the fog.

Lost.

"Stupid! Stupid!" he said, pulling himself out. "You! I should never have listened to you!"

The rat gave a kind of shrug, but also a shrewd look. She'd not been surprised by the severed cable.

"I am sorry your wire broke, but you cannot leave that way open. There are creatures in the Underfog, monsters you do not want to allow into your world."

There it was again. The Underfog. Spirits were real, the dead had their own world, and he had his own part to play.

He had a name, too, but it did not feel right on his tongue, and it stirred things in his blasted mind, brought out memories. A train ride. Brother. The Beatles.

Another Brother, with a broad, charming smile. He stood by, encouraging him to open a hole in a metal box, pull out a golden thread, destroy an entire world.

He sat up, suddenly struck with inspiration.

"It doesn't have to be a door."

He took apart the network of glowing glass hearts, and, straining, he simply shifted the metal frame out of the way, dragging it over decades worth of cables and detritus.

It took a full week to clean out the workshop and make it usable for his purpose. He brought in the warlord's car, covered in decades of dust and spiderweb, tyres deflated, and got to work.

"The House of Torana," Bilben breathed in horror, running her paws over the shiny red body.

"It's not a house. It's just a car."

He stripped out the entire motor and all the other components, pondering the empty engine bay before building a new design. Bilben hovered around helpfully, learning enough to be able to pass the Junkman the right tool most of the time.

The glowing glass hearts went into the car's own empty heart, nestled in a tangle of wires and other components, and then attached to the car itself. A difficult design, but the Junkman had chewed over the problem of the spires and their power for most of a normal lifetime.

It took him one afternoon to replicate what the entire Collegia of the Before had taken years to do. Packing the car full to the ceiling with supplies, the Junkman squeezed in behind the steering wheel.

Perched on top of the passenger seat headrest, Bilben looked forward through the windshield, all of her quivering instances held into this one possibility, this one decision.

"I have every confidence in you, Ray Leicester," she said. The name jangled him to the very soul, even as the rat looked at him innocently. It seemed she knew too many things, like names she had no business knowing.

"I'm the Junkman," he said, turning the key. Golden light spilled out from the sides of the engine bay, and out through the stylised shark gills in the flanks of the car.

He turned on the headlights and pushed the stick forward so that the high beams engaged. They shone on his workshop wall with more of the light, this time blindingly bright.

He shifted the car into gear, and then he paused. He reached over to the glove box, rummaged around, and found a cartridge.

"This is the highest music technology from the world of Before," he told Bilben. "This is called an eight track. It is like a record, but you can play it in your car."

"Eight whole tracks? What a wonder!" Bilben said.

The Junkman slotted the cartridge into a slot in the console, and as AC/DC's "Highway to Hell" played, he drove the muscle car into another dimension.

UNDERFOG

Shifting from spider shape back into a woman of wood, Jenny Rider left the ruined House and the battle between the Jesusmen and the Chain-Folk and ran through the fields of shimmering wheat.

The Farmer's land. She knew his lot had cast in with the Dawn King, drawn in by the endless promises. Jenny remembered similar promises from Papa Lucy and was equal parts sceptic and cynic. She had no friends in that place and knew that whatever she did there would be reported to the force burning through the wood. Overhaeven turncoats also swore for the Dawn King, down here at great expense and peril, all for one thing.

The jawbone she held in her hands.

It was a human jawbone, but it had heft to it, like it was made of iron, or maybe stone. It was odd to look at, and she ran her fingers across the mixture of teeth, an uneven line of horse molars, human teeth, and even the fangs of a dog or a large cat.

The jawbone looked like a key, and it moved around in her hand like a living thing. For one moment, she felt like it regarded her with menace, and ever so slowly it twisted in her grip, as if trying to saw through her palm.

Then, the moment that tooth touched woody flesh, the bone was cooperative, pliant. Trembled slightly in her grip. Perhaps it knew the Cruik she'd been crafted from and was afraid of her?

"Where did the Jesusman find you?" Jenny whispered to herself.

A snarl from the edge of the village, and Jenny saw what Bilben had warned her of. A huge she-wolf, stalking her through the huts and barns.

"I see you, Lupa!" Jenny cried out.

The wolf snarled, eyeing the jawbone in her hands.

"Back, wolf. You cannot have it."

"That does not belong to you," the she-wolf said. "Give it over, else I shall tear off that hand."

Jenny responded by placing the jawbone against her own jaw, holding it in place while she shifted, her wooden flesh moulding across it, her frame quickly expanding with pops and crackles. In moments a wooden horse looked up from the wheat, and as the wolf exploded forward in a fury, Jenny Rider took off in a turf-tearing gallop.

She was Buchephalus, her Seph, the Last True Horse, rendered in woodgrain down to the last sinew, and she was beautiful. Her father's horse, the one that she'd stolen and doomed to an awful death, but in this moment Seph ran again, glorious in every movement. The wolf was a swift predator, but the horse was faster by a whisker, and she led the canine on a frustrating chase around the village, out through fields of stubble, and onto the hardpacked clay where the farming had failed altogether.

Jenny Rider pierced the Underfog at full speed, strength unflagging, even as Lupa the she-wolf drew up short, panting, teats sore from all that jiggling.

Giving a mournful howl at Jenny's back, that suckler of ancient twins turned around, trotting slowly back to Farmer's village, where she had thoughts of nothing but returning to her schoolhouse and curling up behind her desk to sleep.

It took a long time for the golden host to push out of the Oerwoud, stretched out single-file across many miles. They pushed out through the tiny gap that the Joyous Hound had carved for them and formed up on the edge of the cracked clay.

"WHAT HAPPENED TO THE TELLER'S HOUSE?" one of the Princes cried out, pointing at the settling dust. "HE WAS TO GIVE US SAFE PASSAGE."

"EASE OUR WAY!" said the other.

"I know not!" said the Joyous Hound, sniffing at the wind. "Ask the Blackstar, they have eyes unpeered."

"THE BLACKSTAR IS ELSEWHERE."

"Figures. That layabout will give you nothing but songs and excuses. Here, come," and the Joyous Hound gestured towards a high-ranking Taursi, who took a moment to craft an exceptional spy-glass. It was still hot, and the Joyous Hound juggled it in his hands, blowing on it for a moment.

"WE WAIT LONG ENOUGH! REPORT!"

"Fine, as you say," the Hound said, looking over the devastation. He drew in a whistling breath.

"The House is fallen through into Ouroboros's nest. The moths are scattered. I see Chain-Folk running into the hills."

"HMM. THE CHAIN-LORD HAS BETRAYED US, BROTHER."

"INDEED, BROTHER."

"DO WE DIVIDE AND CONQUER?"

"NO. LET THE BLACKSTAR DEAL WITH THE CHAIN-LORD. WE HAVE OUR GREATER TASK."

"Give me the hunt!" the Joyous Hound begged. "I will tear out that traitor's throat in the Dawn King's name!"

"NO! YOU ARE NEEDED HERE!"

"KNOW YOUR PLACE, HOUND."

The Smothered Princes pulled on the Joyous Hound's ears as they berated him, slapping him across the snout and yanking on his fur. Whimpering, he got down on his belly and grovelled.

"ONWARD," the Princes said, driving their force toward the clay nest of Ouroboros. They left the Hound to lay where he was, the force parting around him respectfully.

Finally the Joyous Hound arose with the rear guard and sulked his way towards the great cause, dreaming of all the ways he would destroy first the Blackstar, and then the Smothered Princes.

He dreamt of placing the Master's jawbone directly into the Dawn King's hand, and being seated by his right side, even as the heavens were reordered, the faithless burnt, and the faithful rewarded. The Joyous Hound marched forward, tail wagging.

— 19 —

UNDERFOG

You *invited* the Smothered Princes here?" Lanyard said, eyes narrowed. The entire village was tense, and while they kept their distance for now, that they would strike was inevitable. They would circle, they would draw close, and they would swarm them as one.

Makes sense, Lanyard thought, looking at the wounded House of Torana. *We got rid of their biggest enemy. They're less scared now.*

"Of course," Farmer said. "The Dawn King promised an army from our old enemies. The Princes have forsworn the Lords of Overhaeven and come to set things right. We gave permission for them to enter our lands."

The minotaur was whispering to the slender bird-man, who was bent double and listening, one eye turned toward the living intruders. The cube glided across the clay, forming into a greasy pyramid. Scythes and pitchforks were seen bobbing in the crowd.

Before them all, Mina lay a hand on Lupa's head, her fangs as bared as the wolf's.

"Back," Lanyard said. "We will wipe you out."

"I think not," Mina said. "You are few. Sick and tired."

"Farmer, call this off," Lanyard said. "We leave, and you go back to running your fields."

"We cannot let you go," Farmer said. "You must either swear to serve the Dawn King, or we will do our best to delay you—or even harm you."

"We're not your bloody enemy."

Farmer shook his head sadly, and then raised a hand. The villagers began to encircle the living folks, eyeing them warily, daring each other to be the first to attack. Even with Bogle Hess and Stubs laying down a shot or two, they would be overrun quickly.

That left one option.

"Tilly, you drive."

"What?!"

Lanyard quickly sketched out the marks that formed the jagged palisade, and he threw these out to left and right, but couldn't summon up enough power to complete the barrier. Woozy from the effort of spellcasting, he raised his shotgun in time to take on Lupa, punching the she-wolf in the chest with a point-blank shot. That ancient saviour of twins fell with a whimper and floated off as an empty dog-shaped bag.

Lanyard was too slow to tag Mina, who knocked Stubs's gun aside, tearing out his throat with her teeth. Mem and Lyn fell upon the spirit, stabbing her rapidly with their own little knives.

The spirit knocked the prentices aside with contempt and went toward Bogle Hess, who threw panicked round after panicked round at that advancing horror.

"Stop wasting bloody ammo!" Lanyard yelled and turned around to see how Tilly was doing. She was fighting to open the driver's side door of the House of Torana, and the car was doing its best to close the door on her fingers.

"NO! I CANNOT! I ONLY SERVE GRETEL!" the car cried.

"She's dead! You serve us now! Ah, shitting shit!" Tilly cried, hopping backwards, wincing and sucking on her fingers as the door slammed shut on her grip. The car attempted another slow, hopping getaway.

Shaking his head clear from the magic drain, Lanyard looked back to where Mina advanced on Bogle. Before he could unleash the second shell in his shotgun, he felt a bump from behind him.

Farmer, coming in with arms spread, enveloped Lanyard in an embrace.

"Get off! No funny business!" Lanyard cried, turning around to face him. Then he struggled fiercer as Farmer's arms closed in with the strength of stone, of trees, of a million fields ploughed by these very hands. Hard won muscle, but there was something else to it, something primeval about the man's grip.

Soon he would break through Lanyard's struggling tension, pin his arms to his sides, and then simply crush him to death.

"Damnit, Farmer!" Lanyard yelled, and then rammed his shotgun forward, pulling the trigger. The ancient spirit staggered backwards, clutching at the spreading wound, the line of his worn face open with revelation.

"I remember!"

"Who cares?" Lanyard said, cracking the gun open to feed in fresh shells.

"I was the first," Farmer gasped. "My father called me Adamah."

"You bloody idiot," Lanyard said. "Should have let us go."

"I had to keep my promise," the spirit said. "I broke a promise once and brought on every evil. Souls, death, all of it."

"Shut up and die."

Then he was a film of a Twice-Dead spirit, broken and floating onto Shale, leaving behind a puddle of rich Aether that the land lapped at greedily.

Then Mina was upon Lanyard, howling with wordless anger, her spreading fangs reaching for his throat. Then she stopped, a line of blue spreading across her own neck. Mem and Lyn crawled over the vampire like monkeys, slicing and stabbing, silent except for the childish huffs of their exertions.

Mina fell apart, and then the children fell down in a tangle as her form broke down into a film beneath them.

Behind her, Tilly raked her lance along the side of the House of Torana. The car finally relented, huffing and opening all of its doors.

"In!" she screamed as Lanyard's magical fence began to fail. Bogle and the girls climbed into the backseat, and Lanyard parted the car's hair on his side, climbing into the front passenger seat.

Everything inside the House of Torana was car-shaped, but it was organic, moist and squishy. Lanyard felt like the seat beneath him was a tongue, or maybe a folded liver.

"Go, girl!" he said to Tilly, hearing the shouts of the angry villagers approaching. She pushed down on the accelerator pedal, and Lanyard saw this was a pad of cartilage that left slime on her boots. Gripping the steering wheel of vertebrae tightly, Tilly struggled with the gear stick, which looked like a large toe growing from the steering column.

"HURTS. WHEELS CUT," the car said. It was slow, even slower with all of the occupants weighing down on the flat tyres. Outside, someone was banging on the roof, and Bogle answered this with the crack of a rifle pushed through the curtain of hair.

"Car! What do you need to fix your wounds?" Lanyard called out, speaking into the ear that stood in for a wing-mirror.

"AETHER. BLOOD, EVEN. I WEAKEN."

"Is there a spigot in here? One that Gretel used?"

"YES," the car sulked. It pushed a bony spike out through the dashboard, which Lanyard slammed his hand against with no hesitation.

"Yes, drink deeply, you bloody mosquito," he said, and he felt the blood drain down his arm, trickling into some hidden reservoir. Then the car rose up, tyres reinflated, and when Tilly pushed down on the accelerator pedal, the House of Torana leapt forward, gibbering and chattering away from the doomed House of Adamah.

There was a cigarette lighter in here of sorts, a lump of bone that clicked out when it was red hot, and it worked enough to light a well-earnt cigarette that Lanyard passed around in the car.

"Enjoy it," he said. "That was my last bloody smoke."

The Blackstar received new instructions from the Smothered Princes, and he turned away from his course with some regret. Every waking moment since the Dawn King had revealed himself, the Blackstar had been imposing his will against Bilben, Queen of the Iron Nest, negating every new possibility that she dreamed into being to slow him down.

They'd been playing a grand game of chess against each other, both across the golden sea of Overhaeven, in the darkness of the Aum, and now here in the sepia fugue of the Underfog. Bilben was a worthy opponent and would be right until the moment he wrung her little neck.

The Blackstar was a grand old ghost, in his own words, one of the great intellects of Overhaeven, as well as a cultural force. A rockstar, who'd once stolen into the fleshly realms and become an actual rockstar, just for the stories.

To be turned from his task to hunt down a backsliding warlord felt insulting, to say the least. While the Smothered Princes were above him in the Overhaeven hierarchy, it wasn't by much. As he coasted across the Underfog, he turned his thoughts away from Bilben, mentally tipping over their chessboard in a fit of pique.

Already Bilben was darting about and changing things, but it couldn't be helped. He needed his wits about him, even when chasing down some rebellious spirits. It was dangerous, this place, and while he did not fear any feat of arms, he did not want to lose face by requesting a rescue.

I would drop by a fraction, and the Smothered Princes would rise, and even that damnable Joyous Hound would approach me. Unacceptable.

He knew Ouroboros well, having planted that great gullet beneath the dead lake himself. Not wishing to be eaten by his own monster, he spent a sliver of his own golden fortune to bring forth a throne of black jade, which he slouched across as it floated above the clay. Back in the train of the army, he'd ensorcelled a Taursi general who'd insulted him, binding the creature inside of a ring, and now he leant over the arm of his throne, releasing the spiky warrior to fall down onto the clay.

The Blackstar laughed drolly as Ouroboros seized the Taursi within its tentacles, drawing it beneath the earth to feast upon it.

Creatures like the Blackstar used other senses in the Overhaeven when existing in the abstract, and when he stepped out into a physical realm, the Blackstar always liked to augment his more limited senses. He drew an eye out of his pocket, all that was left of an old foe called the Argus. While killing him he'd lanced 99 of the Argus's eyes, allowing him only the one, and it was this one he raised to his own eye, allowing the optic nerve to wriggle around his eyeball and bind to the nerve there.

There. He saw them scurrying across the hills, Chain-Folk, spirits that enslaved and bled out the other Underfog spirits. While appreciating this philosophy, the Blackstar came in fast, screeching like a banshee from his flying throne.

He carved furrows in the hills with his voice, smashing in their hidey holes and tunnels. Even as the Chain-Folk retaliated with an enormous whip made of Aether, he dodged this lazily, firing golden rounds out of an elephant gun and whooping with every kill.

"Come out and die, Chain-Lord!" the Blackstar shouted, his voice a thunderclap across the flexing hills. "I ask for so little!"

A cavern unsealed, and out came an enormous beast, a bear-shape that wore a living skin, and it howled at the Blackstar. Behind this beast came the spirit of a dead man, enormous, flush with stolen Aether.

The Chain-Lord, one very minor part of the Dawn King's byzantine plan.

"Oh, goody," the Blackstar said, and landed his throne on the ground. Sweeping back his magnificent mane of red hair, he set aside all of his things, placed the Argus back in his pocket, and stepped toward his target empty-handed.

"What is this?" the Chain-Lord demanded. "We've served the Dawn King faithfully! He will hear of this!"

"I doubt it," the Blackstar said drolly. "See, we expected shelter and help at the House of the Accurate Count. We arrive to see it asunder and your people fleeing."

"Not our fault!" the Chain-Lord said, failing to hide a note of panic. "It was the bloody boy, that Jesusman and his crew! They did it!"

"I shall be honest. I am already bored, and I don't care," the Blackstar said, suddenly dashing forward. The bear-beast moved to protect its master, only to scream in pain as the elegant figure carved up its belly with suddenly sharp fingernails, dodging the return blows, and then raking its face open, down to bone.

"You've stuffed a bear into a camel suit!" the Blackstar laughed. "What next? A moon stuffed inside a skull? Such an odd choice!"

The Chain-King lashed at the Blackstar with his Aether-whip, only to find the lash parted by a sharp nail, the severed length wriggling like a cut worm and leaking into the ground.

In another heartbeat, the Blackstar had torn the camel body down the middle, wrenching out a blackening heart. When the skinless bear climbed out and tried to run, the Blackstar destroyed that, too, spilling gallons of Aether onto the ground with one telling blow.

"Come! Try to touch me with your little whip," the Blackstar teased, dancing about majestically. He then ran forward a step, startling the Chain-Lord, and the killer from Overhaeven laughed himself fit to burst.

That was when a rifle shot rang out across the landscape, punching into the Blackstar's shoulder. Another bullet struck him as the first wound was closing. This was a better shot, punching straight through his forehead, but all this did was stagger the Blackstar backward. He shook his head groggily as the wound closed.

"Ah! What an odd headache," he griped. Ignoring the ineffectual whip blows of the Chain-Lord, he reattached the eye of Argus, looking about.

"I spy you, snipers!" he said, calling up his own elephant gun. He dropped one of them with a thunderous golden *crack*, but his smile of satisfaction was short lived as ten other bullets struck his rifle in one instant, shattering it in a wave of radiant heat.

"What matter of army are you?" he called out. They were closing in around him, and while he sang one into atoms with his powerful voice, other shooters were up and out of hiding, running toward him with pistols and other guns blazing.

Real guns. Not imagined creations of clay and Aether. Weapons of cold iron, smuggled into the Underfog from the Prime Realms.

Every bullet was a bee-sting, easily healed but painful, distracting. The attackers repeated their trick, an odd type of magic that concentrated all gunfire on a single spot, and for one odd second the Blackstar felt his physical head simply shatter, which caused him to stagger around comically until it oozed back into place.

What is this gun sorcery? he thought, the moment he could think again. Few weapons across the cosmos had the ability to even give him pause, let alone cause him this much pain.

Then, a ringing blow to the back of the head, and the Blackstar was driven to his knees, gasping. He looked up to see a man wielding a shovel, a heavy looking thing that was equal parts iron and Aether, the digging blade covered with marks and engravings.

"I stole this from the Gravedigger," a spirit said, a human male who stared down at him, intense and mean. "I made some alterations."

The Blackstar opened his mouth to blast this man apart, but the spirit stepped aside and swung the shovel into the front of his face, breaking his nose and laying him flat on his back.

"Do that again and I'll cut your tongue out," he warned.

"Who are you?" the Blackstar managed, genuinely surprised, maybe even slightly fearful. "Just so I can erase your name from all of existence."

"I'm Bauer. I'm a Jesusman. We all are."

He was surrounded by Bauer's companions, all armed with real weapons. Some of them bore tattoos that read B+N, and three of these people were beating and hog-tying the Chain-Lord with a rope.

"A Man of Jesus," the Blackstar said, and instantly fell upon the image in his mind. A minor human godling, recently captured by the Smothered Princes. Previously tasked with keeping the human race under lock and key.

"Where is Jesus?"

"Never heard of her," said the Blackstar.

"Now see, that won't do," Bauer said, and whistled between his teeth. Instantly his people pounced on the Blackstar, rolling him face first into the clay, wrapping wrists, forearms, and legs in a thick, itchy rope.

The Blackstar flexed his considerable willpower to end the farce, deciding he would shatter the fibres of the rope, fly directly upward, and then sing this entire group of gunmen into dust.

"I think I'll kill you all now," the Blackstar said, but to his surprise his willpower did nothing. He was still bound and pressed against the ground.

"Let me know how that goes," Bauer said, and started digging a hole in that breathing clay.

"What have you done!" the Blackstar said. "Know this: if you harm me, the Dawn King will avenge me!"

"Your Dawn King doesn't give two shits about you," Bauer said, still digging. The Blackstar tried to blast around him with his sonic death, to scratch at the ropes with his claws, but he could effect no change whatsoever. The very fibre of the rope was heavily enchanted, and the Blackstar dimly recognised it as Allcatch, a highly illegal item in the Overhaeven. When bound with this, even a god was next to useless.

"You invite your destruction by owning this!" the Blackstar cried.

"So, this is where you tell me what I want to know. I have my own source, but I don't believe just any bastard. Always double-check things."

"Oh, well, in that case I shall tell you whatever you wish to know," the Blackstar said, feigning wide-eyed compliance. Bauer smacked him again with the shovel, bringing a trickle of blood from his nose.

"So, are you going to tell me where to find Jesus? Lanyard Everett? Jenny Rider? The jawbone?"

"I will tell you," the Blackstar said. "They are all hiding inside of my anus. No, they are inside yours. Feel free to investigate it."

Bauer lifted the shovel again, but after reading the Blackstar's face carefully he made his decision. He kicked the Blackstar into the hole, and without further ceremony, buried him alive.

BEFORE/UNDERFOG

Forced to bear its master's killers, the House of Torana blasted across the landscape, whimpering and moaning. It remembered back to when it had simply been "Gretel's car," a fast machine painted in a red so eye-catching that it stood out.

Which was bad for a serious career criminal like Gretel Sparks. At the first sign of her car, certain people would run from her, not wanting any more bones broken. At least once a week a cop would try to pull her over, but thankfully the illegally modified muscle car could outpace any squad car.

Later, Gretel had converted the old petrol guzzler into an Overhaeven-fuelled light show. She missed the guttural snarling of the old eight-cylinder motor, but there was much more power to be had from that bizarre energy source that only magicians and other eggheads understood.

Aurum, they called the stuff.

She wasn't a necromancer or even magically talented, but Gretel Sparks ended up shifting bodily into the Underfog all the same. More an unhappy accident than anything, Gretel had been outpacing the typical Friday night pursuit, and she was sliding through the streets, laughing, pedal to the floor.

Under the hood, the golden light hummed and spilled out, brighter and brighter the more she pushed the pedal into the floor.

Ahead was one of the street-corner power stations, and in that second it underwent a power surge, climbing in temperature. Gretel made a stupid mistake and left the road, colliding directly with the power station—and driving right through it. Instead of an explosion destroying an entire city block, she was driving through a weird type of fog.

"Am I dead?" she asked the car, which didn't talk yet. "Is this the afterlife?"

When she blasted out of the Edgemist and into the Underfog, Gretel found a strange new land, and that her bright red Torana still brought all the bad sorts of attention. Still, she made the best of things. She had a box full of eight-tracks, a trunk full of drugs and booze, and enough firepower to start a small war.

She fought that war, every step of the way. Everything wanted to either use her, scam her, or steal her flesh, and so she started lashing out at everything just to save time.

It was exhausting. She never slept, simply snorted more powder and kept on the move. She'd been a big girl in the Before, but she quickly wasted away, and was desperate for food and water when she learnt about the Half-Buried.

They were an order of spirits who'd found the best way to resist the temptation of the final shore of death, which called to all these Once-Dead spirits. Torsos buried from the waist-down, they were wise and often visited. They had all the answers that she needed, and under gunpoint they helped her to carry out the necessary spell.

Firstly, there was no going back, and she accepted this. She needed to die, and the Half-Buried showed her how to step aside from her flesh, in one painless instant.

"Well, that's a waste," she said, looking down on her body, laying slumped against the car. What started as a terrifying art project became a vehicle, and under the tutelage of the Half-Buried, Gretel joined the car and the body into a hideous amalgam, the metal frame buried underneath her stretched out flesh. This upgraded vehicle was something that could run on Aether, given that her tank of Aurum was running low.

Of course, the car had a brain, which was somewhere in the centre console, and Gretel finally had the daughter she'd never been able to have in life. Having learnt some of the politics of the Underfog, Gretel decided to put out her shingle straight away, and declared that she was her own House. She was the House of Torana, but in practice she was simply a more interesting bandit who rode around the deadlands in her own corpse.

The House of Torana held hundreds of years of memories in her simple mind, that mass of sticky gristle in the centre console. She remembered the way that Gretel had held her steering wheel, spoken to her, raised her as her own. She was orphaned now, this monster car, blinded and forced to carry those who had her mother's blue blood on their hands.

"HATE YOU!" the car yowled, fishtailing at random, jerking the steering wheel out of Tilly's grip to hit stones and other rough patches of ground. As she left Adamah's ruined fields in her wake, the House of Torana fought the grip of her driver, steering them over so slightly to a place Gretel had always avoided.

"WE GO TO THE FIELDS OF HAYAVEN!" the House screamed, and then it roared over the last hill, launching them all into a plain of mud, thick freezing muck that ran for miles. She chose to ignore Tilly's foot jamming down on the brake pedal, and the House of Torana span her wheels, churning and sliding through the mud.

Whooping and yelling, the House of Torana finally came to a stop, bogged in mud up and into the undercarriage. As far as cars went, this one was completely and utterly stuck.

Lanyard and the others climbed out of the car, cursing and sliding around in the mud themselves. The car laughed at them, rolling its one good eye around and wheezing with glee.

"Cars are nothing but fucking trouble," Lanyard grunted. Tilly made to spear the House through the other eye, but Lanyard shook his head.

"No, we still need this bloody thing," he said. "Come on, it's time I taught you how to unbog a car."

"Are you serious? Look at that mess! It's stuck. We're miles from the dry clay."

"It's only a few hundred yards. Stop your bloody whingeing and get to work, girl."

He walked around the front and carefully got down in the mud, level with the House of Torana's maddened eye.

"Car. You've pissed me off. Remember, you work for me now. I will break you as many times as it takes for the lesson to stick."

The Jesusman drove the butt-end of his shotgun into the car's mouth, snapping one of her teeth loose at the gum line. The House of Torana screamed and wiggled around in the mud, frothing and snapping.

"Do you want another?"

"HATE YOU! KILL YOU!"

Snap. Another tooth went.

"Boss, we-"

"Not now, Bogle. I'm talking to the car."

"We don't know how to get it out of the mud. It's pretty stuck."

"Do I have to do every bloody thing? We dig out the tyres and put fabric under them. Pants, shirt, whatever. A rope around the tow bar. We all pull. This useless piece of shit," and here he broke another tooth, "will go into reverse, *gently*, and it will keep doing that until we are out of the mud."

He raised the shotgun again, the butt plate slimy with the car's blue Aether.

"NO! STOP! PLEASE!"

"Boss! We don't have any rope!" Tilly said.

Peals of laughter nearby, innocent and joyous. They all stopped bickering and saw the twins playing in the mud, throwing it up in the air gleefully, and stomping around until Mem slid over onto her backside. More laughter, this time from everyone.

"Another lesson, girl," Lanyard said, calmly now. "Always use what's around. I can see a rope, can you?"

"Ah. Of course," Tilly said, and got to work all around the fleshy roof of the car, shaving through the long tangles of hair with the sharp edge of her lance. There was a lot of it, knotty and tangled by centuries of whipping about in the funk of the Underfog.

"PLEASE! GRETEL'S HAIR!"

"This is your fault," Lanyard said, plaiting the strands of hair into a useable rope. "Think on this next time you disobey your driver."

"SORRY. I'M SORRY."

They sat inside the car, weaving the hair for hours, finally emerging with a rough length of rope, enough to loop around the tow bar, a plate of sternum with a knob of bone protruding.

Then, they waded out into the muck, digging with their bare hands. When the tyres were revealed, Lanyard used the Mark of Desiccation to dry out as much mud as he could, and then they placed almost every stitch of clothing they had underneath the tyres.

"You, too, Bogle," Lanyard said. "Strip."

"Please," they said. "I'm very uncomfortable."

"Lanyard!" Tilly said, a rare use of his name in front of others. "We've got enough!"

"Fine," he said, and then the real work began. The car rocked back and forth in the mud, wheels flicking mud in all directions, while the five living humans heaved and pulled it back across the slaloming tracks, slipping over themselves every few moments.

It was a miserable, painstaking process. They might not have been dead, but by the time they got the House of Torana back onto dry land, they all wished they were.

"Kurgle," Collybrock warbled mournfully. The bird plodded along a scar in the landscape, marked by the passage of many feet.

Mal rode on her back, but this Mal was hard-eyed, a tousle-haired creature with a dark countenance. Some of the deeper wounds that Kirstl had given him were still seeping, but most of the minor ones were beginning to dry.

This Mal rode alone, but he was far from alone.

When Mal twitched Collybrock's reins this way and that, he was not the one issuing instructions. He was someplace in the back of his own skull, a passive observer, unable to act or even scream.

When the blood stopped satisfying her, and his flesh was merely frustrating, Kirstl had stepped into his body. For all her talk of freeing him from the prison of flesh, she'd gotten scared at the last minute. Instead of spilling his blood and freeing him, she'd moved in herself, a possession that was abrupt and almost complete.

She'd attempted to evict his spirit, but with his last scrap of strength he'd retreated inward, shoring himself up in his own mind. But hour by hour she worked at his defences, and there would come a time when he would be cast out of his own body, wandering the Underfog as a ghost. Watching himself ride away.

"Kurgle. Mal. Maaaal. Maaaaaaal."

"You stupid bird," he heard himself say. "Shut your bloody beak!"

"Mal," Collybrock said with a huff.

Locked in a mental battle with his sweetheart, Mal now knew her better than he ever had in their brief courtship. Their thoughts were laid bare to each other as they battled across his brain, and she was a constant stream of chatter, her dark mockery flickering across his own synapses. This invasion was more survival than evil, but death had twisted Kirstl away from the sweetly cynical girl he'd stolen kisses with.

Come out from there and face me! Kirstl said. *You don't deserve to have this body!*

He didn't respond. Didn't have control of his own tongue anymore, and could only mutter, a passing thought in his own mind. He'd learnt early on that it wasn't wise to respond in any way, as Kirstl was merely sounding him out, using his responses to hone in on whatever part of *himself* that he was hiding in.

Everything about this was animal instinct. Kirstl knowing how to possess a body of flesh, the two souls manoeuvring and stalking each other in the forest of a brain. The two prentice Jesusmen weren't high magicians, but this wasn't a science that you could learn, any more than a beast knew how to burrow, or hunt another beast.

Collybrock left that land of dead wheat farmers and their twisted village, plodding onwards, Kirstl's stolen hands steering them ever away from Lanyard's last known location.

"He can't save you," Kirstl said aloud with Mal's tongue. "He can't even save himself."

Mal did not respond, merely burrowed deeper. He stole around in the dark places of his own mind and did not know if he'd ever be able to drive Kirstl out of his body. She was desperately strong, and afraid. She'd always been fierce-willed, where Mal had been the compliant one, who trotted along behind her with puppy eyes.

Kirstl was always tougher than me, Mal thought. *It should have been me who died.*

Oh, how I agree! Kirstl replied, close to him now. He'd given away his position with his thoughts, and now she was closing in, ready to tear him loose.

He could have turned and fought her. This was his body, his brain, and perhaps he had some hidden advantage in here that he could seize in his favour.

But he was too scared, and so he went deeper, as deep as he could, until even Kirstl couldn't find him. He left her the upper halls of his mind to wander and wail in, while he sank down.

Hours passed. Mal still had the distant sense of what his waking body was doing. Kirstl used his hands to fetch out food and water from the saddlebags, and Collybrock ate sullenly, hunger overriding loyalty.

As the bird reached the muddy outskirts of Hayaven, Mal's body fell asleep in the saddle, a long habit that all bird-riders learnt, and they dreamed then, both Mal and Kirstl.

A memory, fuzzy around the edges but accurate enough. They were both there, both perceiving the dream as themselves but also as one. They walked the streets of Crosspoint, the First City, sent from the Lodge on some errand but stealing a moment for themselves.

The first of many stolen moments, where Mal had used Lanyard's trade scrip to buy Kirstl a bag of sweets. He earnt a cuffing for that, but had called it worthwhile for the kiss she'd given him.

Kirstl relived the feeling of the sticky sugar on her fingers and the giddy sensation as they walked together. He leaned into her shoulder. She reached up to place her sticky palms on his cheeks and drew him in for a lingering kiss...

Then they both remembered that other lingering kiss, the moment her Twice-Dead ghost had lapped greedily at his blood and tore at his flesh. Angry, hungry, desperate to not be destroyed utterly.

Mal and Kirstl sprang apart in the marketplace, fists raised, circling each other. As always, prentices weren't trusted with guns, and weren't allowed blades outside of the training grounds.

"You're hiding down here," Kirstl said dully. Then everything swayed around them, the buildings in the market tilting and then righting.

In the waking world, Collybrock had just stumbled across a muddy suckhole, and Mal's physical body lurched around in the saddle, almost falling out. He was close to waking, even as the two selves within his body warred.

Eyes wide, Mal made to rise out of the dream, to seize back his own body, but Kirstl saw this and came in hard with fists and feet and teeth. These blows didn't cause pain exactly, but he couldn't set his feet on that unseen stairway back into his waking mind, and so they were stuck in the dream, ducking and weaving through a dream market.

"It's just not fair!" Kirstl cried, lashing out. "I didn't get to fight those things."

"The Serene tricked us," Mal said.

"I just—I just died. For no damn reason."

Mal backed up slightly and held up his hands, palms facing her. He got down lower, reaching for something on the ground, and Kirstl tensed up, expecting a weapon, looking around for one of her own, something in the logic of this dream that she could use to win.

He got back up with the bag of sweets that Kirstl had dropped. Nodding at her warily, he walked over to the stone steps that led into a burnt ruin, all that remained of the old public library. He sat down there, as they'd done on a happier day.

Kirstl watched him as he ate first one sweet and then another. He relaxed and looked at the fuzzy-edged memory that was somehow a dream.

"What are you doing?" Kirstl shrieked. "Get up and fight me!"

"Don't want to," Mal said through a mouthful of sweets.

She stormed over in a rage, falling all over herself and him as she ran up the steps to slap at him, pull his hair, knock the sweets out of his hands. He did not even resist.

"Damn you!" Kirstl sobbed mid-punch, and she slumped to one side, now sitting next to Mal. They sat together for a long moment.

"The sweets taste real here," he said. "Or real enough."

"Do you feel that?" she said. "We're stuck in this place now."

"It's me. I'm keeping us here. Figured it out."

"You bastard. I won't go back out. I'll fight you every inch of the way."

"So, we've got a problem needs solving," Mal said, and in that instant, he had the shade of Lanyard about him, hard-won wisdom that he could apply to deadly problems upon command.

"You will need to find me another body," Kirstl said quietly. "Go back and kill one of the others, and do it secret. I'll take them over, and then we can be together again."

"But we're already together."

"What do you–oh."

"There's room enough for both of us in here," he said, tapping his head. "We take it in turns to move the body. And we can be together, *really* together, in this place. In our dreams."

"How do I know you won't trick me? As soon as I let go, you can push me out of this body."

"I won't trick you. Because I love you."

She wept then.

"I'm sorry. I'm so sorry for what I did to you. I was scared. I couldn't control it."

"I know."

"But I hurt you."

"It's okay."

"Will this really work?"

"I want to find out."

They kissed deeply, and then Mal woke up in the saddle, fully in control of his body. He'd been beaten and bled, mauled and terrified, but had won through all of it, found the one solution that Jesusmen always overlooked.

It was submission and love.

You really did it, he heard Kirstl whisper in his thoughts. *You said you were going to save me, and you did it.*

"I know," Mal said with a smile, turning Collybrock around. "I'll see you tonight."

— INTERLUDE —

Between the time that Lanyard destroyed Papa Lucy with his holy shotgun and the time that the Dawn King sent an army to burn Crosspoint, the Boneman awoke in his bed.

He didn't really sleep, not anymore, but he still enjoyed the feel of a soft mattress from the Before, clean cotton sheets, and a thick quilt. Sometimes he would drift away while staring at the ceiling, into memories of the Before, of people long dead now.

His bed was one of the few comforts he allowed himself, and apart from a writing desk, an overstuffed bookcase, and a small collection of curios, his palatial rooms were bare.

Everything else he did without, and he gave away his fortune to the city's poor. It was all penance for what his brother had done, what he himself had done in his brother's name, and still it would never be enough.

He was back in his old house in Crosspoint, now also home to the Boneguard, his personal bodyguards. Like it or not, he was still a living god to these people, and they liked ceremony. He sent his soldiers out to help the city watch and put them to work on civic projects, and otherwise ignored them as they attempted to protect an ancient magician who did not need the protection.

That day the Boneman had a meeting with the Jesusmen, and he looked forward to it. Lanyard and Tilly had their own interests, of course, but they were good people, perhaps friends even. Certainly they were allies when he needed them to be.

He stepped out of the front of his compound to find passers-by kneeling, bowing, all of the stuff he found intolerable. Lucy had loved all this kowtowing, but the Boneman just wanted to conduct his public service, his *penance*, and not be bothered or worshipped by people.

"My lord, my lord!" someone in the press shouted at him. It was a woman holding up a screaming baby with a painful looking rash down one side of its face.

"Back!" one of the Boneguard shouted, rifle raised to push the woman back into the crowd. Instantly the Boneman was there, freezing the overzealous guard in place with a brush of his fingers, and he slid past him to see the mother and baby.

"You should go to the clinic," he said kindly. "They will always see you."

"I couldn't afford it," the mother said shamefully. "They turned me away."

"The clinics are all free," he said coldly, and the woman blanched. "No, my dear, I'm not mad at you. Please, let me see the little one."

The baby fell into a bunch-faced howl at the sight of the skeletal face looming over him, but the Boneman was used to this. No number of lollipops and stickers would help with the younger ones. He brushed his bony fingertips across the infant's face, and the rash faded as he channelled the healing magic.

"There you go. No, no that's not necessary," he said as the woman tried to give him a snared lizard as payment. "Feed your family with that."

"Lord! My lord!" someone else cried, and the Boneman sighed. His medics were trying to make money on the sly. Once more, corrupt fingers were plucking away at everything he'd built to service and compensate his brother's victims.

By the time he'd healed everyone in the crowd with an ailment, he was over an hour late to his meeting. The Jesusmen at the steps to the lodge offered a sharp salute, and he nodded back. By long arrangement his own Boneguard waited outside, their hard-won concession a largely ceremonial and heavily armed "aide" who followed the magician inside.

In the Lodge, the Jesusmen were at their lessons. He saw children beating other children bloody, and then swapping places. He saw a man at a gun range, trying for accuracy while someone was whipping his back. He saw a room full of prentices studying their books, even as the teacher shot a pistol at random into the floor, trying to break their concentration.

All of it was necessary.

He was ushered into the inner sanctum, a place of bullet boxes and gun racks. Tilly sat behind the big desk, fingers stained with ink as she scratched through yet another ledger, its cousins on the shelf behind her.

"Hey, Sol," she said warmly, pushing aside the paperwork and coming around the desk. It was Lanyard's desk but in practice actually hers, a pretentious gift from the Leicesterites that they'd found in the bleedthroughs. She and Lanyard had already wrecked it with scratches and spilled drinks. On the front of the desk was a panel, carved with an eagle that clutched arrows and olive branches in either talon, and a tarnished plaque from the Before with only two words still visible upon it: RESOLUTE and UNITED.

She always embraced him tightly. He appreciated the friendly squeeze of pressure around his upper arms and ribcage, a simple pleasure he missed more than most things.

"I am sorry for being so late," he said.

"Lanyard's not even here yet," she said, dismissing this with a wave.

"Let's be honest, young Tilly, he has you running the Order, and he's wise to do so."

"Sure, if you call counting tins of food and boxes of bullets running anything. I'm a bloody quartermaster."

"Not how he tells it."

Tilly laughed.

"So, how is it going here? Really?"

"It's hard," Tilly admitted. "The world veil is still a mess, all across the Now."

"The attacks?"

"Increasing. We have teams of Jesusmen operating out of Quarterbrook and Mawson, and we can reinforce them from here, but–it's bad out there, Sol."

The Boneman had walked through the aftermaths of the massacres, outposts torn apart by predators from other worlds. Blood and flesh splattered everywhere, or worse, the survivors who didn't appear to have been touched, but who were never the same afterwards, falling into violence, trauma, and even catatonia.

Papa Lucy's attempts to breach Overhaeven and destroy the Now had greatly weakened the world veil. Where once the monsters from beyond had struggled to enter the Now, they were freely entering and hunting the settlers.

"Is there anything else your Order needs?" the Boneman said, and meant it.

"Stop it, Sol," Tilly said quietly. "Of course we need things, but so do others. We'll make do."

He'd poured a fortune into bringing the Order of the Jesusmen back into operation and funded most of their upkeep from his own pocket, even diverting the town taxes their way. Crosspoint was still nominally the capital city, and tributes were required by ancient agreement from the other towns. This, too, he dipped into to equip the Jesusmen.

The towns were getting restless and were holding back some of the agreed tribute from the Boneman. He could not blame them. Even fifteen years later, Papa Lucy's war against Overhaeven was still felt. The madman had depopulated entire regions and caused mass starvation when he took most of their supplies.

The Boneman still sent out relief caravans to the towns whenever he could, but they were never enough. The food, the medicine, even comforts were needed all across the Now, and he was perceived to be giving them to a favoured group.

Even when they saved lives or gave bullets to the dying when they were too late, the Jesusmen were still despised. Although their legal status was renewed, lone Jesusmen still vanished in lonely places.

They chatted for a long time, the skeletal magician and the scarred young woman with a heavy burden, and then Lanyard Everett appeared, stomping heavily through the halls with a cigarette clenched between his teeth.

"Bloody Yulio," he said. "He's off his game today. Bastard couldn't hit the straight side of a barn, let alone a bloody man on a rope."

He stuck his Bowie knife into the antique desk and sank into the chair next to Tilly's, sloshing a pour of rotgut booze into a dirty glass.

Lanyard and the girl even sat alike, and if the Boneman could have smiled he would have.

The old man liked to use stories from his own life as parables and lessons for the prentices, and even fully minted Jesusmen who needed refreshers. Sometimes they would hang a prentice, just for a few moments, and invite the senior Jesusmen to shoot rifles at the rope in an attempt to "save" the dangling child. Others would scream and clang pots and pans, or even slap the rifleman, and they were still expected to make the shot, without hesitation.

"I understand why you must terrify your recruits, but hanging them, Lanyard?" the Boneman said.

"They need to know what's out there for them," Lanyard grunted. "We've found more than one prentice strangled or stabbed, even here in Crosspoint."

"The prentices get a bag of sweets if they get themselves loose from the hang-rope," Tilly said. "I did it once. Broke my thumb, but I got my hands free and then I climbed up the rope to undo the slipknot."

"While Bogle Hess missed every single shot," Lanyard said.

"You certainly are a tough breed," the Boneman conceded. "Training them like they're Spartans."

"We have to. They have the toughest job in the world. If they're not tough enough, people will die."

An awkward pause, and they'd been having more lately. The Boneman shifted about in his chair, searching for the right words.

"I need to go away for a while."

"Going on a holiday?" Tilly quipped, with a nervous note that the Boneman noticed.

"No. I have some personal business."

"Don't you drop your bloody bundle," Lanyard said. "We're barely holding things together here."

The Boneman leaned forward, touching skeletal fingers to the edge of the desk. He regarded them both with his soft brown eyes, the only human thing left to him.

"I will be away for a while. I do not know how long."

The two Jesusmen regarded him with borderline insolence.

"The Moot and the Bailiff have their instructions from me, and now I give you yours. The Order will provide support to the town watches in Crosspoint, Quarterbrook, and Mawson. The crooked mobs have been cutting the telegraph wires, and I want you to catch them."

"We're not bloody lawmen," Lanyard thundered. "We've got one job, and we're doing it."

"I have repealed the laws, given you everything you needed to bring the Order back," the Boneman argued. "You can walk a beat when we need you to."

"Stop it," Tilly said. "I'm sick of the pissing contests between you two."

"I don't have the equipment to win that," the Boneman said. After a long moment, Lanyard burst out with laughter, that rarest of sounds, and the moment had passed.

"Sol, what's really going on?" Tilly asked.

"I wish I could tell you," he said sadly. "It might be nothing, or it might be everything."

"You inscrutable fuck," Lanyard said. "If you need us to, we will ride with you, guns blazing. Just talk plainly."

"Let me have my mysteries," the Boneman said. "This is my burden, and I've already asked you to carry so much."

"Yep," Tilly said with a laugh. "Inscrutable fuck."

The Boneman left several sealed envelopes on his desk, addressed to the Moot, the Bailiff, the Chief of the Boneguard, and a few other notables in Crosspoint. None of these people was anything approaching a friend, and this made him deeply sad.

Once, I had a family, he thought. *A wife, a brother, fierce friends.*

Lanyard and Tilly were friends, allies even, but they were fatalistic, already doomed in their own eyes. He missed that other kind of friend, the bright optimists from that old, soft world, who'd viewed this dusty exile as a problem a group of smart allies could simply solve.

Now, he was a bony relic that brought moments of wonder in a dour world. He thought of how many guards he needed to walk anywhere in the city, and the frustrating slowness of it all, the needs of everyone he felt responsible for. The Far-Doors felt too easy for an old soul bearing a penance, but he took one today, tearing a slice in the air of his bedroom and emerging with nothing but the clothes on his back.

He stepped through the other side of the Far-Door and onto the site of the Crossing, the fused stone that marked the first steps into the Now. He settled down on crossed legs and watched as the sun sank into the horizon.

Below him, Crosspoint shrugged into its night-time blanket of drunken laughter, casual murder, and cries of misery. Public places were lit with a fortune in Taursi starglass, but apart from the rare electrical glow from rich houses, Crosspoint was darkness and bolted doors.

No wonder some leave to roam, the Boneman thought. *Sure, there's possible danger outside, but there's definitely danger in here.*

As instructed, the Boneman waited for the dawn. He didn't have the eyelids to blink and was forced to endure the bright sliver of the sun cresting the horizon. He watched it intently, wanted the pain.

Waited for the voice.

The sun was almost fully risen before it talked to the Boneman, and he sagged with relief.

You have made the necessary arrangements? the voice said.

"I have," the Boneman said. "I have left my duties with others."

Good. Did you give the instructions to the Jesusmen?

"Yes. Was it necessary to insult them so?"

Don't question me, just do as I say.

"I'm sorry. Yes, I have done everything I had to."

Good. Now go to Cavecanem.

Mystified, the Boneman nodded. He took a shadow-road through the Greygulf, bending the exit point to take him where he wanted, and once more thinking of penance. They'd ruined the place with all their schemes and dimension hopping, and where it had been vital and wild, it was now a sterile wasteland, empty save for the monsters sneaking through it, stalking prey and being stalked in turn.

He emerged minutes later in the red hills of the Harkaways. Once more it was a thriving campsite, and the Boneman slipped past the ablutions block and the rows of tents and swags. A few early risers looked at him with shock and muttering, and while a few chose to bow, most simply held their mugs of tea and blinked at the sight.

The Boneman received further instructions.

He repeated the climb he'd once taken with a skeletal horse, up to the craggy heights of the tallest hill. Here was a rock formation that looked a little like a howling dog, with a deep cave in place of its throat.

Cavecanem. Or, in one of the dead languages of the Before, Cave Canem. *Beware of the Dog.*

The Boneman sighed, remembering Lucy's love of the pun. He walked past a large sign that stressed the cave was off limits to all but the Boneman himself. A large metal grate sealed off the mouth of the "dog," complete with a gate and a big padlock that someone had recently tried to hacksaw open, judging by the broken blade on the ground.

The Boneman was thankful. If the graverobber had broken through, there were more severe protective measures ahead, and he didn't want Lucy to put any more blood on his hands.

The padlock was a fake. He'd brought a team of Tinkermen up here to install this barrier, and the whole thing swung outwards on a hidden hinge. Steel tongues bit deep into the rock, and with a mystical pass of his hand they slid aside with a loud CHUNK.

Now go and fetch it.

"Please. This upsets me greatly."

You said you would obey. Is this obedience?

Head slumped, the Boneman stepped forward into the cave, quieting the various traps and enchantments that he'd placed there himself. These were as much for the occupant of this place as they were for robbers, the greatest and hopefully most unnecessary of precautions.

With a Witchlight bobbing over his head, he walked through the illusory walls and into the inner sanctum of Papa Lucy's original resting place. The Boneman had stripped out all of Lucy's hoarded wealth, using it to fund various civic or compassionate projects, until all that was left in the chamber was Lucy's sarcophagus.

The Boneman crept forward, mind reeling. He put his bony grip on the very edge of the sarcophagus, gathered his courage, and then looked down.

Within was the original mortal remains of Luciano Pappagallo, suspended in honey, body wreathed in coils of long hair. He'd been brought low by outlaw Jesusmen and dragged himself here, mortally wounded, patient enough to hope that the magic would repair his wounded body.

The magic had failed, and this body had died.

Last time the Boneman stood here, he'd been dragged into another world-ending scheme, and had fallen for all of it. He looked back down at his brother, sleeping peacefully in sweetness, and still he felt terrified.

He'd betrayed his brother. Sent him down to the Underfog. Followed him to the final shore of Shale to finish the job.

Do it, the voice in his head said. *Do it!*

Watching with horrid fascination, he plunged his hand deep into the honey, pushing aside the hair, reaching up towards Lucy's face. Pausing with revulsion and terror, the Boneman touched his brother's cheek, the merest brush of fingertip against preserved flesh.

Suddenly the body of Papa Lucy sat bolt-upright in the sarcophagus, head, torso, and arms flying free of the honey with a goopy slopping sound, and the Boneman backed away in terror, crying out, caught in a nightmare.

Do not run, the voice said. *Look.*

The corpse's head lolled to one side, and then gave one great convulsion, spewing out gallons of honey through gold-tinged lips. Then, the body of Papa Lucy sank back down into an endless amber slumber.

"Must have been a nervous reaction," the Boneman said to himself. "The dead brain finally firing off its last neurons."

If you say so.

It took him a very long minute before he worked up the courage to try again, but this time when he touched his brother's face the corpse did not so much as twitch. Whispering the spell, the Boneman reached through the skin of his check, through muscle and sinew, until he took hold of the jawbone of the world's greatest magician.

For anyone else, it would have been near impossible to tear out a human mandible from a freshly preserved corpse, but the Boneman spoke to the bone, easing the connections up around the ear on both sides, and the whole jaw slid out through a flap of skin, teeth and all. The bottom half of Papa Lucy's face flopped down like a deflated balloon, slowly sinking down until the loose skin rested across his throat.

The Boneman was left holding a perfect jawbone, complete with the gleaming teeth that had smiled his way in and out of trouble, over and over. Still perfect, hundreds of years later.

Now bend it, the voice said. *Flatten it all out.*

The Boneman did as instructed, pulling the curve of the jaw until it was one straight line, soothing the stressed calcium that wanted to shatter and insisting that no, it had never been curved around to form a chin, it had always been this way.

The voice in his mind continued to offer instruction. He followed it, working the bone like it was a white clay, making one end of the mandible into a handle and the other into a sharp point.

You brought them? They are exact to my specifications?

"Yes. Of course," the Boneman said, and pulled out a folded over handkerchief from his pocket. He unfolded it to find a nightmare of dog fangs, horse molars, and others he couldn't even recognise.

He got to work, there in the tomb, easing out Lucy's teeth, and he slid these extras into the jawbone, convincing it that these had always been here, that the owner of the jaw had sprouted that huge, crunching horse molar, the cat fangs, the bigger teeth from a dog or even a wolf. There was an order in which they needed to be arranged, and the different heights made the tooth side look like a jagged knife, or maybe the notched side of a key.

The jawbone felt heavy with the hum of potential, and the Boneman thought back to his Collegia days, to lessons around foci and the ways these could exponentially increase a magic. Jawbones had long held a fashionable place as a sorcerous charm, being the grinder of food, the mover of lips for speech, the foundation for a human face and the soul that animated it.

This jawbone had come from no less than the most brilliant magician of an age now gone. Whatever his new master wanted this magical focus for, it was going to blow the fucking roof off.

Yes. That is most satisfactory to the task. Now, take it up in my name, and proceed to the Underfog.

"I am sorry. I cannot do that."

WHAT? You dare? I demand your total obedience, in this and all things!

"I'm sorry. What I meant to say was that I am no longer permitted to enter the Underfog. My family made...made many enemies. Lucy nearly wrecked the place when he visited. My deal with the Houses and the Lords of the Underfog was for safe passage, and they agreed that I was not to return until my appointed time."

So break that agreement. This supersedes that.

"The moment I am seen, all of the Underfog will hunt me and destroy me. They would take this," and he waggled the jawbone, "and use it for themselves."

A moment of sullen silence, and the Boneman took it gratefully.

Very well. I shall change the plan, just for you. You will go to Overhaeven and join the freedom fighters there. When we are ready, I will send you a courier to bear the jawbone, and you will give this to them without hesitation.

"Of course," the Boneman said.

It would go easier if I could send one of my golden warriors down with the jawbone, but they cannot move it through the damned world veil!

The Boneman opened another shadow-road then, but this one led into the Greygulf and then upwards, into the golden seas of the Overhaeven.

"Is it really true?" the Boneman asked. "That she survived the destruction of the Cruik?"

I said so. Do not question my answers!

"I am sorry, but it is a hard concept to grasp. I was there, and I acted hastily. The final ocean destroyed her and the Cruik utterly."

You are a fool and you understand nothing. Shale is dangerous, yes, and nothing comes out of it unchanged, but some few do survive those black waters.

"Please speak plainly to me. Does the soul of Baertha Hann still exist? Can I bring my wife back?"

Yes.

The Boneman wept then, moisture running down his hard cheekbones and dripping all over his teeth.

"Thank you, Dawn King," the Boneman said. "Your House is glorious, and I have sworn to you."

He was betrayed in that place of gold and multidimensional concepts. Clever as he was, the Boneman was no match for those who schemed in more than one instance of themselves. He was undone, and the Dawn King did not appear to sanction or even observe this execution.

After all this time, and a life that was near legendary, Sol Pappagallo met his end in a factional coup, between two groups of Dawn King adherents. He was snuffed out much like a fly who entered the wrong house, confused and lost, swatted by something beyond its simple understanding.

All of the Dawn King's promises, unfulfilled.

Dirty liar. He USED me.

Much like that final moment at the Waking City, the Boneman had come to his senses. There he had finally struck down his brother, but in here his defiance was more measured. Rather than give the jawbone to the selected courier, a spirit named the Gravedigger, he'd insisted on a meeting regarding his estate, and then jammed the key into Lanyard Everett's mind.

The forces that murdered the Boneman left him in that bubble of dream, one of billions on the edge of the Golden Sea. These were nothing to make and a nuisance to unmake, and so they were a peculiar type of pollution in a realm beyond the physical.

His killers left his remains in that lingering nightmare, but forgot this one truth:

Bones knit.

A finger joint slowly rolled towards its neighbour and connected as if magnetised. Shattered ribs rose up like the arch of a bridge, jagged ends slowly fusing together. The skull slowly puffed out like a souffle, the cracked geography of his own tectonic plates slowly righting itself.

It took weeks for the bones to heal from the brutal beating, and here was a second truth: bones don't always knit perfectly. Every movement was difficult and lurching. Without flesh he rarely felt pain now, but the nerves that still remained in his bones were transmitting a constant signal to his brain, itself a creeping organ that regrew from a splatter of fatty gristle, sprouting optic nerves and finally budding out a new pair of eyes.

Awareness. Memory. The Boneman walked through the corridors of centuries, his soul having never left the mincemeat of synapses and cerebrospinal fluid. As in the bone cairn his brother had left him in, he was always aware, each thought dragging on, a mind operating at a geological pace.

Calcium is in stone, stone is in bone, I am bone and I'm alone, the Boneman mused, half-crazed in the silence. *I cooked twice in the flame, and I was never the same.*

Back in the Collegia, Sol Pappagallo had been part of the research team for the Methuselah treatment, manipulated into the position by his brother. There was the treatment available to the public, but he'd developed a new strain, one the ethics board refused to sign off on.

Badgered into self-experimenting by Lucy, Sol administered it safely. Lucy tested it by severing his brother's pinkie finger, and they watched in joy as it slowly grew back.

That was mere months before their exile and the destruction of all of Sol's notes, the confiscation of his equipment. Lucy never got his cure-all, but soon they all had bigger problems.

Worlds burn, I burn, never learn.

Finally the Boneman rose. He was back in his own head, looking around at the dream he'd been trapped in.

The Dawn King had used him and abandoned him, just like his brother did. He'd never intended to bring his wife back to him. The Boneman walked around the bubble of the physical space, the dream he'd used to pass the jawbone directly to Lanyard.

His captors had pulled the scenery from his memories, and it was Crosspoint true in every detail. He tried to open a shadow-road into the Greygulf and found the option impossible to reach. This space was as secure as any jail cell.

He explored every inch, looking for something they'd overlooked. Perhaps a mile or two away from the town walls the physical space ended abruptly, everything beyond that the merest of brush-strokes and unformed.

So they ripped this place out of my head, holus-bolus, the Boneman pondered. *Dropped it here as a convincing dream-space to do the handover of the jawbone.*

If there's anything I've learnt about Overhaevians, it is that they are as lazy as they are proud.

The search was painful and long, his twisted body hitching with every step, but it was there, at the facsimile of the Crossing. The scar was a weak point in the world veil, and so he'd subconsciously conceived of it being the same here too.

It was a herculean effort, days of staring clench-jawed at one spot, but the Boneman finally forced it open, a gap barely big enough to crawl and slide through, a birth canal that dropped him out of the sphere and into the Golden Sea. There, he changed into his preferred symbol, a cheerful Día de los Muertos skull.

All around him was chaos, a civil war raging. The golden waters were aflame, in places coated with oil slicks, unrefined Aether, even bubbles of Nothing that raged and sizzled at everything that fell into them. Creatures of unimaginable power warred in ways that were hard to perceive, the losers mere husks floating in the light, and through these the Boneman moved and swam, making for one of the public transport nodes that Jesus had shown him on a previous visit.

He visualised the movement, his candied skull racing through the thick gold, but he'd been spotted. Waves of Dawn King cultists gave chase, already focusing their weapons on him.

John Leicester and Jesus had briefed him on what to expect here, and some means of self-defence in this antagonistic and alien environment. He changed his sigil to a fish, doubled-back and ate one of the pursuers, a sharp feather that scratched at his insides even as he destroyed it, consumed it.

Another enemy tore at his flanks just by deciding that he should suffer such a wound. The Boneman reiterated the thought that no, he should not be harmed in any way, and the enemies counteracted that, and so the back and forth went in a nest of contrary assertions.

He ended up wounded, and badly. He just wasn't strong enough to fight these ancient celestial beings, not en masse.

Even as he was struck again, he impressed the thought upon each of his pursuers that they were now all candied Day of the Dead skulls, and they promptly tore each other apart.

The scale of the civil war was mind boggling, with billions of combatants fighting, each one a being more powerful than the greatest of the Collegia. He was harrowed across multiple dimensions, and even jerked around in time itself, sent forward and backward.

Then he saw them come out like a burning hammer, an entire wave of beings formed into cheery-faced sun icons, burning through their enemies, setting the very Golden Sea on fire in their wake. A crack force sworn to the Dawn King, finally laying claim to Overhaeven, and everything else scattered or was destroyed.

Go! the Boneman thought to himself, pushing through a cluster of abandoned dreamspaces that crackled and popped as the flames washed over them. As he left the cover to flee to the transport node, the Boneman saw another sigil there, a large-eared rat.

It struck him, but it was more of a gentle brush than an injury. This touch set him to humming, just for a moment, and then all was well. Their sigils circled, rat and skull, and then the rat fled from the advancing suns without a further move. The Boneman fled, too, disturbed for a moment by this odd encounter, but more shaken at the scale of the destruction.

He finally fell out of the Sea and into a public transport node, a black void with a sense of "floor" and "up," and he immediately fell back into his set physical form.

He raised a hand to open a shadow-road and blinked. *Blinked.* He felt the thin skin of an eyelid closing down across sclera, cornea, and lens, and then open again. Moisture washed across eyes that had stared unblinking for far too long.

The outstretched hand was not a skeletal tree of digits, but it had flesh, pink and new, and fingernails that already needed trimming. He looked down to see his body restored to him, skin and muscles, and he even felt hair on his head, thick and full. He felt across his stomach and heard the rumble of a hungry belly, felt for a pulse and found one.

Calling up the shadow-road, he ran forward, immediately regretting the action. The muscles were still new, barely adhered to bone, and the bones had knitted wrong from his recent obliteration. Every movement was a hitching agony, and even with his body restored, he wondered if he would ever be right, if he could repair this deeper damage.

How has this happened? he thought. Somehow, that frantic swim through the Golden Sea had given him back everything that had been taken from him by Turtwurdigan, but he'd swum through the Golden Sea before, a nervous visitor guarded and escorted to meetings.

Was it the rat?

Sol Pappagallo was hungry and naked, and undeniably alive. For the first time in hundreds of years, he wasn't even cold.

PART THREE

CHESS IN A GOLDEN SEA

— 21 —

UNDERFOG

Collybrock plodded along, warbling pitifully. Sometimes the grip on the reins felt different, the commands either stilted or confident, but it was still the boy on her back, and his wounds were healing, as were hers.

The bird was at ease now that the war inside her master was resolved, but she was thirsty, barely able to break into a trot when threats appeared. Mal had given the last dribble from his water canteen to the bird this morning, despite the ache in his own throat.

We have to go back, Kirstl said inside Mal's mind. *Find Lanyard and his camp.*

"I'm lost," Mal said. "Can't find my way around this place."

Don't you know tracking? Lanyard must have taught you something out there.

"If there was a sun. Tracks to follow. Look there."

Kirstl looked through the same eyes that Mal did, toward the wake of their travel. They were skirting the very edge of the mud fields, looking for a landmark, anything to point them in the right direction. Behind them, the bouncing pattern of Collybrock's big-toed tracks in the damp clay, and moments later the Underfog itself erased them.

It's like the writing thing, Kirstl said. *Things just get wiped away down here.*

Before coming to their strange new arrangement, Mal and Kirstl had fought and wandered for days, and neither was sure where they'd ended up. Mal wanted to strike out away from the mud plane, while Kirstl suggested skirting it, looking for something pointing back towards the wheat fields and the village.

Like any couple forced to share a space during a fraught journey, they argued, wallowed in sullen silences, and endlessly weighed their options.

"I can bleed Collybrock for sustenance."

What? No!

"It's an old bird-rider's trick. I don't want to, but it will keep us alive."

Doesn't change the fact that your bird needs water.

"Lanyard will find me," Mal said again. "He won't stop till he does."

He's probably dead already.

Collybrock warbled, her eyes half shut, tired legs churning along the edge of the muddy expanse, the tracks perhaps too close to being a written letter or a sign and thus ruthlessly erased. Drowsy and thirsty, Mal nodded off in the saddle—and that is how they missed the strange sight of a living car in the distance, bogged in the mud, a handful of figures struggling to free it.

Lanyard Everett was within a mile of his lost prentice, but he was so focused on fighting through mud and hauling on the ropes that not once did he look behind him, not till long after both bird and boy were gone.

"Maaal! Kurgle!"

Collybrock gave a low warning rumble, and this stirred Mal from his sleep, from a lovely dream-space that Kirstl had spent the day preparing by way of apology. Mal did not want to leave the dream of the sumptuous feast in a palace, and he allowed Kirstl to step back in control of their shared body.

She woke with a start to see that they'd veered away from the muddy plains, now a distant brown smudge right on the horizon.

They'd been drowsing for hours. Ahead, the ground rose into a series of sharp peaks, the clay pinched and baked into an unclimbable fence that stretched for miles. The sky was fading into the bruised purple of night, and soon the range was a jagged silhouette.

"Okay, so we're not going that way."

Look there, Mal said from the depths of their shared mind. There were bright flashes of blue running along the base of the range, points that flared and vanished almost instantly. One would flash and be answered a moment later by its fellows, a susurrating pattern washing outwards. Other times they flashed chaotically, as if in a disagreement.

"Do we go there?" Kirstl said.

Absolutely, Mal said. *Look how Collybrock has perked her head back. She's scented water.*

"Can we drink it?"

Dead if we don't. Might as well try.

Kirstl dug in their heels, and the bird trotted forward with renewed energy, warbling.

"Drink. Drink!" Collybrock said.

The blue lights darted about, either in play or in hunting, and Mal and Kirstl were in agreement–they were just too tired now to care. Soon the range was looming above them, crags and sheer faces tinged with the weak purple of the Underfog night.

They were noticed. Collybrock gave off a warning cry as the lights rushed towards them. She looked back to her rider for commands, and Kirstl hesitated.

Here, let me forward, Mal said. *I'm better at this part.*

"Gladly," she said, and retreated back into their brain, letting the boy forward. He shrugged into his own muscles as if climbing into a suit, clicked his tongue, and tapped Collybrock's neck with a staccato of fingers. This meant *stop, make ready, lash out with your claws if I say so.*

They'd lost every weapon but the one that they sat on. Collybrock still had the downy feathers of a youngster in places, but she was savage when ordered, having torn apart the sacks of offal they trained the birds on.

The ground this close to the range was loose stone, and the spirits of small creatures emerged from their hiding places as the other creatures approached. The hidden beasts gave the bird a wide berth, and Mal caught flashes of creatures that might have been lizards or bugs, and stranger beings with shells and scuttling legs and eyes that whipped around on stalks.

They all shared one thing in common: they were prey, and they knew it. Which made the other creatures predators.

Blue lights rushed in from all directions, and then Mal whistled. Collybrock hunched down low, one leg stretched forward, ready to scratch the first creature to close in.

It's too dark! Call forth a light!

He summoned the appropriate mark, but formed it wrong, and it fell into a faint orange ember and then nothing. The unseen creatures paused at this, but at the failure they crept in closer. Collybrock quivered with anticipation.

Stop mucking around and cast the spell! Kirstl called. She'd been a bit better at working marks than Mal, but not by much, and he couldn't waste the precious moments needed to swap her back into control of their one body.

Mal had always struggled in the magical classes back at the Lodge, and it was only when he'd been out on his own with Lanyard that he'd finally found his way, gently coached toward his potential. He remembered those gentle campfires where Lanyard watched him sadly, some other memory in his head, while he taught him what he needed to do his job.

"I won't always be around," he'd chided Mal once, showing him again how to call up a light. Mal did not believe the rough words or understand the love behind them. *"When I'm not here, who will bloody show you how to do this? Get it right!"*

In this dark moment Mal found a calmness, and he formed a perfect mark, shaping a Witchlight above his palm, and it was so bright that it illuminated the entire plain, washing across the side of the range. He could clearly see the large force of hunters moving in, now terrified and reeling from magic he'd commanded.

They were an odd array of creatures that looked like smoky crystals moving on cilia, each beast about the size of a large dog. Some were diamond shaped, others pyramids, some spheres formed of pentagons or triangles.

Collybrock started toward the nearest one, beak open and hissing, and it withdrew the cilia inside the crystal, moving away in a bouncing, rolling motion, clacking against its neighbours.

All of them kept their distance as Mal swept the Witchlight to left and right. The creatures clattered left and right, but they did not flee, still greatly interested in the living creatures that visited their odd landscape.

"We don't want trouble," Mal said. "We're just looking for water."

One of the creatures came slowly forward, teased on by the cilia of its brethren. It stood still well out of reach of Collybrock's beak, and then drew up as tall as it could on the wriggling vines of various limbs. Its sides were diamond shapes, and as it turned one to face Mal, a word flashed across it in the bright blue of Aether.

Alive?

Almost instantly, the word vanished as the Underfog imposed its rule.

"Yes, alive," Mal said. "We're alive, and we're lost and thirsty. Please, show us where the water is."

Dawn King?

The words sank into the smoke. After a long moment, Mal shook his head. Who knew if these rock people were friendly with the one they hunted?

"No, we are not with the Dawn King. Look, what are you exactly?"

Many-Faced, it replied, and this was true enough, each one a gem that flashed triangular, square-edges, diamond shapes, tumbling and crashing with its neighbours.

More rapid blue flashing, as the creatures "spoke" with each other. Finally their spokesperson turned back to them and flashed up one final phrase:

B+N?

Before and Now. The catchcry and symbol of the Jesusman order. Mal nodded vigorously, and lifted up his short shirtsleeve to reveal his own prentice tattoo, the B+N set within a simple circle.

B+N! the creature displayed, the same instruction washing out through the crowd in a wave of words.

Come!

Yes, come!

They immediately started rolling and bouncing away toward the range, clearing a path for Mal to follow on his bird. The sound of the creatures on the move was deafening, as they crashed together like a herd of violent rocks.

The creatures began to funnel through an unseen pass, a hairline crack in the impenetrable face of the range. Excited words bounced back and forth as the herd poured through this and then out of sight.

"Where are you taking us?" Mal asked their speaker, who waited near Collybrock, still mindful of the claws.

Bauer! B+N!

Mal's heart leapt. He'd heard many stories of this man from Lanyard, the steady trigger finger that severed his noose, one of the few lone paladins who'd kept the evil things at bay during the dark years. The old man who'd taught the old man everything he knew. The one who'd climbed back from death to finish this education when Papa Lucy nearly destroyed the Now.

"Oh yes. We are absolutely going with you."

It happened very suddenly. One moment the narrow ravine was echoing with the clatter of dozens of Many-Faced bodies, with Collybrock squawking and swearing whenever one was underfoot, and then everything was silence, complete and overwhelming.

Mal tried to ask their host what was going on, and while his lungs flexed and pushed air through his voice box and out past tongue and lips, no sound emerged at all. In a panic, he leant down from the saddle, daring to touch the rock-beast to get its attention.

Bor Shaon, it displayed back, flicking cilia around to indicate everything. *No noise. Quiet place.*

Collybrock darted her head around and looked to her rider, unnerved by the mysterious silence. Mal felt around his ears, clicking his fingers near his eardrums. Nothing.

There was a faint glow in the ravine ahead, and they rounded a sharp bend to find a bright light fixed to the stone of the wall itself, a mote of sunshine that pushed back the gloom. When Mal's eyes adjusted, he looked in surprise to see the Mark of Light, a four-foot-high sigil carved deep into the rock. A Jesusman sign, firm and fixed, unable to be erased by the record-killing Underfog. Beneath this was a deep cistern, filled to the brim with fresh water, and both boy and bird fell over themselves to quench their thirsts.

It tastes real, Kirstl said in his mind. *Not poisonous. Why has Lanyard's old bossman put a cistern of water in here?*

Mal forced himself to stop. Thirsty idiots were known to hurt themselves by over-drinking when the water finally came. He tried to whistle at Collybrock with no effect and ended up having to push Collybrock away from the trough, her beak splashing around in complete silence. He felt the vibrations of her disappointed grumbling up and down her neck, her beak parted wide to utter some swear word at him, but no sound came out.

There was a gunrack next to the cistern, and it was real metal, firm to the touch. No clay, no Aether, just iron. A padlock had been opened, the hasp thrown wide, and all the firearms removed.

What the hell kind of operation is Bauer running? Kirstl asked.

He came back up to the Now once, Lanyard told me. Maybe he's been up there a few times. Brought back some things.

But water? What does a ghost want with water?

They don't need it, but living visitors do.

Squinting over the sparking flashes of the chattering Many-Faced, Mal could see another weak glow, further down the ravine. The Jesusman had planted more lights along the way.

The brush of a blue tentacle against his leg, and Mal looked down to see his Many-Faced friend rolling and bouncing with excitement.

Long walk! Great reward!

Mal tried to make himself understood but couldn't pass on anything to the polyhedron. All he could do was ride on in that great flashing company of rocks, passing more of the strange waystations left by the ghost of a Jesusman. Crates filled with hard tack and Before tins of baked beans and jellied meat, on which Mal and Collybrock gorged themselves. Medical supplies. Clothes and blankets. Bundles of firewood, kindling and matches. Fuel canisters. And always water, great cisterns of the stuff, and bottles and skins to carry it in.

The ravine went on and on, until Collybrock refused to walk another step. Even as the Many-Faced begged them to travel on, Mal indicated with gestures that they needed rest, and they slept by a fire that crackled silently, surrounded by the restless shifting of their alien guides.

He walked with Kirstl in his dreams that night, arm in arm through a grand house she'd spent the day building in the depths of his mind.

"We could marry in here," she said, on a flower strewn terrace filled with faceless guests, a minister waiting by an arch. "Be together forever."

"We already are," he said, but they tried their hand at a dozen different weddings, and honeymoons equally as languid as they were confused.

Mal woke to the pale mahogany of the Underfog dawn and loaded up Collybrock with as much gear as she could bear, trying to hang the bundled waterskins with equal weight on each side. In the end he dismounted and walked alongside her, trudging for hours until the ravine suddenly opened up.

The Pits! his host flashed on one of its faces.

Bor Shaon! Guests and tales!

A cratered landscape as far as he could see. Here were many stones slowly crawling around through the dust, edges unformed, their flanks only able to flash stutters of blue. The larvae of the Many-Faced, and the adults returned with prey caught out in the ranges, peeling aside panels to pour in half-digested meat.

The horde of Many-Faced peeled apart then, reorganising themselves into smaller family units, rolling into protective cairns that piled above the young.

Mal watched as two families formed an alliance and rolled towards another family, circling and finally pouncing on it, cracking apart the adults and finally the juvenile, which they ate.

His guide still rolled patiently alongside him, and when Mal tapped on his upper panel, the creature waved a handful of tentacles in excitement.

Great battle! Justice!

Mal shook his head.

Bauer permits. Culture/Law.

The Many-Faced paused only for a few hours, and then the juveniles were allowed to wander their creche-lands in peace, the adults reforming into the larger pack. Some of the victors paused briefly to lay a clutch of new eggs, which they abandoned on the ground, racing to catch up to the others.

The Before had a moon, a little larger than the weak rock that tumbled around the Now, and the great magicians of that dead world had walked around on its surface, planting flags and floating lightly upon it. Mal had marvelled over the photos of this in an old book in the Lodge, and Bor Shaon looked just like this place. Rocks. White dust. Craters, deep enough to swallow Crosspoint.

He followed his merrily bouncing guides as they crossed this barren surface. Looking down over the lip of one crater, Mal wondered if he would even survive such a grinding, bouncing fall.

A disagreement flared amongst the Many-Faced, and then they reached a consensus, switching directions and leading Mal up a small hillock, topped with a flat stone. As they approached, Mal felt a small tickle run up his spine, and then he saw it.

A ring of Jesusmarks around the base of the hill, but then there was more. Overhaeven sigils. Other squiggles like the stomping of some alien bird. Mal urged Collybrock to step over that line, and then it happened.

The sound of her foot crunching into the dust and stone. The huff of her breath, and then an excited caw as she realised that she could hear once more.

"What is this?" Mal said aloud, voice dry from days of unuse.

Bauer's rock! the guide said.

"What happens now?"

Wait. He comes.

Mal spent two nights on top of the tor, and despite his initial misgivings he slept on the flat rock. Beneath him the Many-Faced played at some kind of sport, a complicated checkers game with themselves as the pieces, and he could not comprehend their rules.

"Heavy!" Collybrock scolded, still looking at the pile of gear on the ground. She rolled around in the white dust, fluffing it into her feathers, and she spent some time darting back out into the silent plain, playing with the Many-Faced who'd been eliminated from the game.

Then he saw them. A great host, hundreds strong, kicking up a plume of dust that he could see for miles. Mal did not bother to hide and stood atop the rock, waiting.

Who are they? Kirstl asked.

"Stuffed if I know," was all he said.

If it's not Bauer, we're dead.

"If it is, we might still be," Mal said. "We don't know if he's friendly...or if this place has turned him."

The advancing force was close enough now for Mal to see motorbikes, other riding birds, and an overloaded buggy running it hell-for-leather towards them. They were Once-Dead spirits, driving real machines, riding on flesh and blood birds. He'd seen this calm bravado in the field before, the menace that hid behind cigarettes and gallows wit. Mal knew them as the spirits of Jesusmen, and this was confirmed as they pulled up to the hill and set bikes on kickstands, ran a line to tie up the birds, and hustled into the ring of sound with armloads of gear.

"At last! Fella can go loopy out in that!" one joked.

"You bloody talk too much anyway."

"Boil the kettle will you?"

For now they acknowledged him with winks but nothing else. Mal saw prominent marks tattooed onto skin, and the older spirits wore Jesus tattoos on their faces and necks, showing they'd lived long before Papa Lucy's pogrom.

They hustled a prisoner up into the camp. Mal recognised it as one of the Chain-Folk who'd pursued them to the Oerwoud, but this figure seemed important, vibrating with menace, and wrapped with a rope that seemed to wriggle and constantly adjust, tightening wherever needed.

Next came the driver of the buggy, the spirit of a rangy old man, wearing a stolen Leicesterite hat with a heavy gun on each hip. He walked up to the stone and rapped it with a knuckle, looking up at the boy.

"You're Lanyard's lad, aren't you?" he said.

Mal nodded.

"Don't suppose you know where my bloody prentice fetched up, do you? Lanyard is many things, but he's never on fucking time. Or where he's meant to be."

"We got separated," Mal said. "He was back there in the big forest, past the wheat fields."

"Well, lucky you took the right turn, sunshine," Bauer said. "Folks who go the other way hit the House of Avadon, and those beak-faced bastards will shoot you first, and then nick your bird."

Mal had many questions, but he was struck mute by the larger-than-life presence of Bauer. He took in the stacks of rifles, some of them futuristic weapons that hummed with Aurum, and flesh and blood birds that even now were ripping into bags of fodder.

"How did you get all this stuff down here?" he finally asked.

"Dug some holes," Bauer said, indicating the enormous shovel strapped to his back. "Climbed through. Killed any witnesses."

Mal nodded nervously.

"Mal!" a familiar voice said, and he found himself in a tangle of strong arms and a bristly moustache as Yulio gripped him tightly.

"Yulio, you're dead," Mal said.

"Too right. I died bringing down a great big bloody tower. My ghost was about to get eaten by a beastie until Bauer's folks came into the tunnels to pull me out."

The big rifleman smiled at Mal, now holding him at arm's length.

"You've seen some hard times out here, lad. You know that the old man was worried sick about you."

"I had to go after my girl."

YOUR WIFE! Kirstl scolded.

"Fair enough. Salty old bastard wouldn't know love if it punched him in the bad eye."

"Prentice," Bauer said formally to Mal. "Round up that bird of yours and make your camp tidy. Then you can get to work bringing over the ammo."

"But–but Lanyard is my master," Mal protested.

"And I'm his, so now you do as I say."

Shaking his head, Mal went down to do as instructed. By the time he'd tied up an excited Collybrock with his neighbours and came back up the hill with a box of bullets, Bauer had shifted a machine gun from his buggy onto the flat rock that had been Mal's bed. The ghost of a long-dead prentice was running around the fortification, using a can of spray paint to daub enormous marks on the wall.

As Mal placed the box of bullets on the stack, he looked up to see a blur of grey and brown emerge from Bauer's shirt. It spiralled around the shovel and finally settled on the tool's blade, twitching and speaking down at the old Jesusman.

"It's fucking Bilben," Mal said, and then suddenly he lost control of his own body as Kirstl surged forward, seizing command with great fury.

Once more they relived the memory of The Serene's escape attempt, the secret bargain made by this rat beast to take the Jesusmen's big lizard in exchange for assistance—and then the moment the deal was changed.

The heart-breaking moment where Kirstl had been seized, dissected, stitched into an escape tunnel.

With nothing more than hands bunched into fists, Kirstl sent Mal charging up the hill toward the Jesusman and the large-eared rat spirit, unleashing a low bellow of anger, the need for revenge.

"Mal?" the rat twittered, even as the boy fell upon her, snatching at her with his face twisted in an angry sneer, pushing around the amused Bauer to try to snatch the rat.

"Don't you harm my bloody adviser," Bauer said, laughing as Bilben easily dodged every clumsy attempt to snatch her.

— 22 —

UNDERFOG/OVERHAEVEN

At the same time she dodged Mal's snatching hands, Bilben was also watching Lanyard haul the House of Torana from the mud of Hayaven. She watched from her hiding spot as the group beat the car into submission, climbed in, and drove in the opposite direction from the one Mal and Kirstl had taken.

This, she had not predicted.

"The House of Avadon it is, then," she said mournfully.

Concurrently, Bilben was a sigil in the Golden Sea, and she watched as the candied skull of the Boneman entered a public transport node.

As he left the theoretical and the metaphysical, he took on his physical form, but this time he wore flesh and skin, hair and organs, his body a machine of blood and oxygen.

She absorbed the Methuselah treatment she'd stolen from him in passing, and slowly fed some into the thing that she carried, which throbbed in pain and pleasure.

More? it said. She ignored the request.

The blazing suns that represented the Dawn King loyalists roared past her, hunting for any heretics. They passed by Bilben, saw her, and did not harm her.

In yet another place at that same moment, Bilben crept around the edges of the Oerwoud, stealing through the invaders from Overhaeven, shifting and twisting around the crowd of hooves and feet, until she found the Gravedigger's cohort.

He had a peculiar sorcery and was able to tunnel back into the lands of life with his shovels and picks, emerging from both grave and greypot, either returning spirits who'd paid him well or stealing things that the dead needed.

He was most useful.

Also, the Gravedigger knew too much.

The obese spirit sweated with the Aether gained by a millennium or more of ill-deeds. A stray moth licked at his temple, only to be swatted by an enormous, calloused hand.

With a shudder, Bilben postponed that particular plot and made for the assigned meeting place, just inside the Oerwoud. While the Smothered Princes began their negotiations with Ouroboros to cross its nest, the Joyous Hound appeared, looming over the rat.

"The Blackstar?" he asked in a whuffing rumble, the weight of dust and time behind it. An incredibly old enmity.

"Bound with Allcatch. Buried in a deep hole."

"Ho! You meet your bargains well, Queen of the Iron Nest," the Joyous Hound said. "Come, before those two shake a deal loose from yonder guardian."

He smuggled Bilben through the ranks of the host and into the baggage train, past weapons of humming Aurum, around the libraries and artful banners they thought to taunt holdout Underfog residents with, and into the cavalry squares.

They came upon the horse-spider with the precious prisoners, but ignored Horace Rider, human and frail. The Joyous Hound leaned in closely to the glass case as if examining the captured godlings and whispered to Bilben.

"Can you do it?"

"Sure," she said, pressing her paws against the glass, and the two tokens slowly floated her way. She shuddered with change and possibility, and then withdrew her paws, visibly exhausted, and slid them into her marsupial pouch.

"You said you could do it!" the Joyous Hound scoffed. "Looks like you wasted a perfectly good favour."

"But I did do it," she said. "Look closely."

He leaned in and whuffed with appreciation.

"Who are these new ones?"

"Nobodies, and now they pose as the Jesus and John Leicester."

The sigils of the real godlings were now in her pouch, as they were in all instances of her pouch, and no less trapped than they were behind Taursi glass.

"Ho! We all but dangle from the strings of your plots, little Queen," the Joyous Hound chortled.

At the same time, Bilben rode in the front seat of an incredibly fast car, burning across the plains between the Edgemist and the Oerwoud.

"This music is very aggressive. Loud and tribal," she complained to the Junkman.

"I have more," he said, and inserted a new eight-track for a band called Abba. After a few songs the rodent was swaying and smiling happily.

There was a main road through the Oerwoud, and she urged the Junkman to stick to it and simply drive fast. The Aurum-fuelled beast of a car leapt forward at the slightest touch to the accelerator, and they swept through that dream of all forests and none, Adamah's attempt to keep the old enemy at bay.

"Stop!" Bilben said, and the man braked so suddenly that she ended in a tangle on the floor, every possibility agreeing that she would end up there.

"Wait for a few minutes," she said. "The Smothered Princes are still in our way."

"Princes?"

"Long story. We will avoid them."

"So where should I drive now?" he said happily, revving the engine.

"We're going to a beach," Bilben said. The Junkman found the edge of another memory then, of being in a car at a beach, with Abba playing on the radio. Brother was there, but Brother was kinder, and everything was okay.

Bilben placed her paws across the pouch on her belly and felt the satisfaction of a plan unfolding.

While this happened, another Bilben watched Jenny Rider enter the House of Avadon. Jenny was powerful and fast, but those who lived in Avadon had suffered under the Cruik and turned on her the moment they saw her woodgrain skin.

Bilben helped her from hiding, hindering the town militia, delaying and confusing communications, and jamming the mechanisms on the gates so they could not close flush.

Jenny Rider scraped her flanks while wriggling through the tight gap, but she escaped that wicked keep. Bilben watched her go, when all she wanted to do was take the jawbone from her hands.

"Not yet," she whispered to herself. "Trust the plan."

Elsewhere, another instance of Bilben released the sigils of Jesus and John Leicester in a lonely room. She shook them out like wet clothes until they became as people once more, and they fell gasping on the ground, panting and three-dimensional.

This was not the plan, and more of an insurance policy.

At the same time, Bilben held a photograph with curling edges, and she placed it in a hidden cache. Not too obvious, but visible on a deeper search.

She could not rely on old memories, and knew that sometimes these needed a prod. If she could manipulate love and amity to achieve her goals, then this was worth doing too.

While she placed the photograph, Bilben was also at Shale. Her host had given her a generous apartment to prepare her nest, but it was a long way from what she was used to. No attendants, no sacrifices, no scribes to record her every utterance. She'd made her choice, of course, but now she missed the Iron Nest greatly, its comforts, its strength.

She could feel the pressure in her lower belly and knew the egg was coming soon. Not a child of love this time, but a baby born of necessity. Both bargaining chip and desperate gamble.

The father was waiting in the next room.

— 23 —

UNDERFOG

Tilly drove the House of Torana through the bruised night, hollow-eyed and exhausted. The twins and Bogle Hess slept in an exhausted tangle in the backseat, but Lanyard sat awake in the passenger seat, wincing at every bump.

"First bit of honest work and that's you tired out, right boss?" Tilly teased.

"It's not that," Lanyard said. "I don't have any bloody liver-root left. My insides are throbbing like a bastard."

"You silly old twit. I told you to retire years ago."

"And I told you, I retire on the end of a bullet."

They watched the hellish landscape peel by. Tilly had found the headlight switch, something like a nipple or a wart, and squeezing it sent a bright blue light through the House of Torana's remaining eye.

"Boss, do you have a plan?" Tilly said. "We're lost. Fuck all weapons, no food, water, nothing."

"We're not bloody lost. We get around the muck and then we go," and he took a beat, found a spot on the horizon, "that way."

"Lanyard Everett, you are not telling me everything."

"Oh."

"If you know something, if you have anything, you bring me in on it," Tilly said, hands clenching the gristly steering wheel till her knuckles showed. "You owe me. You owe them back there."

Lanyard sighed and shifted around in his seat.

"I went to the Boneman when this happened," he said, pointing to his cataracted eye. "Didn't want to go blind. Hoped he had a magic spell could fix this."

"Did he?"

"Nope. Not for that. Only the surgeons in the Collegia could fix a clouded eye. But he had an idea."

Lanyard closed his eyes and then looked towards Tilly, eyes still pressed firmly tight.

"I can still see you. Like an outline, all in green. If you're a mile or two away, you become a little dancing blob of green on the horizon. All the Jesusmen look like this to me, even those who don't know they belong to us yet."

"You can *find* us? All of us?"

"It used to work. Down here, it's getting more useless by the second."

"This how you saw Yulio? Up in that tower?"

He nodded and was silent for a long moment.

"Girl, listen. I lost Mal yesterday."

"He might be okay," she said, patting him on the shoulder. The House of Torana chose that second to fight her, slaloming left and right before making another run for the mud of Hayaven. Lanyard stuck a knife deep in the meat of the dashboard, and the car yowled pitifully, once more submitting to Tilly's control.

"Look. You don't need to say anything," Tilly said. Lanyard snarled, wiping his blade dry on his sleeve.

"Thought you wanted to hear my plan."

"Don't be a dickhead."

"This sees enemies too," he said, pointing to his milky eye. "Anyone who means me immediate harm shows up in red. Even if they are hiding behind something. Won more than one fight because of this eye."

"Why did you keep it a secret? From me? I could have used this. Every time a prentice goes missing, I assume Witches or worse, and I don't bloody sleep, Lanyard!"

"It's your own damn fault, harping on about my age. I need every dirty trick just to keep alive out there, and I didn't want to give you any more ammunition."

"Probably wise. Okay, you can see an enemy. Go on."

"Ever since we stepped out of the Edgemist, I have seen a pillar of red on the horizon. I quietly checked with Yulio and a few others, and none of them saw this. That is an enemy that is constantly intending me immediate harm."

"Dawn King?"

"Smart money says yes. So yes, I have a plan: get around the mud and kill that bastard."

"Best plan I can think of."

Tilly drove through the Underfog night, until dawn painted the landscape with the faded brown of an old photograph. Now they were following the outer curve of Hayaven, but where the mud ended lay a cliff that dropped for miles, with no bottom to it. The House of Torana's one weak headlight would have had no hope of spotting that in the gloom, and if they'd been an hour earlier, they'd have been over that edge and falling forever, dying of thirst in the car, rotting into skeletons and still falling.

"SHACHAT," the House of Torana said. "BIG PIT. GRETEL THREW IN MANY."

Between the Pit and Hayaven was a city, squatting on top of a narrow causeway. The blue twinkle of Aether danced across thick walls and figures moved behind the parapet.

They had guns here. Big cannons, churning gats from the Before, bombards and ballistae, pivot guns that glowed with golden Aurum. The walls were thick, and while they shifted and pulsed, they held a consistent form. A lot of minds and Aether went into the crafting and shaping of the structure, and the domed towers behind it.

The double gates, thick and bound in iron.

A big settlement, perhaps half the size of Crosspoint. There was a type of dock on the mud side of the city walls, and with the dawn dozens of big, stilted walkers went out into the muck of Hayaven, bearing riders who poled the mud. Others were strapped to the underbellies of the huge insects, sifting through the mud with sieves.

Suddenly, the House of Torana revved and moaned, and the noise carried across the plain. As one, the guards on the walls looked toward them, and Lanyard saw them all instantly light up in red. Behind the wall were more outlines, hundreds of shapes, maybe thousands, rushing for weapons and defensive posts. Enemies.

"WE COME, HOUSE OF AVADON!" the car roared, laughing and laughing. Tight lipped, Tilly accidentally brushed the accelerator pedal, and the House of Torana responded, revving and inching forward, ready for a mad suicidal dash.

"You stupid bloody car," Lanyard said, even as the House of Torana laughed at them. "They'll kill you too."

They prepared their meagre arsenal. Tilly climbed up onto the lip of the driver's side window, reaching up to untie her lance from the remaining locks of hair that held it in place. Bracing it against the side of the car, she was as ready as any bird-rider ever to go jousting.

Then in a brown-grey blur, a rat was on the hood of the House of Torana, twitching its whiskers. It met Lanyard's eyes and gave something that might have been a mousy smile.

With a wordless snarl Lanyard snatched Bilben by the neck. The rat offered no resistance.

"I am very glad I found you," she said.

"I feel the same," Lanyard said, increasing the pressure around her little neck. Still she did not attempt to escape, simply watching him impassively.

Tilly nudged Lanyard in the ribs, and he released the rat with a heavy sigh.

"Got a bloody nerve showing your face, rat," Lanyard said. "Been following us?"

"Yes," she admitted, seated on the dashboard. "I wish to serve you once more."

"Because that worked out so bloody well," Tilly said. "How many did we lose because of your advice?"

"Not my fault. I reckoned on a bargain for your lizard; it was The Serene who altered the deal. Friends, I saved *all* of your lives that day!"

"You saved fuck all," Lanyard said. "It's only us in this car, and my boy on his bird somewhere else. Give me one reason not to pass you back to the twins and their knives."

Three sets of eyes stared darkly from the backseat, and Bilben licked her lips nervously.

"You can't just drive straight into the House of Avadon."

"We've got no bloody choice!" Lanyard said.

"Forgive me, Jesusman, but you look at things wrong. Look upon the guns that will chew you and your fine vehicle into paste. Those stilted beasts there are just as dangerous, as is anything else bred in the Palace of the King of the Birds."

"The—the what?"

"You may not be able to see, but those gunners have beaks and wings. Hawk and ibis-faced snipers are waiting for you to get just a little closer. Some of them may even take to wing and drop things on you from above."

"Well, sounds like we are fucked, then," Tilly moaned, tapping the lance on the hood. The car moaned its annoyance.

"Not at all. Why, not even a day earlier I helped Jenny Rider slip through this very city."

"You have got a lot of explaining to do," Lanyard said darkly.

"Seems all I do is talk, and advise, and still I get regarded in this poor light," Bilben said. "I have yet to tell you a single falsehood, have only served, and still you quibble and threaten to strangle me! Keep this going and I might just leave you to perish."

"I doubt you would," Lanyard said. "See, you still haven't said what you want from us yet."

"Yes, I did. I hoped to call upon you for a favour at an appropriate time. Nothing too pressing."

"I could drive this car through your bloody terms, rat! A favour could be anything. We refuse."

"Fine, then," the rat said. "Look, they're sighting in on you."

Perhaps a hundred paces away, an outcropping of stone exploded into dust as a shell landed into it. A real explosive round, erupting with a flash of flame.

"The King of Avadon has a healthy trade with the Gravedigger, who brings him all manner of shiny bullets and trinkets to line his nest. Look, another close shot!"

The mortar fire was getting closer and closer now, sending up plumes of dust and falling clay. The birds had their range fixed. Tilly looked frantically to Lanyard, who snarled.

"Fine. You can have your bloody favour, then. Show us the way through this, and you can have two favours and a kiss from Bogle Hess in the back there."

"Drive!" Bilben said. Tilly punched down the pedal, and the gibbering car roared with excitement, leaping forward when its wheels gained traction in the shifting dust.

"Where do we go?" Tilly cried.

"Straight at that gate—and put your seatbelts on!" Bilben said, ignoring Lanyard's filthy glare. Shells were landing around them with earnest now, and a stray bullet hit the House of Torana right on the snout, sending a spray of Aether back through the open windshield.

Bilben paced back and forth on the dashboard, finally setting on a spot that looked right, and then the rat latched on with her teeth, savaging the meat of the car. The House of Torana roared out with pain, even as Tilly steered them around the crater where some other soul had met their end.

Then the strangeness happened. Even as Tilly twitched the steering wheel left, she saw a second set of hands twitching the wheel right, and then a third keeping it fixed straight ahead, and then there were three, six, nine different versions of the House of Torana blasting towards the walls of Avadon.

"What are you doing?" Lanyard demanded of Bilben, who could only mumble through her grip on the car's skin. In a car running parallel with them, another version of Lanyard was chasing the rat up and down the dashboard with a flickering knife. To their left, Lanyard was driving, with Mal in the passenger seat and no one else in the car. To their right, a bunch of young prentices crowded the backseat while Yulio sped them toward the city.

Bilben was perfectly still, latched onto the car, but the other instances of the House of Torana twitched and wove together like the rat often did with herself, endless decisions and variations and alterations of how she thought time should unfold.

A whole army of cars came at the city, weaving in and out of each other. The guns of the city opened up in earnest, and some of these other Houses of Torana erupted in flames and spilt wreckage as a round hit, or rolled flipping, the driver taken out by snipers on the walls.

Tilly drove straight at the gate.

The walls loomed above them, and Lanyard caught a glimpse of the beak-faced gunners above, some of whom were now taking to wing, long-limbed and clutching at guns.

"AVADON!" the House of Torana cried, and then it crashed into the front gate at full speed.

By all rights it should have ended in a crumple of metal and meat, with the humans inside just as dead, but the House of Torana remembered Gretel's lessons: how to move fast, how slamming into something and really meaning it had a special kind of power down here.

The car that had rammed its way into the Underfog hit the double doors centre on, punching through them like a big boot through a flimsy door. Lanyard and the others shook around, and Bilben lost her grip on the dashboard, falling down to the floor.

The dozens of other instances of the car winked out of existence, and suddenly they were on their own in the streets of the House of Avadon, their own car roaring in victory.

Before them, pedestrians scattered in a flap of squawking and dropped feathers, taking to tall buildings that were a honeycomb of oversized nests. Others were flightless and darted down side streets or hid in what looked to be shops or restaurants. Storks and gulls, ducks and eagles, even butterflies and escapee moths from the House of the Accurate Count—all manner of winged beast fled their approach, each a mixture of human and animal. On the ground level, stables were opening, and the spirits of dead riding birds emerged, bearing ibis-faced men and women.

Bullets and rocks rained down on them from all directions, the House of Torana taking the brunt of it. Lanyard and Bogle Hess fired at their pursuit, and even the twins took apart one creature who tried to fly through the window and get to them with its own dagger.

"Everything's a bloody bird," Lanyard said.

"Do they take turns shitting on the statues?" Bogle Hess said from the backseat, earning a rare laugh from Lanyard.

"Where now?" Tilly asked Bilben, who scrambled up from the floor and onto the steering wheel.

"I don't know, I'm lost," the rat said, crying out as a rock fell onto the roof. "Let the car have its head, defend yourself!"

It was a city of marvels, but they only caught glimpses of it as they fought for every inch of their way. The House of Torana punched gleefully through buildings, casting them aside as destroyed ideas, wasted willpower, and the car made a new road that might take years to repair.

"Lanyard," Tilly warned, and then a second later the stilted walkers were upon them, kicking the car in the sides and trying to press down on their roof. Tilly stabbed up and got one creature in the underbelly, while Lanyard sent up a mark that exploded in a cloud of cloying gas, sending the beasts coughing and away.

"Look at that," Lanyard said, pointing out the biggest building at the centre of the city, a rotund barrel that pulsed with veins of Aether.

"Yes, that is the Palace of the King of the Birds," Bilben said.

"Looks like a bloody birdcage, that does."

Suddenly, a wall, and the House of Torana leapt into it gleefully, parting that mind-set masonry with style. Doors were meant to open, but walls were not, and this time the collision knocked Lanyard and the others into each other, banging heads and limbs, bloodying noses.

The car was a wreck, limping along from the city.

"Get out! Run!" Bilben said, but Lanyard ignored this, spiking his hand on the car's spigot. After a moment Tilly pushed him aside to do the same. Even as the screeching pursuit from the House of Avadon got close, the car uncrumpled from within, repaired and once more roadworthy.

They took to the causeway, leaving the wreckage of the House of Avadon behind them.

"You know, the Boneman got through there once by asking politely," Bilben said.

"Not in the mood for fucking politeness," Lanyard said.

"My family ran an egg farm, back near Rosenthrall," Bogle Hess said, steering the House of Torana across miles of rolling sands. "Gull eggs, cockatoo eggs, riding-bird eggs. If it fell out of a cloaca and into a nest, they farmed it."

The dunes moved slowly, like an ocean, and it took every ounce of concentration just to avoid ploughing into the drift.

In the backseat, Tilly snored while the twins put her long hair into braids. Lanyard had taken his own turn behind the wheel, but the constant ballet of pedals, gearstick, and steering wheel wracked his insides with pain, and he didn't trust himself not to wreck them.

"Did eggs make them rich?" Lanyard grunted.

"Pa crossed the Water Barons and got his farm burnt down. Glad I got to see that city full of birds, though. Felt a bit like being home again."

Bilben stirred muzzily on Bogle's shoulder, keeping warm in the layers of wrapping that the ex-leper wore.

"Your family would have lost all their birds to the King of Avadon. He speaks their names in whispers and then makes them into men, even as he makes men into birds."

"I hope Mal does not pass this way," Lanyard said. "The boy loves that bird of his."

"I know, I know," Bilben said with a stretch and a yawn. "That's why I sent him north, through Bauer's lands."

"You fucking what?" Lanyard said, even as Bilben realised her mistake. Bogle and Lanyard snatched at her, and the rat wriggled out and through the open window, falling into darkness and sand.

Bogle fought to get the car back under control, and Tilly stirred with a curse as all three of them slid around in the backseat.

"Get your bloody act together," Tilly cried out. "You got a bandage over your eyes now?"

"It was Bilben!" Lanyard said. "She said she sent Mal north, to meet with Bauer."

"She fucking what?"

Once they'd traversed the desert, the sands gave way to a dull black glass, peppered with monoliths that punched through the surface in random places. Some of the obelisks leaned like drunkards, while others had collapsed and shattered into shards.

"I TIRE," the car whined. "GRETEL ALLOWS REST!"

"Gretel's dead," Lanyard replied, but ordered a halt all the same. They climbed out of the slimy seats, mud-spattered and weary, and leaned against a collapsed monolith. It had borne writing once, and the ghosts of these markings could still be seen, an absence deep beneath the surface.

Slow movement swirled and roiled beneath them, a large dark shape underneath inches of glass. Perhaps a cloud or the slow passage of a beast beyond their understanding, and the shifting forms passed them by, uncaring or mindless. Once Lanyard thought he'd seen an eye blinking in the distance, but then it was gone and just another distant thunderhead in some other place.

The twins climbed all over the structure, playing some whispered game of their own making while the rest leaned against the rock.

"It's warm," Tilly said. The fallen obelisk felt like a stone that had been baking in the Now sun for hours, then allowed to cool off in the dusk.

Lanyard allowed his people to rest on the warm rock, but he stayed awake, gun in hand, watching for the signs of an approaching enemy, wary of whatever world lay beneath them. Apart from the beacon of hatred on the horizon, there was nothing hunting them now, but still he stayed awake, shotgun in the crook of his elbow.

Then for a long moment he drowsed, eyelids closing, and he woke to see the House of Torana slowly clambering up the side of the rock, mouth spread wide, slavering as it climbed toward the sleepers. Instantly he was on his feet, slamming the gun butt against the car's face and calling up marks of pain and confusion.

"I thought you'd learnt that lesson, car!" Lanyard shouted, face flecked with a mixture of blood and Aether. "Do we need to tie you up each evening?"

"I'M SO HUNGRY," the car moaned. "PLEASE."

"So are we, but you don't see us eating each other, do you?"

"GIVE ME THE MEAT."

"No!" The crack of a gunstock across the nose, and then the car fell into a whimpering silence. He looked up to see the horrified faces of his people, stirred from sleep.

"What?" he said.

He looked around to see a spirit standing above the body of Bogle Hess. The nude apparition was mutilated in every way. Bite marks on the arms and lower legs, thick scar tissue from burns, and entire sections of skin peeled out by a flenser's knife. Hateful words were carved into the meat of bicep, breast, and thigh, a moment before the Underfog erased them.

In life the spirit's breasts and genitals had ended up a mass of white scars, all of the soft tissue cut away and left to heal badly. Then the spirit turned and met Lanyard's eyes, and he saw the Jesusman tattoo on the spirit's shoulder.

Bogle Hess, and there was no mark of leprosy on that blue-tinged spirit skin, nothing but a map of self-loathing for a body that just now had stopped working. The bandaged figure was stone cold dead, and not responding to the frenzied shaking of Tilly.

"Back off," Lanyard whispered to the car, shaking his gun in its direction. He cautiously approached the spirit and its dead home, eyes wide.

"Didn't want to be a bother," Bogle's Once-Dead spirit said.

He saw the smear of blood on the obelisk, pooling around the body.

"Caught a bullet in that bird town?"

"Yep."

Lanyard nodded. He could respect the decision. Behind him, the car whimpered.

"You hated your body?"

"Yes, I did. So very much."

"Do you mind if I feed it to the car?"

A moment, and the mutilated spirit burst into laughter, honest and long.

"No, bossman, I guess I don't mind if you feed it to the car. Go ahead."

They made a deal with the car in the sepia of dawn: they would trade the body of Bogle Hess in exchange for some meat from the car. It agreed to let them sever one of its ears, and they ate the leathery old meat over a Mark of Flame.

"It tastes like metal," Mem complained.

"It tastes like survival," Tilly said.

UNDERFOG

I'll kill you!" Kirstl screamed using Mal's mouth, clambering all over Bauer to try to snatch Bilben. The confused and awkward ballet went on for many long moments until Bauer lost all patience, sending Mal's body backwards with a ringing backhander.

"Enough!" the old Jesusman yelled. "I don't know what's going on, but know your bloody place, prentice."

"But–but she betrayed me. She killed me!" Kirstl cried, wiping away the blood from Mal's lip.

"You strange, bloody boy. You're the only person here with a pulse."

Mal gave comfort to Kirstl, guiding her back to the dreamspace, and then took over control of the body. Calmly he rose and faced the Jesusman and his grim-faced lieutenants.

"You cannot trust Bilben," he said. "She betrayed Lanyard and caused the deaths of many."

"It's true," Bilben said, capering and shifting until she was at Mal's feet, and she regarded them all. "My kind is incapable of lying, and I affirm that you cannot trust me. I did cause the death of Mal's sweetheart and others. I had many predictions for that event, but I got everything wrong."

Bauer ignored Bilben's protestations, choosing instead to walk around Mal, eyeing him carefully.

"There are two of you in there," he finally said. "Saw the change in you just now, like someone else is looking out from those eyes."

Instantly a pistol barrel was underneath Mal's chin, the cold iron pressing up into the meat of his throat. Bauer stared at him with the instant suspicion of the paranoid survivor.

"What are you? How did you steal this body?"

Bilben was between them then, pushing their faces apart frantically, most of her blurred decisions being to stay and protect Mal from the Jesusman.

"I know of this. It is a willing accommodation," Bilben said. "This young man has found his dead sweetheart and given her a home, allowing her to share this body."

"You've got two souls," Bauer said to Mal, deadpan. The boy nodded, the barrel of the pistol cold and hard as it dug into his flesh. A thoughtful look, and then Bauer made the gun disappear.

"It is a simple but powerful spell, and very old," Bilben said. "They are now a Tontine. I am pleased that my failure had at least one good outcome."

"Alright, Tontine. Get back to bloody work. No more fighting and cussing."

Bauer sent Mal back to the unloading of wagons and cars with a swift boot to the arse, already accepting of this newest strangeness.

"Are you sure you didn't intend this as part of your grand game, Bilben?" Bauer asked when the boy was out of earshot. "All chess players sacrifice pieces."

"This chess player made one mistake," Bilben replied.

"Watch that you don't sacrifice me and mine," Bauer said. "Sticking our bloody necks out for you."

"I care about all of your necks, and most especially my own," Bilben said.

They'd gathered enough supplies for Lanyard and his entire order of stranded Jesusmen, and the spirits watched cynically as one boy and his bird ate the food meant for dozens.

The Many-Faced were able to digest the solid food from the Now, and the dead Jesusmen made a merry sport of tossing out food to the polyhedral beasts, who flashed words of gratitude, demands for more, and anger at neighbours who took more than the perceived fair share.

"You lot! Stop wasting food!" Bauer roared, startling Mal. The boy had been about to share his own meal with a smaller pyramid who'd been affecting a limp. At Bauer's shouting the creature recovered well enough and scuttled off at great speed.

"Boy, come with me," Bauer said to Mal. "Thought you might like to hear this."

Mystified, Mal trotted along behind the grizzled spirit.

Bauer's Jesusmen had the enormous Chain-Lord pinned to the flat rock on the hilltop, pitons through wrists and ankles. Someone had already slit his gut open, the rock slick with treacle-thick Aether, and the knife that rested in his guts wiggled around as he laughed.

"Shut up," Bauer barked. "Tell me again."

"You saved the boy that day," the Chain-Lord told Bauer. "He's your responsibility now."

"Lanyard has a car," Bilben said with a distant look on her face, perched on the end of Bauer's stolen shovel. "He approaches the House of Avadon. He is under fire. I am in place. I am assisting him now."

"How?" Mal said.

"Best not to ask her, lad. The answer will do your bloody head in."

Bauer returned to the mutilated figure on the rock and pushed the dagger in with all his weight, stirring the exposed guts around like a pot full of pasta. The Chain-Lord winced, teeth drawn tight in a sickening grin.

"You had my lad and his people caught up at the bloody moth tower," Bauer said. "Easy pickings, right?"

"The Dawn King will avenge me!" the Chain-Lord said.

"Nah. See, you got greedy and stupid, and you made a bad deal."

Bauer cut upwards, breaking open the Chain-Lord's breastbone. He reached down and opened him up like a rusty old gate.

"I must have killed dozens of men like you, back in my day," Bauer said, hacking away at tissue and gristle, pulling out organs. "Evil doers. All power, but no vision, no real ambition beyond what a beast already knows."

"Fuck you, Jesusman," the Chain-Lord said weakly, even his powerful spirit finally failing before his injuries.

"Before I begin, before I really bring the hurt, Bilben here has something to tell you," Bauer said. "You know her kind cannot utter a falsehood. Mal, you listen too."

Bilben climbed down from the shovel and onto the stone, deftly dodging past gore and guts, until she was perched next to the Chain-Lord's face, leaning over his lipless face to pronounce his doom, and with each word his defiance finally led into fear.

"You have lost everything to a lie, master of the Chain-Folk," Bilben said. "All of your stolen Aether, all of your slaves and servants, all of it gone now. You have sworn yourselves in service to the Dawn King, but the truth is this: the Dawn King simply does not exist."

At the top of the hill, the riding birds of Bauer's camp were gorging themselves on the body of the Chain-Lord, the rock still slick with the gore that was his sorry ending.

"I can't draw you a map, so clean out your ears and bloody well listen," Bauer said.

The spirits of every Once-Dead Jesusman were gathered up and ready here, each one dark-eyed and patient. Mal sat amongst them, and already felt he'd been adopted as some sort of bizarre mascot, the only living human in the squad.

His mind was still reeling from Bilben's revelation. There was no Dawn King. There was nothing but a complicated plan, and now he and Kirstl were caught up in it.

"An army from Overhaeven comes our way. Bilben has seen them marching upon the Farmer's lands, but the Many-Faced here have spotted their scouts as far as the edge of Hayaven."

Bauer looked over his crew.

"Some of them will get through the muck, or over it, and there's nothing we can do about that. But it will slow them down. Others will hit the House of Avadon, and you know what they say about the enemy of my enemy. They'll put up a hard fight, enough to slow them down, at least."

Mal thought about Lanyard and was glad to know that at least his bossman was still alive. *If I get through this, I'll need to track him down, tell him the truth.*

He's not going to like it.

"So that leaves the pass, Bor Shaon, and us," Bauer continued. "It's the easiest way through to the Glasslands, and so most of their mob are going to come this way."

Bauer reached down and hauled Mal to his feet, patting him on the shoulder.

"When we heard the survivors of the order had entered the Underfog, I was hoping we'd have more help from Lanyard. We got one hungry boy and his bird."

The Jesusmen laughed, and even Bauer cracked a faint smile.

"Folks, we're gonna do this the tough way. We're not going to stop them. You know this. All we are doing here is buying Bilben enough time."

Mal nodded. Bilben was preening her fur on the hood of a buggy, and it was hard to imagine the enormous web of intrigue spreading out from this one small creature. Play upon counterplay, a plot spreading from here to Overhaeven.

She'd started a cult, used it to start a civil war in Overhaeven, and drawn the bulk of their forces down into the Now and the Underfog.

Now she was moving the last few pieces in place, preparing to reveal herself and attack the real enemy, and she was close to winning this game. Bauer and his people agreed, and so their one job was to buy her the time.

The Dawn King simply does not exist.

"You can leave if you want. Go and find Lanyard and his car."

Mal shook his head.

"Well, you're not going to do fuck-all without so much as an apple knife. If you're to fight with us, you'll need a weapon."

"Is it a gun?" Kirstl said, suddenly surging forward in their shared body.

"No. I'm not your master, and it's not my place to give you one. With a tough little bird like you've got, you're better off having one of these anyways."

Bauer handed Mal a lance, fresh from the forge. It was short but weighty, and had a sharp blade welded to each end, complete with a crossbar to stop the lance penetrating too deeply.

"Welcome to our ranks, Prentice Mal and Prentice Kirstl," Bauer said, and sent Mal back to sit with the other ancient warriors, who clapped him on the shoulders and welcomed him warmly.

"We'll plug the pass. Put more marks on the walls. Send snipers up to shoot them from above. Give back inch by bloody inch, until we're out in Bor Shaon and running around in the silence."

"Then we run rings around them. Use our marks when their magics won't even work. Let them fail at giving orders, while we communicate with handsign. People, we've been drilling at this for decades. Don't you dare bloody let me down now."

"Yes, boss," came the grumbled response.

"First things first. Mal, come here."

The boy came forward, beaming, new lance safely ensconced in a case built just for it.

"See all that shit you unpacked? Time to start packing it again. Don't you give me that bloody look, an order is an order!"

The small defending force made for the pass as quickly as they could, birds and bikes and smoky buggies blasting silently across the plains. Alongside them rolled hundreds of the Many-Faced, clans drawn in from distant grounds, and they flashed in a silent cacophony of words, tentacles touching.

Battle! Ally! one of the Many-Faced flashed to Mal, who could only nod back.

Kill!

Spiny beasts! another added to many affirmations.

Eat the glass? one asked Mal, and he shook his head.

Lulled by the bird's motions, he fell into a doze and instantly joined Kirstl in their dreamspace. She'd spent her time well, and in the centre of a black room she'd constructed a scaled down version of the landscape that they could look down on as if they were eagles. With a bit of concentration Mal found he could fly his eagle closer and be as if in that place, looking around at the terrain.

"We've beaten the system," Kirstl said with glee. "This is a record that the Underfog can't erase. We have a map that is even better than something on paper."

Mal looked at everything and was confused. There were things here Kirstl couldn't possibly know of. Other Houses, dotted around the Edgemist. A big area called the Glasslands, and the sickle curve of Shale, the Final Shore.

"Please don't be mad," Kirstl said, reading his face and surface thoughts. "We have a visitor."

The big-eared rat climbed onto the table and smiled up at Mal.

"You're not here," he said, and the rat shook her head. Kirstl looked intrigued by the whole situation, when earlier she'd been raging at her perceived killer.

Mal stared at her suspiciously, and suddenly in the dream he had the double-bladed lance on his hip. Bilben was there, not a fuzz-edged dream fragment, but a genuine intruder inside of his own brain, his own self.

"Forgive me, but I simply had to step inside the brain of a Tontine, and I was stunned at what I found. The unique potentials, a place we can record information. It's truly extraordinary."

"Did you arrange for this?" he said. "Did you trick us into becoming this?"

"This, I did not arrange. That is truth. It was a possibility that I identified after The Serene's betrayal, and I allowed it to play out."

Mal pulled out his lance and became the eagle, flying across the landscape at Bilben, who dodged and wove around his deadly thrusts.

"Mal, stop," Kirstl said, flying next to him. "She didn't kill me. And sure, she's taking advantage of us, but this is excellent news. We can make a real difference for Bauer. We can find Lanyard—and maybe even a way out of here."

They hovered together above that perfect map of the Underfog. Everything from the Edgemist through to Shale, where the black waters raced upwards. Mal thought that if he looked upward and followed that vertical sheet of water as far as it went, he would lose his mind. Bilben ran one paw through Hayaven, and it came up dripping with muck.

"Legend here has it that the Farmer raised the mud fields, the pit, the causeway the birds stole, the mountain range, all of it. It was a last line of defence, should Overhaeven get through."

"It's a kill box," Mal said.

"Excellent! That is indeed what this all is. Now mark this well," and here the rat plucked a piece of clay from the map, moulding it into a rough figure of a shepherd's staff. Bilben placed this figure right on the edge of Shale, out in the water itself.

"This is what everyone is really coming for."

Bauer led his group through the ravine to the very edge of the silence, and then pulled back half a mile. The Jesusmen set their ambush here. These Once-Dead paladins dug stake-lined pits, crafted jagged palisades out of mark magic, and set to painting marks of paralysis and pain with spray paint and paint rollers dipped in tar.

Others climbed the sheer wall with ropes and piton, setting up sniper nests from above. Flinty eyes peered over trenches and ramparts dug with magic. A machine gun was set in a nest, and mortars behind that.

Then, the waiting. Mal sat on Collybrock with the other bird riders, just behind the gunner's nest. They were there to help when the first rank was overrun, and to pull out as many people as possible, wounded or not. The buggies and bikes were ready to go, pointed towards the depths of Bor Shaon.

Be ready! Hold! Bauer signalled, and the order went up and down the lines. Ahead, they watched the throat of the pass, the curve where the enemy would come.

Mal was terrified, and he missed Lanyard then, missed the way he loved him without showing love. The old Jesusman had struck off his chains and kept the horrors away, even as he prenticed him into a world of nothing but horror.

Lanyard would have faced this moment calmly, and the calm would have been infectious. As it was, Mal wanted to be violently ill, and had run to the toilet pit so much that the dead Jesusmen had taken to mocking him with the count.

Kirstl was just as scared as Mal, and they took it in turns to be present while the other retreated away from the pumping of adrenaline and blood, the feelings of queasiness, the trembling limbs.

This is all we ever wanted, she told Mal. *Battles.*

I've changed my mind, Mal said. *Let's go back to the Now. Move to the bird-yards near Langenfell or Rosenthrall. Race Collybrock in the junior categories.*

Do you even have the breeder's papers for Collybrock?

Nope. Lanyard took her egg at gunpoint. When he freed me.

You'll only be able to race the Inland circuits, then.

No thanks. Those dirty bastards hurt their birds.

Guess we're stuck sharing a Jesusman, then, Kirstl said.

A flicker of movement in the pass, and a hundred rifles were raised up, held ready, waiting for that perfect killing moment. Another hand sign, and fingers came away from triggers as a handful of Many-Faced scouts came tumbling up the pass, waving their tentacles frantically, flashing out blue words that were too small to read.

Then an avalanche of gold and glass came pouring towards them. First came a shock force of Taursi on their horse-spiders, heavily armoured in glass kilts and barding, and beyond them more riders, and then infantry, thousands upon thousands of invaders from the Golden Sea.

Fire! The Jesusman hit them with one devastating wave of gunfire, chewing apart the vanguard, armour splintering and starred. The Taursi were surprised and confused, and milled about for a moment before reacting, allowing the Jesusmen to send another volley at the next rank.

Now the snipers joined in, and their job was simple. They had to strike the blasting caps that set off the buried caches of explosives. The Taursi cavalry was trying to turn back now, routed in seconds, and then the sudden explosions decimated them. They swirled about, unable to retreat beyond those still advancing, struggling to regroup and push forward. In silence, no orders were coming from their leaders, and their confusion was killing them.

Machine gun! someone signalled, and the enormous weapon chattered away silently, sweeping the Taursi line left to right, chewing apart the retreating vanguard.

We'll be okay! Kirstl cheered, but Mal wasn't so sure. The enemy just kept coming. The machine gun overheated, and they had to change the barrels. The snipers ran out of explosives to set off and were now taking out individual targets.

Then the Taursi got close enough to unleash their battle-glass, and they huffed out their spines until they glowed red hot, tearing out glass jags from the glands in their forearms. Even here in the sepia gloom, the battleglass shone brightly, arcing up and into the front trenches of the Jesusmen.

The first row of riflemen was torn apart in moments, guns clattering to the earth as their Twice-Dead spirits floated past in a film of disbelief. Above, the snipers were unable to do anything but die valiantly, shooting on until the glass jags pinned them to the canyon wall like bugs.

Mal looked around with terror, wondering when his orders would come. Bauer was stalking around by the machine gun nest, hand-signing impatiently as the crew worked to fix the gun. Now the mortars came in, hammering the oncoming Taursi as quickly as the crew could load in bombs.

They were close now, and started triggering the Jesus marks set in place for them. Flame erupted, pure and hot, and some were afflicted by a madness that caused them to turn on their comrades. Bauer played every wonderful and terrible trick in the Jesusman arsenal, and still it wasn't enough.

Fall back, the order came. *Second position.*

A mad rush, as the other trenches were abandoned, Once-Dead Jesusmen racing for the waiting buggies, birds, and bikes. Bauer and the gun-crew attempted to transport the half-repaired machine gun but were forced to leave it behind, running ahead of a hail of deadly glass.

All of that frantic motion, and not a single sound. Two riflemen scrambled onto Collybrock's harness, and she turned around to give Mal the stink-eye. *Heavy!* she tried to squawk, but Bor Shaon robbed the bird of a good sulk.

They rode for one frantic mile, the other birds similarly overloaded, and came to the next lot of trenches, these more dug in. When the buggies and birds cleared the trenchwork, the boards that served as makeshift bridges were pulled aside. The riflemen took up their guns again, ready to repeat the first trick.

Snipers were already here and waiting, aiming at the next lot of buried explosives. Bauer had spent years preparing for this fight, but there was only so much he could steal from the lands of the living. Overhaeven had laid many traps and protections around the Underfog, and each trip with his stolen shovel risked his neck.

There were more explosives, of course.

They waited for many long minutes, but the pursuit came slowly. Soon, it was clear why: the shock troops and even the normal cavalry had stood aside, sending forward the infantry as cannon fodder.

Bauer looked satisfied at this, and gave the mortar crews the sign to open fire when the enemy came into range. Knowing they were dead here, the Taursi warriors charged, sharp slivers of glass singing forward too early, piercing nothing but the clay underfoot.

The snipers obliterated great clusters of infantry with each true shot to a blasting cap. Marks high up in the cliff face sent down sheets of rock at Bauer's command, crushing the enemy, and the rear guard had worked up a rudimentary shield of magic to protect the first ranks, hopefully for a volley or two anyway.

Still they came on. Thousands of the spiny-backed warriors, edging closer by the minute, climbing over their own dead kin and reaching toward the Jesusman front lines. Without the machine gun, there was little they could do to keep them back, and as the shield failed and the glass came in, Bauer ordered another fallback. More dead Jesusmen floated from that first trench toward Shale, and they had to abandon the guns and run.

Third position! came the call. Mal only had one passenger this time, the spirit of a fierce-looking woman with only one eye and Jesusman tatts across her chin. She pointed frantically, as if Mal didn't understand his one job.

Go! Quickly! the woman mouthed.

The third position was at the mouth of Bor Shaon itself, and they'd brought down enough rock with Jesus marks and explosives to make a fortification here, a thick wall to plug the pass.

When they were through, the last lot of explosives were used to drop the gateway through the wall, sealing the pass completely and leaving only a solid mass of stone.

Mal reined in to let his passenger disembark. She went quickly with the others, scrambling up ladders to get to the top of the rough-shaped wall, rifle already out and aiming. He took up a position with the other bird riders, and now his job had changed. If the Overhaeven forces broke through, his responsibility was to dog their journey, lead them around in circles, strike and retreat, as often as he could until he was cut down himself.

All to buy Bilben the time that she needs, Mal said.

I believe her plan, Kirstl replied.

I believe we're all being played.

He drew the beautiful double-bladed lance from its sheath and tested the balance. Perfect. An edge you could shave with, and unlike his first lance, Bauer's people had patiently crafted the marks into the steel, adding sigils that neither Mal nor Kirstl recognised.

The pursuit was close now, and barely a minute-count had passed when the waiting shooters opened fire from the wall-top, sweeping the front lines with gunfire.

A pause. Above, Bauer held up a fist, making the Mark of Many Triggers, and every rifleman struck the same target at the same time. Again, and then again, the ripple of gunfire slowed down to these single moments, crashing thunder realised in silence.

Uh oh. Big enemies, Kirstl said.

The Taursi filled the air with glittering glass, and Mal could only watch in detached horror as those on the wall were peppered with the shards. More glass tore through the air, this reaching up and over the walls, and it fell among the ranks of bird riders and those in the waiting machines.

Collybrock hopped around like mad, squawking silently, and Mal spotted a long glass sliver buried in her side. Without thinking he plucked it loose, slicing up his own palm on the edge.

Hold! came the signal from the Once-Dead riders next to him. *Hold!*

The torn spirits of broken Jesusmen floated past them, shocked, mouths working like landed fish, clean kills. Some had been butchered more messily, torn into strips of gauze by the glass and sent wafting towards Shale.

Then the wall visibly shook, spilling Jesusmen in all directions. On the top Bauer continued to resist, even as he flashed orders to those below.

Be ready! Prepare to retreat!

A golden lash fell on the stone, and another, and it shaved away the rock with every stroke, a sharp axe driving through seasoned wood. With one more mighty blow, the bright whip carved a breach through the wall, and then the defenders were off and running for the buggies and bikes, reaching for the hands of bird riders.

Then Bauer himself was climbing up and into Collybrock's saddle. Mal looked past him to see an enormous figure striding through the breach, a hound-headed man in a kilt, laying waste to everything with a golden whip, growing with every step. Through his broad legs flooded the Taursi cavalry, pushing out of the kill-trap, their numbers barely dented by the best efforts of Bauer's killers.

More monsters were climbing over the wall and through the gap. Eyes surrounded by flapping wings. Golden wheels studded with eyes, interlocked and rotating. A goat larger than a car, flames belching from its mouth.

Watch out for those two boys, Kirstl said. *They killed so many of our kids. Evil bastards!*

A heavy slap on the shoulder from Bauer. The rest of the birds were already off and running, while Mal was gawping at monsters. With a flick of the reins he launched Collybrock towards the others, sharp battle glass falling in their wake.

— 25 —

UNDERFOG

E ven as the Jesusmen set off down to the ravine to poke at the Overhaeven army, Bilben met with the clan leaders of the Many-Faced on the hill where sound worked. These small folk had learnt most of the written languages throughout history, enough to make the literate understand them, but much like she'd learnt the language of The Serene, Bilben had also been patient enough to dig deeper.

It wasn't just about the words that appeared on their faces. That was the most superficial level of their language, but Bilben found more. Their pose with their wriggling cilia. What surface temperature they allowed themselves. And all of this was affected by the speaker's natural shape and what clan they belonged to.

The end result was that she could have a much deeper conversation with their leaders. Even as they adored the Jesusmen and their ways, they trusted Bilben.

So, you have investigated thoroughly and find this necessary? [Query, relevance, disbelief], she interpreted the Many-Faced as saying. Anyone else would have only seen the word *Necessary?*

"It is necessary and very important. A great honour to your clan if you do this."

This is a strange request, and it puts many of us at risk. If they come back down the pass, we will be kill/hurt/shame [Assertion, vehement, worry]

"This is why the Jesusmen lead them on a merry chase. They will keep them away from you long enough. But you will need to move fast, my brave friends."

Bauer has been very kind/wise/friend. What gifts will you give us to risk our warriors? [Bargain, appeal, cost]

"All of the flesh outside of the hearts is yours."

We can already get that flesh! [Obvious, pressure, bored]

"Bring me what I ask, and the Iron Nest will swear fealty to the Many-Faced."

Even as the wall fell and the Jesusmen were routed, the bargain was struck, and the Many-Faced went racing across the white dust of Bor Shaon, the wiggling rock shapes waiting for the bulk of the Overhaeven force to emerge from the tunnel in pursuit of the Jesusmen. It took them hours to fully emerge from the tunnel, but only when the last runt of a Taursi came through with the baggage train did the Many-Faced enter themselves, rolling back through the acres of carnage.

Bilben watched a lot, listened more, and noticed things that the larger creatures ignored. Sometimes Overhaeven warriors came here for sport, and she'd seen them fall once or twice on the other side of the Oerwoud. She'd noted this well.

The invaders differed from everything else in the Underfog. When the forms they wore died, they did not step into a Once-Death or even a Twice-Death. They simply ended and fell to the ground as so much dead meat. Nothing about them went to Shale, which helped her postulate today's theory.

The call had gone wide, and all of the Many-Faced clans had come to earn a favour from the infamous Bilben. Less than an hour later, they returned in their thousands, churning across the plain, holding up their grisly trophies.

Each of the Many-Faced held one Taursi heart in its tentacles, using the rest of its appendages to propel itself as fast as it could. Straight across the plains of silence. To the Glasslands—and to Shale itself.

Satisfied with her work, Bilben ended this instance of herself with a happy sigh.

"HO! SPARE US!" one of the Smothered Princes laughed.

"WE ARE YOUR FAITHFUL SERVANTS!" the other tittered.

Behind them, the House of Adamah was revealed to the world, reduced to ashes and unravelling clay. The murdered villagers floated past the golden army, their Twice-Dead skins flickering and drifting like a school of horrified fish.

"BROTHER, SEE HOW THEY KEEP THEIR OATHS."

"THEY POINT THE WAY TOWARDS SHALE!"

The golden army rumbled forward, unopposed. Occasional spirits were seen fleeing for safety, their rude settlements already settling down into the clay. The Princes sent forth the Ophanim and the Seraphim to hunt them down, the flying eyes and blazing wheels eliminating all witnesses quickly.

"They relied overmuch on their forest to keep us out," the Joyous Hound laughed. "Watch them scatter!"

"DOG, DO NOT DEIGN TO MOCK ON OUR LEVEL."

"OUR MOCKERY IS ABOVE YOURS. RETURN TO YOUR TASKS."

The Joyous Hound stalked away bitterly, ears held erect. He would turn on them soon, and the Princes knew this all too well. Still, they'd been young boys before the pillows were pressed against their faces, and they could not help but tease and prod the old death-taker.

During the earlier aborted invasion, Overhaeven had recorded a map of the Underfog onto a two-inch thick golden tablet. None of their kind had been able to pierce the Oerwoud, but they'd bought the information with promises of salvation and return to life–promises as empty as the eyes of the invaders when they murdered the turncoat Underfog spirits.

This flexing and breathing geography had changed in places, but Adamah's defences still stood. The Smothered Princes drew up short at the edge of Hayaven and brought in their generals and godlings to issue orders.

"OUR INFANTRY WILL DROWN IN THE MUCK, NO MATTER HOW LIGHTLY THEY TREAD," one Prince told the Taursi generals.

"TWO PATHS FOR US, THEN. AN EVEN DIVISION OF OUR FORCE," his brother offered.

"LEFTWARDS, THROUGH TO BAR SHAON. JOYOUS HOUND, YOU SHALL LEAD THEM THROUGH. WE EXPECT RESISTANCE. JESUSMEN."

"I exist to serve," the Hound said through gritted fangs.

"RIGHTWARDS, THE OTHER HALF SHALL LAY SIEGE TO THE HOUSE OF AVADON, AND WIN THROUGH TO THE GLASS PLAIN. BLACKSTAR, YOU SHALL LEAD THEM."

Silence.

"BLACKSTAR, WE SUMMON YOU! RETURN FROM YOUR ERRAND AND ATTEND US!"

Silence.

"It seems you have been betrayed, masters," the Joyous Hound said. "Who knows how the Blackstar acts against you now?"

"FINAL CHANCE, BLACKSTAR."

Nothing but the nervous shifting of soldiers answered the summons. The Smothered Princes crackled with anger, like the build up toward a lightning strike.

"I should command all of the foot," the Joyous Hound said. "I have served and succeeded at all tasks."

"BARE AMBITION, AS BARE AS YOUR FANGS!"

"It is my right to seek elevation. You know this!"

"FINE. WIN THROUGH AT YOUR ASSIGNED TASK, AND WE SHALL RAISE YOU BY ONE INTEGER."

"You are as generous as you are wise," the Joyous Hound said with a bow. "See fit to grant me the Ophanim and the Seraphim, and I will end this swiftly."

"YOU MAY HAVE ONE OF EACH, AND ONE PICK FROM THE GODLINGS. WE REQUIRE THE REST."

The Hound had his own loyal underling, a mute creature known only as Old Goat, and he took half the foot and the cavalry north, towards the pass and Bor Shaon.

"APART THEN, BROTHER?"

"NECESSARY."

One brother went south to the House of Avadon to force a way through, and took many of the godlings, as well as the Gravedigger, with the hope this turncoat spirit would prove a useful sapper. The other brother took the straight path, borne up by the Ophanim and Seraphim, lifted bodily across the muck of Hayaven.

He would petition the Dawn King directly.

He'd breathed in softness and flesh once, up until the rough men had pushed pillows into their faces, and then he was reborn through light and fire, both he and his brother, given a sigil and a rank, and ambition long denied them.

He'd been the second boy (*Richard*, a small voice said, but the name meant nothing now). Life was a series of closed doors, quiet hands, servants, and whispers.

A sanctuary. A tower. Murder.

When he looked upon the stout walls of the House of Avadon, he remembered other castles, the gates always opened to him, right up until the final gate closed.

"It's the gate, Lord," he heard someone say, and snapped out of this reverie. It was the Gravedigger, shovel coated with sod.

"WHAT? REPEAT YOURSELF."

"Someone's already wrecked their bloody gate. They're repairing it."

Suspecting everything from the Blackstar to Bilben, the Smothered Prince ordered his group forward en masse. Guns crashed thunder, and the King of the Birds was on the wall himself, finally erasing the broken gate altogether and frantically replacing it with a seamless wall of stone.

The King's feathered knights clashed with Seraphim high in the sky, guns and holy fire crashing back and forth. Below, the guns on the walls chewed through the Taursi ranks. The Prince stepped forward over the paste of his soldier's bodies, ignoring every bullet and shell that glanced from his own flesh.

"COME OUT, YON CHICKS AND HATCHLINGS. YOU ARE MINE NOW."

It took some time, but soon the defenders milled about in confusion and horror as the young of the House came up to the walls, drawn by the Prince's seductive power, flinging themselves down to their deaths.

"OPEN PASSAGE TO US NOW, KING!" he yelled, but the King of the Birds was gone, back to his grand palace to quiver and sing his final and most beautiful song.

Within the hour, the Ophanim had cracked through the wall, the wheels spinning and grinding like some metaphysical tool, the Gravedigger and his crew weakening the foundations. Over half the

Taursi had fallen during the brutal siege, and they took out their fury on the birds inside, bringing them down with glass as the Seraphim circled above to catch any escapees.

They left the House of Avadon a smouldering ruin, but the Prince left the Palace of the King of the Birds intact, as it reminded him of another squat tower, a beautiful cage where beautiful people died. He personally attended to the King, pressing a pillow over his perfect face, and it was more the idea than the need for oxygen that ended the bird monarch's existence.

There was no more bird song, nothing but the tramping march of the victors, following the flood of Twice-Dead spirits toward Shale. Toward the Dawn King.

The other Prince (*Edward*, you were) had never seen such a great field of mud before. He'd been sheltered, carefully fed learning and literature, but before being smothered in the Tower, he'd read some accounts of the battles of the old kings, and some of the older guards told tales—quietly, lest they be flogged and dismissed from service.

Where others had ploughed fields, his father had left battlegrounds churned with equal parts mud, blood, shit, and piss, the dead heaped for miles. The boy Prince had been bothered by dreams of these stories, crying out and causing certain old storytellers to receive that dreaded flogging, but even these dreams did not chill him as what he saw below him now: Hayaven, the mud fields of Adamah, thick like the gravy on a king's plate. He could sense the depths of the mud, a sea that bred worms and worse monsters, and if he were to fall even he might never escape from the suck of that mire.

It would draw him in, encase his face, his nose and mouth, smothering him, stopping the flow of air…

"GRIP ME WELL! DO NOT LET ME FALL!" he yelped in a panic to the two Seraphim holding him. Below, the trio of Ophanim he'd taken skipped gleefully across the surface of the mud, unbothered by it. Their circular bodies spun only in the sense of motion and weren't truly wheels.

"We, of course, are in your service, Lord," one of the angels said, but there was a moment when their grip shifted, and the Prince regretted saying anything. He'd planted the idea in their minds.

"Lord, all servants deserve rewards, though. We labour long and ask for so little."

The grip shifted again. A threat, phrased in servility. Everyone in Overhaeven played this game, and none better than the Smothered Princes.

"I SHALL GIVE YOU A FULL TWO INTEGERS RAISE IF YOU BRING ME OVER SAFELY."

"If this were for the Joyous Hound or someone equally low, that would be an appropriate fare. You are so much more of an important personage, oh Lord! Humbly, we request three integers."

"FINE. IT IS DONE."

The Seraphim preened and rustled in their cleverness, and gripped their prize tightly, delivering him with full speed and safety to the other side of the Hayaven. As the Prince touched the smooth onyx of the Glasslands, the two Seraphim servants arranged themselves before him, bowing respectfully.

"I GRANT YOU THREE INTEGERS," he said, word and will enforcing this rise in the hierarchy. Normally such a number required decades of hard graft, but these Seraphim had earnt in one flight. The other Seraphim fluttered and hummed in jealousy and annoyance.

"We demand servants now, as is our right," the two Seraphim said, looking to their fellows, even as the Prince slammed forward in a blur of motion, plunging his hands into their central eyes.

"Pity! Spare us, we beg!" they cried, but the Prince was a flurry of tearing and burning, a machine of murder unleashed. In moments he stood above a smear of flesh and feathers, coated in gore.

"DOES ANYBODY ELSE DEMAND AN INTEGER OR A SERVANT?" he asked the remaining angels, who quivered before his wrath.

"ON TO THE DAWN KING, THEN, WHO GIVES ONLY THE REWARDS WE JUSTLY DESERVE."

The Blackstar stirred furiously against the press of his grave, frustrated that a low-grade sorcerer had tricked him. The Jesusman had tamped the clay down tightly, and he could feel the earth in his nostrils, slowly filling his mouth and throat.

The Allcatch rope that bound him was a powerful thing, soaked in Aurum, each strand of fibre crafted from the essence of an Overhaeven being. It was a dark and criminal magic, and one of the few things his kind agreed about.

Owning or making Allcatch invited destruction, and all would turn upon you.

Still, there were those who persisted, weaving these in secret, odd little knitting circles dedicated to this dark craft. The Blackstar knew this because he was the master of one such cabal, and had bound enemies before, risky as this was.

This was how he knew that this particular rope was one of his own devising, as he fumbled with the yarns and the twist of strands. It shifted as he examined it, defeating any attempt to unpick the notes or even the fibres, but eventually he found it, the maker's mark encoded into the weave.

It was a song, one he'd written for the Beatles of one world, but kept for himself when he'd walked as a rockstar and a friend of the famous. He plucked away at the notes with the edge of a thumb, the way a guitarist without a pick makes do, and parted the Allcatch effortlessly.

He erupted from his grave with screeching fury, looking for an enemy to annihilate, and found nothing but the meat of the dead camel, the furrows of his previous assault already slowly being erased.

Frowning, he called up his flying throne and took to the skies, placing the Eye of Argus to his face. He rose up, saw the destruction of the Houses of Adamah and Avadon, the battle against the Jesusmen in Bor Shaon, and his masters converging on Shale towards the stronghold of the Dawn King.

He found it, there on the final shore.

He looked closer, then closer again. Suddenly he drew back with a panic and tore the Eye of Argus from his socket.

"It is a trap! A bloody trap!"

He wheeled about, pointing the throne away from the chaos of their ambitious invasion, and tried to punch through the ceiling of the Underfog. He failed. The sepia sky was an eggshell that kept out intruders, and so there was only one thing for it.

He flew back to Oerwoud, the magic keeping his throne afloat failing before he could cross the nest of Ouroboros. The jaws of the trap were closing in, and he felt his magic failing, felt the connection to the Golden Sea growing thin.

"Bilben. You clever little bitch," he said.

His throne crumbling behind him on the cracked clay, the Blackstar ran the gauntlet of Ouroboros, his treacherous pet finally turning on him, and he was forced to hack it apart, but his claws were less razor sharp, his movements not so spry.

He survived the crossing, but was huffing with the exertion, his excellent outfit coated in gore, his magnificent mane of hair tousled and ratty.

"This is a fucking travesty," the Blackstar said, jogging to the Oerwoud, only to find the Joyous Hound's little pathway already sealed over, as if he hadn't chopped and complained his way through mere days ago.

He was forced to pace back and forth, finally tracking down the one path open to dead spirits, but it slammed shut as he approached it, trees and vines interlocking so tightly he would never win through.

A trick, then. He stilled his heart with a thought, and through willpower he emerged as the facsimile of a Once-Dead spirit. The pathway opened, and he dragged his own corpse through the Oerwoud, stumbling with every step.

Emerging on the far side, he climbed back into his physical form. It felt like sliding into a damp wetsuit, difficult and awkward. His strength was fading fast.

Reaching for the heavens, the Blackstar punched a way skyward, failing two times before he made a connection and slid back up into Overhaeven like an exhausted fish caught on a hook.

"Clever little bitch," he whispered.

UNDERFOG

J enny ran at a full gallop, still wearing the skin of a wooden horse, her horse. Bilben had been at the House of Avadon as promised...and yet Jenny had still suffered injuries and her wounded flanks oozed sap.

She was free now. She ran on, knowing the importance of what she carried, what the jawbone was truly capable of. The possibility of changes for good that she carried across the Glasslands and to its final destination.

Bilben had made her a promise, and it was such a small thing.

"There's your chance, get that jawbone!" the rat had said, back when moths and slavers fought and the House of the Accurate Count fell. "Take it to Shale."

"What then?" she said.

"You give it to me."

"Why don't you go and get it? Carry it yourself."

"Because they are all expecting that. Go!"

She ran and ran, the jawbone hidden in her own wooden skull, Bilben's earlier promise running through her head.

Deliver the jawbone, and you shall have Papa Lucy.

She'd agreed to help in Bilben's sprawling plan, but the chance for revenge blinded her to the details. At that point, Jenny simply did not care. Even here, the smell of Papa Lucy was driving her crazy. He'd tricked everyone, but he would never trick her again.

Her hooves clattered against the dark glass like four beating hammers, and she rode through an avenue of tilting obelisks, startling whenever another Twice-Dead spirit flew past her, faster still.

She saw the bird soldiers from Avadon, Jesusmen spirits, Many-Faced, and villagers from across the Underfog. They all were converging into one trail now, like a pale blue string of flags showing her the way. She ran when the sepia of day turned to the burgundy of night, her eyes still sure in the gloom.

Shale. The stronghold of the Dawn King. The New Iron Nest.

Then a car leapt out at her, a living creature with mouth wide and snarling, and someone was shouting, and a gun went off. She shied off to one side, hooves scrabbling to gain purchase, and she went down with a huge CRACK, even as a rope landed around her neck.

"You bloody idiot, Bogle!" a man yelled. "I said no guns."

She tried to rise and found one of her legs was broken down by the ankle, the hoof now only connected by a wobbling sinew. Closing her eyes, she tried to shift back into her usual form, the girl-shape of Jenny Rider, but she found a new problem.

She was stuck. Try as she might, she could not change from her horse form.

"Easy," she heard a young woman say, slowly reeling in the rope. They were closing around her, and she realised with shock that all but one of them were alive, not spirits. She recognised the House of Torana, that growling servant of Gretel, but the car's master was nowhere to be seen.

Then he was before her, hands raised up, watching her warily: Lanyard Everett. Those same hands had ended her life with a blade, back in the Now.

Stop, help me, she tried to say, but it came out as a raspy horse cry, her vocal cords things of sap and bark.

"It's injured," the girl said again, and she recognised Tilly, the prentice, now full grown. She was accompanied by two twin girls and a spirit swaddled with bandages, rifle held level.

"RIDE HER! RIDE HER!" the House of Torana barked out mockingly.

Jenny tried to stand again, and the pain was intense. She let out a scream that became a shrill whinny.

The bandaged figure called Bogle held the gun out.

"It's always a kindness when a bird breaks a leg that way," Bogle said. "Quick and merciful."

"No," Lanyard said. "Car, come shine your light on the horse."

"RIDE HER!" the House of Torana called out again. Jenny watched Lanyard's face change as the gloomy headlight revealed that her horse form was made of wood, her fur swirls of grain, the mane and tail neat bundles of fine twigs.

"The car's saying Rider," Lanyard said. "Jenny Rider."

Jenny was trying her best to communicate with the Jesusmen, but all she could do was whinny and stamp out in frustration. Sometimes her skin would shift, but almost immediately every change in form she tried slammed her back down into the horse shape.

"You're definitely Jenny Rider?" Lanyard asked.

She nodded mournfully.

"What happened to the jawbone?"

She nodded faster, and then laid her head flat against the glass, scraping it back and forth. Opened her mouth. Lanyard looked in as carefully as a bird rider doing a beak inspection.

"The jawbone's stuck in there. It's part of her now."

Even as they worked to repair the horse, Lanyard and Tilly had a running argument. He wanted to veer off at top speed towards Mal, whom he could see on the horizon through his cataract.

"We don't know how far away he is," Tilly said. "Only so much blood we can feed the car, and we're starving and thirsty."

"Toughen up, girl," Lanyard said, knowing he'd already lost this argument.

"You know the Dawn King is closer. Bauer will watch Mal for now, but we've got a bloody job to finish."

Tilly and the girls were working on a type of splint for Jenny, using splinters of rock and some leftover rope from the car, but it wouldn't bear Jenny's weight. Bogle was rummaging around in the trunk of the car and emerged with success.

"Toolbox!" Bogle said, a remnant from the days that the House of Torana had been a true car. There were other things in here, cutting tools, slicing tools, most with the stains of old blood still upon them.

A clawhammer and nails, finally turned to repair instead of destruction and torture.

Jenny cried out with pain as they made her a new leg, using a sawn up axe-handle and long roofing nails. It was thick and ungainly, but it held her weight, and she was soon game enough to trot around on it.

"Look at that," Mem said, pointing to the repair. "It's all healing."

The wood they'd added to Jenny's leg was already melting into the neighbouring pieces, the metal of the nails sealed over and hidden by bark. Sap ran over the whole joint, and soon there was only a faint scar to show where she'd broken.

"You okay to run on that?" Lanyard asked. Jenny nodded.

"Good. Because you're too fucking big to fit in the car."

They were fellow travellers now, these former enemies, and car and horse kept pace in companionable silence, the car happy enough now that it had been fed on Bogle's flesh.

"The jawbone pointing you towards the Dawn King?" Lanyard said, leaning out the window. Frustrated by her animal form, Jenny shook her head.

"Well, you can travel with us for now. I know my enemy is that way," he said, pointing unerringly without looking. "Dawn King's going down."

Jenny gave an amused snort.

"What's that supposed to mean?"

"It means that you've misunderstood everything," Bilben suddenly said from atop Jenny's wooden rump.

"Bilben!" Lanyard shouted, and he and Bogle had their guns up and out the window, even as Tilly swerved away from the horse. The large-eared rat was a shifting blur, and then it was on the dash in front of Lanyard.

"Really, I wish you would stop doing that. We need to have a civilised dialogue, and if you would just allow me to explain–"

The car erupted with yelling and snatching hands, and the rat simply dodged every attempt by the Jesusmen to seize it, easily staying clear of their grasps. Eventually they were all reduced to glaring sullenly at the rat, who twitched and cleaned its whiskers on the steering wheel.

"Got that out of your systems? Okay. Now, I appreciate you are frustrated with my methods, but I am not your enemy."

"You made a bad deal. Got my people killed."

"Lost some lives, saved others."

"You lied about Mal, about bloody Bauer!"

"I cannot lie. I simply did not mention them, and you did not directly ask me about them."

"You hair-splitting little bastard!"

"I work with what I have. Now listen to me well. You are the second group to arrive, and so you just became very important to the plan."

"What bloody plan?"

"I am wary of saying much. It may affect the outcome. Simply put, I advise that you head towards the enemy you see. Jenny here is headed toward the same place. She bears the jawbone you brought, and it has a specific purpose."

"What is the purpose of the jawbone?" Tilly said suddenly.

"See? Now you are learning. If you ask something directly, you will get a true answer. The jawbone is both gift and compass, key and ingredient, meant for a sleeping brother and a patient father."

"Stop it!"

"I do not lie."

"You also do not answer."

"Here is the only answer that matters. Overhaeven is a parasite that feeds off the rest of the universe. We have the chance now to throw them off for good, destroy them utterly. Whatever I do in pursuit of this goal is for the greater good. I have nothing but the ability to weave out a plan—a grand plan that not even those robbers of golden light can undo."

"Well, tell me the plan."

"Drive that way."

The large-eared rodent had laid out her plans across the multiverse like a huge fishing net, and hands stronger than hers were starting to drag in the catch. Everything was converging on Shale, the final beach, and Lanyard and Jenny were the next to arrive.

It was a beach of thunderous waves and black water, and the shore was heaped with rocks that were jagged, alien looking things. Lanyard saw one that reminded him of the rock he'd driven into Bauer's skull, and he supposed that every evil rock ended up here.

The black surf went out and curved up, and then the ocean itself was rising up into the sky, a sheet of black water that stretched up and up, even the sepia of dawn giving way to the impossible water of Shale.

"Where does it go?" Lanyard asked.

"Overhaeven," Bilben said, surprising everyone with the simple answer. "Watch, and wait for some poor soul. Look."

A cluster of Twice-Dead spirits came washing across the landscape. They moved feebly and frantically now, party balloons trying to resist the push of the wind, but they were driven down onto the rocks, scratched and torn, and then finally swallowed up by a wave.

The waters sparked a sudden bright blue as they swallowed up the last of the Aether, and then the water was less black there, and more a pulse of blue pushing backwards, climbing upwards, and lost to sight as it began to climb the watery stair.

"There it goes," Bilben said. "They get everything out of this place. Whatever gets spilled into the ground washes up here, too, through the aquifers, running out through the sands. Every last drop."

The sound of the car's back door opening, closing gently.

"Before Overhaeven, this was a merry place of sand and fond farewells. Beautiful clear water, and how the other spirits would wave them goodbye as they set off, happy, free, absorbed into the universe once more!"

Bogle Hess was stumbling forward, drawn toward the ocean as if in a trance.

"You might want to stop your friend there. It's hard for new spirits to resist this."

Lanyard and Tilly were out and pinning down Bogle, who cried out in denial, reaching for the black waters, the oblivion, the utter undoing of self that it promised.

"So, you can see that this was once paradise, and it was stolen. Overhaeven came, set itself above all, and caught every dead thing in a sieve, taking their souls and distilling them."

"Bloody thieves," Lanyard said, wrestling Bogle over and hogtying them.

"Down in the cold, where the blue turns to gold," the rat slowly sang.

"I know that song," Tilly said. "Heard it on a record."

"I am sure. Fed the truth to a musician once, little clues in his sleep. The Golden Sea. All of it."

"How long have you been planning this?"

"Since the day Overhaeven dreamt itself into being and took over," Bilben said. "I was there that day. I–I was one of them."

The Jesusmen said nothing.

"We were wrong. I have caused much misery."

"You should hurl yourself into that bloody sea," Lanyard muttered.

"I did once," Bilben admitted. "I was sad, guilty. Ran into the waters and hoped for the end. It doesn't work for my kind."

Bilben walked past them, weaving through the rocks in her own ratty way, blinking into the spray. Then she dived into the water with an almighty splash and bobbed around.

"You can see it does not harm me, but we barred the Taursi from it for their own safety."

Behind her, a great commotion and thrashing in the waves, and something rose in the foam, rose out of the waters. Bilben climbed out of the water to rejoin the Jesusmen and watched.

"I did not die, but I found something in there. I found a friend—a very clever friend."

It was a building, a patchwork construction of what looked to be driftwood, bleached and worn, built to an enormous scale. Water spilled from tall towers and turrets, and wing after wing rose, connecting together until a grand mansion stood before them, completely realised in that water battered wood. The towers had a slight curve, and each of the crenelations ended in a hook, like a beckoning finger.

An enormous drawbridge fell down across the rocks, allowing safe passage into the broad front archway, and it was only then that

Lanyard realised where he'd seen this structure before. It was in Crosspoint, and he'd seen it countless times.

The home of the new Moot, a mansion which was previously owned by none other than Papa Lucy.

Jenny screeched in rage and fury, eyes widened, snorting, hooves suddenly a-clatter as she raced down toward the beach. Bilben watched this with hands folded, and she did not say a single word.

Even as the Blackstar rose toward Overhaeven, Sol made his escape to the Greygulf, which was as far ahead as he was able to plan.

Everything hurt in his new body. It was like stepping back in time to his twenties, hair thick and full, no paunch, skin tight and free of imperfections. A true gift! He was starting to feel cold again, the stale winds of the Greygulf washing across his naked body.

Sol had hidden caches across this industrial wasteland, but two had been discovered and pilfered by Witches or worse. He lucked out on the third try, down in the cellar of the old Terminus, the connecting spire of the shadow-roads, where the Jesusman Neville lost his mind and his way.

Everything else worth a damn had been carted out of here by Lanyard's people years ago, but Sol found the hidden panel easily enough, sliding across the bolt that only magic could move.

Clothes, wrapped in an oil-skin coat. Good hiking boots. A pistol and ammunition. Focus stones and magical augments from the Collegia. Canned food, most of it rusted through now and spoiled, and a good whisky that he looked forward to enjoying.

"I haven't had a good drink for so long," Sol said to himself with a smile. It then occurred to him that he was not the Boneman anymore. He felt like he'd lost something in the Golden Sea, something important, but it was worth it just to see his hands, feel the flesh across his cheekbones, and know that he was finally back, finally *alive*.

He dressed in the jeans and shirt, warming up once he shrugged into the oilskin. As he sat down to lace up the boots, he saw it in the back of the cavity, pinned up and hard to see.

A photograph. On hands and knees he crawled forward, hardly daring to breathe, and he slowly plucked it from the old adhesive. An edge crumbled in his hands, and his heart hammered.

It was all of them, their happy little gang of plotters and misfits, in the final days of the Before. Sol, Lucy, John, and Hesus, laughing by the beach. Baertha lay across their arms, hamming it up, one arm raised with a ballerina's grace.

"Oh, my love," he whispered. He missed her to the point of physical pain. There was so much potential to all of the friends in that photo, but most of all in the face of Baertha Pappagallo, and she was like the focal point of a Renaissance painting, face alive with love, light, and joy, even with such a heavy task ahead of them.

Sol and Lucy were grinning elbow to elbow in the pose, holding up the woman that they would both love in their own way, and he had to wonder which was the most poisonous: Lucy's use of the Cruik to ruin her, body and soul, or his own slow stifling of such a free spirit, confining her to the top of a pedestal and not much more.

In the photo there was a car behind them, John's beautiful old Ford Falcon, the hood open despite it being in perfect order. A figure was poking around with the insides and was caught looking up at the camera as if surprised.

"John's brother," Sol said after a moment. "Ray, that was his name. Poor bloke."

He remembered Ray in the invalid tents after the Crossing, his long climb back to recovery, how he'd finally sent him off to hide. The Junkman, vanished somewhere in the wilderness, but safe from Lucy, safe even from John's misguided kindnesses.

Sol found a mouldering beach-chair in the wreckage and sat down in the cellar, eating a cold can of baked beans and washing it down with whisky. With food, shelter, and warmth to hand, he had the bottom of Maslow's pyramid covered, and his brain could move onto that all-important question: *What now?*

There was nothing left for him in the Now; who would believe him, coming back as a living man and claiming to be the Boneman? All that waited for him in Overhaeven was discovery and destruction, and though the Witches had mostly been exterminated here, the Greygulf was still a dangerous place to linger—and certainly a lonely place to starve.

His captors had let loose some information as they prepared him for destruction, giddy with hubris and success. John and Hesus, captured and sent down to the Underfog, to feed whatever scheme the Dawn King had down there.

Sol had made promises when last he visited, but supposed the people he'd sworn these to were no longer there, or no longer in power. Even if he could not escape the Underfog, it was the right thing to do—even with the promise of his new body and a new chance at life.

In his mind, it was all settled. The last of the necromancers was returning to the land of the dead. He would do everything he could to fight the golden armies, free his friends, find Lanyard and the Jesusmen.

Most of all, he was going to find the Dawn King and make him pay for his seductive lies. Baertha was gone, but Sol remained, and now he knew that penance and vengeance were as good as the same thing.

Sol preferred the traditional approach into the Underfog. He dropped through into the Aum, the place of darkness and whispers, and then made his petition to enter the Underfog itself.

Nothing. The Lords of the Underfog were silent.

Sol pushed through the barrier, and it was easier than it should have been, the sheerest curtain between darkness and the fog of the Edgemist, and no one observed his entry into the lands of the Once-Dead.

He'd been a strange figure on his last visit, a walking skeleton that was still technically alive, and the Lords had been confused on how to handle him. It went well for him that he was there to deal with his destructive brother, but his existence insulted many.

A great delegation came for him, holding court on this side of the Oerwoud. Old Paeter and his gang of vampires. The Farmer, the Gravedigger, the Teller, the King of the Birds, Gretel and her House of Torana, the Sleepers of the Glasslands, even the Many-Faced, all of them in a furious debate over this odd necromancer, the brother of Papa Lucy no less. Even the Chain-Folk sent a cautious representative, lurking in the wings with a set of shackles should the Boneman wander too close.

It seemed like an easy agreement to make at the time. As the Boneman, he had no reason ever to want to return to the Underfog, save for when his life ended, and so he agreed to the terms of entry. Deal with his brother and leave, never to return, on penalty of destruction in the waters of Shale.

Sol watched for Old Paeter, the sinister lurker who pounced on newcomers in these lands, but saw no one. Great hordes of Chain-Folk were sometimes seen roaming and warring in these plains, but Sol faced nothing more than a quiet and uneventful walk through the breathing landscape. He knew the old necromancer trick, and stepped in rhythm with the "breaths," sliding swiftly across the Underfog.

"Argh!"

A biting pain in his foot, and he was forced to stop, hopping madly on the spot. Taursi battle-glass, straight through the sole of his thick boots and into the flesh of his foot. He extracted it and whispered a spell to clean and close the wound, then looked at the remnants of the great battle around him.

The bodies of many Taursi soldiers littered the ground, most torn apart with great violence, still fallen in their ranks. They'd been marching on Oerwoud, and something destroyed them with great prejudice.

He approached the eternal forest slowly, but nothing rushed out at him, and his quiet little magics revealed no hidden foe. Normally this place was as lousy with the Once-Dead spirits as there were fleas on a dog, but it felt abandoned.

There was a path through the Oerwoud that opened for spirits, but it closed itself against any intruders. An old defence planted by the Farmer, and Sol knew the trick for a living man to bluff his way through. He simply thought about plants, and how happy they made him. Remembered geraniums, grass, bonsai trees, all of it, and the Oerwoud opened for him readily enough.

Sometimes there'd been predators here, lurking in the Oerwoud, but apart from the shifting of the plants it was as empty as everything else. If the Dawn King cultists had pushed a way through, they'd scared the lurkers and hunters into flight.

Risking the fast travel again, Sol slid through the montage of plant growth to emerge to the strangest of sights. The House of the Accurate Count had vanished. The cracked clay around it had erupted, revealing the tentacles of the beast that had once slept at the House's root, Ouroboros.

A red muscle car was trying to escape from the grip of a tentacle, wheels spinning madly, the golden light of an Aurum engine spilling from under the car and out of the exhaust pipe.

Sliding forward in rhythm with the land, Sol walked easily over the traps Ouroboros had set, and then he was standing next to the car, laying gentle hands on the tentacles spiralling around it, using flesh and nerve to convince the distant brain that this was not food, this was distasteful, poisonous, bad. The tentacles unravelled quickly, drawing back into the ground, and the car jerked forward several feet.

The driver jammed down on the brakes and then leant out of the window, looking back at the retreating monster. He met Sol's eyes for a brief instance before looking away, mouth working and trying to form a response.

A gust of wind tickled the driver's thick mane of hair. Free as he was, the driver of the red car seemed powerless to move.

"Are you okay?" Sol ventured.

The man nodded and turned the engine off. The ratchet of the handbrake followed a moment later.

"What are you doing?" Sol said, but the man ignored him. He was adjusting his seat and mirrors, checking his seat belt strap, and then he held his hands at 10 and 2 on the steering wheel. He turned the key back on, and when the Aurum engine hummed back into life he clicked on the right indicator, which flashed and ticked all alone in that desolate place.

He checked his blind spot, released the handbrake, and then imme-diately stalled the engine. With an anguished cry the driver slapped himself in the head, and kept striking himself, faster and faster.

"No. Stop," Sol said, leaning in to prevent the man from hitting himself, gently holding his wrists. "Please don't hurt yourself. Breathe. You're okay."

He saw it then, in the nose, the set of the jaw, the thick mane of hair. Remembered the moments when a dear friend dealt with his overwhelmed brother.

"You're Ray Leicester," he said, and then the man started screaming.

"I'm not! I'm not him!"

"Okay," Sol said, backing away a step, hands raised with palms outward.

"I'm the Junkman. Only the Junkman."

"You are. I remember you."

"I don't remember you."

"Sol. A friend of your brother."

"Brother!" he screamed. "No!"

Sol decided it was best to stop speaking altogether, and he let the Junkman work through his agitation. A few minutes later calm returned, and the Junkman leaned across, opening the passenger door, pushing a pile of boxes outside to make room. Model plane kits, tins of baked beans, comic books, and other ephemera, all of it slid out onto the ground.

"You can get in if you want," he told Sol, who walked around and climbed into the vehicle. The muscle car was in pristine condition, either a perfect bleedthrough or a patient resurrection, and Sol marvelled at this glimpse of a world long gone.

Then there was a rat with large ears suddenly sitting in his lap, and Sol cried out in panic.

"Perhaps a bit unnecessary," the rat said to him. "After all, last time I saw you, you were a set of bones in need of a friend. I spoke on your behalf, though it earnt me wide scorn and a burnt bridge or two."

"Bilben of the Iron Nest," Sol said, remembering.

Once more the Junkman went through his pre-driving checklist, as flawless as any well-studied driving student, and this time the car did not stall.

"How did Ouroboros catch you?" he said. "I remember the stories, that you see all ways, plan for all things. That does not ring true."

"The probabilities are shrinking. I could see everything once. Now, my eyes are little better than years."

"What does that mean?"

"Forgive me for being rude, but I'm about to do something strenuous somewhere else. I don't feel like talking," Bilben said, and curled up in his lap, immediately asleep.

"Where are you driving to?" Sol asked the Junkman.

"Going to the beach, she says. Drive to the mud, she says, and then go left, go through a skinny gap. Find a quiet place, and then a very black place, and then there's a beach."

"Do you know where the Dawn King is?"

"Don't know who that is. I'm just driving now. Seatbelts please."

Sol was suspicious, but even though this meeting felt contrived, he buckled in. He was hypnotised by the nostalgia, and he felt a little closer to Baertha in that moment, as if Crossing and Cruik and cuckolding had never happened. He was able to marinate himself in those distant memories, think back to the fast group of friends once captured in a crumbling photograph. The two men from a dead world drove through the emptiness of the Underfog, the rat sleeping on innocently.

"Going to the beach," Sol mused.

— 27 —

UNDERFOG

The retreat became a running battle, and Mal was breathing frantically, riding low in the saddle. Taursi glass flashed by in waves, and he'd caught more than one jag as the spider-horse cavalry kept pace with the bird riders.

Taursi blood ran down his lance, but these were the pure warriors of Overhaeven, and their fluids were thick and golden. Mal thought the echidna-faced warriors were terrifying, fixing him with eyes of purest black as they came in with glass-tipped spears, quills spread and glowing red hot. In the killing moments, Kirstl came forward in their mind, and it was her will that drove the lance most often, killing while Mal watched mutely.

I just wanted a bird, he realised. *I just wanted Lanyard to be my dad and get me out my chains. Not this.*

Bauer's plan to run rings around this enemy had failed like so many plans did. The army from Overhaeven was as fast as they were, and even the infantry could keep up with Bauer's brace of birds. They were hounding them left and right, rounding them up like sheep.

Ahead, the cars and bikes doubled back, guns flashing death in the unnatural quiet, and the Taursi lancers met them on their spider-horse mounts, waves of glass scarring windshields and throats alike.

The Jesusmen threw around marks, the contortion of hands and fingers bringing forth symbols to blind and confuse the enemy, flashes of pain and bright light, even fire to turn an enemy into a running candle. But there was always a cost, and Mal remembered another lesson of Lanyard's, delivered around a lonely campfire.

Magic is like a gun running low on bullets, he'd said. *Never fire that gun completely dry because the last bullet is always meant for you.*

Mal saw bike riders toppling out and onto the ground, drained from their efforts against the huge, rolling horde, the last of their magic winking out. Others caught on fire when their magic went off too early, entire buggies and cars going up in flames.

It was a strange sight to see their two armies racing across this silent moonscape, weapons flashing back and forth, the filmy sheaths of the Twice-Dead Jesusmen floating towards Shale, the shattered spirits a river of blue that stretched out over miles.

Mal could feel the movement of Bauer shifting around and was glad for the silence as the old Jesusman unleashed a chattering assault rifle right by his ears. Bauer tossed it aside when he was out of ammunition, and then he was pitching grenades left and right, blowing Taursi and mount alike into oblivion.

Oh shit, Kirstl said, and Mal saw it then. Ahead, the enormous jackal-man and his burning goat lay in wait, deposited in their path by the winged eye-beast. At their feet, the linked golden wheels churned up the white dust, ready to race forward and grind them to oblivion.

Mal looked up to Bauer, who lay a firm hand on his shoulder, squeezing gently. At this point there was nothing much that needed to be said, and he was again grateful for the silence, that there was no need to fill this final ride with words of bravery, of goodbye or regret.

But one look at Bauer's grim face reinforced this truth of Jesusmen. They didn't waste words when bullets would do, and Bauer was as likely to have kept his own counsel on this mad, final charge into their deaths.

Come in here, Kirstl said. *Quickly.*

I'm too busy dying, sweetheart, Mal said, looking as the big dog-man unfurled his bright whip, but then he closed his eyes and relaxed. He let Kirstl drag him in deeply. He was only dimly aware of Collybrock thundering away beneath him, of Bauer clutching at his back.

He opened his eyes to see that he walked the war-room with Kirstl and Bilben, and looked down on that map as if an eagle just hovering above. He had a front row seat to that final glorious charge, could see the Jesusmen funnelled towards certain doom and embracing it with gusto.

"You all did it," Bilben said proudly. "They've been fooled. Look!"

Sliding back across the dust and craters, Mal looked at the pass with its shattered wall and saw the Many-Faced pouring out through the gap, holding up grisly trophies as their tentacles propelled them across Bor Shaon. Mal realised the string of Twice-Dead Jesusmen and the Many-Faced were both heading in the same direction.

"Bilben," he said slowly. "Why are they taking Taursi hearts to Shale?"

"It's the plan, boy! And it's working!"

"You've lost your bloody mind, rat. And Bauer, he's lost everything. We did this for meat?"

"They have to get them to Shale," Kirstl said. "The hearts can fix everything!"

"You wanted to throttle her yesterday, and now she's infected you with her bullshit," Mal began, but the rat pulled him close, and she seemed bigger then, all snout and whiskers and eyes.

"Appreciate what you are seeing, boy," she said. "Bauer and his people are about to be destroyed for a greater cause."

"Well, that's great."

"Stop being facetious and pay attention. You are not an acceptable casualty in this charge, so you are not going to be there."

"What the hell do you mean?"

"It will cost me greatly. This cannot happen again. You are to deliver a message—and deliver it you shall."

"Run your own letters," Mal said, but she ignored him.

"Your job is simple," she said. "Tell Lanyard Everett of the many ways that I have betrayed you today."

Bilben seemed to envelope Mal, and then he was back in the saddle, Bauer on his back, but this time Bilben rode with them, and then suddenly there were two Collybrocks, pulling apart with a sickening lurch, but this time he wasn't carrying Bauer. Everything stopped. The flying glass, the cracking whip of the kilted dog-god, the weaving bikes and cars, all of it frozen in place.

Then Collybrock was moving backward, even as everything struggled to move forward again, one or two seconds jerkily moving backward and forward in place. Mal saw himself weaving in and out of the press, moving faster, and then everything blurred, and then he was back at the ravine, waiting for the wall to crumble, lined up with the bird riders and ready to evacuate the defenders.

Mal could only watch as he took up the reins and wheeled Collybrock's head in the other direction.

Kirstl. Kirstl! Stop that!

I'm not doing it, she said in a panic. Mal felt his body sit up high in the saddle, and he dug in his heels, flicking the reins, clicking his tongue to issue the command for fast trot.

Bilben, please! Mal cried out. *Stop this.*

He did the most unforgiveable thing a Jesusman could do. When the trouble came knocking, Mal ran. The older Jesusmen cried out in disbelief and cursed him for being a coward. Even Bauer caught wind of the disturbance and looked down on Mal from on top of the wall.

Mal caught the moment when the god with the whip caught Bauer around the throat, pulling him down to the other side, and he went over without complaint, doing nothing in his last moment but stare down at Lanyard's failed prentice, condemning Mal in silence, and then he was gone.

"Damn you, Bilben!" Mal said some hours later, when he was finally able to wrest back control of his body. Crying messily, he yanked back on the reins, wheeling Collybrock around.

No, stop, Kirstl said. *We can't go back.*

"We have to," Mal sniffed. "That's our place."

We can't go back because they're all dead now. See?

She seized his arm for a minute, pointing, indicating a distant smudge of blue on the horizon. It was a river of destroyed spirits washing across the ground, forming a straight line towards Shale.

The ground had changed slowly, the ground-bone-dust style of Bor Shaon changing to fused glass, miles and miles of it, growing darker with every step. The Glasslands. Mal realised he could hear again, heard the click of Collybrock as she shifted from foot to foot.

"Come with me," Mal said, and shifted inward, pushing down to the dreamspace, breaking in to face that treacherous rat in her war-room. He came in scowling, imagining his wicked little lance in his hands, but the room was abandoned, the map slowly drifting apart.

Kirstl bore an identical lance to Mal, and she stalked murderously through the wreckage of the dreamspace, poking her blade into hidden corners, trying to flush Bilben out.

"Come out, rat!" she yelled. "I spoke for you! You won me bloody over, and now you'll pay!"

Nothing. The tiny schemer was long gone. The details of everything Bilben had made in here were already fuzzing over in the nature of a dream just woken from, but enough remained to make out the smoking ruins of the House of Avadon, the chaos in Bor Shaon, and always that final shore, beckoning them, closer now than ever.

Everything converged on this location, trails of ants drawn to sugar. The spirits of dead Jesusmen, the Taursi, a huge rolling horde of the Many-Faced, and the besiegers of the House of Avadon. In the logic of a dream each group became a chess piece, the Underfog now a sprawling board that Mal and Kirstl walked upon.

"Let's go," Mal said, and they slid across the black squares, winning through to the final two rows of the board, everything beyond this the void, the climbing water, the utter destruction that was Shale.

There was a castle piece here, tall and dominating, and a row of smaller pieces set to defending it, likenesses carved into the wood by a masterful hand. Bogle Hess, the twins Mem and Lyn, Tilly...and there was Lanyard, grimmer still as a statue.

There were more. Jesus himself. John Leicester. And in front of them all, unassuming and clutching her paws, a pawn piece carved to represent Bilben.

Kirstl knocked it over with her lance, and she and Mal took out their frustrations until it was a pile of wood chips.

A sound behind them, and they saw pieces sliding out from the muck of Hayaven, moving toward them. A golden piece, flanked by winged beasts and wheels, and heading to Shale at great speed. A Smothered Prince.

There they were on the board, too, a boy on a bird, right in their way.

"Wake up," Kirstl said, shaking Mal fast. "Wake up and ride!"

Mal woke in the saddle, alone on the vast black plain, and he turned in a panic towards the far end of Hayaven. He thought he could see a golden glow on the horizon, and he knew that if that creepy little god-boy called to him, he would answer that summons, he and Kirstl both.

He needed to go, right now. Save himself. Save Lanyard, warn him about the enemies closing in on them. Warn him about Bilben.

"Come on, girl," he said, patting Collybrock on the flanks. She was hanging her head, sides heaving from her epic trot, and her knees were giving, which usually meant a bird was about to sit down and ignore its owner. She was obedient and faithful, but he'd driven her too far.

"Rest. Sore," she said.

"Please. I need you to run for me one last time, and then you can rest."

"No! Tired!"

Collybrock sank to her haunches, head and neck laying flush with the slick glass. She huffed out a bellows of disappointment and lay still.

"Come on!" Mal said, yanking up on the reins. "Up!"

"Rest," the bird gargled.

"I have never whipped you once! I've fed you well! You lazy bloody beast."

"Mal can walk," Collybrock said.

He sank down next to his bird, barking with laughter. Even as doom approached, birds would be birds. Mal watched philosophically as separate points of light began to fuzz the horizon, like three false dawns. The trident of the Overhaeven invaders, closing in on everyone left whom he cared about.

"Right, bird. You can have five minutes, but then you'd better run like racing stock. We've got a job to do."

Collybrock let out a rumbling fart and then a snore.

Mal and Kirstl spent their last five minutes together well, casting aside Bilben's schemes to share a few moments of paradise in their dreamspace. They played at leaving the Jesusmen and running a wayhouse as husband and wife. Got into the glamourous world of bird racing. Took over as the new Lanyard and Tilly, running the

Lodge in Crosspoint. Lived in the Before, eating plentifully from a fridgerator and breeding countless children.

Then the dream had to end, and Mal was up, rummaging through saddlebags, booting Collybrock to her feet.

"Wake up," he said, smiling at her attempts to ignore him and bury her head deep beneath her wings. He finally coaxed her out with the last of the food and water, and she fell on it with snapping beak and groans of satisfaction.

"You need it more than me, girl."

The glow from the approaching Prince was bright now, and Mal tightened the girth, set the saddle with excited hands. She rose to her feet, and they were ready to race for their lives.

"Sun," Collybrock said, looking toward the glow.

"That's not the sun, girl. Go, go!"

Collybrock started off slow, but she built up her pace to a fast trot that ate up miles, huffing and bouncing across the slick surface of the Glasslands. Mal sat down low, pushing her for more and more speed.

Shapes appeared ahead and soon revealed themselves to be columns, obelisks carved like black gravestones, details of names and designs smudged by an unkind thumb. In places the obelisks were leaning over or had fallen altogether. They formed broad avenues, a grid that stretched as far as he could see.

Underneath the glass, dark shapes moved slowly, as if clouds or large, slow fish. The ground felt solid and firm, but Mal knew this glass could fail, and wondered for a nervous moment if there were places he and Collybrock might fall through.

"Come on, girl," Mal said, leaning forward, patting her neck. She picked up the pace, and even in this peril part of Mal could pretend that he and Collybrock were running the racetracks of Langenfell and Rosenthrall, the stone markers the edge of the track, an unseen audience cheering them on.

There. The spark of a visible glow on the horizon, and then a great light went up, arcing into the air. A signal, answered a moment later by the other wings of the invading force.

"Lanyard," Mal said through gritted teeth. "We've gotta warn him."

Surely he saw it, too, Kirstl said.

"Bilben is probably spinning him lies. Telling him help is on the way or something. We need to get there now!"

Collybrock had burnt through her initial burst of speed, and was back to plodding along faithfully, a trot that would get you where you were going if you had plenty of time. Mal started to strip away the gear from her saddle, casting it away to reduce the weight she was carrying. His sleeping roll, a set of cooking pans, kindling and logs for a campfire, all of it fell to the ground as he sawed away at the straps with his blade.

"Go, girl, you can do this," he said. He emptied his pockets, threw away his hat and pack of clothes, and after a moment of heartache he even threw away his precious new lance, which clattered and tinkled merrily on the glass in their wake.

"We don't deserve to keep it," he said to justify this to Kirstl, who said nothing.

Perhaps a few miles back, he saw an obelisk erupt into a pillar of fire, and then another one. The invaders behind him sent up a flare and were answered by the other converging parties.

Collybrock was huffing now, struggling to keep up this pace, and Mal knew that he was done, that his message wouldn't get through. This group would overtake them soon enough, and he had no doubt of the sport and joy they would take from a lone boy riding a bird in the dark.

More obelisks exploded in the landscape, and one erupted into flames, tipping over with a heavy crash. There was a sense of timelessness about the Glasslands, and here the Prince was destroying the place out of hand, much like a naughty boy with a stick might strike the heads from flowers as he walks past a well-kept garden.

"Please, girl, we've got to keep moving," Mal begged, and he fed a trickle of his own vitality into her, the mark winking briefly in the darkness.

The smallest of lights, but in all of that black it was enough.

"HO AHEAD!" a booming voice echoed across the landscape. "WAIT FOR ME, LITTLE SHOOTING STAR. I AM COMING!"

The ground shivered with the thunder of their approach. A burning wheel bounced left and right like an excited puppy, knocking over pillars, and winged beasts bore the Prince above the ground, homing in on them fast.

You had to throw away your only weapon, Kirstl said dryly. Even now, Mal urged Collybrock on, the lessons of resisting to the utmost driven into him. Never giving up, fighting for every breath and heartbeat, knowing that defeat sometimes held a surprise victory.

"A LITTLE JESUSMAN!" the Prince cried. "SHALL WE SING TO YOU? SUMMON YOU TO OUR BOSOM?"

His servants tittered with laughter, the sound a cacophony of church bells, the baying of hounds on the hunt, the scrape of mountain ranges grinding together deep underground.

"NO, I SHALL HUNT YOU! RUN, RUN WITH ALL HASTE!"

The wings deposited the Prince on the ground, and he ran after Mal, the cherubic child now glowing with so much light that it sent shadows dancing between the rows of columns. Even without his servants to bear him he was fast, as swift as Collybrock.

This was it. The moment every bird rider lived for, fantasised about. A race at high stakes—but this wasn't for a rich purse or a place in a prestigious stable.

The stakes were no less than *everything*, and Mal was already losing. Collybrock was already burning through the spark of energy he'd shared with her, her legs beginning to wobble. He gave her another bit of himself through a mark, as large as he could spare, and almost fell from the saddle, instantly dizzy, barely able to hold on.

It was just enough to keep Collybrock ahead of the Prince, and she drew ahead of him by a whisker.

"STAY BACK! THIS ONE IS MY PRIZE ALONE!" the Prince yelled out when one of the winged beasts got too close, and he struck it from the sky with a beam of violet energy.

"Keep going, girl," Mal whispered, clutching her around the neck. He loved this bird so very dearly, and at the end he even considered tossing himself to the Prince, allowing Collybrock to escape. Would her empty saddle and flapping reins give Lanyard the warning he needed? Would Tilly and Lanyard be able to prise some secrets out of the bird's simple mind?

He was ready to do it. Ready to leap backwards in a flurry of defiant fists and chokeholds, whatever moment he could win before the Prince recovered and enchanted him.

Wait, Kirstl said. *Look at the Prince. Don't give up yet.*

"COME HERE! LET ME PLUCK YOUR FEATHERS, BIRD, AND STRING YOUR GUTS AROUND YONDER COLUMNS!" the Prince said. Mal heard it then. A gasp, as the golden godling began to flag, holding his hand to his side. A stitch?

Collybrock drew ahead by another whisker, and then another. Mal smiled.

"You're piss weak," he called out over his shoulder. "You call that a race?"

Collybrock lifted her neck, perking her head back. She'd scented water, dead ahead. *Shale.* But all he could see in the gloom was endless columns, the shadows cast by the Prince, and the large shapes moving slowly beneath the glass. It might be miles yet before they reached the shore, to whatever fortress Lanyard was defending.

Miles that Collybrock simply did not have in the tank. The bird needed a week in the stables and a veterinarian to properly suture all of her wounds. The energy he'd been feeding her through the mark was a false vitality, and her muscles were still burning, her lungs still heaving. If Mal pushed her much further, there was the very real chance she could die.

His magic was beginning to fail now. The Prince still kept pace, little limbs blurring, and he gained by a step, and then another. Sweet little lips curved up into an evil smile.

"THERE IT IS," he said. "THE WEAKNESS OF PISS!"

Mal suddenly jinked left, putting a column in between them. The Prince was forced to slide around to keep up. And then Mal leapt Collybrock up and over a fallen obelisk, forcing the Prince to scramble up behind them.

"HO, THE INVENTIVENESS OF A GOOD PREY!"

This was it, the final endgame of the chase, and it could only end in Collybrock falling and the Prince destroying them—but like a mouse fleeing a snake, they could not give up, not until the moment the jaws closed around them.

Then they were amongst an entire field of figures, hundreds of people buried in the glass. Their arms were laid across to their shoulders in the manner of the dead put to rest, and they swayed slowly, as if with a tide or the breeze.

They opened their eyes as one and cried out in alarm.

Mal remembered the Boneman's tales of the Underfog, and his stories of the Half-Buried, the caste of monks who'd finally given Papa Lucy the location of the Cruik. He'd always imagined them pressed into soil or sod, but he supposed this made as much sense as anything down here.

Collybrock flinched, but he pressed her on, whispered words of encouragement, and ran through the ranks of the Half-Buried, who called out to him as he fled.

"Living flesh!"

"You should not be here. Leave!"

"I am a friend of the Boneman," Mal called out. "Please, please save me! Overhaeven comes!"

A silent conference, and then they nodded as one. As the Prince ran through their field of hands and arms, the buried monks snatched out at him, grabbing at his legs and ankles, even as he destroyed them utterly with violet fury.

"YOU CHEAT!" he called out to Mal, who responded with an upright middle finger.

Collybrock reached the far end of the Half-Buried lands. She could only huff and grumble, slowing down to a pained walk.

"Get off," she complained, and Mal slid out of the saddle, pulling her along by the reins. The Prince was furious now, destroying every last one of the Half-Buried, and his wheel and his flying eyes were joining in, churning the ancient order into nothing. Twice-Dead by the score flew past Mal, pained and shocked, their eternal rest undone in seconds.

"YOU DARE TO TOUCH ME?" the Prince screamed.

The Half-Buried had spent decades slowly drilling into the glass, placing themselves inside to remain in situ—a process taking centuries—and now they were suddenly gone. The destruction of their order had happened in seconds, leaving a field riddled with deep holes.

Around the Prince, cracks in the surface spread, each footstep exacerbating this rapid destruction, as if he dared to run over thin ice. A loud snap echoed against the obelisks, and then another.

Suddenly the surface of the Glasslands broke, plunging the golden Prince into the abyss below. He roared in disbelief for many moments, plummeting an impossible distance toward that place of flames.

"We did it," Mal said in shock, looking at the wreckage of the Half-Buried's lands, and then down into the sharp-edged pit that looked deep into a place of eye-twisting strangeness. Layers of black cloud-beasts floated as far down as he could see, ringed with eyes, all of them mating or killing each other, dividing into more of the creatures. Below their language of lightning and division, Mal caught glimpses of a dark land, veined with flaming rivers, and the twinkle of well-lit settlements.

Another secret world? Kirstl said. *What in the bright blue fuck?*

"GET HIM."

The ringing of bells, the blinding flare of light, and then the Smothered Prince soared back out of the pit, borne aloft by his winged servants, and he rode the spinning wheels, eyes ablaze with vengeance.

Then, he gave a chilling smile.

The Prince began his secret song, and Mal was filled with joy and belonging. He dropped Collybrock's reins and walked towards the curly-haired cherub, who beckoned him onward, inviting him to step into the pit and let it swallow him.

"It's beautiful," Mal said.

So beautiful, Kirstl agreed.

His feet approaching the very edge of the shattered glass, Mal cried out in denial as an immense, dark shape rushed forward, slamming him backward. He slid across the glass, which flexed and bowed yet did not break, and still he struggled to rise, crawling toward the song.

The creatures that swam below the Glasslands rose up, squeezing through the pit like a pair of hands, and they enveloped the Smothered Prince and his servants, drawing them downward, sealing over the glass as they pulled them under.

Freed of the siren song, Mal could only watch, chilled to his very being as the Smothered Prince was drawn deep into that place of clouds and fire, the cloud-creatures slowly drawing him into themselves, his golden glow eventually snuffed out.

— 28 —

UNDERFOG

The remaining Smothered Prince fell to his feet on the other side of the House of Avadon, screaming so loudly that several Taursi keeled over dead, heads shattered from the sheer force of such grief.

They'd died together once, under the pillows pressed by rough hands, but now he was alone, so utterly alone.

(I was Richard, he was Edward.)

He'd always been the second, the spare to the heir. Now he was the only one left, the only survivor of their bizarre journey through death and beyond, their selection for Overhaeven, and the jostling for power since, the guzzling from the Golden Sea, the siphoning of that sweet nectar from the rest of an unsuspecting universe.

"WE ARE AS MOSQUITOES, DEAR BROTHER!" Edward had declared, and in that instant they'd been transformed from victims into predators. All of the injustices they'd faced in life fuelled them into greater heights of depravity.

There were others in the newly minted realm of Overhaeven who'd known their world, and other worlds, and worlds beyond that, and it was a cosmic accident more than anything, a sideways shift from the normal places the dead went.

Before, there were places for the living. A place for the good. A place for redeeming evil ones. Beyond that, a universe that absorbed those who'd learnt their lessons or lived their fill, absorbing them all to start again.

Then came an alliance, a cabal of dead spirits, both good and evil, attempting to break back into Life. Their attempt went awry, shunting them all to an empty place filled with refugee souls, starving and angry.

There was a powerful magic in twins, and so of course the Smothered Princes had fallen into the scheme and thus into that blister between the realms.

They'd found a secret prison, a place of sand and utter darkness. The Taursi were here, moaning in the dark, imprisoned with their fallen leader, the crooked staff that they still ferried around like a standard. The Cruik seized on this new opportunity to escape.

Invasion. Wars. Raids against the other worlds, driven by hunger, and they were rebuffed at every turn, by foul Adamah and others, until they devised a smarter way: using the final shore of Gan-Eden against it.

Rising along the edges of the old realms, the conspirators used the waters to siphon stolen Aether up and into a new reservoir, refining it into Aurum along the way. Then to safeguard their theft, they made a hard boundary around both the Gan-Eden and the prison underneath the dark glass.

The lords of this new realm decided that they needed to prevent record-keeping and written communication amongst their prisoners, a most powerful spell to foil any attempt at organising resistance or revenge. It was always a source of amusement to the Princes, who valued their own literacy and thought of the illiterate as peasants.

As the conspirators took their place as rulers of the universe, they were all finally forced to evict the Cruik, which wanted to set itself above them all. This took a furious battle that destroyed half their number before they trapped it in the Underfog, broken and beaten.

In place of kings or democracy, they developed a byzantine system of treachery and promotions, integers, gifts and punishments. A hierarchy, and the Princes benefited well from this.

Then came the reaping of the spoils. A refined source of power and knowledge, pleasure and addiction, every drop of it stolen.

"AND WHY NOT US?" Edward chortled. "WE ARE THE MOST CLEVER. THE STRONGEST."

Then came the people of Before, quietly drilling into the bottom of the Golden Sea to fuel their own world, and the punishment was decided on by the Lords of Overhaeven. Thieves. They would roast slowly, like the Witches of old, and then choke out in their own stolen heat.

A solid plan, until Papa Lucy sped things up, yanking on the thread and burning his own world to a cinder, seeking to enter the Golden Sea himself. Some called for his admittance, while others feared him, and then came that disaster at the Waking City where he nearly broke in.

All of it shook up their happy centuries of bloated leeching from the rest of the universe, and they were addicted to this Aurum they'd stolen and refined. The hierarchy was more restless than ever.

"WHAT SHALL WE DO WHEN THE NEXT PAPA LUCY APPEARS?" Edward had said.

"HE IS DESTROYED. WE FEAST ON HIM EVEN NOW," Richard said, but he was not so sure. The humans of the Now were hardy and resourceful, and so they needed wardens, rules. Bars.

The Jesus and John Leicester, and later the Boneman, were forced into imprisoning their own, knowing that the alternative was widespread destruction.

Some wanted to wipe out the Now, especially the Blackstar, who once was ranked over the Princes and now answered to them. He pressed them, but they resisted, fearing the loss of face and integers should they fail.

"I HAVE AN ANSWER!" Edward said once, while they circled in the Aurum, their joint sigil of crownlets circling and scheming.

"ANY ANSWER IS GOOD AT THIS POINT."

"THE DAWN KING! HE HAS CLAIMED ABOVE AND BELOW, LEFT AND RIGHT! HE WILL ABOLISH THE HIERARCHY. ONCE THE UNIVERSE IS CLAIMED, HE PROMISES TO DISSOLVE HIMSELF AFTER THE REVOLUTION, AND GIFT EVERYTHING TO HIS FAVOURED HEIR!"

"A BOLD CLAIM! BE CAREFUL WHO YOU MEET WITH, BROTHER. IT COULD BE A SUBTERFUGE."

"I HAVE NOT MET WITH HIM. I HEARD IT FROM THE JOYOUS HOUND AND HIS OLD GOAT, WHO HAS ALREADY SWORN TO HIM."

"WHERE DID THE HOUND MEET HIM?"

"I DON'T KNOW! HE COULD BE ANY OF US!"

There were hundreds of similar conversations, none of them originating with anyone who'd seen or indeed met with the Dawn King. A few investigated the Dawn King, such as The Hidden Agatha, and they vanished, presumed murdered or bound in Allcatch.

"I DO NOT CARE WHO IT IS," Edward scoffed. "WE SHOULD SWEAR TO THE DAWN KING NOW, OR MISS OUT."

And so they did, bringing their integers and their forces to the cause, joining the greedy rush that led to civil war, answering to every request that came second or third hand.

"THE DAWN KING SAYS TO KILL EVERY HERETIC IN THE GOLDEN SEA!"

"THE DAWN KING SAID TO BURN THE NOW! EVERY CITY!"

"THE DAWN KING COMMANDS THAT WE BRING THE JAWBONE INTO THE UNDERFOG! DELIVER IT INTO HIS HANDS!"

When pressed, none could remember who'd given the order, or accused another of relaying it to them, and so it went, right until the moment a brother lay weeping on a causeway in the Underfog. Mourning the death of his twin.

"Lord, may I approach?" one of the Seraph said cautiously, knowing it invited destruction. The Prince nodded gravely, hands twitching and clenching into fists, little golden tears falling from his face.

"We have seen more flares from the Joyous Hound. He has pressed through and approaches Shale."

"LET HIM HAVE IT. NOTHING MATTERS NOW."

"We—my sisters and I are in agreement on this. The Joyous Hound cannot be the master of all creation. Certainly not the Old Goat, should he fail."

These old turncoats knew the Underfog well, from its previous incarnation as the place for the good and the revered. Angels, they'd been known as. Servants of the Most High, that long-vanished maker of the cosmos, and they'd tired of the instructions and restrictions they'd been left with. They wanted plunder and rewards, and went with those who promised such. They killed their counterparts who stood against the defection.

Now they served a grieving brother and regretted many of their decisions.

"We heard the Dawn King awaits us at Shale," one of the Ophan said with a grinding squeak of iron bands, "ready to give out the greatest prize!"

"I heard whoever hands the jawbone to him takes all!"

"WHERE DID YOU HEAR THIS?" the Prince demanded, and suddenly his angels and Taursi officers could not answer as to how.

"FIND THE JESUSMAN NOW," he said. "GET THE JAWBONE BEFORE THE BLOODY DOG CAN."

"I received intelligence earlier," one Taursi said tersely, all clad in glass plate and the shining bands of office. "The jawbone fell into the hands of a spirit named Jenny Rider."

"DID YOU THINK TO PASS THIS ON?" the Prince thundered.

"I did, my Lord," he said fearfully. "I told your brother, and–and the Joyous Hound and the Blackstar. You were beating my previous superior to death."

The Prince stretched a hand out lazily, disintegrating the Taursi in a beam of violet light. His glass kilt and breastplate fell to the ground, the bands of office clattering atop it.

"YOU. TAKE UP HIS COMMAND," the Prince said to the nearest Taursi. "GRAVEDIGGER. GRAVEDIGGER! BRING ME HORACE RIDER!"

The obese spirit approached, hauling the terrified man along by his elbows and then depositing him at the feet of his master. His nightshirt was spoiled with sweat and bodily filth, his hair caked and out in all directions, and he was ill, hacking and coughing, feet bloated from advanced riverlung. It was unlikely he would live out the week, especially down here.

The Prince pondered this scene, suddenly puzzled. He remembered their joy at acquiring this prize, and earlier hearing this as a good plan, a great decision. But it wasn't his brother who said this. Not the Hound. Certainly not the Blackstar, and the Old Goat had merely belched and farted away malevolently, wreathed in flame as usual.

It was certainly too handy that they now had a needed hostage.

"GRAVEDIGGER, WHO GAVE THE ORDER TO SEIZE THIS ONE?"

The fat spirit licked his lips, suddenly nervous.

"You did?"

"I DO NOT REMEMBER GIVING THE ORDER."

"My lord, I remember now! I was certainly told to fetch this one! Highest orders! Came from the Dawn King himself!"

"NO. WHO SPOKE THE ORDER TO YOU?"

"Forgive me. I–I just do not know."

The Prince thundered and buzzed in place, and that sickening feeling came back, a memory long since suppressed, the turning of a loving uncle into a killer, the closing of a tower door.

Betrayal.

"BILBEN. BILBEN HAS SHOWN HER HAND!" he roared. "BLACKSTAR, ANSWER TO YOUR FAILURES!"

The Blackstar did not answer.

"She won't mind," the Junkman said. "Once she's asleep, she sleeps through anything."

Sol held a fortune's worth of eight-track cartridges in his hand, music he'd long thought lost. The Bee Gees. Elvis Presley. Aretha Franklin. Lots of AC/DC.

"Do you have any Beatles? I remember you were such a fan."

"No. NO!" the Junkman shouted, suddenly clenching the wheel and his jaw equally tight. Bilben stirred a little but did not wake.

"Okay," Sol soothed. "Do you want to hear something else instead?"

The Junkman nodded, and Sol slid Fleetwood Mac's *Rumours* into the slot. Soon peace returned to the car, and Sol felt equal parts guilt and sorrow for his fellow traveller. He remembered well that fateful evening of their first meeting, the concert on the TV, his brother's sour gibes at the autistic mechanic.

We did this to you, he said. *My brother used you, burnt out your beautiful mind, and now you even hate your favourite band because of us.*

The Underfog slid by them with tremendous speed, and Sol remembered his other visits here, the painful progress across the numerous petty kingdoms. Months lost to each crossing. Tribute to this House, and missions on behalf of the other, and the land itself slowed any visitors down. Danger with every step. Robbers, vampires, and worse.

Lucy himself had pushed hard against this place each time and been slowed down for years due to his stubbornness against a realm that was equally stubborn.

Now, Sol was blasting across it in a car filled with tunes, with no one to stop them, and it was bloody *awesome*.

The headlights picked out the very edge of Hayaven, that sea of mud. Once he'd petitioned the King of Birds to allow him the use of a stilt-walker to search it for signs of his brother, and more than once he'd had to flee from the beasts that swam through the muck. No vehicle short of an aircraft could hope to safely cross it.

"Drive to the mud, she says, and then go left, go through a skinny gap," the Junkman said. Then he was pulling up the handbrake and yanking the wheel hard left, sliding dangerously close to the edge of the sucking mud, powering through a turn worthy of a stunt driver.

"You're amazing," Sol said, and meant it. "You used to be terrified of a train ride, and now you can drive like Peter Brock when you put your mind to it."

"I do not have my driver's licence," the Junkman said, suddenly worried. "I am very sorry if I get you into trouble."

"We won't get in trouble, mate," Sol said kindly. "There are no policemen anymore. No road rules that ever stuck. Just do your thing."

"What is my thing?" he said, puzzled.

"I mean, do whatever you like. That's what we do now."

"But there are meant to be rules," the Junkman said. "It doesn't make sense otherwise."

They listened to *Dark Side of the Moon* and *Led Zeppelin II* before they found the ravine, and their course became treacherous as the headlights picked out Taursi corpses and battleglass littered everywhere. A battle, with trench work and diggings, the signs of explosions. Nearby, an emptied cache of goods, and Jesus symbols carved into the canyon walls.

"Bauer," Sol muttered, remembering Lanyard's tales of the master returning to finish his training. "So you kept up the good work after all."

Once the Junkman popped a tyre on a sharp Taursi spine, and Sol got out to stretch his legs while Ray changed the tyre. Investigating the Taursi corpses, Sol noticed one strange fact: each had its chest torn apart with great force and the heart removed.

"Hardly necessary, Bauer," he said with an eyebrow raised. The Junkman replaced the jack in the trunk and stood next to Sol, looking calmly over the field of dead flesh.

"I won't be able to drive over that," he said after a moment. "All the tyres will pop, and I have already used the spare."

"Don't worry," Sol said, sitting on the hood. "Drive slowly, and I'll clear the way."

Taursi were strange creatures, souls bound into flesh and bone, and they were incredibly easy to raise from death. With simple motions he invited the dead to stand, and then to step aside, and the car drove through a sea of puzzled faces, snouts drooping, dead and blasted eyes watching their progress towards the first section of earthwork.

Then the stereo cut out halfway through. While he could feel the humming of the Aurum engine beneath him, he couldn't hear it, and the groaning of the dead fell to instant silence.

They'd crossed the boundary of Bor Shaon.

The Junkman spent a long time in confusion and stopped the car, crying out, touching his mouth and ears. Only through hand signals and reassurances could Sol persuade him to get back into the car and drive.

Bilben slept on, curled into a tight ball.

Their passage through the ravine was painfully slow. Sol had to carefully collapse the trenches and earthwork that blocked their car, unable to call upon more powerful magics that required vocalisation.

Finally, they reached a wall that had once plugged the end of the ravine. It was shattered, broken enough in the centre that they could drive straight through it. The dead Taursi were more spread out here.

In complete silence they drove across something like the moon, complete with craters and white chalky dust, but if anyone had passed this place, the Underfog had already erased their tracks.

The Junkman looked around wildly, unsure of where to drive now, and he looked to Sol with pleading eyes. Sol gestured onwards, knowing the edges of this place had a way of ejecting you into the Glasslands no matter which way you went. The Junkman nodded, and put his foot to the floor, sending them both back into their seats with the sudden acceleration. Sol looked nervously at a crater that the Junkman drove around and noticed it was miles deep. He wondered if they'd ever be able to get out if they drifted into one.

Please slow down, he mouthed to the Junkman, who ignored him, frantically shifting through gears, sliding and driving through the moonscape as anxiously as if something was chasing him. He kept trying to talk in phrases Sol couldn't read, upset that he couldn't hear his own voice.

Then Sol saw what spooked the Junkman. An enormous force of Taursi warriors circling the lip of a crater, kitted in shining glass plate, and before them a burning goat and a dog-man with a golden whip, who immediately wheeled and began to chase the car.

Sol recognised the Joyous Hound and the Old Goat.

The Junkman yanked his wheel again, spraying the advancing warriors with white dust as he turned a hard right. He punched the accelerator down hard.

Please drive faster! Sol said.

For one awful moment the loping echidna warriors kept pace on their spider-horses, with the Overhaeven Lords driving them on, the winged eyes and burning wheels looming large. Pedal down, engine humming bright gold with energy, and the Junkman shifting up and into top gear, the little muscle car shaking all around them.

Soon there was only the flying beasts behind them, and even these began to tire. Then they were finally alone, but still the Junkman kept the accelerator floored, terrified by the size of the army chasing them.

"-drive faster," Sol heard himself say, and the dust gave way to the onyx of the Glasslands. Once more T-Rex was thumping out of the stereo, the endless loop of the eight-track cassette still playing.

"We can talk," the Junkman said. "I can hear again. I did not like when I could not talk and I could not hear."

"Me neither, mate," Sol said, looking in his side mirror for signs of the pursuing army. "We should not stop."

"Not yet, anyways," Bilben said with a stretch and a yawn. "When we see the big stone columns, start counting. Tell me when we hit the three-hundred and seventy-fifth row."

She returned to sleep and would not stir to the prods of Sol's finger.

Sol remembered these obelisks from his last visit. He suspected they were boundary markers or maybe memorials of important figures, but the records were smudged. Below, he saw the shifting shapes that had puzzled many necromancers.

The muscle car roared between the monuments at great speed, headlights causing the shadows to shift in all directions. Expecting an enemy behind every turn, Sol readied both pistol and spell, and suddenly they jerked to a sliding, squealing stop across the glass.

"Three hundred and seventy-five," the Junkman said.

"Good," Bilben said with a yawn. "Now, turn left. The trailer should be somewhere near."

"What are you talking about?" Sol said.

"The trailer I instructed Bauer to hide here," Bilben said impatiently. "With the tools and the telegraph wire."

"Well, that explains everything."

At the mention of tools, the Junkman perked up. Wrenching them left, he drove them at a great velocity toward the next destination.

Sure enough, there was a large car trailer here, in near perfect condition, tyres inflated and jockey wheel installed. In the back was an enormous spool of wire—maybe miles of the stuff—a generator, drums of diesel, and dozens of diamond-tipped industrial drills.

Without questioning anything about this find, the Junkman backed the muscle car up, Sol directing him with hand signals. Between them they wrestled the trailer onto the car's hitch, which sank under the heavy load.

"Good thing I talked that idiot into selling you his best car for a song," Bilben said. "I always saw you needing the strongest motor from this point on."

"You got me my car?"

"Sweet boy, I've been working this plot for a long time. Now don't panic, because we're about to have a lot of visitors, bearing many gifts."

Suddenly they were caught up in a flood of bizarrely shaped figures that pushed out through the columns and around the car, polyhedral rocks with waving tentacles, their polished-gem faces flashing excited words.

Bilben!

We come!

Arrived fast!

Many gifts!

With a panicked cry, the Junkman climbed up onto his car roof and refused to come down. Sol was initially surprised but had met the Many-Faced before. They were a long way from their hunting lands in Bor Shaon, and another mystery was explained as they held aloft their grisly trophies.

Taursi hearts, pale without blood.

"Get down from there and open your trunk, Junkman," Bilben said. "They need somewhere to put the hearts."

Emptying his trunk of knick-knacks and various broken machines, the Junkman watched sadly as the Many-Faced packed it to the brim with slimy meat. Hundreds, thousands of hearts, packed into every cubic inch of the available space.

"Pack them in. Don't waste any," Bilben instructed. "Put the rest in the backseat."

"Please. The upholstery is mint condition."

"Not anymore."

— 29 —

UNDERFOG

Jenny raced across the drawbridge, nostrils flared, huffing and stamping, her horse-self ready to unleash tonnes of murder in all directions.

She'd never visited Crosspoint, but had seen a book of sketches, all of the public buildings erected by Papa Lucy and his cronies, and recognised this as a facsimile of that tyrant's own house, of the house the Cruik had imprisoned her spirit in, before she escaped on Lucy's trail.

Everything was cobbled together driftwood, artfully placed to resemble a stone construction. There was the courtyard with the fountain, ringed by the villa itself, by the colonnaded terrace where the Cruik's victims had gone to dissolve. She'd had a friend in here, a man with a dog, who gave out gentle warnings and then left.

She destroyed the fountain with her hooves, kicked out a column, and cried and cried out in an echoing screech.

A footstep behind her, and she wheeled, rearing up, lashing out hooves. She clipped Lanyard, who fell backward with blood streaming from his forehead.

The others looked at her. The girl from the Waking City who'd become a woman, with two younger girls, and a bandaged spirit. Behind, the creeping car, tongue lolling from its awful face.

She tried to speak an apology to Lanyard, but gave more horsey cries, and then she was running up a broad stairway, nostrils drawing in air.

Everywhere, the arrogant stink of Papa Lucy, but up here most of all. On top of the banister Bilben stood, waving her paws frantically.

"This way!" she said. "Quickly! Don't forget what I promised you."

Deliver the jawbone, and you shall have…

She reeled down a hallway, following the capering of the large-eared rodent, resenting the big horse frame she was trapped in. The jawbone ached and throbbed in her skull, and all she wanted was for someone to prise it out, free her from whatever it was doing to her.

"Jenny, wait!" she heard Lanyard say, accompanied by the thumping of his own feet up the stairs and the clatter of his disciples.

"RIDER!" the car cried out mockingly, from down below, unable to ascend the stairs.

"Don't listen to them!" Bilben said, gesturing to a room. "Quickly now, we're close!"

Jenny paused on the threshold then, looking back at Lanyard, who stopped, hands raised.

"What are you doing here, rat?"

"The right thing," she said, launching up onto Jenny's back, sinking her teeth into her rump. Startled, the horse ran through the door, and it closed by itself with a resounding slam.

A moment later, sap oozed around the edges of the frame, hardening instantly into wood, and even as Lanyard and the others beat against it there was no door at all.

"This way," Bilben said into Jenny's ear. "So close. You will get everything you were promised, dear girl."

Panicked neighing. Scrabbling of hooves. An inexorable pull.

They were in a stately courtroom, with rows of columns supporting a lofty roof. At the end rose a set of low steps with a large wooden box at the top, and Jenny was dragged toward these, a defiant racehorse on an invisible lead rope, unable to resist.

"Shh, girl, let's get that nasty thing out of you."

Why? she wanted to say. The jawbone throbbed. She reared, and fought, and tired, even as the Jesusmen without thudded at the wall where a door had been.

Soon, she was like every broken horse. Head hung low, defeated, ready for bridle and saddle, and then she was going up the steps, one unsteady foot after another, and then she was above the wooden box.

Above the sarcophagus.

It was one piece of driftwood, carved and shaped to resemble both the coffin and the man within it, arms crossed in the peaceful pose of the dead. Jenny looked down in horror, a whimper building in her throat.

It was Papa Lucy.

She cried out, and his wooden eyes flew open.

"Let's get that out of you," Bilben said, reaching down from the top of Jenny's head, paws pushing in and through her skin, and then she seized the jawbone, yanking it out with surprising strength.

Jenny fell across the sarcophagus, her limbs shrinking, head snapping back into her usual shape. She couldn't move, couldn't speak, her tongue flat against her teeth. She saw Bilben drag the jawbone over to Papa Lucy's carved chest, holding it like a dagger over his heart.

She stabbed down once, and bone met wood with an awful sawing crunch and a series of ratchetting clicks. The rat pushed until the jawbone was buried in as deep as it could go.

Bilben turned the jawbone like a key. With the sound of wood fibres separating, Papa Lucy sat bolt upright. He looked at Jenny, and his mouth opened in a broad smile.

In the next room, Bilben was also hunched over in her nest, finally able to relieve the pressure in her belly. One iron egg slid out of her, pocked and dark, and it landed with a heavy thud into the padding she'd torn for herself.

Her baby, her final baby. In the last moment she'd passed the last of the stolen Methuselah treatment into the egg, and it was done.

In life, her kind laid eggs that took one thousand years to hatch, the hatchling old and hungry by the time it ground its way out—but here there was no time to waste, not with the enemy approaching.

A doorway irised open in the wood, and Papa Lucy appeared from his grand hall, Jenny Rider slung over his shoulder. The jawbone was in his hand now, the wound in his chest oozing sap.

"Faithful Bilben," he said weakly, casting Jenny Rider to the floor without further ceremony. "How was the birth?"

"It went well," she said, nudging the egg over with her nose. "One perfect egg, as promised."

"Shame I didn't bring any bacon," Papa Lucy said, plucking up the egg with a smile. With a motion he drew a table and chair flowing up and out of the floor, and then he sat himself as if about to eat a meal. A small egg cup rose from the table surface, and he deposited the egg within.

"A thousand years for my egg to be ready? I prefer three minutes or less," Lucy said. He drew the edge of the jawbone along the shell, carving easily through the iron and into the pale red centre.

Placing the jawbone on the table, he peeled off the iron shell with his fingers, whistling merrily through wooden lips and giving off a recorder screech. Soon he had the egg unpeeled, and he looked at it with wonder.

Gently applying his thumbs, he massaged the egg, and paused his whistling to blow into it, inflating it like a balloon—and then suddenly he was holding a throbbing heart, all red and vital.

He placed it over the hole in his chest, and it ran inside like an egg yolk, the wound sealing over. His woodgrain body started to run together, the silver-brown of driftwood becoming the first flush of a fleshy colour.

"Ooh, almost forgot," he said, pushing the jawbone in through his skin, and the fangs and horse molars fell out in his hands, now so many leftovers. After an awkward moment that resembled the fitting of false teeth, Papa Lucy once more flashed his winning white smile.

"Winners are grinners," he told Bilben. "So, how do you feel after all that?"

"Spent," she admitted, moving slowly out of her nest. No more flickering, no more time shifting, just a tired old rat.

"Good," he said, pouncing on her and snatching her up. She tried to escape, but found she could not.

"Damn it all!" Lanyard yelled out, crashing into the wall where a door had been. Tilly and the others applied boot and fist to no avail, but finally Lanyard thought to crash the butt of his gun against the wall, hoped the sorcery carved into the stock would tell.

Everything around them shivered, and the *tok* of the metal buttplate meeting the wood echoed around the halls of the wooden mansion, as if the first stroke of a lumberjack taking a chip out of a tree.

Lanyard struck again, and again, and Tilly drove her lance deeply into bark and wood, carving out divots, pulling away great ropes of sap that coated her blade. Mem and Lyn took to carving out the outline of the vanished door with their Jesus-marked knives, and they began to win through.

That was when the stair behind them started to seal over like a throat caught around a fishbone, and wooden shapes flowed out of the walls and floor, slowly reaching for the intruders, each a hook with a perfect curl at the end.

"It's beautiful," Jesus said. "They've completely captured the vibe of a disgraced soldier's messy flat."

After being shaken out of their two-dimensional forms and left here to inflate, John and Jesus found themselves in a new prison, a wooden replica of John Leicester's flat in Ur-Sydney. The site of so much of their plotting—and friendship in a dark hour. Even the windows pretended to show the expensive view of the harbour, the bridge and the Opera House, realised as a flat panel carved and covered in lacquer.

Every attempt to use magic was rebuffed, as if they were completely separate from a universe where that worked.

"This is so creepy," John said, examining a cupboard full of wooden pots and pans, the refrigerator full of perfectly carved wooden food. The door seemed fused to the wall around it, and the windows were merely decorative panels.

After their capture in Overhaeven, the pair had been taken elsewhere, but in a two-dimensional form, and the third dimension from outside their prison had been almost impossible to sense.

Like seeing time or smelling numbers, the Boneman had once described the sensation.

Then, scrabbling hands removed them, placing them somewhere warm and soft, and then the same hands shaking them out in here.

"Are we in Overhaeven?"

"I don't think so," John replied. "Once that creature released us, we just sort of popped back out into the third dimension. Like a souffle."

"Yeah, normally takes a will to force that change," Jesus said.

"Catch," John said, casting a wooden beer bottle to Jesus, who caught it and smiled wryly.

"Ha ha."

"Gotta be a bottle opener in here somewhere."

Then the door was a door, and it flew open to reveal Papa Lucy, all black curls and open shirt, smiling widely.

"What's the buzz, losers?" he said, swanning inside. With a gesture he closed the door, fusing it shut.

"What the hell is this?" John Leicester said, and he came for Lucy with fists raised. Lucy stopped him in place with a gesture and pulled out a chair from the table with an invisible hand.

"This might look like your place, but you're in my house," Lucy said. "Sit down. You, too, you miserable shit."

Jesus stared pure venom at Papa Lucy, reaching for magic that wasn't there. The last time they'd faced off had been at Sad Plain, and they'd destroyed an entire Taursi city during their battle, waking the Mother of Glass and bringing the attention of Overhaeven to their feud.

"Sit down or I'll sit you down," Lucy said. Jesus sat after a long moment, still gripping the faux beer with a trembling hand.

"You were destroyed," John said. "Drowned in the waters of Shale by your own brother."

"Speaking of Sol, he'll be along shortly. Oh, I assure you, John, it was a painful dip, but not enough to end me. You will have to try much harder than that."

He placed a crystal container on the table, inside it a swirling token from Overhaeven. The sigil of a large-eared rat, tumbling over endlessly. The other two looked at the prison nervously, not wanting to re-enter one.

Jesus recognised the sigil at once. The Queen of the Iron Nest, a plotter par excellence. It was she who'd passed on information about the Dawn King to both he and John, back in Overhaeven. She who'd planted the trap they'd been caught in.

"And so Bilben's scheming ends," Lucy said. "Bloody mouse was less accurate than a fifty-cent fortune teller. So forget whatever she whispered, and listen to me. Today, our Family is reunited. Best buddies, just hanging."

"Go fuck yourself," Jesus said.

"We were friends once, yes?"

The other two said nothing. Lucy laughed.

"Bound by a great threat, and our little council of geniuses answered it."

"You caused it!" Jesus cried out. "You burnt the whole world, you bloody monster!"

"Save me your po-faced sanctimony, you bloody coward. That world was on the way out and I did it a favour. Lame horse, meet shotgun. And I'd do it all again."

"What do you actually want?" John said.

"Call me nostalgic, but I want to work together again," Lucy said. "I was kinda hoping to talk you around."

"Work together?" Jesus spluttered.

"I was hoping we could let our bygones go off and fuck themselves, but that's not going to happen," Lucy said. "Pity. Sometimes I missed you guys, even after you started being dicks."

"We are remembering events a whole lot differently," John said.

"Well, here's another thing. As my old dad said, we don't have to like each other to work together. Do this one thing with me, and we can go our separate ways."

"Here it comes, Hesus," John said. "More of his Machiavellian bullshit."

"Oh, not me. Bilben was the one who did all that stuff," Lucy said, tapping on the glass container with the rat sigil. "I'm changing the plan."

"Just tell us," Jesus said.

"We separate Overhaeven from the planes. Cast it aside and let it starve. Reorder all of existence back to how it used to be. Be fucking heroes and get laid."

"Simple?" John said.

"You pair of bloody pissants. It's simple because we don't have to figure that bit out. That's for Ray to do."

"Ray?" John whispered, wide-eyed. "He's here?"

"On his way with Sol. Got some choice words for my own fucking brother, let me tell you that for free."

"So Ray and Sol are here, and they work for you," Jesus said dryly. "What about Baertha, is she next door warming your bed?"

"You shut your mouth," Lucy said, looming over the table.

"Was it you cuckolded your own brother, or was it the Cruik that did that bad business?"

"That's between me and Sol."

"We should have put you down years ago," Jesus began, and cried out as Lucy made a gesture, slamming his head down against the table. John twitched, and Lucy raised his other hand, freezing him in place.

Jesus sneered, and Lucy banged his head against the table again. Jesus rose up, blood now trickling down his nose.

"So where is she, then?" Jesus said. Once more the gesture, and this time Papa Lucy bounced his head against the table a few times, only letting him rise up when his face was a mess, lips split, one eye closing over.

"Baertha is gone," Lucy said after a long moment, once the sudden rage washed out of him. "After my arsehole brother pushed me into the waters of Shale, he cast the Cruik in. Baertha's soul went into the dark water, same as everyone else. She's dead, gone, fucking extinct."

"You came back though," John said cautiously.

"Because I'm strong," Lucy said. "I refused to be a part of their fucking punch bowl. No one else ever managed this."

"You are a shining example of willpower," Jesus ventured, "but why are we down here? Apart from this delightful reunion."

"Professor Hesus, you just went to the top of the class," Lucy said with a wide grin. "Our one job is to hold off an invading Overhaeven host while Ray and Sol do some nerd bullshit."

"Hold off an Overhaeven army? You cannot be serious. There are only three of us."

"You forget my secret weapon," Lucy said with a smile. "Come and meet her."

The door opened, and John and Jesus found they could leave their chairs. There were rooms beyond the one they were in, and Lucy moved the walls around with the tips of his fingers until he was happy with the arrangement. Lucy beckoned them on with the crook of a finger, and they followed him into a grand hall, a cathedral to Papa Lucy. The columns writhed with carvings of the gorgeous women he'd fucked, friezes spoke of his supposed deeds, and a ridiculous, oversized throne loomed over the room on a dais, underneath a tapestry moulded masterfully from wood, shaped to look like fabric as if a Renaissance master had been put to the task.

On it loomed a new coat of arms, but in place of a shield was a large breast, bearing a phallus crossed with the Cruik as if they were a pair of swords. John groaned out loud at the sight.

Then a moan, and the two friends spotted her, almost blending into all of that driftwood. A woman made of wood lay on the floor, groaning and unable to move herself.

"Here she is!" Lucy said brightly, scooping her up and holding her upright. "Guys, this is Jenny. She's my new main squeeze."

"You...you bastard," she managed, trembling.

"I get a lot of that, to which I say look around you! I've never lied about what I am, about what I do."

"Are you okay?" Jesus asked her.

"No," she moaned.

"I gave her a job to do once," Lucy said. "One job! And she fucked it up! Not only that, she had the balls to try to kill my Once-Dead arse. Then, if you still doubt the majestic heft of her swaying testicles, she even broke out of the Cruik and followed me down here!"

Lucy gestured all around, at his wooden fantasy house.

"Obviously, I salvaged what I could of my favourite walking stick. But here's the thing: Jenny here has got something very special in her still."

He grabbed her by the throat and squeezed tightly, and she cried out, mouth in an O, and they were all powerless to move or stop him as he stretched her neck up and over, bending her head down, pushed in her shoulders and hips, and ran his hands right down to her feet, pushing, twisting, moulding, until the girl was gone.

Papa Lucy held up the Cruik in his hands, face alight with mad triumph.

Bogle Hess noticed the driftwood castle closing in on them far too late and raised the alarm. Lanyard and the others turned from hacking open the doorway to see dozens of raised hooks, reaching for them, the wood creaking and flexing all around them like a ship under sail.

The Jesusmen answered with bullet and blade, mark and curse word, but they were in the heart of the beast. Even as some of the hooks were turned aside, burnt and broken, more still seized at hand and throat until all of the invaders were pinned to the wall. The opposite wall pressed against them, and then they were no more than knots in the wood, with a little air to breathe and not much else.

"TRAPPED!" came the muffled voice of the House of Torana from somewhere nearby.

"Not helpful, car," Lanyard groaned.

UNDERFOG

Slow Ride" by Foghat was playing on the stereo when Sol and the Junkman blasted out of the Glasslands, the muscle car hauling a heavy and bizarre load. Bauer had tied down the spool of telegraph wire securely, but it had a worrying tilt to it as the Junkman slid around a corner, one of the trailer wheels briefly lifting off the ground.

In the backseat and down in the floor wells, hundreds of dead hearts slid around with a squelch, and the Junkman moaned in dismay.

"That will never come out of the carpet, never!" he said.

Behind them, two converging armies, glittering even in the gloom of the deep Underfog. Taursi stretched out by the thousands, with cavalry, and even crews hauling strange glass weapons on sleds.

Above flew the flickering squadrons of defected angels, and belches of flame and golden light from three of the Lords of Overhaeven, and all of it heading in to form a single gleaming point.

A spearhead, ready to thrust at a wooden castle, perched on the edge of a rocky beach.

"Where do we go now?" The Junkman said to Bilben, who sat atop the steering wheel. She was quivering and timeshifting in place, little microshifts that did nothing.

"Pretty soon I will be betrayed and captured, so listen good," she said. "It's all about a fat stack of Taursi hearts and this wire. Main reason we lured the Overhaeven host down here."

"What then?" the Junkman asked.

"Somehow you two use this equipment and this knowledge to separate Shale from the Underfog."

"We're going to excise an entire beach from the land it's stuck to? How is that even possible?"

"Look, I run out of time very soon. Can't see or affect anything past this point. Everything points to you two being here, with exactly this equipment. So work it out!"

With a rumbling clatter, the Many-Faced caught up to them, and they kept pace even at this rattling speed, the comet tail to the red car that was its centre. They were loyal and brave, and Sol wondered how many of them would be destroyed today.

"He comes! He wakes!" Bilben said excitedly.

"Who?" Sol said.

Bilben did not answer, merely considering Sol with a sad look on her face. Then she was gone.

"SEND UP THE FLARE," the remaining Smothered Prince said. "ORDER THE JOYOUS HOUND TO HALT."

Nodding, the Taursi general passed the order to the nearest signaller, a young female who bowed deeply. Spreading her spines out wide, she used them to radiate heat, drew in more, held it as long as she could, until she was white hot down to her bones, a magnesium frame that melted away all of her flesh.

At the last moment of her life she released all of her battle-glass in one glorious arc, a shining star that shot across the sky, visible for miles.

The Prince had already turned away from this sacrifice, clicking his fingers imperiously toward the Gravedigger. The bloated spirit approached with his sullen crew in tow, all dusty clothes and picks, all of them tense in the face of the grieving golden boy.

"THIS IS AN OBVIOUS SNARE THAT BILBEN WISHES TO PLACE AROUND OUR THROAT," he said. "WE HAVE ALL BEEN PLAYED, AND MASTERFULLY."

"Are you foreswearing the Dawn King, then?" the Gravedigger said. "Dangerous words, those. He's asked for his jawbone to be fetched for him."

"Yeah, that's the Dawn King's house, that," one of his underlings murmured in agreement. "Everyone knows that."

"YOU BLOODY FOOLS!" the Prince shouted, a wind of his wrath whipping through the camp. "THERE IS NO DAWN KING!"

His words sank in, and the camp became restless. His Taursi honked mournfully to each other. The angels circled in their own cacophonous conferences. The Once-Dead spirits who'd sworn to their flag were eyeing everyone, weapons to hand. Discipline and order were falling apart visibly.

"So what now? Do you lot turn around and go home, then?" the Gravedigger said. "That's a right mess you've left me and mine in. I was promised certain things."

"WATCH YOUR GREEDY FINGERS, LEST YOU BECOME A CAUTIONARY TALE," the Prince said. "AS FOR YOU ALL, YES, WE WERE LURED DOWN HERE. A TRAP CERTAINLY AWAITS."

The Prince stepped over to Horace Rider, who was blubbering and holding out his bound hands, pleading wordlessly. The boy grew larger and tousled the old man's hair affectionately.

"I HAVE REACHED A CONCLUSION REGARDING YOUR DAUGHTER. THUS, I MOST CERTAINLY STILL HAVE A USE FOR YOU," the Prince said with a chilling smile.

The wood flexed and pulsed around them, and soon Lanyard and his crew were fed up through the floor of a grand hall, still held fast with staves and hooks. Even the House of Torana was brought up, gibbering madly, meaty wheels spinning in place.

Lanyard took in the tacky grandeur, and the three figures who stood before him, infamous from statue and carving—and once in the sights of his shotgun.

Papa Lucy, John Leicester, and the Jesus.

"You should have stayed dead in the water," Lanyard said to Papa Lucy. "John Leicester, you're trapped in a rock head. As for you, Jesus, you've never so much as shown your bloody face to us."

Tilly looked with fear at John Leicester. In that moment she went from a scarred veteran of a hundred battles to the tough little girl Lanyard rescued from a death cult.

"They're not gods, girl," Lanyard said. "Just sad old bastards with ambition."

Lucy leaned back, booming with laughter, honest and loud, and basked in the echo.

"Seems he has our numbers, gentleman."

Jesus and John Leicester stood helplessly by this scene, unable or unwilling to act against Lucy. Jesus looked to Lanyard and gave a little shake of his head.

They're prisoners, too, Lanyard realised.

"Where is Jenny Rider?" Lanyard pressed.

"Show some bloody manners, mate," Lucy said. "Don't come barging into my throne room demanding answers. Do you really want to know where she is?"

Lanyard glared.

Papa Lucy held the Cruik sideways on his index finger, at the point of perfect balance. He let the staff with its maddening hook float a full inch above his hands, the whole time giving Lanyard his most winning smile.

"I've always loved a girl with curves," he said, and Lanyard thrashed around in his bonds.

"Alright, amusing as this is, I've got shit to do, so it's time to assign everyone their jobs. You, too, Jesusmen."

"What?" Tilly said. "We are not working for you!"

"I think you'll find it in your best interest. I certainly don't like you lot, but we've got a mutual enemy out there, sniffing at our trousers."

"The Dawn King."

"Incorrect. There's no Dawn King."

"Bullshit! They came to Crosspoint," Tilly said. "They wiped us out."

"But did you see a Dawn King? No, you can thank Bilben for that. Just a ruse to empty all the heavy hitters out of Overhaeven—and trust me, that place is fucked."

Tilly looked to Lanyard, who didn't have any of the answers.

"So here's the deal," Papa Lucy continued. "I'm going to let you go, all of you. There's another car coming, and it's got my brother and John's brother in it. Meet them. Do whatever they say."

"The Boneman?" Lanyard said. "He's dead."

"Death's often a temporary condition, dickhead," Lucy said. "Fair warning: he's put on a bit of weight since you saw him last."

"I'll find a way back in here," Lanyard said, as they sunk back into the floor. "Gonna end you for good this time."

"Hey, that's fair enough," Lucy said. "Tell you what, you help me take down Overhaeven, and I'll let you have your shot."

They sank downwards, but suddenly Papa Lucy darted forward and kicked Lanyard in the side of the head.

"That's for shooting me in the face, you prick."

The Joyous Hound swore when he saw the flare from one of the Princes, ordering him to halt his advance.

Frustrated, he drew up with a scowl, lashing a nearby obsidian column with his whip until it was dust.

He could see the great castle ahead and knew that the Dawn King was there, waiting for his most loyal servant, the one he would name his heir.

So close!

The Hound had held judgement over the dead once, and he knew the smell of marrow well. He'd been able to smell the jawbone for days now, just a faint whiff as if the wind was teasing him with it. This close, he knew it was somewhere near or in that castle.

The Princes are wrong-footing me, seeking to seize the great prize for themselves! I brought them into the cause, and this is how they repay me!

When the Boneman tricked them and gave the jawbone to another, the Hound had been the first to charge into the Underfog, on the quest to seize it back to give to his true lord and master.

"I deserve to be the lord and master," the Joyous Hound muttered.

"My Lord?" the signaller said.

"What?"

"They are awaiting your reply."

"Oh. Tell them I have halted the advance and await further orders."

"It has been an honour to serve you, my Lord."

The Taursi self-immolated, sending the coded flash across the Underfog skies. Nearby, the burning goat farted, looking at the Hound sourly.

"Don't look at me like that, Goat. Of course I lied. Everyone, move like the chariots of old! We're getting to that jawbone first!"

"Well, would you look at that," Papa Lucy mused from the top of the driftwood castle. "Bilben was right. They're taking the bait."

He caressed the Cruik greedily, watching the movement of the Overhaeven forces, eyes glowing with an enchantment. John and Jesus were next to him, unpacking a crate of scavenged Collegia artefacts. Staves, wands, devices of brass and crystal, others with wires and switches. They set these out across the battlements, ready to be seized up at a moment's notice.

"So if I follow you, this man Bauer is sworn to my old Order," Jesus said. "He stole a shovel from this Gravedigger, and he's been getting you supplies from the Now."

"You don't even know your cannon fodder by name?" Lucy scolded. "Sure glad I'm not a Jesusman!"

"Lucy, you are such an arsehole."

"At least I'm not an absent manager. And Bauer wasn't getting me supplies, he was running around after Bilben. I was preoccupied, what with being fucking dead."

"Hey, I think this one was mine once," John said, lifting up a mystical focus with a gun-stock style handle attached to it.

"There's a plaque on it," Jesus said. "'To J.L., Welcome to the Other Side. Love From Your New Family.'"

"That's right," John said with a wry smile. "You guys got me this when I started my Army attachment with the Collegia."

The two old friends shared a smile.

"I suppose most of our old things are scattered around still," John said. "Hey, remember your old motorcycle?"

"The one that Baertha wrapped around a telegraph post?"

"And then she walked away without a scratch. Can't believe you still spoke to her after that."

"It was just a bike," Jesus said.

"Heart-warming stuff," Lucy mocked, blinking away the enchantment on his eyes. "Now, if you've finished pulling each other's dicks, let's get this party started."

Papa Lucy raised the Cruik, and Jesus felt it then, as the entire wooden castle shifted around underneath them. Looking over the parapet, he saw the castle rising up, with a thousand hook-ended legs scrabbling and pushing them out of the dark waters of death.

The castle made of driftwood began to walk toward the Overhaeven armies, stepping across the shifting stones of the beach, each lurching step the sound of a thousand tree-sized Cruiks striking the earth.

"Grab your scrotums, gents, shit's about to get wild," Papa Lucy said, wild-eyed and grinning.

Below, Jesus saw his disciples leaving in their bizarre meat-vehicle, cutting a hard right to avoid the crushing feet of Papa Lucy's castle.

How do people still march under my name, follow my teachings? he wondered. *It was only ever meant to be a temporary thing. Raise an army of middling sorcerers. Get the people safely across the Greygulf, keep them safe. Disband, and be bloody farmers and blacksmiths.*

From what he'd seen and heard, Jesus realised it wasn't about him at all now, and perhaps it had never been. These Jesusmen had a skillset and a credo, handed down through many hard years. If Jesus himself told a man like Lanyard to lay down his guns and swear off his trade, he would tell him to fuck off, and be right to do so.

"Good luck, Lanyard," he whispered.

They'd only ridden a short distance from where the Prince had fallen through the Glasslands. Mal feared the thinness of the glass beneath them. Collybrock sat down with a rebellious squawk and refused to move, and boy and bird slumped against each other, dozing in exhaustion, a five-minute break dipping into the edges of a true sleep.

Come on lazybones, we've got to keep moving! Kirstl said. Even in their dreamspace, Mal was buried deep in a fluffy bed and could not be roused. Cursing laziness and men in general, Kirstl slid into Mal's tired body and opened their eyes.

"Oh," she said through his mouth, realizing the deep exhaustion in his flesh. Groaning, she rose to their shared feet and looked around.

There it was again. More flares, converging from two different locations. Collybrock wouldn't stir, even to a prodding in the ribs from Mal's boot, and she needed more information. Digging through the saddlebags, she saw that Bauer's people had equipped them with bandages and medicine, blankets, a strange type of squirming rope, and a handkerchief full of random loose bullets for the gun they so desperately needed. Underneath all this was a farglass, brass tubes filled with powerful lenses.

There was a column nearby, sunken and on a tilt, and she scrambled up its side, grabbing for handholds and cutting Mal's hands more than once on the sharp edges of the broken stone. The tip of the obelisk had a flat edge that she could squat upon, and she carefully extended the farglass, scanning the horizon.

Kirstl had only learnt a few of the Jesusmen's spells, but she'd mastered the Mark of Farsight, and placed it upon the brass tube of the farglass. A moment later she placed it upon her own eye for good measure.

"Now I'll be able to see a flea scratching its arse on the moon," she said with satisfaction.

That was when Kirstl realised they'd been sleeping in the centre of a shitstorm. Two shining armies, even in the gloom of the Overhaeven night, with thousands of glass-plated Taursi on the move. Above them circled burning wheels and flying eyes, signalling to each other with bright rockets of some sort.

Ahead, there was the black coast of Shale, the death that had once called to her so strongly, and there was a mansion there, a cobbled thing of driftwood that changed even as she watched it. Now it was a castle, and now it was rising from the waters, stepping forward on a thousand tree sized legs, walking forward to meet the armies.

One Overhaeven host had halted well clear of the castle, but the other charged on heedlessly, abandoning its baggage train in favour of a mad charge. She saw bright lights flashing at the forefront of the charge, and flame, and the flicker of wings and spinning wheels.

Three figures stood on the parapet of the castle, and they unleashed all manner of destruction on the attackers. Jets of fire that stretched out for miles, beams of intense colour, even a creeping fog that washed down from the house to settle across the front ranks of the host.

One of the figures stood up tall, waving a stick, and it seemed like a giant fist was falling upon the shining army, smashing down on it again and again, flattening hundreds of Taursi with every blow.

Still they came on. And still the other force sat back, watching and waiting.

"What the hell do we do?" Kirstl said to herself, and then she caught a vision of something else. A car, bright red, hauling a trailer alongside the beach, and another car driving to meet it—if you could call it a car. It was an obscenity of flesh and machine, and it drove joyously along the shore, flicking up dirt and drifting around rock outcroppings.

The cars met, and after a long moment both vehicles emptied of occupants, the group speaking on the edge of the shore.

"It's Tilly! And Lanyard!" Kirstl cried out. She slid down the obelisk on their backside, shaking Collybrock around by the beak until the bird stirred.

"Get up, you sad excuse for a bird," she said. "We're needed elsewhere. Rest time's done."

"No. Kirgle. Sleep."

"Get up!" she screamed in Collybrock's face, wiggling the beak until the bird snapped out at her, nipping her in the forearm.

"Tired. Angry!"

"Do that again and I'll pluck you bald. Let's go!"

Mal slumbered, oblivious, and Kirstl let her man doze, scrambling up into the saddle, urging their exhausted bird first to a walk, and then back up to a jog.

"Keep moving. That's right."

"Kirgle bad. Bad!"

"Stop your bloody whinging, bird."

As Lucy's mansion grew into a castle with legs and went on the move, all of his furnishings slid around inside. Wooden chairs clattered, statues fell over, and in the false apartment of John Leicester, everything bounced around in a great big racket.

The crystal case sat perfectly still in the centre of the table. The tiny glass prison had the weight of Overhaeven to it and was not so easily disturbed.

It was also completely empty.

— 31 —

UNDERFOG

As Papa Lucy's house rose and went on the attack, Tilly drove the House of Torana through the dunes above Shale, foot to the floor as they sped toward the Boneman.

"I saw him dead," Lanyard said.

"In a dream, though. Where he put a jawbone in your head."

"And that's the weirdest thing about all this?"

Rising over a sandy crest, they finally saw the red car, two figures standing beside it and looking at the attached trailer. Tilly pressed the brakes down, and then again when the House of Torana disagreed with the order.

"CAR!" it called out, jumping around on the spot. "PLAY! PLAY WITH CAR!"

"Shut up, car, and behave your bloody self!" Lanyard said, pushing the prod of his knife up into the roof, just enough for emphasis.

Tilly pulled up alongside, and they took in the horrified looks from the two men as they finally saw what the House of Torana was made out of.

Everyone got out of the living machine, weapons to hand, and the two groups looked at each other for a moment. The pair of men from the red car looked alive, young, and well-fed, with the perfect teeth that spoke of Before-time dentistry.

"Lanyard!" one of them said. "Tilly too! You're alive!"

"Who the hell are you?" Tilly said, leaning on her lance and giving the stranger the stink eye. "Where's the Boneman?"

"I am him," he said.

For a long moment Lanyard stared at the Boneman before finally nodding.

"It's the eyes. Same eyes."

Tilly stared at the stranger until the magical moment that all the suspicion fell out of her face, and then she cast aside her lance, hugging the man fiercely.

"Sol, it's really you," she said. "How? How did you–"

"Get my body back?" he said. "When I escaped from Overhaeven, it was just there. Cost me, though."

"Who cares? You're you!" Tilly said. "Handsome face and all."

"I lost my Methuselah treatment. It's gone. I'm going to grow old… and eventually die."

"So? You lot had your turn and made a pig's ear out of things," Lanyard began before there was a commotion nearby. Bogle Hess was walking back toward the waters of Shale, Mem and Lyn doing their best to slow them down.

"Just let me go," Bogle cried. "I need this so badly. You don't understand."

"Get it together, Bogle," Lanyard said, seizing the spirit roughly and dragging them backward, back into the dunes. "You're not finished fighting yet."

"Please," they whispered.

"It is very tough, my friend," Sol said kindly, touching Bogle on the shoulder. "Few can resist the waters."

"I am just so tired," Bogle said, and all they could do afterward was sit on the sand, knees to their chin, staring out at the rippling black water.

"Who's your friend there?" Lanyard asked Sol. The other man was unpacking various tools from the trailer, and then he popped the trunk open. It was filled to the brim with meat.

"That's Ray Leicester, John Leicester's brother," Sol said, *sotto voce*. "Call him the Junkman."

"Another Leicester?" Tilly said. "We–they never taught us that."

"You have to understand, the religions we made were just put in place to keep everything going. They weren't even remotely accurate to history, the real us."

"Stop talking all this bullshit," Lanyard said. "We're here to help you with whatever needs doing."

"Who sent you? Bilben?"

"Nope. Papa Lucy. Your brother is alive and well, and he's driving that walking castle."

Wide-eyed, Sol took the offered binoculars, standing on top of the car to get a better view.

"We're gonna have to kill him. Again."

"Planning to, mate. Planning to."

"Put the hearts in a pile over there," the Junkman ordered brusquely. He was fussing about with the tools, laying everything out just so.

Everyone was carrying armfuls of meat from the trunk and the backseat. Sol had conjured up a circle of shimmering air to move more of the meat, and this served as a type of wheelbarrow, but loading this up by hand was taking a long time.

"Can we just have shovels?" Mem complained. "This is gross."

"Absolutely not," the Junkman said. "The sharp edge will damage the hearts. If the chambers are pierced, none of this will work."

"So gross," Lyn echoed.

The Junkman spent a long time pacing around the pile of hearts. He picked one up, looked it over. Lined several of them up from smallest to biggest. Unspooled the telegraph wire and made a circle around the hearts to no effect, ran the line to the black waters and carefully placed it in, flinching at the spray when the waves broke. He started the generator, plugging in one of the drills, and made a mess of at least three Taursi hearts before declaring this as pointless.

He was unhurried, approaching Bilben's bizarre puzzle as an intellectual exercise, while everyone else was frantic, expecting to be caught up in the edges of a deadly battle.

"Girl, report," Lanyard called up. Tilly was on top of the car, the binoculars glowing with the Mark of Farsight.

"The horde come out from Bor Shaon have nearly reached the castle. The other mob are staying put."

"Hmm. Might be they'll kill Papa Lucy and do our job for us, Sol," Lanyard said.

"If Lucy has the Cruik again, it will take much more than that," Sol said solemnly, upending the magical disk at the Junkman's feet with a meaty squelch.

The House of Torana kept nuzzling against the muscle car, murmuring in wordless pleasure. Occasionally it came running in, butting the car playfully, leaving dents that drove the Junkman into a rage.

"Get away!" he yelled out, driving the living car away with a boot to the bumper. Popping the hood, he summoned over everyone to observe his homemade engine, the glass hearts glowing softly even with the engine off. Sol whistled at what he saw.

"I took a tour of a car manufacturer back in the Before, when I was in the Collegia's good graces. We designed the engines, and none of them was anything like this."

"What's that supposed to mean?" the Junkman said, bristling. "I did my best!"

"I'm saying it's good, Ray. It's very good. You're years ahead of what whole teams of people could manage."

The Junkman was pleased to hear this and overlooked the use of his name. He began to point out aspects of his engine as the Jesusmen hovered nervously on the perimeter, weapons at the ready.

"I cut these hearts out of the Taursi spires back in the Now," the Junkman said. "I think we gotta make those other hearts like these."

"The spires," Sol breathed. "I studied those for years. Watched the wild tribes forging these out in the hidden places. I did not think to ever break one of them apart."

"I was experimenting," the Junkman said, wrestling with the bolts holding down one of the hearts. "My friend in the mirror told me to do it."

"Your friend in the mirror," Sol said carefully. "Did he look like this?"

A quick contortion of fingers and a quiet word, and an illusory image appeared between Sol's hands, of a handsome face that floated in the darkness, smiling with too many teeth.

A sudden memory came to the Junkman, of sitting on a couch, cruel words coming from those same haughty lips, listening to the music that drove him mad-

He fought the memory down, and with a great effort froze his own hand in place before he could slap himself in the head.

"Yes," he managed with a shudder. "That's him."

Sol looked to the walking castle, now flashing with beams of destruction, and shuddered.

"If there's one thing Lucy knows, it's power. Okay, how can we work with this?"

"We'll compare the glass heart to those hearts over–ah!" the Junkman cried. As soon as the glowing heart was free of the engine, it flew from his hands and bounced across the ground toward the black waters.

As the rest of the hearts in the engine fell dark, the freed heart skipped toward the ocean. A moment before it could fall in, it stopped, hovering just above the rocks, spinning in place.

"Careful!" Sol cried out as the Junkman slipped down over the jagged rocks, getting as close to the heart as he dared. He stared as the heart strained to get to the water, blocked by an invisible barrier.

Then it spun in place, faster and faster, glowing brightly, an arc of Aurum spiralling out of it. Then it suddenly shot downward, blasting through the rocks of Shale and into the beach itself.

Crawling on his belly, trembling at the nearness of the waves, the Junkman looked down into a two-foot-wide hole, and saw the golden gleam of the heart in the distance, still drilling madly downwards.

"Oh no," the Junkman said. "That was part of my car battery."

Sol and Lanyard dragged him backward just in time to dodge a black wave that came crashing in, sizzling as it washed against the heat of the accidental digging.

"The rat said something," Lanyard said. "Said that her buddies in Overhaeven made it so that Taursi couldn't go in that water."

"Still, it's hardly a safety measure," Sol said, looking at the crater. "Hey, Junkman, got an experiment for you. Everyone, actually. Grab a heart and try to lob it in the water."

With great enthusiasm the Jesusmen set to lobbing meat into the ocean, but this time around the fleshy hearts drove into the sharp rocks with great velocity, painting them with gore.

"Okay, experiment over. They've got to be the stone hearts to dig that hole."

"Bogle, no!" Tilly cried.

The Once-Dead spirit of the troubled Jesusman stood overlooking the beach, Taursi heart laying forgotten at their feet. This close to the waters of death, Bogle had lost all control, driving a dagger into their own heart, blue Aether splattering everywhere.

"I'm free," they said with relief, and then Bogle was a broken Twice-Dead shell drifting down and into the water, feeding Overhaeven with a faint flash.

Mem and Lyn were crying, and the Junkman and Sol were staring in shock, but Lanyard had the presence of mind to act. He leapt down on the site of Bogle's suicide, rooting through the fallen stack of bandages and ammunition belts.

He emerged, holding a glowing Taursi heart, the meat now transformed into milky-white stone, and it glowed with the golden light of Aurum. Already it was struggling to fly into the sea, and it took Lanyard and Tilley to wrestle it away to a safe distance.

"Alright, mate, plug this back into your car," Lanyard said, helping to wrestle the new component into the car's battery.

"Oh. I know what to do," the Junkman said.

Even as the war raged and pushed closer towards them, the Junkman tinkered, and Sol remembered. Remembered the day he'd seen this man fix a television he'd never seen. How even with his mind burnt away, he could still pick up the tools, approach a situation by instinct, and simply tinker his way toward an answer.

Even when a problem reached metaphysical levels of confusion, Ray Leicester simply noted the rules of the laws of this bizarre place and adjusted his tinkering accordingly.

The Jesusmen were near the belching generator, using the power tools to drill holes into Taursi hearts, the girls threading them onto the telegraph line as quickly as they could. They spaced the hearts out in five-foot intervals, each secured against a thick knot in the line. Ten seconds per heart was the goal.

The Junkman's car was parked half a mile back from the waters of Shale. Earlier, the House of Torana had roared forward with the loose end of the telegraph wire, unspooling half of the reel, spitting out the wire so that it lay resting in the battering waters of death. After a moment with the wire-cutters, the living car returned to lay another half mile next to the first, panting excitedly like a dog with a tennis ball.

"A GREAT GAME!" the House of Torana cried. Mem and Lyn fed it Taursi hearts when no one was looking, but no one minded. They had enough hearts to do this twice over.

Five-foot intervals. Ten seconds per heart. Knot, drill, thread, repeat. Just over one hundred minutes, and they would have the job done.

The two wires lay by the open hood of the Junkman's car, ready to be connected to the repaired battery. If this worked, it would be the biggest jump-start ever attempted in the history of cars and electricity.

Of course, if they were noticed before they were ready, there was the example of Bogle Hess, and a whole ocean willing to swallow them up.

"THAT DISOBEDIENT HOUND! THAT TRAITOR!" the remaining Smothered Prince raved. "I WILL SEE HIM FLAYED AND STRETCHED OUT ACROSS THE STARS FOR THIS!"

"Do we commit, my Lord?" one of the Ophan said. "He is seeking integers and glory that should be yours!"

"NO. THE HOUND WILL FALL, AND WE SHALL WATCH. THEN WE ATTACK."

They assembled the greater engines here, ones they'd dragged through the Underfog for just such work. The signallers were relegated back into the ammunition caste, and they awaited their flaming deaths with great honour, their brethren honking with admiration as they passed by.

The Prince watched with grim satisfaction as Papa Lucy swept death from the battlements of his stomping castle, the infamous Cruik in his hands, the castle itself walking on hook legs. Satisfied with his conclusion, he hauled Horace Rider up by the elbows, calling for the Seraphim and Ophanim.

"This is definitely in my top three best moments," Lucy whooped, sending out waves of crackling destruction from the Cruik. "I hate to admit that banging my brother's wife is still number one."

"Such an arsehole," Jesus groaned, his powers channelled through a pair of jade carvings, one in each hand. Below, the enemy milled in confusion, several ranks clutching their heads and running around in visible agony.

"Don't just steer us straight into them!" John called out, waving a red-hot sword at the distant enemy, knowing that thousands of mysterious cuts were landing throughout the enemy ranks at random. "Use the terrain. We've got magic, so keep them at a distance."

"Listen here, soldier boy. When you get a magical walking castle, I'll let you make these decisions."

Jesus let out a cry, the carvings overheating and cracking in his hands. Dropping them down, he ran to the next post, seizing up a staff made of latticed metal.

"Oh yeah, I think that one used to have a mop on the end of it," Lucy mocked. "Some beginner's bullshit that I gave the prentices. Your staff's not as good as mine, mate!"

John and Jesus shared a look. They'd seen the Cruik moving as a living woman, forced into the shape by Lucy. He was worse than ever, a monster back from the dead, and here they were, fighting by his side.

"How are they going?" Jesus asked John, who turned an eyeglass over to the beach.

"Well, they're doing something. Got the wires and tools out."

He paused for a long moment, until Lucy snapped at him.

"Stop looking at your long-lost brother and get back to work, John Leicester! We've got enemies to kill!"

Lucy called down lightning and ice, hurled the obelisks of the Glasslands into their ranks, and caused the rank and file to fight each other, all in the space of a few heartbeats.

The Cruik was powerful, terrifying, and seductive, and even those ancient magicians began to covet it, even knowing how corrosive it was. It had been bad enough before, but now there was another element to the artefact.

It had a prisoner in it who desperately needed their help.

Please. Free me! the girl called Jenny said to them both. *I'll serve you if you save me from Papa Lucy.*

"Ha! Neither of you have the balls to take it!" Lucy said when he realised both men were staring at the Cruik.

Jesus cast a charm to keep the whispers and promises of the Cruik at bay and pulled John Leicester backward.

"If we can't free her, we will need to destroy her," Jesus whispered.

"No. We can take down Papa Lucy with that thing."

"Listen to yourself. Sol was the only one strong enough to resist the Cruik. Do not think you are an exception to this!"

Jesus's charm finally won over, and John blinked slowly, common sense returning.

"My thanks," he said, a moment before the whole castle shook underneath them.

The Joyous Hound had reached the castle with the Old Goat, carried aloft by a pair of angels. The Hound was striking the castle with his whip, opening deep wounds with every stroke, the Goat raking its horns upwards.

"Oh yes. Come on up here, you glorious golden fuckers!" Papa Lucy crowed over the side of the castle. The structure lurched again from its wounds, and a blaze of destruction from the Cruik went wide.

"Come on, Jenny, get your shit together," Lucy said, banging the stick against the parapet as if it were a torch with the battery running low. "Well, don't just gawp, you two, bloody kill them!"

A Seraphim bore up the Old Goat and came flapping at Jesus and John, the edges of its feathers like razors. The Goat bucked and belched, kicking and tearing at them both. John fought to free himself from the onslaught of the big beast and reached for that most familiar of soldier-mage spells.

He turned himself into stone.

"No!" Jesus cried, even as he forced the angel back with a breath that became a wind-gust. "Don't go too deep, John, you won't come back out!"

But Sad Plain was ten lifetimes ago, and John Leicester was already in the form, stone clothes flowing as he moved around slowly, trading blows with the Goat, absorbing the horn butts that were like cannon shots on his forearms.

Meanwhile, Lucy battled the Joyous Hound, who lashed down on him again and again with the golden whip, barking with delight at the spray of sparks as whip met staff.

"A fine stick! It has the look of old Aegyptus, and it should be mine. Hand it over and death will be swift!"

"You want me to give a stick to a dog? Okay boy, fetch!" Lucy made to throw the Cruik to his left, and for a moment the Joyous Hound startled, as if ready to chase the staff and seize it up.

"I am no dog! You will die hard for that!"

"Nah. I'm gonna make you gargle your own balls, put your head above my toilet, and make your tail into my toilet brush."

The jackal-god stared at the insult, jaw working as he tried to form a response.

"My Lord! Let me break this foul little man!" the Ophan cried out, charging Lucy with flame and the grinding of metal wheels.

"Oh, you're worse than a fucking fly! Just fuck off!" Papa Lucy said, swatting the flaming wheel aside with contempt. The Ophan came apart as if it was a cheap toy, rims and eyes falling with a clatter and raining down around their feet.

"Heh. That's not union-made," Lucy laughed. "En garde, motherfucker."

Jesus and the Seraph were face to face, the angel trying to carve him apart while he held it at bay with the metal staff, focusing his own considerable sorcery through the entry-level device.

Bend, he insisted. *Flex inwards.*

He forced the Seraph's wings to slowly curl in, sharp edges reaching towards the iris, the sclera, and the lens. When the angel realised it had lost the battle it tried to retreat, but Jesus held it in place, looking at it sadly as he pushed the feathers through, slicing the orb neatly in half.

Next to him, John Leicester already had the Old Goat pinned down to the roof of the castle under his knees, the beast bucking and burning, and then the stone soldier seized it by the horns. With one mighty wrench, he twisted the creature's neck until it broke with a loud snap.

Gasping over their victories, they watched as Papa Lucy wrapped the golden whip around the Joyous Hound's throat, using it to hang him from the parapet, and that old god of death finally experienced his own portfolio.

"Feels good to win, doesn't it boys?" Papa Lucy said.

"Yes," Jesus admitted.

John Leicester tried to move his stone tongue and said nothing at all.

— 32 —

UNDERFOG

"THERE. THE HOUND DANGLES ON HIS OWN LASH," the Prince said with great satisfaction. "NOW WE GO. DRIVE THAT RAT AND HER PET MAGICIAN INTO THE SEA!"

The cavalry began a slow advance, spider-horses guarding the flanks of the Taursi infantry. Firing crews gave the signal and set off their great glass engines, and those Taursi slated for self-sacrifice made one last majestic flight, burning magnesium comets that roared across the Glasslands to rain against the walking castle.

At the top, Papa Lucy formed a great invisible umbrella with the Cruik at its centre, turning away the worst of the damage, but still his castle staggered, many of the legs now burning or missing altogether.

"YES," the Prince said. "NOW, WE ARE GOING TO VISIT YOUR DAUGHTER, SELECTOR."

"Please, don't harm her. I'll give you anything," Horace begged. "The city, the Tower, all of my wealth, you can have it all."

"YOU HAVE NOTHING I EITHER WANT OR NEED," the Prince sneered, and concealed the man within his cloak. With a signal he rose into the air, aloft on a bed of fluttering Seraphim and Ophanim, soaring toward the top of Papa Lucy's walking mansion.

"I DEMAND YOU SURRENDER NOW!" the Prince shouted across a short gap. Papa Lucy, John Leicester, and the Jesus stared at him from the top of the castle, sorcerous foci at the ready, gathering an incredible stock of energy.

"You can't demand jack shit," Papa Lucy scoffed, waggling the Cruik. "You're outgunned mate."

"I WAS NOT ADDRESSING YOU. I WAS SPEAKING TO THE CRUIK."

With a flourish the Smothered Prince twitched back his cloak, and with the legerdemain of the godlike he produced Horace Rider.

In Lucy's hands the Cruik began to shake, and it took all of Lucy's strength to hold it still.

"Now listen here, Jenny," he said. "You work for me. Behave your bloody self."

The crook end began to uncurl, the whole length of the staff moving in a rapid, sinuous motion.

The Smothered Prince smiled.

"I NO LONGER DESIRE YOUR SURRENDER," the Prince said. "I WOULD SEE YOU TURN UPON EACH OTHER."

Slowly, luxuriously, the Smothered Prince dug his fingers into Horace Rider's stomach and pushed. The man screamed, and the boy pushed his fingers in deeper.

"DELICIOUS," he whispered into the man's ear. "SCREAM MORE. A CHOIR OF DELIGHTS."

In Papa Lucy's hands, the Cruik was now a straight line, expanding, the features of a face visible on one end. A mouth was open, issuing a whistle, the shriek of a child honking on a recorder without attempting any specific note.

Now the magicians were unleashing all manner of destruction upon the Prince, and he drew on his reserves, turned aside their worst spells, let one of the Seraph take a death magic meant for him. Still he had enough to remain aloft, and now he gently teased out a rope of intestines, letting yard after yard of guts dangle down toward the ground.

"Stop!" Horace cried. "Please, it hurts so much!"

"YOU ARE A NOVICE TO PAIN," the Prince said, and with a gentle brush of his hands he caused the skin on Horace's arms to slough off, as if an expert flayer had spent hours at his craft.

"No!" a woman cried, and Jenny Rider had broken loose from Lucy, once more a woman realised in wood grain, reaching out for her father with long, hooking arms.

"HERE, TAKE HIM, TAKE YOUR FATHER," the Prince said, before letting the man fall, screaming, plummeting to the ground. It was far, and it was a long moment before he struck the ground, utterly broken. A moment later the dead Selector's spirit went running past the chaos, screaming as he plunged into the surf of Shale, failing to resist that compulsion.

"OOPS!" the Prince said, flying back to his forces, shrugging off the dread magics those in the castle tickled him with. He gave the distraught girl a friendly wave and watched with delight as she ran for the parapets, screaming in anguish. She sprouted a set of wings from her back, but these were not shaped to catch the air. When she stepped over the side, she plummeted to the plains below.

"YOU ARE NO ICARUS!" the Prince laughed. When Jenny struck the ground, the wooden castle shivered, turned around on the spot like a beheaded chicken, and then it collapsed in a mountain of sawdust, shattered beams scattering in all directions.

"Oh crap. Oh, that's not good," Kirstl said. She was close now, in the centre of the two shining armies, and it was going to be a near thing.

She had the perfect vantage point from Collybrock's saddle, watching as the first army destroyed itself against the walking castle, with a handful of odd creatures flying upward in an attempt to board the structure.

They were destroyed in seconds, and the castle turned to the second army, lumbering onward.

All that was left of the first army were scatterings of routed Taursi fleeing for their lives, but many of these were still between her and Lanyard. Some of the Taursi rode on the spider-horses Mal had seen with Lanyard, and she wasn't sure if Collybrock could outpace these should they give chase.

She pulled in behind a fallen obelisk, gathering the courage to move out in the open.

"Think, Kirstl. We can't just sit here."

Mal was still deeply in slumber, and even in the dreamspace she couldn't wake him.

"Looks like it's up to us girls," she told the bird, and that was when she saw the bright weapons of the second army strike the walking castle, making it stagger.

Then a long moment of seeming negotiation with a flying creature, and the Mark of Farsight made Kirstl feel sick to the depths of Mal's stomach. It was a Smothered Prince, carried up by flying monsters, and then he was gutting some poor old man, tearing him apart, before finally casting him to the ground to die.

On the castle the three figures cast every sort of magic against the retreating Prince, and then she saw glimpses of frenzied movement. A staff becoming a snake, and then becoming a woman, and then sprouting wings in an attempt to fly after the Prince. The woman fell like a stone. A moment later, the walking castle began to stagger around like a drunk before completely collapsing.

Then the second army was on the move, toward the fallen castle, and Lanyard and his cars on the beach just beyond this.

"Go, go!" Kirstl said, digging in her heels, and Collybrock loped forward.

"Kirgle. Scared!"

"Me, too, bird, but we can't stop. Go!"

There was a gap between the routed first force and the ruined castle, and Kirstl made for it. She heard the honks as a trio of Taursi infantry spotted her, hurling battleglass in her direction.

One sliver lodged in Mal's bicep, and then they were free of the group, but then came more cries. Kirstl saw with panic that Taursi cavalry were closing in on her, the spider-horses clattering across the glass, riders up and honking excitedly in the saddle.

She turned inward, and even as she steered the riding bird in blind panic, she was into the dreamspace, tearing off the bedding, reimagining the comfy mattress as a bed of nails and the firepit as a slab of freezing stone, and then Mal was up.

"What the hell? I needed a rest."

"We are about to die, Mal, and you are the better bird rider. Don't make me jam you back into the brain because so help me, I will."

"There was a time you wanted to be in charge," Mal moaned, but a moment later he looked out through his own eyes and realised the threat.

Three Taursi cavalry on the left. A dangerous ruin full of sharp wooden jags on his right.

"Collybrock, hutt left!" he cried, and they suddenly steered into the group of Taursi cavalry, the bird huffing out its wings in a threat display.

Mal! What are you doing?

Mal ignored her and then gave three swift taps behind him, on the very top of Collybrock's leg, as he yanked the reins to the right.

The bird gave a leap, slashing out with her razor-sharp claws, and tore open the throat of the nearest spider-horse as she simultaneously snatched the Taursi rider from the saddle in her beak. She then pushed free, completing a right-hand turn.

After a moment, the two remaining riders got over their surprise and fell into a honking pursuit. Collybrock finished savaging the Taursi rider, but Mal tapped her between the shoulder blades twice.

"Give!" he said, and the bird turned her head around to present the dead echidna-man, neck torn apart to the bone. Mal helped himself to a spear and some battleglass, sliding the weapons into his empty lance sheath.

"Now, drop!" he said, and the bird dropped the Taursi, running onward. Another flash of battle-glass, this time lodging in Mal's buttock and leg, and he answered this with one swift cast of his own, a lucky shot that lodged straight into the Taursi's eye, dropping it with an anguished honk.

One left. He wheeled Collybrock around, drawing the spear, and they charged like the jousting knights of the old Before.

A tap and a command, and Collybrock leapt over the enemy at the last moment, and boy and bird fell upon them in a frenzy of beak, claws, and spear.

That was incredible, Kirstl said in awe. *You were born to be a bird rider.*

"I know, love," Mal said.

"Love," Collybrock warbled, blood falling from her beak.

Keep going, Lanyard is straight ahead!

"Lanyard?" Mal said, and then he yanked on the reins, drawing Collybrock to a shuddering stop.

What the hell are you doing? Kirstl said.

Staggering out of the collapsed castle was a woman covered in dust, and she raised a hand at the sight of the bird ridden by the boy.

The same woman who'd sprouted useless wings and fallen from a great height.

"Help me!" she cried out. She looked wounded, and Mal leaned down, hoisting her up into the saddle without hesitation.

Her face ran with tears, but neither Mal nor Kirstl realised that the tears were thick and ran like sap.

Lanyard and his people were perhaps two-thirds of the way through their grisly craft project when Papa Lucy's castle fell.

"We're out of time, Junkman!" he called out. "Is this enough to do what needs doing?"

"I don't know! I didn't have time to sound the depths of the hole. I–I don't have enough information!"

The Junkman began to hit himself in the head, over and over, moaning.

"Hey, pull it together," Lanyard snarled, but then Sol was there, gently holding the Junkman's wrists, gripping him by the shoulder, whispering in his ear. After a few moments he calmed and looked over the work.

"This will work. Or it won't. But the theory is sound."

"It better bloody work," Tilly said, flexing her sore hands.

"Aether can change the hearts," the Junkman began. "And near as we know now, Aurum is refined Aether. It's like diesel is to petrol. Except it's electricity. Except it's actually from souls."

He picked up the jump-start clamps attached to the ends of the telegraph wires, hovering over his glowing engine.

"You can do this, Ray," Sol said kindly.

The Junkman connected the clamps to the car, and suddenly everything was sparks and blindingly bright light, from the engine bay down the wires, and even in the waters of Shale, a lightning show that went on just beneath the surface, running backward and then up the vertical wave, as far as they could see.

Right up to Overhaeven itself.

"Stop it, now!" Lanyard shouted over the crackling chaos. "That's too much."

"A bit more," the Junkman replied, watching the display. After reaching some number in his own internal count, he closed his eyes and reached in, unclipping the jumper cables.

The insane light show subsided to reveal hundreds of glowing Taursi hearts, stone beads tied to a very long string.

They began to move on their own.

"Quickly, everyone, grab the cables!" Lanyard shouted. "Car, get over here now! It's time to play!"

"PLAY!" the House of Torana cried out, and backed itself up obediently, allowing the Jesusmen to tie the telegraph wire to the bone nubs where its trailer hitch once was.

The trailer was already abandoned for the dead, and Sol and the Junkman fastened their own wire to the muscle car's trailer hitch, and then the draw of the hearts gained in strength, slowly dragging the car across the dunes.

"Are you ready, Junkman?" Lanyard called out, as they piled into the cars.

"I have the perfect music ready to play for this," he said, digging out an eight-track and slotting it in.

The first bars of "Born to Be Wild" blasted out as both cars raced in opposite directions along the very edge of the dunes, the string of burning hearts unravelling as it punched downward and into the sharp stones, a knife that blazed and sliced through the ground in their wake.

The Prince's jubilation turned to despair when he saw the light show at Shale, and the penny finally dropped. It wasn't about Papa Lucy and the Cruik, it wasn't about ambushing the strongest Lords of Overhaeven.

Bilben and her conspirators were cutting away Overhaeven, removing it like a wart, and they'd all fallen for it.

"BILBEN! THAT DAMNED RAT, HER PLOTS WITHIN PLOTS!" he screeched.

"What are our orders?" the angels asked. The Taursi were now too terrified to approach the Prince and kept their distance.

"GO AND BLOODY STOP THEM!" he shouted. "OR IT ALL ENDS THIS DAY!"

The slow advance became a rush, and the angels tore forward in a chorus of broken bells and thunder, bearing the golden child as fast as they dared.

Jesus climbed out of a hole in the wreckage, a thick beam the only thing that possibly saved his life. He was bleeding in a dozen places and coughed at the dust sitting in the bottom of his lungs.

"C'mon, John, where are you," he muttered, pulling aside parts of the wreckage, looking at the shining army on the move, the Smothered Prince returning to finish the job. At this stage he would have even been grateful to find Papa Lucy.

The thud of collapsing timbers nearby, and then John Leicester emerged, carrying Papa Lucy over his shoulder. The stone man placed him at Jesus's feet and gestured.

"I told you not to go into that stone," Jesus said. "Can you come back out?"

A shrug.

Papa Lucy looked pale and appeared to have several broken bones. Jesus looked closer and was shocked to see his skin was taking on a wood grain, the man turning into a carved puppet.

"I'd set him on fire if we didn't need him so badly."

The sound of rock grinding on rock, and Jesus realised John was laughing. Looking for bones to set, Jesus noticed that the worst injury was to Lucy's jaw, which was completely dislocated.

"I hope this hurts," he said, pushing it back in with a sickening crunch. Within moments Papa Lucy's flesh regained its colour, and then he was hale and upright, cursing up a storm.

"How bloody dare she? Where is that rotten bitch?"

"Miles away, if she has any sense," Jesus said levelly. Lucy locked stares with the man, and then he was channelling mystical power and forging it into a dozen invisible and equally deadly weapons, enough to kill a lesser man, but Jesus was able to hold these all at bay, the only sign of the immense struggle the set of his jaw, one bead of sweat running down the dust on his face.

"So this was some of the Cruik," Jesus said, indicating the fallen driftwood castle. "No doubt what you were able to fish out of the black waters. Jenny Rider was the rest of it. Am I correct?"

"Broken clock is right twice a day, arsehole."

John Leicester placed a stone hand on Jesus's shoulder, and he found a wellspring of power to draw from. Soon he was able to tip the balance, and Papa Lucy was on the defensive, unable to outmatch the two friends on his own.

"Leave off, Lucy. Yield."

"I've never backed down once, you sanctimonious dog-fucker. What makes you think I'll start with you?"

A light flared in the distance, and then Jesus was forced to divert his energies into a shield, as more Taursi artillery came soaring in, blasting down on the wreckage of the castle and the trio arguing on top of it. It was hard work without a mystical focal point, and John and Papa Lucy both joined in the effort, keeping the energy and the explosions at bay.

"We have larger problems, Lucy," Jesus said. "They come!"

The entire Taursi force was coming their way, but this time they didn't have the Cruik or the small arsenal of Before-time magical gizmos. Nothing but each other.

"Look out, the Smothered Prince is back," Jesus warned, but the Prince and his squadron of angels soared overhead, pushing toward the nearby dunes and Shale, to the two cars rapidly unstitching it all from reality.

"Holy shit, John. Your brother figured it out! Those shits are actually doing it!" Papa Lucy said.

The Taursi came on like a glacier in fast-forward, shining brightly, and Jesus saw it. Where the cars had already unstitched the shoreline, a jagged tear was running all the way up into the heavens. It peeled away a bruised layer and tore down the sepia behind it, revealing a sky of brilliant blue. A beam of sunlight broke through the Underfog murk, finally destroying the stage dressing Overhaeven had slapped across the place.

"We cannot stop the Prince, but we can help here," Jesus said. "Buy them enough time to finish the job."

Papa Lucy nodded. The three friends joined their energies and fought long and hard, taking down as many Taursi as they could. The dead were piled high, but still the enemy came on, finally tagging Jesus and Papa Lucy with their sharp-edged glass.

Their energies began to flag, and Jesus knew their time was measured in perhaps minutes.

"Lucy, I'm glad we got to do this," Jesus called out, snuffing out lives with a pass of his hand. "This seems right, ending it this way."

"I'm not dying here today, Professor Hesus. Soon I'll be balls deep in some strange and nowhere near you."

Then a wave of rocks washed across everything, dragging down the Taursi, and it took Jesus a moment to recognise what he was looking at. The Many-Faced creatures of this realm, rumoured to be the last creation of the enigmatic Farmer.

The glass weapons of the Taursi did nothing against them, and they were helpless to stop the polyhedral shapes from climbing all over them, connecting together to form a type of cairn around each creature, and then unfolding in an eye-twisting way, pushing meat and spine flat with immense force. In less than a minute the Taursi army was crushed, with the Many-Faced reinflating and chasing after the handful of Taursi who'd escaped.

"You were right, Bilben," Papa Lucy said. "Those little bastards are great fun to watch."

Jesus turned from the sight to see Papa Lucy with the infamous rodent now on his shoulder, preening her whiskers.

Bilben had never once been his prisoner.

They'd been played, right from the start. Captured, lured here to bolster Papa Lucy's defences, tricked into working with their worst enemy. Three of the greatest magicians of a dead world, fighting off an army. John and Jesus had performed their parts perfectly, and now they weren't required.

Jesus scrambled to raise his defences, but Lucy struck first, smiling widely, the rat on his shoulder adding her own energies to the assault. Bilben watched impassively as Papa Lucy blasted Jesus into a bloody heap, and then smote John Leicester into dust.

Sitting on the old obelisks that once marked out the rules of the Glasslands and their blessed dead, the Gravedigger and his crew idly watched the trio of sorcerers making their last stand.

"We are support crew only," he said when a Taursi commander honked at him, demanding he join in the fight.

"Those magical fellas may have some valuables on them, boss," one spirit said. "Wands and rings, shrivelled hands in jars, and such."

"You ask me, the real treasure is down in that wrecked castle. Papa Lucy brought a fortune over from the Before."

The Gravedigger was already gathering this fortune in his mind when the Many-Faced appeared from nowhere, instantly washing over the Taursi army, enveloping and crushing them in seconds.

And now, the wave of stones was heading toward them.

"Out of my way!" the Gravedigger roared, pushing his way down the slanted obelisk, and he hit the ground running, already reaching for his shovel. In all his self-serving years in the Underfog, he had never seen the Many-Faced do that, had only ever known them as pointless little hunters.

"They're a bloody defence system," he huffed, and began carving his way through the ground with his shovel. Here the intent meant as much as the digging, which was a good thing for a creature of his immense girth, and he was carving an escape tunnel into the earth at a great rate. He only paused to light his miner's lamp before continuing to dig.

"Boss! Wait for us!" his crew shouted, one stepping into the tunnel after him. Behind him he heard the screams of the others, already being consumed by the beasts.

"Boss, no!" his crewman cried out as he struck away the support beams that were mostly symbological, caving the tunnel in behind him.

He'd lost a fortune today, but at least he was safe. He'd find a way to rebuild and start again. He had caches and even cultists who followed him in the Now, a hideout in the Greygulf, and many in the Overhaeven who owed him favours.

Others won and lost, but the Gravedigger always survived.

His churning shovel hit solid rock with a clang.

"Impossible," he said. This shovel could chew through steel, through magical barriers, even craft tunnels through water. He tried to the left and right, above and below, and every stab struck this frustrating obstacle.

"Damned strange," he said, and turned around to find the tunnel sealing closed behind him. With a panicked cry he made to dig but found the same material filling his tunnel.

The Gravedigger was trapped in a cube barely big enough for him to stand in.

"What is the meaning of this?" he blustered, ringing his shovel against the stone. He knocked away clods of dirt to reveal each face was polished marble, but not a marble that even his sharpest grave-breaking tools could hope to penetrate.

Wiping away more dirt revealed words, and the Gravedigger frantically brushed it away with his hands, letting out a strangled cry when all was revealed.

"THINK ON YOUR SINS," was all the inscription said, and underneath this was the sigil of Bilben, Queen of the Iron Nest.

"You–I–I did everything you asked of me!" the Gravedigger cried out in the tiny space. "I helped to supply the bloody Jesusmen. Got Papa Lucy his magical toys. Found your trailer, the spool of telegraph line, everything you asked for!"

There was no answer, nothing but his own panicked breathing, and the accusing statement carved deep into the wall.

He knew he didn't need to breathe. Knew he was Once-Dead, and the amount of air in this cavity made no difference to him. Regardless of this, he felt dizzy, a tight grip on his chest, and he struggled not to breathe too quickly.

"Let me go! Bilben, you've got to let me go!" he screamed, the sound muffled in the close confines of the crypt. After a moment of panic he unpacked all of his digging equipment, both metaphysical and mundane, and worked furiously, looking for a seam, for some way of escaping. None of it could make a mark on what Bilben had encased him in.

"It's not fair," he whimpered, and then he had nothing but time to think about the nature of fairness, and the realisation that Bilben was simply cleaning house, no more and no less. Eventually his lamp began to run low, and the moment before the lights went out, the walls seemed to close in ever so slightly.

"Not fair."

"Can you go any faster?" Lanyard asked Tilly, who was struggling to keep the House of Torana on track.

"I don't bloody know!" she said. "I don't often drive a living car with a half-mile deep knife attached to it."

"Alright, girl, stow the attitude."

The House of Torana moaned and groaned, wheels sluggish as it fought against the heavy load. The scar from the Junkman's invention glowed white hot, and behind them the gap was expanding, the surrounding earth and rocks falling in.

Above them, there was already a wide tear in the heavens where the sun was shining and the sky was blue, as if several layers of wallpaper were peeling away.

"TIRED. HUNGRY!" the House of Torana cried out, and without further thought, Lanyard, Tilly, and the twins took turns slamming their hands into the spigot. The blood was enough for it to perk up and pick up in speed.

"Boss, trouble behind!" Lyn cried out from the backseat. "Look!"

Lanyard leaned out of the window and looked behind them, past their own gouge in the landscape, and saw the Junkman's bright red muscle car. Flying toward it was one of the Smothered Princes, held aloft by his angels.

"Binoculars, girl!" he called out, and called up the Mark of Farsight. He saw the Taursi army wiped out by some strange defence system of the Underfog and came to his decision.

"Girls, climb out the back and cut that cord. It's slowing us down. Tilly, turn around."

"What? It's working!"

"There's no point if the Smothered Prince kills Sol. He needs us, girl."

Nodding, Tilly worked the squidgy brakes on the living car, even as Mem held Lyn by the ankles out the back window, the other girl sawing away at the cord.

It gave way with a sharp *plink* and instantly burrowed its way into the earth, their attempt to cut Shale from the Underfog ending maybe a mile short of Bor Shaon.

"C'mon, car!" Lanyard urged, reaching out of the window to pat it on the flanks. "Run as fast as you can! Catch up, playtime now!"

"PLAY!" the car yelled, and it raced across the dunes, pudgy little tyres perfectly suited for the terrain. Soon the car was racing alongside the cut the Junkman was making, and Tilly had a heart-stopping moment where she nearly landed them in a spreading sinkhole, an entire dune sliding down into that glowing abyss.

"I'll hold the wheel," Lanyard said, handing Bogle Hess's rifle to Tilly.

"Alright, but I'm no Yulio."

"You're better than an old man with cataracts."

Aiming up at the approaching cluster of angels and the boy they carried, Tilly sent a bullet just wide of a winged eye.

"Give me another!" she said, and Lanyard fished out another precious round, which she fed into the bolt-action. Taking a deep breath, she lined up and squeezed the trigger.

She wasn't to know it, but at the exact moment that Jesus died at Papa Lucy's hands, she made the perfect shot. She pierced a Seraph right through the eyeball, the bullet ricocheting from the Prince's impervious throat to eviscerate the spinning wheels of an Ophan.

The Prince thrashed around angrily, but his own riposte went wild, the violet beams of energy from his hands breaking his companions apart.

He fell to the sands of the dunes from a great height.

Tilly climbed back inside and drove as fast as she could until they were alongside the Junkman's car. Lanyard indicated they should stop, but the best they could manage was the slowest of crawls, the knife of Taursi hearts trying to draw them backward in the spreading chasm.

"What happened to your line?" the Junkman said. "Did it break?"

"No! We're under attack! Sol, get out, we're going to need you."

Mystified, Sol climbed out of the muscle car and stood with the cluster of Jesusmen, who were waiting on the sands with weapons at the ready.

The Smothered Prince came running out of the dunes, petulant and wild, unharmed from his fall. He shrugged off Tilly's rifle shot and the boom of Lanyard's shotgun, but then he staggered a little before falling to the sands, his left leg folding in on itself in a sickening way.

Sol stood next to the warriors, holding a perfectly formed child's femur. The Smothered Prince crawled toward them, and so Sol plucked out the boy's humerus, and then the tree of bones from his left hand. Still the Prince came crawling on, eyes crazed, spewing out magic that Sol did his best to contain.

"I see how you did it, lad," Sol said. "Skin that cannot be broken by any means. Clever, but then here's me with my little bone tricks."

"YOU SHALL SUFFER THE MOST, SOL PAPPAGALLO," the Prince cried out. His eyes flicked to the left then, and Lanyard had the barest second of warning before the Prince cried out to the twins, who were now his servants, body and soul, coming for him and Tilly with knives drawn. He had the barest of moments to hammer the swift little killers in the face with the butt of his shotgun, and he felt the crunch of the gun-butt against their faces right down into the depths of his bitter soul.

"Stay down," he shouted at the girls.

Tilly had the Prince spitted with her lance, and he was cackling up at her, sending a painful magic up through the steel and wracking through her body, but still she held on.

"Sol, help her," Lanyard yelled. Sol reached his hands out into the air as if rummaging around, and came out with a skull, complete with eyeballs.

The boy's head deflated into a pile of skin and golden curls.

"Skull. Now," Lanyard ordered, and Sol sent it bouncing across the sands until the Jesusmen stopped it under his boot.

"Look at that. I'm down to my very last shotgun shell," Lanyard said, watching how the eyes still twitched around the sockets, the jaw still working, tongue still trying to frame a spell, or perhaps some final cutting remark.

Lanyard pulled the trigger and spread that tiny sphere of bone and brain into a spray that covered half a hill.

— 33 —

UNDERFOG/NOW

They gathered on the dunes by the Bor Shaon border, watching as the Junkman peacefully drove his car along the last length of the beach. He looked for all the world like a farmer with a supernatural plough, planting light.

"There it goes!" cried out Sol cheerfully, as the last length cut through, and then they were all up and cheering. No longer tethered to the Underfog, the stones of Shale, the black water, and even the impossibly vertical wave were drifting away, fading through the universe and gone moments later.

What was left behind was beautiful.

A perfect beach, with crisp white sands, with water so blue it would make your heart ache to look upon it. Grasses began to grow on the dunes, and nests full of gull eggs pushed up through the ground as if they'd been bulbs lying dormant for years untold.

The sky was a brilliant blue, with a sun that shone with an intensity that painters and sailors could only dream of. There was a moon, too, a sliver that seemed to be waiting for its turn, suggesting that night would follow day.

Behind them, the Glasslands were gleaming, obelisks slowly righted. The burning lands below now seemed to be in balance with the perfection of this upper realm. Beyond that, the binoculars showed that Hayaven was gone, replaced with a plain full of gleaming, golden cities.

The Junkman drove back over to their group, merrily tooting the horn, and joined their picnic. It was the last of the Junkman's collection of baked beans, and the hungry Jesusmen ate as if it was their finest meal.

They laughed as the House of Torana chased and capered after the perfectly white seagulls, and cried out in horror when it caught one, savaging it to death.

"None of us belongs in a place this nice," Lanyard said, watching the twins chase the car away from the gull nests.

"There are people coming. Riding on a bird," the Junkman told them, immediately shovelling beans into his mouth. Lanyard felt himself standing on unsteady legs and turned to see his boy riding towards him in the distance, his enchantment confirming this.

"Tilly. It's Mal," he said, and then they were up and running across the sands.

"Don't you scold that boy. Just be glad he's alive," Tilly said, but Lanyard waved her off. For the first time in a long time, he smiled.

Mal had a woman riding behind him in the saddle, with poor Collybrock exhausted and in need of grooming, huffing and struggling through the sands.

"Boy," Lanyard called out. "Been looking for you, I have."

Mal fell out of the saddle and ran for Lanyard, and boy and man collided in an awkward embrace.

"I am sorry, boss. So sorry."

"You bloody, bone-headed boy. You could have died."

"I know."

Tilly kept her distance from their embrace, smiling at the display. Each of them would deny the tears and the tight hug to his dying day, and so she gave them their moment.

When Jenny climbed down from Collybrock and waved, Mal made his introductions.

"Boss, I saved this girl from the castle," he said. "Her name's Jenny."

"I know her," Lanyard said with a smile. "Met her a very long time ago. Met her again a short time ago. If we keep on meeting, she might just have to come home with us."

"I might like that," Jenny said cautiously.

They made their plans over lunch. The Junkman believed he could use his Aurum-powered engine to open a gate back through into the

Now, and if that didn't work, Sol could take them through the long way, one at a time.

"Everything we know about the cosmos just changed," the old magician said in wonder. "Overhaeven used to sit above everything, but now we know the truth. They were just parasites. And now they are gone."

He gestured around.

"This is now where souls go. And–and it's perfect."

"There's another place though," Mal said. "I saw it, under the Glasslands. Place where everything's on fire. Clouds eat people. It ate one of the Smothered Princes."

"I spent my whole life studying these other lands, only to learn I know next to nothing," Sol said.

"School sounds like a waste of time," Lanyard said dryly.

Mal found a small amount of liver-root in his saddlebags and made a cup of tea for Lanyard, a little ways away from the group. Both of them knew important words needed saying.

"Thanks, boy," Lanyard said, nursing his chipped enamel mug. "Been in agony for days."

The tick of their little fire, a small mark set to boil the billy. They'd long since run out of firewood, which meant that every cup of tea meant someone got a headache from boiling the water. Today, it was Mal.

"Never thought I'd miss this awful stuff," Lanyard said, sipping with a grimace.

"Boss, I've–I've got a message I was meant to deliver to you. But there's more."

Once again a campfire between master and prentice, but this was an occasion of love, instruction, and honesty, and the rock that Lanyard drove through Bauer and carried around in his heart could now be set aside. Mal told Lanyard everything. About Kirstl's spirit invading his body, and how they'd reached an accommodation. All about Bauer and the battle to slow down the Taursi.

Finally, Bilben's message to Lanyard.

"Tell Lanyard Everett of the many ways I betrayed you today," Mal recited.

"That bloody rat. If she's still here I'll wring her neck."

They looked at the wreckage of Lucy's castle, the one blight on a landscape of perfection.

"Probably a good place to start looking," Lanyard said. "So tell me, boy, what's it like having your sweetheart living inside your head?"

"Different. Nice."

"You're never gonna be able to keep a secret from her."

Damn straight, Kirstl said.

Cries over by the main camp, and Lanyard was instantly on his feet, pain or no, rifle in hand.

"I swear, if that car has eaten something else..."

They drew up short, and Lanyard pushed Mal behind him. Papa Lucy was there, standing with his back to the perfect sea, looking down on their jolly gathering.

Bilben was perched on his shoulder, ears twitching.

With a snarl, Lanyard unleashed a rifle-shot straight toward Lucy's face, which the magician stopped with the palm of his hand and a smile.

"Stay back!" Lanyard warned Tilly, but she came in low with her lance, spinning and slashing. Papa Lucy simply clicked his fingers and the steel glowed white-hot, as if just pulled from the blacksmith's coals, and she dropped it with a cry, both her hands badly burnt.

"Girls, don't," she warned the twins, but they were hiding behind the Junkman. Ray Leicester was frozen in place, trembling and hyperventilating, a wet patch spreading down the front of his pants.

"Good work today, Ray," Lucy said pleasantly. "Didn't think a simpleton would pull this off, but Bilben was hopeful!"

"Leave him alone, Lucy," Sol said.

"You. You can shut your mouth," Lucy said, turning from pleasant to vicious in a heartbeat. "Traitor. Brother killer. I will give that back to you in spades, don't you worry."

Sol readied a spell, but Lucy punched out in his direction, the blows landing, and he struck his brother with invisible fists, again and again, until he fell to his knees with face bloodied, unable to talk.

"Don't worry, you don't get to die yet. Oh, I'm the one who has your Methuselah treatment now. I will make every day of what's left into agony, you bastard of a brother."

Papa Lucy walked closer to their group, hands held low, eyes alight with madness. Suddenly the House of Torana appeared from the dunes where it had been stalking more birds, and it came out roaring, ready to pounce on Papa Lucy.

"Ugly fucking thing," he said, and flipped the car over with one motion, stranding it upside down and on its roof.

"PLEASE," the car cried. "CAN'T MOVE."

"You, I will tame later. Now, where are you, Jenny? Come here and get on your fucking knees."

Jenny Rider stepped out from behind the Junkman's car, looking at Lucy with a mixture of terror and hatred.

"I'll admit, you caught me by surprise, girl. Strong, too, changing back into your shape, but that will not happen again. I won't tell you a second time. Down on your fucking knees."

"No," she said quietly.

"I'm sorry, did I hear you wrong?" Lucy said, cupping an ear. "Because I thought you just said something very stupid."

Jenny stood her ground, and Papa Lucy smiled, a chimpanzee's threat display.

"You promised me the girl, Bilben. My faithful servant, my Cruik. You said you saw it."

"You did have her," the rat quibbled. "It's not my fault you let her go."

"What do you see now?"

"Nothing. This is my first time here. I am close to the end."

"Pointless bloody soothsayer!" Lucy said, but the rat was already gone and scurrying off through the grasses of the dunes.

Jenny slowly stalked forward, hands outstretched. She and Papa Lucy faced each other across the sands, like gunslingers.

"Kids, get in the Junkman's car," Lanyard said quietly, but Papa Lucy slammed the doors shut with a gesture, the doors locking. Then the keys slid out of the Junkman's pocket and flew across into Lucy's hand.

"My car now," Lucy said. "So, Jesusman, I promised you would have your shot at me. How's that working out?"

Lanyard fired the rifle again, and this time Lucy knocked the bullet straight back down the barrel, shattering the gun.

"Piss weak, mate. Okay, Jenny, enough of this. Time for you to get back to work."

She came in closer, hands starting to curl over, stalking in a circle around the smiling Lucy. Then she took three quick steps, hooked hands raised up high, before freezing in place, a puzzled look on her face.

"That's it. Keep going. Lift your arms. Gimme a little wiggle, toots."

Jenny grimaced and struggled, but slowly her arms touched over her head and melted together. Then the rest of her began to flow, twisting and curling, until once more she was the Cruik. The staff stood in a perfect vertical on the sands, the curl of its end sheer perfection, a construct of power and terrifying significance.

"There you are," Papa Lucy said, and then he spared the defeated Jesusmen a look. "Oh, I forgot to mention, I straight up murdered the Jesus a little while ago. John Leicester too. So I guess you all work for me now."

If the Jesusmen were beaten before, they were utterly despondent now. Papa Lucy was despicable, evil, and beyond any resistance they could hope to offer.

"Brother," the Junkman said numbly. "John. You killed Brother. My brother John is dead."

Still laughing at their misery, Lucy walked over toward the Cruik, lust written across his face.

"The Cruik was great before, but now I might just get to fuck it," Lucy said over his shoulder when Mal and Collybrock broke out of cover. They launched themselves out of the dunes and leapt over the House of Torana, hitting the ground at a flat-out run.

Mal snatched the Cruik first, and he aimed it at Papa Lucy, pointing it like a lance.

"Mal, no!" Lanyard yelled. "Put that down, right now!"

Papa Lucy stared at Mal, face twisted with rage, and then he reached out for bird and boy with all of his malevolent energies, every manner of vile sorcery pouring out of his hands and mouth, magic that meant death at a touch.

It all fell aside, unable to touch Mal.

"Do you really want to do this, lad?" Papa Lucy said. "You got lucky, but you can't keep me out forever."

"Surrender, Papa Lucy," Mal said. "Answer for your crimes."

"Crimes," Collybrock echoed.

"Well, if it isn't Bailiff Bird," Papa Lucy mocked, and then suddenly struck forward with the palm of his hand. The spell found a way through the Cruik's protection, and Mal rocked back in the saddle, clearly stunned by the blow.

"Alright, Jenny. It's time you and I have a long and intimate conversation," Papa Lucy said, and went to take the staff from Mal's numb fingers.

Then, the whites of Mal's eyes shifted into focus as Kirstl took over the body. She suddenly lifted the Cruik and slammed it into Papa Lucy's head hard, and then again, and then the magician was down in the sands, the curl of the staff pinning him down.

"You shouldn't treat girls that way," Kirstl said through Mal's mouth. She released the Cruik, which was now unravelling and forming back into Jenny Rider, wrapping her hands around Lucy's throat. Her feet were still the butt of the staff, which beat every bone it could reach, breaking him as brutally as any condemned man was ever broken on a wheel.

"Kill me then, you sad fuckers," he gasped.

"No," Jenny said, a hint of cruelty dancing across her wooden lips. She leant forward and kissed him gently across the forehead.

Then she climbed to her feet and let him be.

"No. No! You twisted little bitch! You can't do this to me!"

Jenny turned away.

"Please. Put it back! You can't understand. It's all I've got."

"Luciano Pappagallo, you've misused your magic your entire life," she said, in a voice that was hers and also not hers. "You no longer deserve to possess it."

He reached up a broken hand, trying to reach for his power, for the tools of his cruelty and vanity, and fell short. For the first time in his life, Papa Lucy wept.

"I was there, Ray," Sol said. "He never left your side after the Crossing. Even with everything that needed doing, all he cared about was you."

"John," the Junkman said, the word sitting foreign in his mouth. "John Leicester."

While the Jesusmen bound up Papa Lucy and made ready to return to the lands of Life, Sol and the Junkman took the car for one last cruise through the Glasslands, heading for the ruins of the castle.

It was beautiful, the boundary between this land and the place of flames below, the obelisks a great record stretching out over many miles. They saw rules regarding this boundary, great lists of names, and words that the obelisks flashed amongst themselves, much like how the Many-Faced communicated. It wasn't a great stretch of the imagination to suppose that Adamah had forged some of the obelisks into that race, the last guard against invasion.

"John was always so proud of you, you know," Sol said. "He had medals, and was going places, and all he could ever talk about was how clever his brother was."

"I know what clever looks like," the Junkman said, bitterness in his voice. "It's people using you for what you know, what you can do. They laugh at you, or don't understand you, or smile and say the polite phrases, but the people always go. Being clever is always being alone."

A long moment. Today, there was no music in the car.

"I'm sorry that's happened to you, I really am." Sol said. "I'm just as guilty of mistreating you, when I sent you away."

"Hiding me from brothers."

"Yes, I hid you from our brothers. I didn't think you had the ability to deal with the situation, but it doesn't make it right."

They were close to the wreckage now, enough to see that the driftwood that was part of the Cruik was slowly decaying, a wind blowing away great drifts of dust. Given enough time, none of this would be left to mar the perfections of this place.

"What will you say if we find him?" Sol asked.

"But he's dead."

"Spirits stay in this place, though."

"They used to. We don't know the rules for this anymore. If you don't know the rules, you can't predict anything. And so it's pointless to talk about something if we don't know the proper rules for it."

Sol smiled.

"You're nervous, aren't you?"

The Junkman nodded.

"He never pitied you, Ray, and he never tried to fix you, to erase your condition. After the Crossing hurt your mind, John only ever tried to bring you back to how you always were."

"I didn't know how to do what Brother asked. He kept pushing me, he always pushed me, just like he always pushed me in the Before!"

Sol watched him carefully, as the memories slid home. The Junkman closed his eyes, breathed deeply, and was a little bit more of Ray Leicester when he reopened them.

"Did he really push you, Ray?"

"No," Ray admitted.

"None of us did. We all loved you. Baertha adored you. Lucy found ways to use you, because he is sick and uses people, but he loved you in his own way."

"Lucy gave me a Messerschmidt model plane for my birthday. We went to the beach in John's car."

"We did. We had a lot of lovely times."

They stopped at the edge of the wreckage and got out, looking around and poking through the planks, and then they heard shouting in the distance. Two spirits were running across the Glasslands, waving at them.

"John!" Ray Leicester cried, running into the arms of his brother.

"The Underfog had an older name, before Overhaeven invaded it," Jesus explained to the others. "It was called Gan-Eden."

Everyone else was packed up and ready to leave. Lanyard, Mal, and the twins were going to take Ray's car back through the Edgemist with his marvellous engine. They'd found the trailer and hitched it back on to carry Collybrock, who warbled and threatened a bound and very nervous Papa Lucy.

Sol was sharing the House of Torana with Jenny Rider and Tilly. The boundary to the Aum was no longer blocked by Overhaeven's sepia fence, and Sol thought he should be able to connect a shadow-road straight through to the Greygulf and back to the Now.

"How people react to this beast when we drive it past them is another problem altogether," Sol said.

"HUNGRY," the House of Torana grumbled.

Jesus came up to Lanyard and his crew and smiled.

"It is a great honour to meet you all," he said. "Truly. You have done hard things in my name, and for so very long. I thank you all."

"Didn't do it to be thanked," Lanyard said huffily. "Just a job."

"Yeah. We stop the monsters till we get stopped, and that's all there is," Mal said.

"Oh," Jesus said, taking in the scars on the lad, the eyes that spoke of trauma and a hidden passenger. "Oh, you poor kid. Back in the Before, you'd have had a proper childhood and grown up in safety. Lanyard, I have something to ask."

"Go on," he said apprehensively.

"I don't want you taking on any more children as prentices for the Jesusman order. Adults only."

"Nope."

"What? It's my order. Got my name on it."

"I don't give a shit, mate. We need these kids. We need everyone."

"I am sorry to hear that," Jesus said with a frown.

"So, you were a professor? In that Collegia?"

"Yes. Yes, I was."

"Think you can actually make a fucking appearance once in a while and teach the kids some things?"

"Yes. Yes, I will."

Jesus and Lanyard shook hands on it. Jesus left his namesakes with a nod and a quizzical expression on his face. He had his answer now as to where he stood.

The living made their final goodbyes with the spirits of Jesus and John Leicester, who were going to stay on as the new guardians of Gan-Eden.

"The dead will still arrive, from all worlds," John said, his spirit no longer bound into stone. "We are going to stay and make sure this place works better. A paradise for souls."

"Then all of my plans have worked perfectly," a high voice said.

Bilben was sitting on the hood of Ray's red muscle-car, cleaning her whiskers and looking around innocently. With a guttural roar, Lanyard lunged on the rat, who allowed herself to be captured.

"You!" he said, squeezing tightly.

"It won't work," Bilben chirped. "I can't die from bullets, or knives, or the fingers of a man who has every reason to throttle me."

Eventually tiring of the effort, Lanyard cast the rodent to the ground.

"You did this," he said. "All of this. The plotting, and manipulating, all your little betrayals."

"Yes, I did," she said. "I had my reasons, and you see them realised. Overhaeven, driven away, the lords of that place scattered or destroyed. The old Houses that corrupted Gan-Eden, also ended. Everything is repaired and made good."

"Made good? My people died because of you! Even the dead Jesusmen fell to your conniving bullshit. I came here with thirty-three Jesusmen, and I'm leaving with five."

"Technically six, with the Tontine there," Bilben said of Mal. "Acceptable casualties for what you've achieved here. A clean slate, the universe put back into order. Every villain brought to the justice they deserve."

"You forgot one villain," Lanyard said. "I don't know how, but we'll find a way to end your miserable little life."

"Oh, I shall tell you how," Bilben said. "Now that my task is done, I submit myself to your justice."

Bilben grew rapidly, the rodent expanding and reforming into a being of absolute glory, an androgynous human perfect in every dimension, skin of deepest grey, their eyes orbs of milky white.

"I have always been able to lie," the creature said. "And this was my greatest lie. I am Bilbenadium, Sworn Sword of the Most High, Queen of the Iron Nest. Assigned to guard Gan-Eden in the Maker's absence."

Lanyard stepped backward with a curse word, reaching for a gun. The angelic being smiled graciously at the reaction.

"Understandable."

"Why the hell did you pretend you were a bloody rat?"

"Because I am a coward."

Bilbenadium turned around to face all of the stunned faces, addressing everyone in a voice that was melodious and resonant, a musical instrument crafted for glorious songs, now turned to oratory.

"My first failure was to allow the rise of the corrupt Houses in Gan-Eden, and the evil spirits that plagued the innocent. When the invaders came from Overhaeven, I abandoned my post, and hid as one of them for countless years.

"I only had the courage to manipulate others from afar. I should have taken up my burning sword and fought to the end, but all I ever managed was to plot a great plan that might repair the damage. This plan would cost others greatly, and I decided that you should all bear that cost.

"Mal. Kirstl. This next task falls to you, as it always was going to. You needed to be a Tontine to defeat Papa Lucy and wield the Cruik, and I made you so."

"But you said you didn't do that."

"A lie," the angelic being said. "I nudged every little stone, caused every little ripple. The stumble of your bird, the biting of your lip, the struggle over your body. Before this even, when The Serene decided to turn on you, and then selecting Kirstl to slay in place of another. All of these events can be placed at my door."

"Mal," Lanyard warned, but already the boy was at the angel in a fury, hammering into their perfect solar plexus with his scrappy punches, tearing and biting, emptying his wrath to no effect.

"Punch her in the dick," Papa Lucy yelled out helpfully from his prison of ropes, shaking with unhinged laughter.

"I told you, Mal, you cannot harm me in these ways. Check your saddlebag."

Puzzled, Mal did so, and emerged with the shifting rope Bauer's people had packed in there. He shook it out to find the rope was alive, shifting in his hands like a snake. At its end was a perfectly tied noose, complete with slipknot.

"I have committed crimes against you, Mal Jesusman. Hurt and killed those you loved. Killed countless others by my scheming and by my inaction. Do you wish to end my existence?"

Mal held the noose, looking at the angel and trembling with rage.

"The Most High laid out the exact condition of my ending, thought I was never permitted to see it. I can only die choking on a rope that cannot be broken, strangled by two hands that are actually four. Years of research proved that I needed a Tontine to die, and a noose of Allcatch. That's the second reason I made you. I killed your sweetheart so that I could die."

The angel knelt in the sand of the dunes, closing their eyes and waiting peacefully for the noose. Mal was in a fury as he slid the knot outwards, trembling.

He paused.

"Lanyard?" Mal said, turning to his master for help.

"Boy, this is your call," Lanyard said, a gentle hand on his shoulder. "We don't hand out justice often, so only you can decide what that looks like today."

Mal set his mouth in a grim line and nodded.

"I know what to do," he said.

The angel Bilbenadium waited for a long moment for the noose and the sweet release of death, only to find that Mal was rapidly hogtying them with the rope of Allcatch, binding them up like a leg of ham.

"What is this?" the angel demanded. "I'm a monster. You're meant to kill me!"

"And why would I give you anything that you want?" Mal said. He fetched Collybrock from the trailer and hooked the noose end to her saddle, using the bird to haul the angel across the ground.

"I enjoyed it, killing your friends," the angel said. "The moment your little girlfriend died. The look on her face! I'd do it all again!"

"Nice try," Mal said. He was trotting Collybrock across the Glasslands now and saw the swirling clouds beneath the clear and shining plain, looked to the living Obelisks around him.

VISITOR! one Obelisk displayed.

YOU SPEAK WITH THE DAMNED?

STATE A NAME.

"No," Mal said, looking down to the distant land of flames. "I want to open up the glass and throw this arsehole down there."

"No! You cannot! I do not belong there, I am the Sworn Sword! My place is to die here!" Bilbenadium moaned.

SOUL ASSIGNED INCORRECTLY?

INCORRECT LOCATION?

"Absolutely," Mal said. "Do the really bad souls go down there?"

YES.

"No! Please! Mal, I'll do anything, I'll get Kirstl her body back. I'll slave for you and your order for ten thousand years. I beg you!"

"Stone, can you take this piece of shit to their new home?"

IS DAMNED?

UNSURE.

CHECKING.

TRUTH IS FOUND

SOUL IS DAMNED.

Mal unhooked the noose from Collybrock's saddle and dropped it to the ground. The thick glass barrier slid open to admit Bilbenadium, who screamed all the way down.

Mal left, and the name BILBENADIUM appeared on that column, from that day until the last day.

The cars were ready to go, and the people packed in.

"Hey, boy," Lanyard said from the front seat. "I've got something for you. For Kirstl too."

He passed over his shotgun, the mean old god-cannon that had been Bauer's, had passed through dozens of hands before that.

"You've earnt your gun today."

"But this is yours," Mal objected.

"Not anymore mate. Not anymore."

The boy held the ancient weapon in wonder. It had a heft to it. Power, the weight of duty, and old blood soaked into every inch of the old etchings. A story he and Kirstl could now add to.

"Seatbelts, everyone," Ray Leicester said, carefully checking his mirrors and seat positioning.

"Mister, can we listen to your radio?" Mem asked.

"The other car didn't have a radio," Lyn added.

Ray rummaged through the glovebox, emerging with an eight-track cartridge. He began the long drive back into the lands of life, blasting "Bat Out of Hell" out of his stereo, foot to the floor.

— EPILOGUE —

OVERHAEVEN

The Blackstar put down the chaos with brutal efficiency. Any being who still swore for the Dawn King was given the choice: renounce this false belief or die.

The fighting still went hard, and a memetic idea spread throughout the Golden Sea.

"The Blackstar wants the prize for himself!"

"A trick! A ruse!"

The Blackstar's attempts to relay the truth of events in the Underfog were ignored or mocked by many, and so the Blackstar resolved himself to escalating the civil war. Total warfare, and those who were traditionally exempt from even arguments were conscripted and forced to fight.

The Blackstar became frustrated with the fluidic hierarchy and dissolved the system of integers and servants, seizing all power for himself. With this unified approach he was able to finally put down those who wore the false sun sigil.

With little more than smoke and mirrors, Bilben had reduced Overhaeven to a battle-scarred ruin, the Aurum in the Golden Sea polluted in many places from the terrible mind-weapons of the civil war. Abandoned dreamspaces were bursting open now, spilling out nightmares to swim in the gold.

It was an absolute mess, but even as the Blackstar plotted his revenge against the Underfog, the unthinkable happened.

Shale separated from the edges of Gan-Eden and The Place Below, some powerful sorcery slicing through it like a knife. In one stroke it was excised, and Overhaeven itself was set adrift from the universe, like a barnacle peeled from the side of a boat with great prejudice.

They were adrift, but the Blackstar's court continued to drain from the Golden Sea, as polluted as those waters now were. The Aurum was beginning to make some sick, and others mad.

Worst of all, the level of the Golden Sea was dropping. They'd always had more Aurum here than they needed, and the Blackstar was reminded of a fish tank he'd kept as a living man, where he'd let the water grow green and evaporate, the fish forced to share a smaller and smaller amount of water, gills struggling.

Other cosmologies were searched out and found wanting. It was only the tree of planes forming out from Gan-Eden that produced the right conditions to make Aether.

"The Most High left only the one garden," the Blackstar admitted, "and we are now walled out from it."

The Blackstar looked out at his starving subjects, their sigils flopping around in a crowded pond of oil-slick muck. Even the culling of the least competent civilians was only doing so much to keep starvation at bay. They were going to need to launch an attack soon—or die.

"Was there anything left in the Shale mechanism?" he asked of the terrified servants grovelling before his throne. It was a last-ditch attempt to extract the remainder of the refined Aurum from the captured souls, a metaphysical squeezing of the pipeline that had connected their parasitical dimension to its victims.

"A little," one reported, and was immediately incinerated on the spot by a furious Blackstar.

"Only a little! I cannot abide this failure!"

"We found something else though, My Lord," another said in terror. "We found someone. A powerful soul that survived the process."

"Great. Another mouth to feed," the Blackstar mocked, but he followed his subjects the same, dipping into the muck of the Golden Sea and rotating downward as his many-pointed sigil.

He saw the new arrival near the inlet at the sea's base, and already it was holding court, gathering sigils about itself. The Blackstar darted forward like a predatory fish, his unfaithful servants scattering in terror.

The newly arrived being was representing itself as the silhouette of a ballerina, mid-pirouette. The star and the dancer rotated around themselves, and the Blackstar realised he was facing a being of immense power.

"I am the Blackstar. Lord of Overhaeven. Submit to my rule or die."

"No. We won't be doing that," the ballerina said. Her voice was a choir of hundreds that caused the sea to shiver. She stretched the points of the Blackstar out until he felt he might come apart at a philosophical level.

"What are you?" the Blackstar said, keeping a wary distance. All he could do now was save face, and he knew he was far outmatched.

"We are Baertha," the ballerina said, forming out into dozens of sigils, hundreds of sigils, and back into the one form that shimmered with immense potential. "You will submit to our rule—or die."

To be continued in Book 3 **"The Bride & The Bird-Man"**

— AUTHOR'S NOTE —

After such an uphill slog with *Papa Lucy and the Boneman*, it's not only been a delight to find such a great publisher to work with, but a seemingly endless stream of accolades for this cross-genre mutant of an idea.

To date, *Papa Lucy & the Boneman* has received a starred review in *Publisher's Weekly* and shortlistings in the Aurealis, Australian Shadows, and Ditmar Awards. Soon it will lurch into life in *Bullets & Bleedthroughs*, a roleplaying game where you get to step into this brutal universe and run with your own stories.

But best of all, the *Papa Lucy* universe seems to have found a small but dedicated gang of fans, and it is my pleasure to dish up deeper and grittier strangeness each time you crack the spine of one of these books...

So now, dear reader, you hold in your hands volume 2, *The Jawbone & The Junkman*. In some ways this was a personal challenge to try and beat the first book in the weirdness stakes, but in other ways I wanted to start exploring the distant corners of this brutal setting and set things up for a brutal showdown with the Lords of Overhaeven.

Being a multifaceted afterlife story, there are many recognisable cultural touchstones in this book, and it was my pleasure to pilfer through the garbage pile of human achievement and history, sifting out various treasures to line my magpie nest with. This alternative universe version of the Beatles is easy of course, but there are many, many others hidden in this text. I hope you enjoy the brainteaser!

I look forward to serving you up the next book in this trilogy, *The Bride and the Bird-Man*, where we rejoin Baertha, that most scorned of brides, who finds herself on an awful throne...

— ABOUT THE AUTHOR —

Jason Fischer is a writer who lives near Adelaide, South Australia. He has won the Colin Thiele Literature Scholarship, an Aurealis Award and the Writers of the Future Contest. In Jason's jack-of-all-trades writing career he has worked on comics, apps, television, short stories, novellas, and novels. Jason also facilitates writing workshops, is an enthusiastic mentor, and loves anything to do with the written or spoken word. Jason is also the founder and CEO of Spectrum Writing, a service that teaches professional writing skills to people on the Autism Spectrum. He plays a LOT of Dungeons and Dragons, has a passion for godawful puns, and is known to sing karaoke until the small hours.